For Mildred & Dan
    From a constituent —
        Dick Scowcroft

21 Sept, 1954

First Family

By Richard Scowcroft

Children of the Covenant

First Family

First Family

BY RICHARD SCOWCROFT

HOUGHTON MIFFLIN COMPANY BOSTON

The Riverside Press Cambridge

The Riverside Press
CAMBRIDGE · MASSACHUSETTS

PRINTED IN THE U.S.A.

For the Family,
from whom one learns these things

Part One

CHAPTER 1

Harriet Gannon had been talking of the lunch for three days. Should it be fried chicken or baked ham? The chicken might taste awfully good — it always did on a train — but there was the ham, bought especially for Jack (heaven only knew what they would feed him back there! Did they really subsist on baked beans, codfish, and Parker House rolls?) Potato salad would be the best — it would keep longer, cold, sealed in a fruit jar at the last minute — and if there were any left after the first night, he could have it for lunch the next day. Did he think some nice celery would taste good and stuffed eggs, and which would taste better, some nice pears or an orange or two? And of course she would make a banana cake because that would please him. But what should it be — ham or chicken?

Jack Gannon III (named after his father, Jack, and his grandfather who had gone to the law to change his name from the un-American Jeremiah to plain, ordinary, democratic Jack)— Jack Gannon III answered her from afar. "Anything, Mother — anything you say — thanks." But which? she insisted. Which? The

3

urgency of her voice seemed not to reach him; he was taken up by this future which was, at best, encroaching much too soon on her world. "Anything'll do."

His sister Edna, whom they called Eddie, argued against the lunch. "If he were going to Harrisville, to Ogden or Pocatello — but *Harvard*, Mother, you can't go to *Harvard* with a shoe box under your arm." Eddie would be a senior at Clark City High. "It's humiliating, it's — well, can't we at least *pretend* we know how to do things?" She appealed finally to her father. "For heaven's sakes, Dad, let him buy his meals. I'll pay for them myself. Must people think we're paupers as well as — " Eddie couldn't find a word.

Flo, the oldest sister, who dropped in every day with her two children, thought that a ham sandwich was easier to eat on a train than a piece of fried chicken. "The chicken could be messy," she said. Seated on the couch in her mother's bedroom, contemplating the grate fire, which they were lighting early this year, she murmured, "The celery hasn't been up to much this year — I'll have Grant call Mr. Inglehart and see if he can get some that's really nice."

Jack Gannon II, "Papa" to Harriet, though to none of their children, clasped his hands behind his tall straight back and said nothing. Those last days before the departure had taken on a solemnity to which the female concern over a box lunch was an irrelevance. Did his father, the first Jack Gannon, worry about a box lunch when he deserted the old world for the new? When Jack I acquired control of the mine in which he had started as a worker, did he have box lunches on his mind? Was the first Jack Gannon pondering the merits of chicken and ham the day he laid the cornerstone for the first — and almost the only — factory that Clark City was ever to have? Papa paced back and forth in his paneled library, past bound sets of Balzac and Dickens and Stoddard's Lectures. The scowling portrait of Jack I, who dominated the room from his gilt frame above the mantel, was a thundering answer to Papa's questions. As were the plaster bust of Ben Franklin, the tinted portrait of Harriet in diamonds and satin and egrets, the sepia photograph of Jack I, trowel in one hand, brick in the other, mustached circle of admirers watching from a respectful distance.

In Papa's own life, there were no single events to parallel the momentousness of the present occasion. He had mainly carried on where his father left off, disposed of the mine at the proper time, maintained the business as something to be proud of. But this house, this wife, these children — it was this aggregate of moments and events, of people and things that he could point to and know that progress had been maintained, that he had not failed. And so, during those last days before the departure, he took to walking about the house, hands behind his back, through the rose room with its damask walls, its chandelier of cut crystal, its plush loveseats and chairs all the way from New York; through the music room with its straight mahogany furniture, hard, green-upholstered — no one could sit on any of it, but Harriet liked to look at it — and the best damned player piano in the town; through the dining room with the heavy oak table that could be stretched to seat eighteen, and the built-in glass cupboards filled with dishes and glassware purchased in San Francisco or New York, or ordered especially from Henry Potter, the local jeweler; through the oak hallway with its ceiling hand painted by an artist for whom Papa had sent all the way East to Chicago. It was all good, in spite of any vague uncomfortable feeling, it was all good, and he would face up to God and Jeremiah and Harriet and the children to say so. Even to himself, by God. And if any more proof were needed, here it was: his oldest boy was about to enter Harvard. The war had been fought and won, really, so that the American Way could endure. Verdun, the Marne, Flanders Field where poppies grow. Jack Gannon III, grandson of an illiterate, penniless Irish immigrant, was going to Harvard. Ham or chicken? What did it matter?

To Louise, who at thirteen was her mother all over again, it mattered very much indeed. Her concern for the lunch was all that made Jack's loss bearable — that and her total faith in the brilliance of his future. To Louise had been granted the privilege of stuffing the eggs. Each egg would be a symbol of her immolation, a tribute to her belief.

But poor Babe, the youngest girl, whose real name, Helen, was marshaled forth only at school and Sunday school and at times of reprimand — poor Babe was so miserable over his departure that she was rendered quite useless. It seemed to her so impossibly sad that one of the family should be leaving — the end of everything good in life. Thanksgiving without all of them was such a sad thought that Babe burst into tears whenever the awful realization came upon her, and Harriet would say that Babe was too big a girl to carry on this way (even at ten, Babe was large for her age — almost as tall as her mother). And Harriet would put her arms around Babe to comfort her and the two of them would cry until Harriet would wipe her eyes on one of those tiny, sweet-smelling handkerchiefs and say she had better go and see what she could do for Jack.

And what of Gus, ten-month-old Gus, who spent most of his days sleeping in the hastily contrived nursery upstairs or lying on his belly, kicking like a turtle, in the center of the living-room rug; what did Gus make of all this? Even a baby can't have been wholly unaware that great events were taking place; surely he must have felt a touch of nervous colic, a bit of gas around the heart, a looseness of the bowels. Did his apparent indifference mean ignorance of this culmination, this beginning; or was it real indifference, a biding of time, a withholding of judgment? Gus, of course, in coming late, a somewhat embarrassing surprise ten years after the youngest child, had missed the preliminaries of growth and acquisition; by the time Gus came to understanding, Jack would be a Harvard graduate, a famous author — or anything else he might choose, and the best dreams of man would have been realized. What to the others seemed climax and fulfillment would be to Gus as ordinary as the telephone, the airplane and the talking picture.

Gus's roots were different and to the others, he himself was to be pretty much of a curiosity the first years of his life, not a younger brother but a toy like the player piano or the stereoscope for the whole family to enjoy. Within a week of his birth, he fell into the hands of a brother and four sisters, who dropped the Arthur that had been selected for his christening, called him Gus after Augustus Caesar, whom he resembled. When Gus wet his pants, it was old Octavius crossing the Tiber.

And while the first-born son moved in a hallowed world, the last-born was allowed to kick and grunt unnoticed in the center of the living-room rug. Ham or chicken? A bone of either would have felt good to his swollen gums.

The afternoon before the departure, Harriet climbed the stairs in search of Jack, in search of work to occupy her mind. His bedroom door was shut, which would not ordinarily stop her, but because she heard Eddie's voice, she knocked before she turned the knob.

"Wait a minute," Jack's voice ordered, and there was the sound of a window opening. When his face appeared through the merest crack of the door, he seemed surprised that it was she. "Oh, it's you, Mother."

"Yes, it's —" But he didn't open the door and she felt called upon to justify her presence. "I thought, if there was anything to do —"

Jack looked over his shoulder and with some reluctance stepped back. "Nothing, Mother — I was just packing — Eddie's been reading —"

The room was filled with smoke, which surprised her because it hadn't occurred to her that Jack was grown up enough to smoke. Then she realized that it was because of the smoke Jack had tried to keep her out and joyous relief swept over her. "I don't mean to break up a party," she explained to Eddie, who was on the bed, leaning against the footboard, a book in her lap. "I just thought —"

"If it's a party, you're invited," Jack said.

She wanted to say that it was all right about the smoking — she wanted to say anything to show her gratitude to Jack. But she wasn't sure yet that she really was invited and she said to Eddie, "Go on with your reading — I'll just fuss around here a little."

Eddie tossed the book aside, stretched her arms.

Jack's clothes, in a confused pile on the floor, surrounded the trunk. Harriet stooped to collect the underwear. "What were you reading, dear?"

"Oh — some poetry." Eddie yawned. "Byron."

"That's nice," Harriet said, wishing Eddie would continue with the reading, wishing Eddie would include her in the world she shared with Jack. Eddie and Jack were so close — she had to remind herself every so often that these relationships between brother and sister were a fine thing, exclusive, secretive though they might be. Jack and Eddie looked like twins. They both had the square faces, the broad foreheads and straight black hair of the Gannons; they both had Harriet's dark eyes and white skin. Jack's cheeks had a blue, shadowed look from the closely shaved black beard, and the circles beneath his eyes were almost blue. His handsomeness was a wonder that never ceased to startle her — she couldn't look at him without being almost immobilized with approval. And Eddie, of course, was the most beautiful of her girls. But Eddie — well, sometimes it was difficult to know how to take her: her attachments were so possessive, her resentment of intrusion so obvious. As a woman, Harriet was quite sure that Eddie never would say, "If it's a party, you're invited" — if the party were with Jack, or with Papa. And it was strange to approach a daughter with a woman's understanding rather than a mother's. Eddie's restlessness, her youth, of course, and since summer, that trying business — but she wouldn't think of that now.

"Don't mind me — just pretend I'm not here," she said brightly. "I have to keep busy," she explained, careful to conceal how terribly true were her words.

"Mother," Eddie said, "I'm going East with Jack. I'll go to Radcliffe — or I may spend a year in New York. I haven't decided yet."

This, of course, was a joke, and so as Harriet gently laid shirts in a trunk drawer, she smiled. "That'll be nice, dear."

"It's true," Eddie exclaimed, clasping her knees to her chin. "If I don't, I shall simply and absolutely die — of — of slow strangulation. I can't breathe in this town!"

Jack had sprawled in an armchair by the window and was gazing tranquilly at yellow leaves that stirred on the tops of branches. "I kinda like it here," he muttered.

"You can't like it here! It's dead — it's finished. There's nothing you can do, nothing you can be. Just marry some fool and have a lot of nasty, screaming brats — and then die. Smother."

"Well," Jack said, "don't marry a fool. And you don't have to have brats. A few of Gus wouldn't be too bad."

"Oh, you can talk," Eddie said, tears coming to her eyes. "You're a *boy* — you can leave. You don't know what it is to be a girl in this town, to know that you never, never, never can get away!"

Jack looked over the back of his chair, tossed her a smile. "Poor old Eddie."

"Jack, if you fail me — " she rubbed the tears from her cheeks, "if you — Look, Jack," she knelt on the bed, facing him, "you can do anything, be anything — anything you want. There's no possibility that isn't open to you. It doesn't matter about me if you can have it — "

"When the right man comes along," Harriet said, hating to interrupt but unable to resist striking a blow, "if you just *wait* — are careful of the kind of young men you go with — everything will work out fine. Won't it, Jack?"

He wasn't listening. He stood against the window frame, gazed out on the autumn day. "Do you suppose I really will be famous?" he mused. "I guess I will — since everyone expects it — "

"You know what Miss Kirkham says." Eddie blew her nose, glanced at her mother.

"Miss Kirkham," Harriet said, quick to the defense, "is the best-educated woman in Clark City."

Miss Kirkham was the high school English teacher who had taught all three of the children — Flo, Eddie, and Jack. And in more than twenty years of teaching, Miss Kirkham had said, she had never seen such a rare talent as Jack's — his name, she predicted, would stand beside those of Sir Walter Scott and Rudyard Kipling.

Jack said that as a matter of fact, he had been thinking of the novel he might write. It would be about a young guy — a sort of extraordinary person living in a very ordinary small Western town. Well, this young guy wouldn't get along too well in this town because he'd be so superior to everyone else in the town — you know, artistic and that sort of thing — that they would naturally resent him, mistrust him. So this young guy would want to get away, go someplace where he'd meet some really interesting people who would understand him. He'd go to New York and have really one hell of a time at first — no money, no one appreciating him. But he'd have a lot of affairs and he'd be developing a philosophy of life —

Jack's face, as he talked, lighted up, his hands mapped out the events of the novel, swept philosophically toward the moment of enlightenment. All this was directed to Eddie, who clutched her shoulders as if she were cold. When he was finished, she lifted her eyes, solemnly. "This young guy," she said, "who goes off to New York, does he have a sister?"

"Poor old Eddie." He put the heel of his palm against her forehead. "Maybe we'd better have her go along to New York too."

Harriet knew that she was excluded from this party but she hadn't liked his novel, it hadn't made sense at all, and she couldn't hold her tongue. "But why do they have to run off to New York?" she asked indignantly. "Why can't they do just as well in the town where they were born, where they belong?" She hugged a suit of Jack's to her. "What about their mother? What about her?"

Dinner that night was made an occasion by the fact of Martha's having cooked a roast, which, unless something extraordinary happened, was Sunday fare. If Harriet was to take full charge of the box lunch, Martha must, she had insisted, cook a last dinner that Jack wouldn't be likely to forget. And so the roast with all the Sunday trimmings and the fruit cocktail served in Harriet's best Bohemian glasses. But with the Sunday food had descended a Sunday pall; Martha's festive dinner made them heavy and sleepy and a little sad, and Jack escaped sooner than he ought on his last night at home.

They heard him wheel his motorcycle out of the garage and were silent till the putt of the motor had faded up the street. Then Harriet, trying to be casual, brushing together a little cone of crumbs, asked Eddie, "What are your plans for this evening?"

Eddie folded her napkin, pushed it in the ring. "I'm going out," she answered.

"Can we go out and play — please," Babe asked. "Just for an hour — for forty-five minutes then — if we don't go far away — please."

"If you don't go far away — I guess."

Babe and Louise jumped up from their chairs and dashed through the kitchen. Eddie, at a slower pace, went through the hall, up the stairs. That left Papa and Harriet in the darkening room with the used plates, the best glassware, the damask, the wedding presents.

Papa squirmed in his chair and gazed out the window. "It must be about seven-thirty," he said.

"I should think it must be all of that," Harriet answered. She listened for a moment to Papa's fingers drumming on the arm of his chair. Then she said, "We should all go to bed early tonight. There's Jack's lunch box to be fixed in the morning."

Harriet finally slipped out of bed at five. Attempts at sleep had been futile — in fact, her nervousness had merely become more intense until she was lying there listening to her heart beat and trying to control the twitching of her eyes. She had the ham in the oven and the banana cake made and she herself was all dressed before any of the others appeared.

Jack was pale and had cut himself shaving and spilled his coffee when it was passed to him. All the rest of them tried not to notice because he merely reflected their own tension. Except Eddie, who said, "Where were you last night?"

Louise brought Gus down, pressed backside against her, hanging over her arms, chewing his gums. Harriet reached hungrily for him, cooed at him, talked their special language, bounced him up and down.

But Gus was hungry for food. He squirmed and stretched and twisted his head to find the bottle and looked at his mother with a pained, tortured face that threatened tears if something were not quickly done. Louise rushed to the icebox, took out a bottle, set it in a pan of water on the stove, rushed back to punch Gus in the stomach and shake her hair at him until he shoved his fist in his mouth and laughed a deep, rumbling laugh.

"Louise'll have ten kids," Jack said with a stiff, pale smile. "Ten kids."

They looked approvingly at Louise — small, the rich long hair, the delicate little face and big eyes and small sloping shoulders and quick nervous hands. Louise was their little sweetheart.

From the front hall came the sound of a door opening and Flo's "Yoo-hoo"; then her redheads, Sammy and Connie, aged two and three, bounded into the room, grinning. They headed first for Papa, then Connie deserted Papa to go over and yank Gus's foot. "Has Uncle Gus had his breakfast?" she asked. "Why is his face so dirty?"

Jack had taught them the "Uncle Gus," though he himself was just plain Jack to them.

"Oh heavens," Harriet said, taking her napkin and wiping Gus's unyielding face, "these children are getting to be as critical of me as my own. Now I'll have to start watching myself around them too."

Flo kissed her father and then her mother. She wore her new fall suit of lavender duvetyn, her new fall hat with a wide embroidered brim that hung low over her eyes. Two children had given Flo a comfortable look, filled out her breasts and hips, rounded her face. Never so striking as Eddie, she had been considered, by the ladies in her mother's club, to be really prettier, to be, certainly, a sweeter girl. If Eddie was all black and white, Flo was shades of tan, honey and molasses.

"You look lovely, Flo," Harriet said in the easy, comfortable way that you talked to Flo. "Just as smart as it can be."

"Grant says that if skirts get one inch nearer the knee, the men — well, I hadn't better say it. You know how he talks."

Yes, they knew.

Flo sat on one of the wicker breakfast-room chairs, crossed her knees. She looked around the circle, rested her eyes on Jack. "Well, Jack?"

In the silence that followed, Harriet felt the tightening at her heart, the shortness of breath, and she nuzzled against Gus's shoulder.

"Why do you go?" Babe blurted out. "Why do you want to leave? I could just die."

Jack glanced quickly at his father, embarrassed. Then back at Babe. "That's how families are, I guess. You grow up and leave. You will too, some day."

"I never will — I'd rather die first. I'm never going to get married or anything. I just couldn't."

"This, Babe," said Flo, "should be the proudest moment of our lives." She flipped a glove at her knee. "I know it is of mine."

Harriet, for reassurance, held Gus against her shoulder, patted him and whispered in his ear. But ten-month-old Gus wriggled, fought, pushed with all his strength, grunted and finally squealed. Sammy, watching in fascination, said, "Uncle Gus didn't like

Grama." And because he could pronounce neither *l* nor *r*, the remark was very comical and made them laugh. Harriet bent her
head and kissed Gus's neck.

Papa leaned back, reached for the gold watch in his vest.

"There are things to be done," Harriet said, observing his gesture. She handed Gus to Louise. "You take Gus, Louise. I have
to get busy."

"Now Mother," Eddie said, "just calm down."

Papa frowned at the empty plate before him, wiped his mouth
on his napkin. "Jack — if you're not too busy — would you mind,
for a moment — in the library?"

Papa closed the door behind them and indicated a leather chair
by the fireplace for Jack. The room seemed to Papa, in pleasant
fancy, a small-scale reproduction of an Eastern men's club — dark
paneled, smelling slightly of Papa's after-dinner cigars and leather
upholstery. In such an atmosphere as this, he felt sure, the distinguished men of the nation settled the world's business, the buying
and selling, the mergers and new enterprise. And particularly on
this morning, the club atmosphere was a pleasing and helpful illusion: it took so much for granted, it denied the necessity of explaining mutual assumptions, of establishing a complex and difficult personal relationship. He and his son and his father (framed
above the mantel) could, as it were, in this oak and leather room,
understand each other.

Papa opened the leather humidor on his desk, hesitated only a
moment before he offered it to Jack. "Cigar?"

Jack, sunk deep in his chair, looked at him with the surprised
eyes of a boy. But Papa kept his gaze steady and his arm extended. Jack didn't accept his gaze; he dropped his eyes, took
from his inner coat pocket a package of cigarettes. "If you don't
mind, Dad — I'll have one of these."

Papa said, "Oh. Not at all." And as, with elaborate delibera-
tion, he peeled the tinfoil from his own cigar, he tried not to feel
rebuffed. "The young fellows these days," he said with assumed
heartiness, "I guess they'd leave cigars for the older boys now."

"Yeah. I guess that's right, Dad."

Papa lit Jack's cigarette and his own cigar with the same match and dropped it into the fireplace. Then, to re-establish order, he said angrily that it looked to him as if the country, unless there was an immediate change of resident in the White House, would be carried by the Democrats to complete ruin. Where was the soundness, he demanded, in handing the country over to a visionary college professor instead of a good solid businessman of the kind that had made this country what it was today? Jack said he supposed Papa was right, but it looked to him as if Wilson's day was about over.

"All these Irish troubles — the Bolsheviks," Papa said, "it doesn't look too good. Prices — housing — and what about our own sheepmen? Charlie Harris was telling me that if we don't get a tariff —" Papa chewed his cigar, swaying on the balls of his feet. "Well, of course it looks bad, but we've had a war, it takes time. With the right administration, we can start looking after America for a while. And I believe in our future, Jack. We've done it before — and now there'll be no stopping us, no limit for men of vision."

"Yeah," Jack said. "You're probably right."

Papa waited for Jack to say more, but Jack stared at the end of his cigarette and was silent.

"Well," Papa said, tugging at the cuff of his shirt, "all that can't be of much interest to you. Other matters — your own future —" Papa hesitated, watched Jack for some sign. "History, mathematics, that sort of thing — they help a man. Education is a great thing. A great thing." His eyes left Jack to caress the beautiful gold and leather bindings of the books that lined his walls. "You'll be a better man for your education, Jack. You'll be a richer man. There's treasure in these books just as surely as in your grandfather's mine or in a machine. Education will provide the tools to dig it out with, the knowledge of how to separate the precious metal from the dross."

Jack stroked his chin, smiled warily. "It's a kind of alchemist's pot, I guess. Put in enough silver dollars and you come out with pure gold."

Papa laughed in pleasure at the joke. He didn't know its meaning, but it was proper that he and his son should share a joke on this occasion, in this room. "Yes," he subsided. "I guess that's just about it."

He felt now that the ice had been broken, as the saying goes, he had started the ball rolling. Ah, but he caught Jack's casual glance at the clock — there was never time! He should have started much sooner; it takes a while to become friends with your son.

"These little talks," he said, "we should have had more of them." He gazed at his feet, somberly aware of the inadequacy of his words. "I hope — we must have them more often."

"Sure, Dad." Jack grasped the arms of the chair to push himself up. "They mean a lot to me."

"I'm not such an old fogy," Papa grinned, jokingly, as to a member of the club, "that I can't remember how it is to be young. Maybe I could help you — we could talk over any problems —"

"You're a great help, Dad." Jack stood up, pulled his coat straight. "No old fogy, you."

"It may be different back there," he said frowning. "You'll be on your own — those Easterners probably won't ever have heard of your grandfather. But I want you to be proud of us, Jack. I want you to remember what your grandfather stood for — he was successful, he made money. There's nothing to be ashamed of — you can have anything they can have —"

"Ashamed? Ah, Dad!"

"Good then." Papa's voice was gruff. "We're proud of you, Jack — your mother and sisters and I. And your grandfather would be, too. I wish he could be here. I wish he could know this." He drew a deep breath and gave Jack his steady gaze. "Is there any advice — anything you'd like to know? Any more problems we could talk over?"

"Not a thing, Dad." Jack's handsome face smiled camaraderie and understanding. "That really takes care of everything."

On the way to the door, back to the world of women and babies and lunch boxes, Papa rested his hand awkwardly on Jack's shoulder. Then he reached for the knob and held the door open for Jack to pass through.

The train was due to leave around noon. By eleven, Harriet was in such a state of nerves that there was, according to her family, no living with her at all. Her own hat and veil pinned on by ten-thirty, her suit coat and bag and white gloves lying ready in the hall, she made the rounds of the upstairs rooms to hurry the others.

"For heaven's sakes, Mother, don't worry," Eddie called from the bathroom. "We've got hours."

"I could do it," said Babe when Harriet took the brush from her and drew it through her gnarled hair, 'if you'd just leave me alone."

And even Martha became a little impatient and said she was perfectly well aware which of Gus's clothes were most suitable for the drive to the railroad station.

"Really, Mother," Louise said, "there's enough time for us all to *walk* to the station."

Of course there was, of course there was — did her children think she had no sense? But they weren't walking — they were riding in the car and so they needed to allow more than enough time. Supposing they had a blowout, or what if a wheel came off? It had happened often enough before. Supposing the car just stopped dead? That too had happened. And even though George was a good mechanic as well as chauffeur, they had to allow plenty of time if they were taking the car.

When she looked into Jack's room to see what she could help him with, the bare furniture, stripped of all his personal belongings, struck her with so sharp a pain that she had to turn around and go out because she knew that if Jack said so much as a word to her, she would cry. And so she called downstairs to Papa to have George bring the car around.

Soon the downstairs hall began filling up. Jack piled his suitcases by the door (the trunk had gone yesterday); Louise and Babe in enormous hair ribbons, white stockings, smocked dresses, sat on the bottom step and teased Connie and Sammy, who shrieked and hid behind the grandfather clock; Flo, before the large hall mirror, pinned on her velvet hat, buttoned the coat to her suit; Eddie swept down the stairs, gowned in her new fall outfit, draped rose dress, spats, swagger stick, veil pinned to her hat. Harriet sat on a stiff hall chair, carrying Gus, who was bundled like an Indian baby. Then Papa appeared angrily from the back part of the house, saying that he was damned if he knew what had happened to that good-for-nothing George. Harriet went pale and said, "See, see what I told you?" And all her children, almost at once, said, "For heaven's sakes, Mother — calm down."

Papa took desperate command and said that there was only one thing to do: Jack would drive to the station, Martha would send George down after them — if he appeared; if he didn't, they would just have to leave the car at the station and walk home, or take the streetcar.

Jack grabbed his suitcases, hurried out toward the back; Harriet said it just went to show — and all the children frowned at her as if she were to blame for the crisis. "When she gets like this, there's nothing you can do about her," Eddie explained to Flo.

With bitterness in her heart, Harriet hefted Gus against her shoulder, sailed out the front door, muttering about children and chauffeurs and about Prohibition — they had said it would take care of people like George — and it was no wonder his poor wife was gray before her time. The others followed her, stood a little apart from her as they waited for the big Peerless to round the corner of the unpaved street.

And there it came — the beautiful, luxurious motorcar (not another like it in the town), shiny (you could say *that* for George), its top down, Jack high in the driver's seat, his cap rather tight on his head against the wind. Papa held Gus while Harriet climbed in the back seat, then handed him over, helped Eddie and Flo in beside their mother. Louise and Babe and Flo's two squeezed into the jump seats. Papa sat in the front beside Jack.

The cortège to the station (for though it was a single motor vehicle, it seemed like more) proceeded on its way. And Harriet had to forget anger and resentment. Certainly no other occasion lifted her pride so much as these drives with her family, when, she was sure, everyone must see that they were the handsomest children in the town. Even the matinées at the Palace when Papa took a box and the whole family was stiffly on display — even that wasn't quite equal; somehow it was the automobile — it lifted them so high, and as they drove along the street, Papa would tip his hat and Harriet would wave a lace handkerchief and Eddie would shake the knob of her swagger stick. And everyone would know that the Gannon family was going someplace. Quite like, she had often imagined, the King and Queen of England and the young princes.

Today, of course, the pleasure was not wholly sweet. The leaves that dropped from the trees to scatter over the lawn of the

Methodist Church and choke up old Mrs. Hanson's birdbath and pile up red and yellow by the schoolhouse steps; Mr. Gierson's lovely brown horse chestnuts which the boys stuffed in their pockets and hollowed out for pipes; the straight row of now-fading marigolds which Mrs. Abbot planted and cared for so beautifully; the scarlet vines of Virginia creeper that covered the City Hall and the catalpa pods that littered its walks — they all spoke of the end of something, of shorter days and longer nights and loneliness and sadness. And you could see by the way Mr. Brown, who kept the grocery store, worked with so much purpose at taking down his awning — hardly bothering to wave at all, by the way Effie March managed to propel her lethargic bulk at a smart pace down the street, by the funereal solemnity with which Mr. Harkington of Harkington's Furniture Emporium tipped his hat, that the new chill in the air and the softer edges of vision had done something to them all, drawn them in, apart, toughened their surfaces, built little walls around them. Henry Potter, busy with his fall window display of jewelry and gift merchandise, waved to them from behind an amber vase of dried cattails.

And then they were at the station, climbing down from the car; Papa was shaking hands with Joe Krump, the stationmaster, Babe and Louise were running to the candy stand to buy Jack a present. The train was not due to leave for another forty minutes.

Harriet sat on a bench, holding Gus, who was so tightly bound in a blanket that he could merely gaze passively at the strange surroundings. In his crocheted bonnet, he looked, Eddie said, more than ever like Augustus Caesar, crowned in laurel after the Battle of Actium. Jack took care of his luggage, then sat beside his mother.

She couldn't trust herself to speak now — the time was too near, the separation, like death, was too inevitable. She rested her hand on his knee and fixed a pale smile on her face and patted him when she felt a lump rising in her throat. He looked grown up — he looked to be a man — but of course he was still a child, her child, and he needed her as much as Gus did. Who would care for him way out there — who would see that he dressed warmly enough and got enough sleep? Within her was a terrible physical need to hover over him as she could hover over Gus, to surround his body with her body to protect him from cold and pain. And

she knew that she must call this whole thing off — he mustn't go —
Eddie said, "In one more minute, Mother will be in tears."
Everyone laughed.

"Lick your lips, Mother," Flo said. "It'll make you feel better."
She reached over to brush some powder from Harriet's forehead.

"I'll have to send her some rouge," Jack said. "We'll paint her
up like a Follies girl. How about that, Dad?"

"Well — " Papa laughed stiffly, "maybe we'd better not do *that*."

Harriet patted Jack's knee and murmured, "I think we should
go down to the train. We want to have plenty of time."

She gave Gus to Papa and they all stood. Harriet put her arm
through Jack's, Flo led her two children, Eddie walked with
Papa, Louise and Babe giggled at the rear, trying to hide Babe's
purchase.

They all climbed onto the train to see Jack's lower berth, for
Papa to say a few words to the porter and give him five dollars,
for Harriet to see what kind of traveling companions Jack would
have for the long trip to Chicago. (And in Chicago, what would
happen? Would he be able to make the change from one railroad
station to the other — without getting hopelessly lost in the
crowded city, without being robbed of his money?) The children
ran up and down the aisle, and had to have many paper cupfuls
of water and peer into the lavatories. And Harriet smiled, she
hoped graciously, at the refined, elderly woman across the aisle
from Jack.

When they got off the train, they saw Grant, Flo's husband,
looking about for them. Harriet smiled weakly, pleased that
Grant had left his work to be here. Grant had been a good marriage for Flo; he came from a lovely family who had built up a
good business and he was quite nice looking, despite his extra
poundage and thinning pink hair.

"Well, how's the Hawvud man?" he asked jovially. "How about
letting me trade places with you, Jackie?"

"Here, Grant, take these children," Flo said. "They're driving
me crazy."

And then Tommy Reed came striding out of the station, lean,
blond Tommy. He wore a turtle-neck sweater, soiled flannel
trousers and tennis shoes, and had his hands in his pockets. Tommy
was like one of her own. His great-grandfather had been a rancher,

his grandfather a rancher and governor, his father a rancher and bank president. Tommy at nineteen had failed geometry and French in his senior year at high school and thus had not graduated and thus was not boarding the train for Harvard with Jack, his oldest and dearest friend. He had been accepted as a special student at the state university, where, he had declared, he would work not so much for a degree as for a *real* education.

"Here's Tommy," Harriet said.

Tommy was as pale and drawn as Jack.

Jack looked at him, grunted, turned away.

"Good morning, good morning, good morning," Tommy said. "And how is everyone on this bright September morning?"

"From appearances," Eddie said briskly, "I should say we're all quite a bit better than you."

"We hate to see him go, Tommy," Harriet said. "It just seems as if — "

She couldn't finish. Tommy went over to her, put his arm around her shoulder, squeezed her. "The way I look at it, Mrs. Gannon," he said, "we aren't losing a son, we're gaining a Harvard man."

Grant had been gazing quizzically from Jack to Tommy. "Say," he asked, "what were you fellows doing last night? You look terrible."

Harriet took Jack's hand and Tommy's in hers. "You boys have been working too hard this summer. I want you to take care of yourselves."

Tommy leaned down and kissed her cheek. "We'll take care of ourselves, Mrs. Gannon."

And now Papa thought Jack had better get on the train — better not be rushed at the last minute. Jack shook hands with Papa, murmured "Thanks," for the hundred-dollar bill Papa slipped into his palm. Then he kissed the children, Sammy, Connie, poked his finger in Gus's blanketed stomach, said, "So long, Emperor"; then Louise, and Babe who smothered him in her bearhug and got his cheek wet with her tears and gave him a movie magazine with Theda Bara on the cover.

"Bye, Eddie," he smiled at her, touched his fist to her chin. Eddie turned her head away, handed him a limp leather copy of the *Rubaiyat*.

"And Flo — "

It was when Flo was giving him the pink candy box of divinity that Harriet started, grew deathly pale, and turned as if she would run toward the station.

"Mother — what's the matter?" Louise screamed.

"Oh heavens," Harriet gasped, "we forgot the lunch — we forgot it — it's in the icebox at home — "

Jack stepped over to her, clasped her arms. "It's all right, Mother — don't worry, don't worry — "

Harriet was crying. "It's that George — that awful drunken bum. And what good's Prohibition if it doesn't stop men like him? I forgot it because of him — "

"Look," Tommy said, "I've got my motorcycle — I'll go back to your place and get it!"

"There isn't time," Harriet sobbed, "it wouldn't do any good — "

"It's all right, Mother, really it is," Jack said. "I can get food on the train."

"Of course you can — " Harriet turned away, tried to stop the flow of tears with her handkerchief. But the food would not be her food — she had been denied this last act of love. There was nothing, now, they could do for Jack — the last thin line to them was broken and he was starting out alone, with nothing even to remind him of a family and a past. What good could possibly come of it?

The porter called "All aboard," and Jack said, "I guess I'd better get on, Mother." He kissed her and she couldn't say anything.

And then they watched Jack through the window and they waved and tried to say things that the window made impossible to hear. Eddie stood on one side of Harriet with her arm around her, Louise and Babe pressed against the other side. Papa held Gus up so he could see Jack through the window. Flo bit her lip to try to keep from crying, Tommy grinned and Grant looked solemn, Sammy sucked his thumb, Connie gazed down at the end of the train to see the engine.

And then with a jerk, the train started and slowly gained momentum. They all waved until the last glimpse of him was cut off. And then they stood quiet for a moment.

F ALL TOOK ITS MEANING that year and its color and its tone from the fact of Jack's absence: fall became the long three months between Jack's departure in September and the day in December when the whole family would drive to the station to welcome him home for the Christmas holidays. Stillness settled over the town, over the hills and mountains that had lost their summer purple in a last cry of color, over the streets that school had robbed of shouting, running youth, over homes that settled into long hours of silence and grew dark early, over people who bundled their bodies in woolen clothes and warmed their blood with steam heat. And though one learned something about peace during those days, they gave rather too much time for thinking, and conversation often lagged at the dinner table.

Babe was in the fourth grade at the Lincoln School, Louise in the seventh. Eddie was in her last year at Clark City High. There had been afternoons at the Golden Rule, outfitting them all with sensible clothes for school, the woolen dresses, the heavy underwear, the flat shoes and cotton stockings that would get them through a Rocky Mountain winter. There had been check-

ups with the dentist and the oculist and new glasses for Babe.
There had been the secret meeting of Eddie and Papa for lunch at
the City House Hotel, and a new gray squirrel coat for Eddie.
The hall table was, to Martha's annoyance, constantly piled with
schoolbooks, and the privacy of Papa's library was forever intruded
upon by someone seeking wisdom in the *Book of Knowledge* or the
Americana. Clark High played — and lost — its first football game.

For Harriet the days passed by in unnoted performance of
duties which kept the house alive and made her necessary to her
children and justified to herself. In the first days — the terribly
lonely ones when Jack had gone and the girls were in school —
the poignant, awful days when it seemed that they had all outgrown her and no one needed her and only Gus drew his suste-
nance from her, in those days she had felt old and a little desperate and would have washed every curtain in the house had
Martha not finally put a stop to her. And of course without Flo,
heaven only knew how she'd have managed. But Flo dropped in
every day with the children, sometimes twice a day, and they
talked over problems, they gossiped and planned in drowsy contentment. When Flo wasn't there and the girls were in school and
Papa was at work and Martha was putting up fruit or busy with
the cleaning, Harriet turned to Gus and had long conversations
with him. Sometimes when she talked to him, it would come over
her that it was not he who depended on her but rather she on him
and she would be so filled with the wonder and the need of him
that she would have to carry him back and forth across the room
— which, of course, the children said was very bad for him.

But soon, gradually, the loneliness faded, the winter activities of
the town took over the unused half of her mind and energies and
made her a whole being once more. Sewing Club started up its bi-
monthly Wednesday luncheons; there were the Tuesday afternoon
meetings of the Women's Auxiliary at the church, an occasional
large tea where one saw all one's friends, an occasional matinée
or evening performance of a New York play at the Palace. There
were Papa's business associates to have in for dinner, sometimes
Easterners or society people from San Francisco; there was the exciting world of Eddie and Clark City High to share in, the polit-
ical and social intrigue of high school seniors, the tempestuous,

restless romances. And there were the cozy, crackling fires in Harriet's bedroom, where she could doze over the *Delineator* and wait for the children to find her after school, their cheeks bursting with oatmeal cookies, and Babe spilling milk on the oriental rug. Then autumn became a warm, rich time, and the new pursuits and the new climate which had seemed at first to separate them brought them really closer together, and their common waiting for Jack's return brought them together. This world that Papa had given her — this fireplace and the rose taffeta window hangings and the little silver-headed jars and the row of babies' pictures above the mahogany bed and her satin wrapper and her *Delineator* — this was her foundation-on-a-rock, her eternity.

But if eternity was long and sure, it was not, she found, for the mother of a family, without its murmurings. There were the nights that she waited up, after Papa had gone to bed and was asleep and breathing heavily, nights when she sat by the window in the dark, wrapped in a blanket, waiting for the automobile to stop in front of the house, for Eddie to step lightly out and run quickly up the steps, for the automobile to rattle off down the street. Then she would fold the blanket, note the time — one-thirty, two, three — and fall wearily, unhappily into bed. One couldn't, of course, talk to Eddie (to imagine the scene actually made Harriet shiver); one could only wait up to see that she was safe and thank God for it.

At least Harriet couldn't talk to her, and neither Jack nor Papa would talk to her. Jack had told Harriet during the summer that Bill Miller was not the sort of person for Eddie to be playing around with, a good sort of fellow with men but not someone you'd want your sister or daughter playing around with.

Why didn't Jack talk to Eddie, Harriet asked. She thought so much of him, she really would pay some attention to what he said. But Jack said it was none of his business whom Eddie played around with.

And Papa, stretched out in the warm bed, slept through the worry and the danger of Bill Miller. Whenever Harriet tried to prod him into action, he would ask who were Bill Miller's parents — which wasn't the point at all. Charlie and Nettie Miller — nothing the matter with Charlie Miller, he'd say. Not Eddie's quality — but the boy, wasn't he the one in the war? *He* must have some spunk and initiative! But initiative for *what?* Maybe it's the wrong *kind* of initiative! Papa would yawn and say that Eddie was a good sensible girl, who could take care of herself, and if there really was cause for worry, it was a mother's job to settle it, a problem between women, hardly something he could discuss with his daughter. And Papa, in a matter of seconds, would fall asleep.

The problem, most certainly a cause for worry, was, as Jack had said, simply that Bill Miller was not the sort of young man one would choose as a companion for a girl of Eddie's background, youth, inexperience. Bill Miller came from a nice enough family (small shopkeepers — his father owned the stationery store), but he had been wild, difficult. Though he was only Jack's age, he had matured early, and while Jack and his friends were just entering high school, Bill had run away from home, lied about his age and enlisted in the army. Then after the mad, glorious excitement of November 11, on the day when Clark City's sons marched in khaki beneath the Welcome Home banners which stretched across Center Street, not the least glorious among those sons was young Bill Miller, Charlie Miller's boy, who had told a lie that he might offer up his life, if need be, for Democracy, that he might battle for his country and return now with ribbons on his chest. If the boys who had grown up with Bill Miller, who had passed listlessly through high school waiting for birthdays that would allow them, too, deeds of glory, if they were somewhat sullen about Bill Miller's heroism, it must be said that their throats were among the few to which Bill Miller's story did not bring a patriotic lump.

When Bill returned to high school, he was two years behind his age group and thus easily the most worldly, the most manly, the most *interesting* boy in his class. He made the first-string football team, right end, and was the only spectacular player on Clark High's mediocre team. He smoked cigarettes and seemed always to have money and drove a chocolate-colored Marmon. He had seen and had adventures in and made frequent reference to Paris — London — and oh wonder! — New York. And as if God had not already been more than good to him, he could play the piano. Added to this were a strong, stocky build, a weather-beaten face

with a frank, sudden smile, straight hair that always needed pushing back off his forehead. He was, to the women of Clark City
High, irresistible.

It was inevitable that after a few months of being seen by the
whole town with girls who were not of the category of "nice girls,"
he should end up being seen with the nicest of the nice girls,
Edna Gannon. The town observed; the town talked. Eventually,
Harriet had to listen.

Wednesday Sewing Club was, as of all good things, purveyor of
the latest goings-on of poor Nettie Miller's boy. Over their
luncheons of scalloped chicken and creamed peas, over their embroidered pillow slips, crocheted chair tidies, knitted pink sweaters for their little grandchildren, the ladies passed words around,
tasted lightly of names and doings that constituted a richer diet
than anything in Fanny Farmer. To Flo Gannon, who was the
first of the second generation on whom membership in the club
had been conferred, the unabashed discussions in which the ladies
engaged had been startling indeed. Victorian, proper, quick to
blush if any husband were so little a gentleman as to utter an off-
color word, the ladies had yet, she found, not borne all those children without knowing where they came from.

It was at Charlotte Cranfeld's way last spring that Julia Harkington had shaken them all with a report that young Bill Miller
had been seen swimming at Whelan's Pond with one of those girls
— naked. Where? How? Who? the ladies wanted to know all at
once. Naked — at Whelan's Pond, Julia repeated. Her daughter,
Ama, had been driving up the canyon with a girl friend and seen
Bill's Marmon parked at Whelan's Pond. No one was about (you
know how willows grow around the Pond) and so Ama and her
friend, crazy the way girls will be, decided to stop the car, take
a peek to see what they could see. And what they saw! Naked —
both of them.

"Naked?" Ruthie Harper had murmured incredulously.

"Not a stitch on!" Julia said, self-righteously.

"But did Ama actually *see* them?" Charlotte Cranfeld asked.
"Or did she just see their clothes lying about?"

"She saw *them*," Julia insisted. Then shaking her head, "My
heart aches for his poor mother."

But the other ladies weren't thinking of Nettie Miller; they were thinking of Julia's daughter, Ama, and what she saw. "She's seen more than's good for her," Charlotte Cranfeld later told her husband. "I shouldn't be surprised if Julia had some trouble with that girl."

During the summer, when Bill Miller had started parking the Marmon before the Gannon residence, Wednesday Sewing Club was (more's the blessing) disbanded. But at the first meeting, late in September, his name came up again.

"That Miller boy — Nettie Miller's son," said Orpha Graves, concentrating so intently on her knitting that she dropped a stitch, "he seems to be settling down some."

Ruthie Harper stared out the window and said she felt they should all remember that it was a fine thing he did — lying and all so as to serve his country.

They all knew, Harriet could tell by the way their eyes avoided her, and had talked it over during long telephone conversations. They all knew, that is, except Julia Harkington, who had been away for the summer and no one had as yet managed to inform her.

"Well," she declared, "even so — he may be fine — but I certainly would hate to see a daughter of mine out with that kind of fellow."

Flo's pretty round face tightened with anger. "Who are we to condemn a person like that?" she demanded warmly. "What do we know about him — aside from cheap gossip that we shouldn't listen to anyway? He's — he's mature, he's very gifted in music — certainly a lot more interesting than most of those high school boys."

Julia looked at her, surprised and hurt. All the other ladies were filled with infinite pity that things had come to such a pass that the Gannon family should have to justify Bill Miller.

Afterwards, in the back seat of the Peerless while George drove them home, Harriet and Flo sat in unhappy silence until Flo said helplessly, "Mother, why does she do it? She must know how people are talking!"

Harriet felt just too depressed, too exhausted by it all to talk about it. She murmured only, "Eddie's very young."

"But eighteen isn't so young! Heavens, I *married* when I was nineteen."

"Well — so did I. And so should Eddie. But, I don't know. Eddie doesn't seem to care about the things we wanted. She's restless — it takes a boy like Bill Miller to keep her interested. He's been away so much."

"Eddie should be talked to," Flo declared. "*You* should talk to her. She needs to be told a few things."

"I?" Harriet held out her hands in despair. "I talk to her? What good would it do? She wouldn't listen to me." She squeezed Flo's hand, and smiled wearily. "Don't let it upset you, Flo. If that's what Eddie wants, well — "

But Harriet did try to talk to Eddie — not about Bill so much as the late hours he brought her home. And of course Eddie silenced her. Eddie wanted to know why she must be spied upon, why her affairs must be the affairs of the whole family, why her life must be interfered with more than anyone else's in the family. Harriet explained that no one was spying on her; one just couldn't help knowing that she came home very late and she was after all still in school.

"For heaven's sakes, Mother," Eddie said coldly. "This isn't the dark ages. Try to remember we're living in nineteen-twenty. I certainly hope that if ever I'm a parent, I'll try to be a little more understanding — "

And so as the fall wore on, Harriet tried to be a little more understanding, tried hard to realize that the nineteen-twenties seemed to be something special that must be coped with, and wondered why, what it was, when life seemed so quickly to have fallen back to normal. She thought about the dark ages, by which Eddie obviously meant the period of Harriet's own youth, and had to repress the wish that the present dawning age of enlightenment were as easy to see by as that historic time when Clark City was a main street and a few farms huddled at the foot of a mountain, and an aged queen cast rays from her quivering lamp as far west as the Rocky Mountains. Eddie continued seeing Bill Miller, oftentimes secretly, Harriet knew, and Harriet sat up to wait and hope.

Eddie's problem was only a part, however, of the larger design that included Louise's election to vice-presidency of the nature

club, Jack's rather vague, rather sad letters from Harvard, Gus's
two weeks of a kidney infection, and Papa's comforting presence,
night after night, bent over his desk in the study, reading the lives
of great men, smoking cigars, storing away in a filing cabinet the
newspaper and magazine clippings or elaborately penned tran-
scriptions of the thoughts, the statements, the incidents that all
added up to the thing a man lived by. If there was worry from
one child, there was comfort from another and that's how it had
always been. The important thing was to have them there, the
children and Papa, making a life for her, needing her.

Later in the fall, too, giving a sense of occasion to the sleepy
little town, reminding them that they were part of a busier world,
was the Benefit Ball given by the affiliated ladies' clubs of Clark
City to raise money for the Charity Hospital. The Benefit Ball
meant silk hats and tails (smelling slightly of moth balls) for the
men, new gowns — gowns or evening frocks or costumes — for the
women; it meant that for the cause of aiding the poor, every respectable citizen of Clark City would do his utmost to prove himself one of the rich.

Not being a respectable citizen of Clark City, Bill Miller had
announced to Edna Gannon that he wouldn't be caught dead at a
Benefit Ball, that he, personally, was going hunting that weekend.
The news could not fail to stir various strong reactions in the Gannon family. Eddie herself was forced to acquire a sudden indifference toward everything connected with the Benefit Ball; Harriet, after her anger had cooled, reasoned with herself that perhaps
Bill Miller's brutal selfishness would indicate to Eddie that he was
not her kind, that his attentions were keeping other, really fine
boys away, that the whole town would now be given evidence of
the questionableness of his intentions. Papa was so disturbed by
Bill Miller's ungentlemanly behavior that he gave Eddie fifty
dollars to buy herself a little something. Louise and Babe admitted
passionately that they would rather die than not be seen at a
Benefit Ball when they grew up.

The one advantage of Bill Miller's insult to Eddie was that it
released Martha for help with the refreshments at the Ball since
now Eddie could stay home with the children. Louise and Babe
squealed with delight when they realized that Eddie, less yielding

to mortality than they, would be there, quite alive, to share the dark house when the grownups had swept out. Flo would drop off Sammy and Connie for the night, and Eddie would think of something to do and — oh golly!

The night of the Ball, the whole family was, of course, gathered in Harriet's and Papa's room, helping, adding to the flutter. Eddie tied Papa's tie and brushed off his shoulders. Louise and Babe pounced upon the gold lace bag of jewelry which Harriet took from the little wall safe, decked themselves in diamonds. The jewels were gifts from Papa, each time Harriet bore him a child, and were named for the inspirer and eventual recipient of the gift. Louise wore Flo's diamond and sapphire bracelet, Eddie's diamond watch; Babe wore Jack's sunburst, her own diamond and emerald lavalier, Gus's earrings. The earrings were for pierced ears so she just dropped them inside her ears. Then Louise had the idea that their clothes should befit their adornment, so they brought armfuls of discarded velvets and taffetas from the box couch in the hall, piled them in the very center of the room where everyone would have to step around them.

When Flo and Grant arrived with the two children and all came up to the bedroom, Harriet was strained and white with nervousness and the wonderful excitement.

"Oh heavens, Flo — " she said without even looking around. Connie and Sammy ran to her to be kissed and she had to turn from the dressing table to say who were Grama's sweethearts.

"There's no hurry, Mother," Flo said, while Grant complained heartily that he sure hated to get into one of these monkey suits.

"You both look very grand," Eddie said, swooping Sammy off the floor. "Don't they, Red?" She blew into his neck; he giggled and squirmed to get free.

"Let me look at you, dear."

Flo slipped her coat off so that Harriet could see the lavender chiffon and silver metal-cloth, draped about her hips, draped in a tight skirt that revealed one ankle.

"She looks like a shady lady," Grant said, "showing off her legs that way."

Papa smiled uncertainly at Grant's special kind of wit, and Harriet shook her head with concern. "I guess we'll all be getting around to that from the looks of things."

"You're all going to be shady ladies?" Grant hooted. And Eddie said, "Speak for yourself, Mother."

Harriet looked quickly at Papa. "Now Grant," she chided. "You look lovely, Flo. I'll stop in and tell Mr. Hart next time I'm in town. He just knows what you can wear."

Then Harriet stood up, ready for her jewelry.

"Oh heck," said Babe, stumbling on high heels, dragging, tripping over the skirt of an old velvet afternoon dress of Harriet's. "I wish you didn't have to go." She reluctantly gave up the sunburst and the lavalier and one of the earrings, but the other one was gone. Everyone searched the room, Eddie and Louise and Grant knelt on the floor to look.

"Really, Helen, I wish you'd be more careful," Harriet said.

Babe, hearing the name Helen, was immediately on the defensive. "I couldn't help it," she whined. "Golly, I'm always blamed for everything."

Papa sighed and muttered to himself. Then Flo discovered that Sammy had the earring clutched in his hand, and everyone laughed with the release of nervous tension and Grant said disgustedly that sometimes he wished he'd remained a bachelor.

Harriet stood before the long mirror, putting on the jewelry that Papa had given her. Everyone watched quietly as if this were a rite, as if Harriet in the white satin beaded dress were somehow anointed. When she was finished, they all regarded her in silence, until Flo went over to push Harriet's hair just a little more off the forehead, Eddie brushed a streak of powder from her neck, Louise pulled at her corsets, smoothed the satin over her hips. Then they all said she looked lovely.

Lights went off, room after room, as they proceeded to depart, until, in the whole big house, only the downstairs hall light was on by which the party people could take a last look at themselves in the hall mirror. Harriet kissed the younger children, and then, impulsively, kissed Eddie and patted her shoulder, and Papa and Flo said good-bye to her as if she were being very brave. Eddie and Louise and Babe and Connie and Sammy stood by the door, watching George help the people into the Peerless. All the white-gloved hands waved from the car, and as the car drove off, emptiness swept through the house.

This was the time when childhood seemed a horrible desert, too lonely and drab, really, to be borne. With a fervency of anguish, Louise and Babe wished that they were old, old, old. Sammy, with a hurt, forsaken look, put his thumb in his mouth and turned his back on the others. Connie moved over to Eddie, clutched her hand. They all waited helplessly for Eddie to say something, to do something, to take them out of this desperate loneness.

Eddie came through. "Well, kids," she said, embracing them all with her voice, bringing them together, bringing back security. "Why don't we make some fudge?"

Without a word, Sammy took his thumb from his mouth and trotted toward the kitchen. Louise clapped her hands together with a prolonged "Oooo." Babe strangled Eddie in an embrace and said, "Oh Eddie, I just love you!"

In the coziness of the kitchen, with the smell of fudge cooking and Eddie's voice reading *Romeo and Juliet,* the world became an enchanted place again. Outside, far away, was the Benefit Ball, but here were Montagus and Capulets, dressed in finery that resembled quite a bit Mother's satin gown and Dad's tails, here was young worshipful love and a dark-haired, slim, yummy man, and a melting maid who resembled quite a bit Louise and Babe leaning over the oak banister in the hall.

"'O! Swear not by the moon,'" Eddie read in a throbbing voice as she let a few drops of fudge fall into a cup of cold water, "'the inconstant moon, That monthly changes in her circled orb, Lest that thy love prove likewise variable.'" She poked the balls of fudge, licked her finger. Then in her deep, exciting Romeo voice, she whispered, "'What shall I swear by?'"

Sammy and Connie were both too sleepy to give very much to Shakespeare, but they watched with drugged stares as Eddie poured the fudge onto the platter, and came to life somewhat when Eddie passed the empty pan and two spoons. Louise and Babe listened enraptured, asked Eddie please to skip the dull parts when the nurse or the friar came in but to read all the speeches of

Mercutio, who, they agreed, was the image of Tommy Reed, and, of course, all the love parts.

"'It was the nightingale, and not the lark, That pierc'd the fearful hollow of thine ear,'" Eddie sighed, as the fudge cooled, and the grownups danced away the night at the Benefit Ball.

Time passed, Sammy dozed, the fudge was quite ready to be stirred, Louise and Babe wept quiet tears as Romeo clasped his death cup.

"'Eyes, look your last!'" Eddie cried passionately. "'Arms, take your last embrace! and, lips, O you The doors of breath, seal with a righteous kiss A dateless bargain to engrossing death!'"

The doorbell rang, cutting off her words, bringing a startled question to their faces.

"Who could that be?" Eddie asked, annoyed. Babe jumped up but Eddie said, "I'd better go." She walked through the dark dining room and the dimly lit hall with Babe tagging behind her.

Bill Miller was at the door. When Eddie saw him, she said only "Oh," leaned against the door.

"You wouldn't ask me in, I suppose," Bill said, in his rasping voice.

Eddie waited, biting her lip. Then she stepped aside.

Bill was dressed in a leather jacket, khaki pants, boots. His hair was mussed — he brushed it smooth as he came in.

Eddie stood with her arms folded, looking at him. He returned her gaze with equal coldness.

"The car broke down," he said finally. When she made no comment, he added, "It can happen, you know."

Eddie shrugged her shoulders.

Then Bill noticed Babe and his expression changed. He grinned, slipped his hands into his back pockets. "Hi there, Beautiful."

Babe, in the velvet dress, high heels, and old feather boa tied around her neck, swished her hips, lowered her eyes.

"What the hell," Bill said, "won't any of the gorgeous Gannons speak to me?"

Babe grew very red, murmured "Hello," then covered her face with her hands.

Bill turned his grin to Eddie, then back to Babe. He walked

over to her, put his arm around her shoulder, squeezed her. "Why don't you teach your big sister some manners? You're the only Gannon I've ever met who isn't a stuffed shirt."

This was too much for Babe; no one had ever given her such a tribute. She twisted about so actively that she stumbled on the velvet skirt, collapsed to the floor. Laughing shrilly, she said, "Oh gosh, I'm dumb."

Eddie turned from Babe's exquisite embarrassment to Bill's smirk. "Why don't you go?"

"Why don't you come with me?" he asked.

Louise appeared in the doorway from the dining room, pale and troubled.

"Ah," Bill said, holding out his hands in amazement, "is there no end to the ravishing beauties in this house?"

The remark drew more laughter from Babe, sprawled on the floor, but not so much as a glance from Louise.

"Eddie," she said quietly, "Sammy's asleep. I think we should put them to bed."

"Would you mind taking them up, Louise? Babe, get off the floor and help her. I'll be up in a minute."

But Eddie didn't go up. Louise and Babe settled Flo's children in Jack's bed, and Louise looked in on Gus. They waited for Eddie, and when they came downstairs, they couldn't find her in any of the rooms.

They were both frightened, because they had never been left at home alone, and the house seemed very dark and empty and the three children upstairs seemed very far away. Babe's first impulse was to whimper, but then she remembered the unstirred fudge in the kitchen and the thought gave her courage.

They stirred the fudge for a while until their arms became tired and the fudge was nowhere near stiff — it hadn't even lost its gloss. Then Babe burst into tears and said she was going to bed and that she just hated Eddie. Louise told her not to be a silly little crybaby. Babe said she hated Louise too and stomped off to bed.

Louise was really alone now. She left the fudge on the kitchen table, made her way fearfully through the dining room to the hall. By the grandfather clock, it was eleven. She sat on the steps, her eyes fixed to the front door. She rubbed her arms, tried not to think of the shadows pouring out of Papa's study, out of the music room, down the stairs. She hummed and she counted and she recited Robert Louis Stevenson, and she thought about Christmas. But the autumn night kept forcing itself into her mind.

Shortly after midnight, she heard voices on the porch — Harriet's, then Papa's, and Grant's loud laugh. The twelve strokes of the clock had suggested such terrors of rattling chains and dying groans that now, with everything all right, she started to cry. She ran to the door, threw her arms around Harriet, sobbed into the white fur collar of her coat.

"Louise — what is it?" Harriet gasped, with sudden terrible knowledge that Gus had been kidnapped, Babe had cut an artery, Eddie had eloped.

"Nothing — nothing, nothing," Louise stammered. "Everything's all right — I'll be all right — "

"Louise dear, darling, there there, don't cry," Harriet patted her, wiped away the tears with her own handkerchief.

"Where's Eddie?" Flo asked suddenly.

"I don't know — she went out, I guess — with Bill Miller."

The four grownups looked at each other. Flo said, "You see, Mother?"

Papa asked, miserably, "Should I go out and look for them?"

Harriet shook her head. "Why don't you take Louise upstairs. I'll wait for Eddie."

The Benefit Ball was over. The tails could return to moth balls, the gowns to garment bags, and the Charity Hospital would have a new kitchen from the proceeds of the evening. And so it had been for twenty-one years, and if Eddie had attended, as she should have, everything would be all right now, nothing could have gone wrong. And Jack —

The kitchen door slammed. Eddie's hurried steps brought her to the front hall. "Oh, you're back — " She looked anxiously at the faces.

"Thanks for looking after my children, Eddie," Flo said. "I appreciate it very much."

Eddie's worried expression turned to anger. "You might try looking after them yourself sometime, for a change."

"Eddie, please," Harriet said. "At least let's not quarrel."

Papa put his arm around Louise, spoke without looking up. "You shouldn't have done that, Eddie."

"I didn't do anything, Dad. I was in back the whole time. I didn't leave them — "

Flo kissed Harriet and Papa good night, patted Louise and thanked her. "I'll pick up the children in the morning," she said. She and Grant left without a word to Eddie. Then Papa took Louise up to bed.

"Well?" Eddie said defiantly when she was alone with Harriet.

"Eddie — can't you see?" Harriet asked, too tired to discuss it now. "You're hurting yourself as much as you're hurting me — you're as much a part of the family as I am. If you can't see that, what is there — "

Tears of anger and vexation came to Eddie's eyes. "Why can't I lead my own life? Why do I have to be told what I can do or what I can't do? You treat me like a child — or like one of those simpering little things when you were young. Times have changed — "

Hanging up the white satin dress, taking down her hair, turning off the light and slipping into bed beside Papa, Harriet wondered how many times she would be hearing that these were new days, that things were different now.

Oct, brought Hallowe'en with pumpkins and masks and ghost drapery. Then November hurried the year on to its close, with only the barrier of Thanksgiving before the arduous preparation for Christmas could begin. Hardly was the last bite of nut and date pudding swallowed, the last Bohemian glass returned to its shelf in the dining room, the last damask napkin sorted out for the wash, than Christmas came sweeping in.

The secretive trips down town, the telephoning and late hours squinting over a needle, the sore feet and stuffed closets were a prelude little conducive, one would think, to good will toward men. But with the sore feet came an intoxication of the spirits, with the snow, brilliant and golden in the day, blue and glistening at night, came a richer awareness, a sharpening of life after the soft, sad days of autumn. If Clark City knew not quite how to cope with the subtleties of autumn, the rigor of a really bad winter renewed each man's faith in himself, reminded him that this was pioneer country, this was pioneer stock.

The first week in December, Center Street decked itself with garlands of colored lights and the two pine trees in City Hall park acquired lights and stars. And then the merchants of Clark City offered their wares: the Golden Rule and Hart's Drygoods featured nighties and kimonos for ladies, gloves and mufflers for men, Tinker Toys and Meccano sets and dolls and sets of dishes for children; Mr. Potter filled his window with Swiss watches, bronze incense burners, cut glass; Harkington's Furniture Emporium offered a three-piece living-room suite of a shiny red material, sprinkled with Christmas-tree snow, exclaimed over by ecstatic cardboard figures; Miller's stationery had special gift boxes — either of cedar, or cardboard with a hand painted landscape — containing different pastel tints of paper, a sealing wax set, and a small bottle of scented powder. These were Clark City's gifts of Orient rare, of myrrh and frankincense. During business hours, Center Street was festive: Mr. Hart, Mr. Potter, and Mr. Harkington were harrassed and affable. When darkness settled and the stores closed and the customers went home, the strings of lights and the two pine trees shining valiantly under the vast sky drew the town into a tight, lonely oneness, as if this were indeed the furthest outpost of civilization.

Harriet bought the biggest Christmas tree she could find, ordered an eighteen-pound turkey, continued filling her closet and the little glass conservatory downstairs with her purchases — and counted the days and then the hours until Jack's return.

Jack too was looking forward to Christmas — so he said in his letters. He said also that he missed everyone, that Boston was a disappointing place, that he seemed to be doing all right in his work, that he guessed Harvard was all right. Considering that Jack was to be their author, Harriet found the letters, precious and watched for as they were, surprisingly uncommunicative. Did they give him enough to eat, she would write. What sort of room did he have? Had he met a lot of nice boys from good families? What had the teachers said about his writing? The food wasn't so good, he wrote, but the room was all right — except if he'd known anything about it, he'd never have been in a dormitory — it was kind of hard to meet people — those he had met seemed to be all right. He hadn't written much — the literary magazine seemed to be more of a club than a school publication — it seemed kind of hard to break in. Mostly he thanked her for the oatmeal cookies she had sent or told her not to worry — everything was fine. Or he'd say that he guessed you had to leave home before you really appreciated it and that Christmas couldn't come too soon for him. What he said in his letters to Eddie, Harriet never knew; the entire family read all of Harriet's mail but their own was of course private and they resented even her curiosity. The one note to Papa was an apologetic few lines saying that, darn it, he hated having to do this, but everything seemed to cost so much more in the East and unless you were going to turn into a grind and not know anybody, well, you just needed a bigger allowance. The letters did little to take the place of him. He lived in a world which she couldn't even imagine and all he ever told her about it was not to worry — everything was all right.

On the morning of December twenty-second, the whole family, Gus included, Flo, Grant, and their two, climbed into the Peerless and drove to the station. The ground was covered with deep snow and Harriet reminded George twice that he wasn't to drive more than ten miles an hour. Inside the steamy, hot station, they stamped their feet on the cement, and Joe Krump came out of his stationmaster's office to shake hands with Papa and say he guessed Papa must be pretty proud to have a boy at Harvard. He tipped his visor at Harriet and said Merry Christmas, these were happy times.

The clanging of the locomotive bell drew them outside to watch the train slowly pull in and jerk to a stop. And Jack was home again. Thinner? Somewhat drawn? What was the good of all that education if it ruined a boy's health?

Harriet held on to his arm as if someone might whisk him off again and driving home, driving through the town for Jack to admire the strings of lights and the City Hall Christmas trees, she communicated with him in the only language she could summon, an occasional pat on his gloved hand.

Once at home, however, their shyness left them. When Jack came downstairs wearing a sweater, carrying a little lavender box of Louis Sherry candy for Harriet, she just had to hug him. And Babe grabbed at him from the rear for a throttling embrace.

"Hey! My gosh. Do you women want to kill me?"

"Jack," Babe beat her fists together, "could we please — would you please — please — please help us with the tree this afternoon? Mother wouldn't let us till you got here."

He pulled her braid, plucked her glasses down her nose. "Okay, kid." He swatted her behind and Harriet took his arm to lead him to the living room.

And there they all were, Papa standing by the fireplace, Gus on the floor, the girls and Grant on the loveseats, waiting, and Flo's youngsters investigating the boxes of decorations that surrounded the tall bare fir tree. Harriet, having them together once more, felt so proud she could burst.

"Well," said Flo, with her warm smile. "Now tell us *everything*, simply *everything*."

"Everything?" Jack whistled. "But Flo, that's not simple."

"How's Harvard?" Eddie asked. "Is it heaven?"

Jack snickered, looked briefly at his father. "Well, hardly. Depends on what you mean, I guess."

"But you *know* what I mean. Is it — " Eddie leaned her elbow against the loveseat, pushed her fingers through her hair. "Oh, Jack — is it cosmopolitan and do the boys talk about books and invite the girls to their rooms for tea? — with chaperones, of course."

"Well — not too much of that tea. Lots of books, I guess — that is, among a certain class. And yeah, sure, girls go to the rooms sometimes."

"How's your work coming?" Harriet asked. They would, she knew, have to drag it out of him. He was not one to boast of scholastic attainment. "I guess it isn't time yet for the prizes."

Color seemed to come to his pale cheeks, very becoming color, she thought. "It takes time — college is different. I wanted to talk to you about that, Dad. Lots of fellows have trouble the first few semesters. We haven't had exams yet — but, well — we shouldn't really expect too much."

Harriet smiled. That was his way — as Miss Kirkham said, he was, intellectually speaking, the most self-effacing boy she had ever encountered. "We aren't worried," she said. "None of us."

"In fact," Jack hurried on, "it's pretty academic and some of the fellows have been thinking that college isn't the best way to get an education — pretty removed from life, and, well, you know —"

"College is a fine thing," Papa proclaimed soberly. "A fine thing. No one, I suppose, would go so far as to say it's useful, as experience in business is useful, but it's — it's important."

This, for Papa, was a speech and nothing but the deepest conviction could have drawn it from him. Now, deflated, he looked for confirmation.

"You're perfectly right, Dad," Flo seconded him. "There are other values — *besides* business. Honestly, I think it's perfectly wonderful what Jack's doing."

"But what *is* he doing?" Eddie said. "Jack, what *are* you doing?"

Jack frowned, rearranged himself in his chair. "I go to classes, I — " he brightened, "Say! have you ever heard about those glass flowers? Marvelous collection — nothing like it in the world."

"Tell us something about your friends," Papa suggested. "What kind of contacts have you made?"

This really was what they all wanted to hear — the weekend parties at Long Island estates, the coming-out parties in Boston and New York, the boys whose fathers were senators, leaders of business, writers, the girls whose fathers controlled Wall Street. "Yes, Jack," Harriet beamed, "tell us about them."

"There isn't," Jack said, "a lot to tell." He sat back in his chair, kept his eyes on his hands that hung limp between his knees. "The fellow I see most of — my best friend, I guess you'd say — is my roommate. His name's Dave. Dave Archer."

"Where's he from, dear?" Harriet inquired.

"North Dakota. I guess his Dad's pretty rich — you never see any of it on Dave, though."

They waited and finally Papa said, "Any others?"

Jack rubbed his eyes. "Well, there's a fellow I play handball with sometimes — he's from Pittsfield, Massachusetts. And then you meet different ones, of course — eating — or out. There's a little place down behind the Copley where you're apt to run into Harvard men."

"But what about your classes?" Eddie asked. "The people you discuss things with? The people who believe in — in the League of Nations and vote for Wilson — the radicals? Or the young poets?"

"Gosh, Eddie, you don't understand. It's different there. You don't speak to anyone unless you're introduced and there's no one in a class to introduce you."

Harriet smiled, trying to think of the right thing to say, watching Gus's grunting attempts at a crawl. Then Papa cleared his throat and said, "Well — these things take time. Easterners — we all know how they are and New Englanders are famous for their — reserve."

"Of course they are, dear," Harriet said.

"You don't suppose — " Papa paused. "Do you think that being a Westerner — "

"I don't know, Dad." Jack leaned his elbows on his knees. "I just think maybe it's a mistake, that's all. I wanted to talk to you about that. Harvard's too old — they have some funny ideas. I think maybe, for a fellow like me, with all that money you're spending — "

"The money's worth it, Jack." Papa's forehead was wrinkled, he pressed his thumb into his chin. "You know what I think the trouble is? I think maybe you've been working too hard — you're worried about those examinations."

"Of course that's it," Harriet said. "I could have told you that. Why Miss Kirkham used to say that — "

"It just takes time," Eddie interrupted her. "He's only been there three months."

"Of course it does," Flo said. "And I think he's done just grand. After all, three months isn't very long."

When Martha came in, wiping her beaming red face on her apron, to say that luncheon was on the table, they were all, except Jack, thoroughly happy, and it was up to them to see that Jack relaxed, to take his mind off those examinations.

Grant, stretching and groaning, said, "Hey Jack, how about those Boston fillies?"

"They exist," Jack said.

But that was no kind of talk. Harriet took his arm, and as she led him to the dining room, she patted his hand. "Now, dear, what was it you were going to tell me about those glass flowers? I want to hear all about them."

Martha had been sure that Jack wouldn't have eaten a decent bite of food since he left home, and so she staggered in with a platter heaped with leg of lamb, roasted potatoes and onions, and then the gravy and creamed peas, fruit salad, muffins, and chocolate cake. She brought milk for Sammy, Connie and Jack.

Over the food, they discussed the party.

"Ah, the party," Jack said.

"We thought it would be nice to have it before Christmas this year," Harriet said. "That way all your friends will know you're back and will want to do nice things for you."

Eddie broke in bitterly, "We thought it would be nice to have it before Christmas because the Hoopers stole New Year's Eve. They started inviting people practically last summer."

Jack grinned. "Muriel Hooper?"

"Did you know Muriel, dear?" Harriet asked. "We thought it was odd — they must know that New Year's Eve has always been our night."

"It's to be in their *ball*room — the invitations were hand written in green ink. Ballroom!" Eddie scoffed. "It's that clammy room in the basement with water pipes across the ceiling. You'd think that at least people wouldn't have to be entertained down with the plumbing."

"Well, I don't know," Flo said, "maybe it'll be nicer having ours before Christmas for a change. It seems to me people are a little tired by New Year's Eve and don't really notice how much work you've gone to. This way we'll get them when they're fresh, start things rolling — "

Flo was right, of course, but a tradition, after all! Confetti and serpentine at midnight, snappers and paper hats and horns — this, since Flo was at the Lincoln School, had climaxed the season. The new party dress which each girl in Clark City received for Christmas had its first showing New Year's Eve at the Gannons'; the new Ingersoll watches of the boys ticked the evening away. Drugstore perfume and gift-package hair oil, initialed handkerchiefs from the Golden Rule, new pen and pencil sets drawn from inner pockets to check off numbers on the dance programs. It was hard to see the Hoopers taking all this.

Papa couldn't understand how Caleb Hooper would allow his wife and daughter to do such a thing. "I've had lunch with Caleb Hooper, oh — several times," he said, troubled. "Caleb and I served on the Liberty Bond Committee together. I thought Caleb was a gentleman. Caleb shouldn't have let this happen."

"But he's not a gentleman, Dad. They're complete trash," Eddie exploded. "Just because Mr. Hooper makes money out of the war, they think they can entertain the whole town in their privy. Oh, I hate this town — I despise it."

"Why does anyone go to their old party?" Babe demanded. "I'd kill myself before I'd go."

"Well," Harriet said, "maybe it will be a nice change to have ours before Christmas — to be the first rather than the last." To herself, she did have to admit that the Hoopers seemed to have come up in the world with the war. But one needn't believe the stories one heard.

"It'll be interesting," Jack murmured, "to see Muriel Hooper again."

After lunch, Papa and Grant had to get back to their offices and Flo had to take Sammy and Connie home for their naps. Eddie asked Jack if he didn't want to come downtown with her to buy some new rolls for the player piano; but Jack stretched happily over his full stomach and said he guessed he'd get at that tree. Louise and Babe said "Goody," and rushed off to make things ready.

"How about you, Mother?" Jack asked. "You better come in and talk to me."

"I shouldn't — there's so much to be done — " But his wanting her was such happiness that she yielded without conscience.

In the living room, Louise stretched the tree lights across the floor to test the globes and Babe was pasting loops of red and green paper to make a long, unlovely chain for the tree. The Santa Clauses and bells and candy canes and birds and glittering tree balls lay in tissue paper in boxes. Already Babe had spread gray dingy cotton at the base of the tree and arranged the sparkly paper houses and steepled church and pine trees in sooty snow.

"Shall I just be lazy?" Harriet asked. "Shall I just sit here and watch?"

Jack held her face between his two hands and kissed her; Louise stopped her work to clear a place for Harriet to sit. "Ah, I'm spoiled, spoiled," Harriet complained blissfully.

Babe held up the chain she was working on and said, "Look what I made."

"Very fine," Jack said, struggling to set up the ladder beside the tree.

"I don't think it is." Babe grinned with bravado. "I think it's dumb." She pulled at the two ends of the chain until one of the loops broke, then she dropped the chain, covered her mouth with her hands, and gurgled.

"Don't be so silly, Babe," Louise said, looking uncomfortably at Jack. "Be your age."

Babe reddened, glanced quickly at all their faces, stuck her tongue out at Louise.

"How does Eddie look to you, dear?" Harriet asked. She tried to catch Babe's eye to frown at her.

"Eddie? Just the same — meaning fine, I guess."

"I wondered if she didn't look a little strained, tired. I hope you'll have a chance to talk to her while you're here."

"Probably have a lot of chances."

"What Mother means," Louise said, handing Jack the string of lights, "is that you should tell Eddie she can't go out with Bill Miller."

Jack frowned. "He still hanging around?"

"I'm afraid so." Harriet made little tucks in her skirt. "Not serious, I'm sure — she's just young, but if you — "

"It is too serious," Babe said. "I bet they get married."

Had Babe been nearer, Harriet would have stroked her hair with a certain parental touch, but Babe was at a distance and would not even allow Harriet to catch her eye.

Then they heard Tommy Reed's voice, joking with Martha in the kitchen.

"Just if you have a chance," Harriet said, "when you're talking to her sometime."

Tommy slouched into the room, chewing gum, an old fur hunting cap perched on his head. He stared for a moment at Jack on the ladder, then nodding in his direction, asked, "Who's the character trying to climb the pine trees?"

Babe giggled. "You crazy."

"Has he changed, Tommy?" Harriet asked. "Does he look older?"

Tommy strained his eyes. "From here it looks like old John Harvard himself."

"Same old joker, same old clown." Jack leaned his elbow on the top of the ladder. "I figured a college education might have a maturing influence, but" — he held out a hand toward Harriet — "you see, Mother, if that's a product of the American university system, there's no point in my keeping on."

"I guess you boys wish we'd leave," Harriet said. "I guess you'd like to talk."

"Reed, do we want this lovely lady to leave?" Jack demanded.

Tommy stood at attention. "We do not."

"Reed, out of all the lovely women in the world, which one would we rather have share our secrets?"

Tommy grabbed the fur cap from his head and made a sweeping bow before Harriet.

"Oh — " It was shameful how delicious these boys could make her feel. At her age, and so giddy. "Well, just for a minute then."

"Now if Reed will haul his fat — if Reed will come over here, he can make himself useful."

"Why don't I help Babe here?" Tommy asked. He replaced the cap on his head and sprawled on the floor. "How's about it, Babe? I cut and you paste."

"Well, Tommy," Harriet said, "how are things with you?"

"It's the war, they tell me, Mrs. Gannon." He concentrated on his cutting. "That's what my English teacher says. It's always the war. How's Harvard?"

"Terrible. How's State?"

"Ah, wonderful. Ah, the lovely coeds. Ah, the love. You approve of love, don't you, Mrs. Gannon?"

Harriet felt herself blush. "He doesn't think it's terrible at all, Tommy. He's just tired — he's been working too hard."

"Yeah — I figured he probably had been." Tommy sat up, bit his tongue as he cut a long strip of green paper. "That could be the war, though. They say it's ruined our generation. They say it's worse for those of us who didn't get in. We aren't part of our generation."

"I was in the ROTC."

"You know how he is, Tommy — he wouldn't admit he was doing well even if he was at the top of his class."

"Is that how Jack is?" Tommy compared his own strips of paper with those Babe had cut. "I guess you're right. They don't give Phi Bete to freshmen, do they, Gannon?"

"Naw — and anyway, I'm against those Greek-letter organizations. Pretty frivolous, it seems to me."

"What about the Great American Novel? How's that coming along?"

"Jesus, Reed — these things take time. You gotta live, drink deep of the Pierian spring. I'm just a kid — no experience."

"Trouble with you, Gannon — you just ain't part of your generation."

"Mother," Babe said, without looking up from her work, "what are they talking about?"

"What a question!" Tommy said. "Babe, sometimes you disgust me. Weezie, tell your sister what we were talking about."

"What were you?"

"The Magna Charta, of course." Tommy snickered. "That King John — he was a great old guy. He really was."

Harriet searched for a question that would draw her in again. "Who's your partner for tomorrow night, Tommy?"

"Tomorrow night . . . ah, the Gannon party. Well, I thought I'd come alone, Mrs. Gannon. Hey look," he said to Babe, "why don't you let me paste for a while? I'm getting tired of my job. How about you, Jack?"

"Well, I thought I'd come alone too. You gotta have some stags." He backed down the ladder and stood off to survey his light arrangement. "Did Eddie invite Muriel, Mother?"

"Muriel Hooper? Yes, dear. After her invitations arrived — "

"Muriel Hooper," Tommy said. "Well, well."

Jack stood in front of Harriet, his hand stretched through his open collar to rub his chest. "Here's how I look at life, Mother: you have it only once, you don't know for how long and so it's a duty and an obligation to make it rich and wonderful. Open your arms to it — embrace it all. No experience should go untasted — no segment of life unexplored. And it's a sin to shut yourself inside brick walls — even if they do have ivy on them."

Was he serious about this? It would break Papa's heart.

"Hey Jack," Tommy said, "was you ever shot down over France — in a aireoplane? Bombs screaming around you — machine guns — " he held up his two arms vibrating with the stuttering of the gun, "ak-k-k-k-k-k — beautiful German spy in a parachute beside you? Hell, you missed all that — you don't stand a chance — "

Jack grinned and Harriet knew that everything would be all right. "If you'll ask Eddie to dance with you tomorrow night — both of you — "

"Hasn't Eddie a date?" Jack asked.

"Yes — of course. But she's so fond of you two. I'd like her to have a chance to talk to you." And now she must go. They had done more than their duty. "There are things to attend to."

By seven o'clock the night of December 23, every light in the Gannon household was turned on, the rugs were rolled, the floors waxed, the doors between rooms opened wide, the creamed chicken was bubbling on the stove, and Louise and Babe Gannon were fighting over who should have the first use of the bathroom. The contest was not without point; the long stream of bathers had practically emptied the hot-water tank and the loser would have to bring a kettle of boiling water from the kitchen.

Harriet sat before her dressing table, powdering her neck, puffing out her hair, adorning herself with jewels — all in bitter solitude. Papa was in the room, encasing himself in his tuxedo, but Harriet was not speaking to Papa. Nor was she to Jack, Eddie, Louise, or Babe. She was on very good terms with Gus, whom she had sought out many times during the wretched day to whisper to and squeeze; and when Flo arrived, she would speak to Flo, but to none of the others.

All day long they had criticized every move she made, and if she was a little irritable, heaven only knew she had a right to be. The work had to be done; standing around talk-talk-talking all day would certainly accomplish very little indeed, and the thought of Eddie's constant admonitions to be calm brought out a film of perspiration on Harriet's forehead and the back of her neck that undid all the work of her powderpuff.

The climax had come in the late afternoon when the evening paper arrived and Jack had seen his picture on the front page. "Harvard Boy Home on Vacation," it said. Could she help it if they had used an old picture out of the high-school year book? The picture was their idea, not hers. All she had done was mail in a little article to the *Clark City Sentinel*, anonymously, giving a brief review of his high-school career, hinting at Miss Kirkham's prognostications of his future, welcoming him home on behalf of

all his Clark City friends, who, the article said, were proud of the
fine record he was making at Harvard and were all anxious to see
him. It was just a little surprise she had planned for him, nothing
more. And certainly a little advertising never hurt anybody. And
as a matter of fact, it was a nice little article; while she was working on it, the thought had occurred to her that it was probably
from her side of the family Jack got his literary talent.

But the storm it had aroused! You'd have thought she had com-
mitted murder — or worse. That cold, icy expression — she had
seen the same thing on his father — the command, please, for God's
sake, not to meddle in his affairs. Eddie looking on as if Harriet
were some impossibly strange or repulsive object; and Babe, in-
furiatingly, saying she didn't understand how her mother could
have been capable of such a thing. And did Papa say a word in
her defense? All of them taking Jack's side, against her: if Jack
had been pleased, they too would have been pleased, but she, of
course, was always wrong.

Sitting before her mirror, seeing her eyes grow moist, seeing
the depth of sadness on the face that was after all not so young
as it once had been, Harriet was swept with such pity that she
had to bite her lip to keep the tears from falling and spoiling her
face. Don't meddle in my affairs, Jack had said. As easy as that.
For nineteen years he could use her, then cut her off when he was
through. None of them stopped to think that she might have had
something quite different from this — that she had had plenty of
other chances. If she had married Alf Reinhart, for instance, she
might have lived in Venice, California, and been a real lady of
leisure. But no — she had chosen Papa and them. And they had
all rejected her, all of them.

Harriet stood (more of this kind of thinking and she'd have to
take an aspirin and go to bed) and surveyed herself in the long
mirror. What she saw was, she knew, charming and appealing.
She was small but the white satin gown gave her dignity. And
little matter that her eyes were red — it wouldn't hurt the family
to know. Without a word to Papa, she swept out of the room,
down the hallway, down the stairs. While the others were dressing, she would make a final survey of the house in peace, start the
fires, check the lights.

She lit the wood fire in the library grate, the thick red candles on the mantel. This was the only room in which the rug had been left; this would be their cozy-corner. Jack had tied mistletoe from the chandeliers of all the downstairs rooms, in all the doorways. There was a wreath in the window, a silver dish of holly on Papa's desk. Harriet poked and pulled at the holly, shifted the angle of her portrait on the desk, and with a quick look round, passed through the brightly lighted hall (sliding a little on the powdered wax) into the music room.

Here from the pile of boxes on the piano, she selected "Dardanella," fitted the roll into the drawer under the keyboard so that when the guests arrived, just a turn of a switch would start the music for dancing. She straightened the wreath in the window, checked the mistletoe, passed through the open doorway to the living room.

But here she had to stop. This was too lovely — all her efficiency left her, all her grief. Only the tree lights were on, shining red, blue, and gold through tinsel, icicles, glittering ornaments. The village at the base of the tree cast little glowing lights and blue shadows on the cotton snow, on the great pile of wrapped packages that circled the tree. Pools of soft light shone from the waxed floor, and in the mirror above the fireplace, were reflected the red and blue and gold of the tree. The rose plush loveseats and stiff little chairs gleamed primly in the soft glow, and the crystal dishes on the mahogany tables caught the light like prisms.

She was aware of another pattern unfolding, living itself out at this moment. It was always this way at Christmas: after the preliminary rush and exhaustion, the nervous part was suddenly over and at that precise moment you realized that now was the time — the feeling spread through you in a single moment that it was Christmas. And at that moment, you lost your identity in a mass of feeling, the past Christmases, the little town of Bethlehem, the three wise men and Scrooge and Papa and the kiddies. From then on, Christmas would mean watching all the others. But Christmas really came to you when you were alone, at a time like this, before the others arrived.

Harriet took it all in, the room, the Christmas tree, the snow outside, the Christmas party about to begin inside. She lit the candles on the mantel, on the mahogany tables. And she caught a glimpse of herself in the mirror, alone in the great shining room, before she departed for the dining room.

The table was set with the finest that money could buy: the cut-glass punch bowl and candelabra that the men at the mine had given Grampa Gannon, the drawnwork tablecloth that she had smuggled in from Mexico, the silver compotes and trays Papa and the kiddies had bought her for anniversaries and birthdays. Martha's Christmas present to the family, a huge poinsettia, stood in a cut-glass bowl in the center of the table. Because more than a hundred had been invited, the creamed chicken in patty shells would have to be served on paper plates. But behind the glass doors of the china cabinet, stacks of Haviland and Rosenthal stood ready testimony that here was quality. Why the little Hoopers should want to have a party after this, Harriet didn't know; but as she lit the candles on the table, she felt kindly disposed toward the Hoopers, toward all mankind, indeed.

In the kitchen, Harriet wanted to share a little of what she felt with Martha. "It's lovely, Martha — the whole house. I'm satisfied! We did a good job. I think the party will be a success."

But Martha was taking a gloomy view of things. Ten dozen patty shells, besides all those chickens to stew, had made the world look pretty grim. "Enjoy yourselves," she sighed, "take your pleasures while you can. It won't be long before the Bolsheviks will be after us and then I don't know where we'll be."

Harriet smiled her most reassuring smile though really she didn't know why Martha had to say these things. "Papa says we aren't to worry, Martha. He says he thinks now everything will clear up. I'll send him down to explain all about it." She scooped a spoonful of the creamed chicken, blew on it, tasted. "Mm — that's lovely, Martha." And she left Martha, whose hair was straggling and whose feet were swollen. "Don't you worry, Martha," she called, seeking comfort in her own cheerfulness.

When the first guests arrived (a sallow, pompous boy who won the oratorical contest at high school and a flat girl with huge rats in her hair) Harriet greeted them at the door, directed the young man to Jack's room, the young lady to Eddie's room to leave their wraps, and while they were upstairs, she turned on the piano to let the rolling chords of "Dardanella" sweep through the house.

Babe and Louise bounded down the stairs in white dresses, hair ribbons, black patent leather slippers — Babe to answer the door, Louise to change the music, and, when the time came, serve punch.

"Oh golly, Mother, do we look all right?" Babe demanded breathlessly.

Babe's hair could have used some parental disciplining, but to mention the fact would be to remind them that during the latter part of the afternoon, all relations between parent and children had ceased. "Fine," Harriet said, with just enough lack of enthusiasm to show she hadn't quite forgotten. Babe dashed to the mirror to look at herself and try to smooth her hair down with her hands. "Oh golly," she said, and ran to the door to admit the new arrivals. Louise looked at her mother in rapt wonder, then came over and kissed her cheek. "You look just beautiful, Mother." And Harriet knew why the trouble and despair were worth it all.

The guests arrived, stamping their feet, making self-conscious greetings on their way upstairs to those already acclimated. Papa and Harriet stood before the big mirror to shake the hands of the young people, to tell them to enjoy themselves. When more and more arrived and the hall began to fill up, they moved to the stair landing which overlooked the hall like a balcony. From here they could watch the gaiety below, smile and nod and wave a handkerchief like the King and Queen in the Pathé News.

It was a lovely sight, the girls in their pretty new dresses and corsages of sweet peas or pink roses, the boys in their best Sunday suits and slicked hair. Some of the boys would try to dance their girls under the mistletoe, but the girls would squeal and run away. Then the boys would dance them into the living room where the lights were not so bright.

Muriel Hooper arrived with Richard Rice, one of Jack's friends. She wore a black velvet coat with a silver fox collar and carried three long ostrich feathers, not a fan but apparently serving as one. Her hair, puffed out on all sides, was glued to her forehead in elaborate bangs and a braid of gold metal cloth crossed the crown of her head. People turned to look at her. No one came up to speak. Jack danced by, didn't stop to welcome her as really he should, but said something which made her laugh.

On her way upstairs, she stopped to speak to Harriet and Papa.

"Gee, Mrs. Gannon," she said, "it's simply wonderful to be here." She took a quick survey over her shoulder. "It looks like a scrumptious party — and look at you! Really — isn't she perfect, Mr. Gannon?" Richard was jogging her elbow. She frowned at him. "Wait a minute, can't you?" Then leaning toward Harriet, pressing her hand, Muriel whispered, "Why are boys always so darned impatient?" This started Muriel laughing again, and all the way upstairs, into Eddie's room, the laughter continued.

"Caleb Hooper's daughter," Papa murmured, and Harriet nodded.

"Dardanella," "Margie," "Japanese Sandman" — all the latest tunes — the young people checked them off on their dance programs. Before each number, there was scurrying around to find partners, then a lull until Louise pulled the switch. Dancing by, different ones would comment on the perfection of the party; whenever Tommy Reed danced by, he would wave one arm and shout, *"Merry Christmas to all and to all a good-night."* And whatever girl was dancing with him would slap his shoulder, scold, "Oh Tommy," and share her disgusted smile with Papa and Harriet.

Papa was taking particular pleasure in Tommy; he would shift about, wave self-consciously, then rub his hands together. "That's a fine boy," he said again and again.

Surveying them all, thinking it over for a while, Harriet finally had to admit, to herself and to Papa, that their children were the most attractive on the floor. Jack, in the tuxedo they had bought him for Flo's wedding, was so utterly handsome — certainly with that fine forehead and straight black hair, he'd be the one you'd pick out of any group. And it was perfectly clear that half the girls on the dance floor were wild about him. Eddie was the only real beauty there. And she was smart. The beautiful bouffant dress of luminous taffeta, the corsage of violets and deep red roses that Bill Miller had sent her, the way she danced, dignified and graceful — people who had seen Irene Castle had said she was exactly Eddie's type, maybe not even so striking. They had told Harriet that more than once. And Flo — her figure wasn't what it had once been, but she was a dear thing and she looked lovely. She was busy seeing that everyone had a good time and whenever she passed her parents, she waved and smiled and in a loud whisper informed them that everything was just gorgeous. Grant was perhaps being a little foolish, dancing with the younger girls, but it was nice that he was enjoying himself.

It was getting on to ten-thirty before Bill Miller arrived — almost time for the refreshments. He dropped his coat in a corner and didn't so much as look up to where Papa and Harriet were standing. He wore a tuxedo (he and Jack were the only young people in tuxedos) but the trousers needed pressing, the tie was about to come untied, and his hair needed a comb through it. He stood by the door, his hands in his pockets, stared at the dancers, and when any of them spoke to him, he muttered something without looking at them.

With his entrance, Harriet felt as if someone had suddenly turned the lights down or muffled the music. She had known he would be there, of course; she had prepared herself for it, but now that she saw him, the evening that had been pure enjoyment became overshadowed, complex. Why had he not come up and spoken to them? Eddie had undoubtedly told him of their feeling toward him, but he was their guest, you don't go into people's homes showing so much resentment. At least you pretend. His open antagonism was frightening; his stolid square bulk gave her a moment of panic. He had such power to hurt her — he was like a force of nature before which she was utterly helpless.

Eddie was off dancing someplace, but Jack came up to Bill, held out his hand. Bill seemed embarrassed. He reached toward his tie, then shook hands, pushed his hand through his hair. For a moment they talked — Bill would be asking how was Harvard and Jack would be saying fine, how had the football gone. Harriet watched and breathed easier. Her side was winning. Like the Bolsheviks, she thought. If they actually *should* come over, something fine, the better upbringing, the essential better breeding of her class must triumph. She must remember to explain it that way to Martha.

The thought of Martha reminded her that it was time to do something about the food. She looked at her little diamond watch and held Papa's arm and they descended the stairs.

In the dining room, by the door that led to the little glass conservatory, Jack was talking to Muriel Hooper and she was holding her feathers to his lips to watch his breath flutter through them. Seeing Harriet and Papa, she hailed them. "Honestly," she cried out, "what has happened to this boy?"

"Why, has something happened, Muriel?" Harriet asked.

"He's *terrible* — he's perfectly *awful*," Muriel gasped. "He was bad enough *before* — but the things they've taught him at *Harvard!*"

Harriet felt herself tighten with disapproval and then to keep from being the intolerant meddler Eddie considered her, she had to smile her implication in Muriel's little joke. "You scold him for me, Muriel, while I see to the food."

"Well, I don't know if I trust myself with him," Muriel said, goaded on now. "Maybe I should trade men with you, Mrs. Gannon. Or are all the Gannon men like that?"

Harriet managed the merest smile and sailed off to the kitchen, leaving Papa to disentangle himself as he might. Muriel was obviously everything that Eddie said she was, and what would happen to the poor boys with the girls flaunting themselves this way? Jack, Harriet remembered uneasily, had seemed more amused than embarrassed or disgusted.

Later, when the food was served and the young people had taken the paper plates into the living room or library, or had seated themselves on the stairs, Harriet saw Tommy Reed coming from the back hall that led to the basement.

"Where have you been, Tommy? You haven't been in the basement?"

"Just looking around, Mrs. Gannon." He rubbed his finger along his nose. "Could I please have three plates of food?"

While Louise served punch, the player piano was to take a rest. Let them eat in peace, Harriet had said. But when a live musician took over, you could hardly go in and tell him to stop that noise. He played the same piece over and over, "The Love Nest," the sheet music was on the piano. Nothing else, just "The Love Nest."

Passing ice cream to the young people in the rose room, Harriet observed through the open door that the musician was Bill Miller, and his audience, consisting of one, was Babe Gannon.

"Helen dear," Harriet called, "wouldn't you like to help a little?"

If Babe heard, she pretended not to. She sat on the bench beside Bill, slumped forward in ten-year-old ecstasy, her clasped hands hanging down between her knees.

"Helen is very fond of music," Harriet explained nervously to Nancy Barton and Allen Cram. They both smiled and nodded.

Harriet found Eddie, whispered, "Tell Babe I want her. She can pass cookies."

"I'll pass them," Eddie said with a blank stare that defied Harriet to say more.

"Well —" Harriet bit her lip, gave in. "Is everything all right?"

"It's a lovely party. I'm having a lovely time."

She spoke the words with such cold precision that Harriet was startled. Eddie swept off to the dining room, head high, for the cookies. Eddie was obviously not having a lovely time at all, but her coldness, bless Heaven! was not directed at her mother. Well! Harriet said. Well, well!

There were only four dances left on the program after refreshments — the party would end almost on the dot of twelve. Harriet and Papa didn't take their place on the stairs but moved among the guests, receiving compliments, wishing Merry Christmases, sending greetings home to the parents. "It's been just perfect!" wailed the girls. "You bet," added the boys.

Harriet tried to keep her eye on Eddie. Eddie was dancing every dance, talking with almost excessive animation to any boy, every boy but Bill Miller. As far as Harriet knew, she hadn't spoken a dozen words to him. And he had danced with no one, had talked only with some of the boys. At one point, she had seen him take a package from his coat pocket and go outside with two of the boys. And why was that? Was it too stuffy, she asked Papa. Papa was afraid that it might mean cigarettes, but Bill kept going out with different ones of the boys and staying only a moment.

The last dance, the dance when each girl should dance with her partner, and certainly Bill Miller had been asked as Eddie's partner, Eddie was no place to be seen. Bill was there by the door, hands in his pockets, his face somewhat redder, his clothes even mussier than when he arrived. He stood there through about half the roll, then he did something surprising. He asked Babe to dance.

Babe had been leaning against the doorway to the music room, gaping, with her mouth slightly open, at the dancers. When Bill came up to her, she blushed deeply, and instead of saying she had never danced before in her life, followed him wordlessly onto the floor. One of the boys shouted "Bravo," and the dancers cleared a space so they could watch.

Harriet, seeing them, felt the vague fear again. There was something not quite nice about this. Had it been Tommy Reed who had asked her, that would have been cute and sweet, and fun to see Babe get such a thrill. But this was different. He wasn't doing it for Babe's pleasure. And poor Babe — her white stockings were bunched and soiled at the knees and she wasn't a graceful child. They would probably fall, the way they were stumbling about — he seemed none too steady himself. She was red, and whenever they stumbled, she laughed so hard that little bubbles formed in the corners of her mouth. And the way she looked at him, the red-faced ecstasy — it was almost painful to watch. He didn't look at her so much as at the grownups on the floor and his expression said that he was highly pleased with himself.

And where was Eddie all this time? Harriet looked through the crowd for her, stepped into the other rooms. Forgetting her tired feet in the anxiety that grew in her, she hurried upstairs to search the bedrooms.

They were in her room, Flo and Eddie. Flo was holding a washcloth against Eddie's eyes.

"Good heavens, is anything wrong? What's happened?"

"It's all right, Mother," Flo said. "Eddie's just upset."

Eddie held the washcloth away. "Flo's trying to make me presentable." She managed two notes of a laugh, then burst once more into tears. "Oh damn — give me that cloth, Flo."

She sat on the bed and wept into the washcloth.

"Bill's been running a saloon out on the front porch," Flo said. "We had an anonymous call — some friends, so they said. They weren't very pleasant."

"I don't mind about me," Eddie said brokenly, "but that he

could do this to my family — to our Christmas party — Does he
think we're the Hoopers?" She sobbed miserably. "For heaven's
sakes, Flo, make me stop."

Harriet looked up at Flo for a reflection of her own surprise.
She sat on the bed beside Eddie, took her hand. "Everything's all
right, Eddie, if you're all right. I think it's been a lovely party."

Eddie threw her arms around Harriet. "Don't be sweet to me,
Mother. Just tell me how awful I've been, but don't be sweet."

"You'd better go back down, Mother. The party's almost over.
I'll take care of Eddie."

Standing beside Papa and Jack, saying good-bye to the guests,
Harriet agreed with every one of them that it had been a lovely
party; in fact, she did not always wait for the guest to make the
first statement of that fact. Bill Miller had departed, without a
word to anyone, and now the air was clear — he'd never be there
again, if she knew Eddie. These were stages the young people
went through — Eddie's rebellions, Jack's impatience with Harvard
— and you wouldn't want your children to lack spunk and spirit.
But Eddie would meet some nice young man now — the *right* kind
of young man — and Jack would finish Harvard with flying colors.
After all, things don't change much, order restores itself. The end
of the party was like the beginning. The young people, bundled
up, went out into the snowy night, laughing, excited, calling back
and forth to each other. It had been an occasion.

Then it was locking up, blowing out the candles, turning off the
lights.

In the music room, spread limp against the piano, a sad frazzled
remnant of the party, Babe Gannon had sat out the end of the
party in solitude.

"Babe!" Harriet exclaimed. "What are you doing here all by
yourself?"

Babe lifted her head, squinted through puffy eyes, brushed the
loose hair away from her face.

"The party's over," Harriet said. "Now for bed."

Babe sat there, staring at the keyboard.

"Time for bed now," Harriet repeated. "Did you have a good
time, dear?"

Babe looked up, took a deep breath. Then she drooped forward, buried her head in her arms. From the bottom of her soul, she drew a sigh. "Oh golly," she murmured.

The party was the first rite of Christmas. The next day was an unvaried repetition of every twenty-fourth of December the family had ever known. The pies went in the oven, the pudding went in the oven; the turkey, plump and naked, sat on the kitchen table for the admiration and whistles of all passers-by, while its innards boiled in a little pan on the stove. Louise and Babe broke the bread for dressing. Martha scraped the celery and wrapped it in a wet towel.

Every member of the family made at least one hurried, secret trip down town. At ten o'clock, Tommy Reed called for Jack and they went down together to help each other buy presents for their families, to select the tie that each should give the other. They had a turkey sandwich in Hart's basement where they ran into Eddie, laden with packages. They bought her a hot tamale smothered in chili.

At four o'clock, when Papa came home early from the office, his arms full, he found Jack and Tommy stretched on the floor listening to the player piano. Because it was the day before Christmas, he invited them into his library for cigars and port, and because Jack had been so worried about his examinations, Papa gave him a hundred dollars to help him relax.

Dinner was at five-thirty — a lamb chop, boiled potato, canned peas, bottled peaches. Harriet sent Martha to bed, and the whole family helped with the dishes. Jack didn't do much, mainly stood around and flipped his towel at his sisters. Then he stretched — said he guessed he'd be going — he had a date. He kissed his mother — said he guessed she was about the prettiest gal he'd ever seen. And told his father to take it easy. And told Eddie to get some beauty sleep — she could use it. And told Louise and Babe not to wake him before ten-thirty the next morning.

Before Jack left, he and the girls had to go upstairs for a stocking to hang on the chair that tradition had made his own for Christmas day. And Jack said it wasn't fair — his didn't hold as much as the girls'.

Then Harriet and Papa and the girls sat in the living room with just the tree lights on, not saying much, just looking at the tree and at the packages. Soon Harriet began to yawn — Santa Claus, Eddie always said, got sleepy early the night before Christmas. The girls withdrew reluctantly, hating to leave the warm light of the tree for the cold white light upstairs, wanting to hold on to the lovely moments, to retard time just for a little. Upstairs, while they got into bed, they heard the carolers outside and pretended they heard sleigh bells on the roof.

At twelve-thirty, Jack slipped quietly in the front door, up the steps, down the hall to Louise's room where Babe would also be spending the night. He looked at the dear little girls sound asleep, took hold of the bedclothes, pulled them back. The dear little girls were fully clothed, except for shoes, and screaming, "Darn you, Jack — leave us alone — you woke us up —" "Yeah, sure," Jack said. "Come on — off with the clothes —" "But it takes so long to dress in the morning —" "Off with the clothes." While they undressed, they both stated emphatically that they just hated Jack — he was the meanest thing they ever saw.

At five o'clock, Babe was up, making the rounds of the bedrooms to see if anyone was awake. At 5.15, Louise was on a similar mission. At 5.30, Babe retraced her steps, making certain that a door banged, that she bumped into a chair or two. From the darkness in her parents' room came Harriet's weak voice, "What time is it, darling?" "Merry Christmas," Babe shouted, and from the other end of the hall came Louise's bounding steps. "Merry Christmas, everybody."

"What time is it?" Papa's sleepy, grumbling voice asked.

"It's late, Dad," Louise groaned. "Get up, hurry, or it'll be light."

"Well, it isn't now. Turn on the light so we can see."

Eddie appeared in the doorway, yawning, her bathrobe pulled around her, her hair down her back. "Merry Christmas, everybody."

"My God," said Papa, "it's only five-thirty."

"Hurry, Dad," Babe pleaded. "You're always the slowest one."

"Oh golly — I'd better phone Flo." Louise dashed down the hall to the upstairs extension.

"I'll start in on Jack," Babe said with slightly diminished spirits.

She crossed the hall to his room, opened the door, and in her loudest whisper, called, "Jack, are you awake?" No answer. She thought for a moment, closed the door quietly, tiptoed down the hall, then ran back shouting "Merry Christmas Jack," and opened his door with all the noise she could command. Then she whispered, "Jack, are you awake?"

From his bed came a low mumbling. "Go away."

"He's awake, everybody," Babe cried out. She turned on his light, dashed to his bed.

"For God's sake, turn off that light — do you want to ruin me?"

"Everyone's up — practically dressed. Hurry hurry hurry."

Jack sat up, blinking at the light. He looked at his watch, sank back, moaning, "Oh my God, Oh my God."

"Now *hurry*," Babe ordered, and rushed off to dress.

She was back in exactly three minutes, dressed and braiding her hair and crying, "Mother, come and make Jack get up!" Louise followed after her, saying, "Jack, if you don't get up I'll never speak to you again as long as I live."

"Well, how can I get up with all you women fussing around?"

Suspiciously they withdrew. "Now *hurry*," Babe said, closing the door. "Remember — you promised."

By the time Flo and her two children had arrived and rushed up the stairs calling their Merry Christmases, Jack was up and dressed in pants and sweater. He wasn't shaved — they had to make at least one concession to Jack. He yawned and grumbled and scratched his head.

Babe and Louise were counting off steps, oldest to youngest. Sammy was considered still too young to lead the procession and so Connie would be first, then Babe, Louise, Eddie, Jack, and Flo carrying Sammy. Harriet had taken Gus downstairs and Papa had followed to turn on the tree lights and start the fire in the grate. And then the breathless moment, waiting for the signal from downstairs, the signal that would open the door on Christmas, that would put an end to anticipation for another year.

Harriet's voice, "All right, kiddies," started them running down the stairs, as fast as Connie could run, across the hall, through the music room. Squeals of delight from Louise and Babe when they beheld how thoroughly Santa had visited this year.

Harriet stood with Gus in her arms, watched the expressions, listened for exclamations. Gus chewed at his finger and twisted around so that he could keep his eye on the tree. Papa stood stiff and formal but cracked his knuckles behind his back. In the doorway from the dining room, Martha stood, wearing her best church dress.

"Oh golly, Mother, it's just beautiful —" Babe held up the red taffeta party dress, swished it about for sound. "How did Santa *know* — it's *just* what I wanted!"

Louise's eyes filled with tears when they beheld the white fur muff and scarf. "Oh gee," she gasped.

Eddie's big present was a hope chest. Inside was a pair of pillow slips Harriet had embroidered. "She's started in on me," Eddie said to Flo. "She won't be at peace till I'm out of the way now."

"I thought it was something you could always use," Harriet began, justifying herself. "You could put your fur coat in it — you could —"

Eddie kissed her cheek. "It's beautiful, Mother. I'm thrilled to death with it."

Jack's big present was a set of the Harvard Classics. He looked at the books, lifted the cover of one, said nothing. He tried on fur-lined gloves and turned to his mother with a smile. "These are fine — just fit."

For Flo, there was a little finger ring, diamond and sapphires. Flo burst into tears when she saw it. "Mother — you shouldn't have —" She put her arms around Harriet. Harriet's eyes filled with tears. "Well, Flo, we wanted you to have it."

And there were the other presents, the add-a-pearl necklaces for the younger girls, the satin night gowns for the older ones. The underwear and silk stockings and perfume and bath salts. Jack's ties and socks and underwear and cashmere sweater, and stationery with his name and the Harvard seal in crimson. The toys for Connie and Sammy — dolls, baby carriage, building blocks, fire engine. The electric train for Gus. The five-hundred-dollar check for each of them.

And then there were the presents they gave each other, the packages under the tree, the diamond jewelry Babe had bought everyone at Woolworth's, the satin and lace garters Louise had made for the girls, the scarf she had knitted for Jack. Gus's presents were there, with cards written in his mother's hand — girdles for his older sisters, shoe brush for Jack, handkerchief boxes for Louise and Babe. He, in turn, received mechanical toys and picture books, a red ball, a clown that sat back up when you pushed him over. Gus paid little attention to any of the gifts he received. What he liked best was an old curling kid he pulled from the back of his mother's hair — the soft leather was nice to chew.

And there were presents for Harriet and Papa. For Harriet, the beaded bag and satin negligée, the box of creams, the bath salts and powder and perfume, the gold locket with eight sections for pictures of Papa and the kiddies. Papa received cigars and a white silk muffler, velvet smoking jacket, jade cuff links.

And then the initialed handkerchiefs for Martha, the box of candy, the toilet water, the flannel nightgown, the renewal to her astrology magazine, the check in an envelope.

"It's been the best Christmas we've ever had," they all said. "Everything's been just perfect."

It was what they said every year, and then they looked at each other's presents and thanked each other once again and whatever they had received was precisely what they had wanted.

Grant arrived about ten, drank a cup of coffee, opened the ties and socks on his and Flo's chair, then stretched out on the floor to play with Gus's train. Tommy dropped in shortly thereafter to pick up his tie and deliver Jack's. He joined Grant on the floor. At eleven, when George dropped in for his check, he watched out of the corner of his eye the clumsy maneuvering of the two non-mechanics. "Lemme take a look at that," he said, finally yielding to desire. Until dinner was announced and Tommy and George had to leave, the three men kept Gus's train burning up the tracks; now and again, to keep Gus from fussing, they rolled the red ball at him.

Dinner was a repetition of Thanksgiving — the most of the best, the damask and Bohemian glasses and whatever goes with a turkey. And Papa prayed, to give his thanks for the day and for the wife that had been granted him and for the blessing that the children had been. And over the dessert, when he filled the wine-glasses with port for the grownups, he said, "To all of us — and the merriest Christmas we've ever had."

This Christmas was actually rather a special occasion because it was Gus's first conscious one, and as he sat at the table in his high chair, chewing a piece of toast, spitting, blowing out his lips, they couldn't imagine how they could ever have thought Christmas was fun before Gus shared it.

"It wasn't all of us in the old days before the emperor," Jack said. "We needed old Gus here to complete the triumvirate."

"I'm going to pretend we never had a Christmas without Gus," Babe said.

So significant did Gus's presence seem to Harriet that that night, after the dinner and the long afternoon of people coming and going and the turkey sandwiches in the evening and the final withdrawal from the living room, after she was in bed and the lights all off, she felt she must go and see Gus. She slipped out of bed, put on her bathrobe, went to his room. He was awake, lying quiet in the dark. She picked him up, kissed the soft creases of his neck. And then she felt he must want another look at the tree.

When she reached the bottom of the stairs, she could see that the tree lights were on. In the living room, Louise was snuggled on one of the loveseats, her hands in the fur muff.

"You should be in bed," Harriet said. "It's late — you'll catch cold." She sat beside Louise, put one arm around her; the other cradled Gus. She felt Louise's face against hers, felt that it was damp. "You've been crying," she said. "You should be in bed asleep."

Gus was quiet, sucking his thumb, watching the tree. The fire in the grate was almost out, only a few red coals.

"I don't want it to end," Louise said. "I don't want it to end — ever."

"There'll be others," Harriet said. She kissed the top of Gus's head. "There'll be others."

Part Two

A BARE TWO WEEKS before the country was to be mourning the man whose election to the presidency had returned the world to "normalcy," Harriet Gannon had an appointment of some moment. For who could tell? Perhaps her younger son might himself be President some day. If, indeed, he were, this day would be an important one not only to Gus and to his family, but to the nation and to the world at large. Gus, for the first time in his life, was to have his picture taken.

It was a July morning in 1923, hot, hardly a breeze to stir the curtains at the open windows in the rose room. The vegetable man, calling his wares from the street, was as wilted as the lettuce in his wagon, and his poor horse clopped at a tired pace down the street. One of the neighbor's children, one who sometimes played with Gus, though he was older, sat on the curb and let the water in the gutter run over his feet and the legs of his overalls. And his mother, hanging up a wash in the back yard, straightened up between pieces, rubbing her back, losing herself in a daydream.

It was a day for starched linen, for straw hat and white shoes and white stockings, for a touch of cologne on the temples, for a dash of cologne on a handkerchief.

Harriet had ordered the car for ten, and at ten, she and Gus stood hand in hand on the porch, waiting for Frank to drive it around. Frank was Japanese. His real name, something quite unlike Frank, had been too much for Harriet, and not since the first day had he been called anything but Frank. The first day was shortly after the horrible accident in which George had overturned the Peerless, killing himself, wrecking the car. His wife, poor thing, had had to go out by the day and all because of that awful booze. Frank could help Martha in the kitchen as well as drive the motorcar, and the new Packard seemed to give less trouble than the old Peerless.

The car appeared from around the corner, and Frank helped them in, saying something agreeable but incomprehensible. The town, as they drove along, was clean, dappled with color and shadow. Roses were out and petunias, delphinium, sweet william and phlox; the box elders and maples were heavy and lush with foliage. Harriet chattered about Mrs. Abbot's lovely garden, about chances for a break in the hot spell and the President's lovely vacation in cool Alaska. She talked on uninterrupted, because, though Gus could talk, he didn't much, and Frank had discovered early that since Harriet could understand not a word he said, it was usually simpler merely to nod and grin.

"Pick us up in half an hour, Frank," she told him when he pulled up in front of Mr. Watson's studio. "It might be a good idea if you went now for the groceries — Martha would appreciate it."

Frank muttered a few words, gesticulating, affable. Harriet smiled vaguely. "Well — yes, you just pick up the groceries — that'd be lovely."

Mr. Watson was a Clark City landmark, who, like the City Hall and the monument in Pioneer Park, was beginning to show the weathering of years. He had photographed Harriet as a bride and all her children from the time of birth till they were old enough to rebel against the sylvan backdrop and velvet, fringed couch. Harriet felt comfortable about Mr. Watson: he had aged more than she and he remembered her from better days. "And he gets a nice likeness," she would insist to Papa. Also, Mr. Watson would not only listen while she talked about her kiddies, but he showed an active interest in them.

"Mrs. Gannon," he said, in a voice weighted with incredulity, as if he hadn't expected to see her at all, as if he hadn't talked to her on the phone yesterday when she made the appointment. "My dear friend, Mrs. Gannon!" He pressed her hand in his, and drew back to get a look at her. Then he knelt down to be level with Gus. "And this is the new one!" he exclaimed, with the same note of surprise.

"Well, not so new," Harriet said. "He's my baby, Mr. Watson, but he's three — three and a half. I guess he'll be the last." She gave a little embarrassed laugh and fumbled with the neck of her dress.

Mr. Watson stood up and with a wide gesture ushered them into the studio. "Come in, Mrs. Gannon, come in, come in."

The studio was shabby and dusty; the wicker furniture in the waiting room had, through years of service, acquired a beaten look, and the dusty collection of photographs on shelves recorded somewhat ingloriously the births, high-school commencements, marriages, and wedding anniversaries of Clark City's undistinguished citizenry. Mr. Watson was himself a worn remnant; the thin strings of hair, the shiny vest and watch chain with elk's tooth indicated that here was a man who would have no weapons against the get-up-and-go of the younger competition down the street. Like the pictures on his shelves, he looked out from a world of gray shadows and brown sunlight.

Behind a velvet curtain was the studio itself, bare, its only furnishings the velvet couch against the forest scene of grays and greens, a small dressing table with a worn hairbrush, lights and the aged camera which created immortality by the squeeze of a rubber syringe.

"It hasn't changed," Harriet said, nostalgically, "not in all these years."

Mr. Watson smiled, resigned and sad, arranged his lights, then approached Gus like a man who has faced too many losing battles. "This is our little fellow who's going to have his picture taken," he said with tired joviality. "We're a fine, brave little fellow, aren't we, Mrs. Gannon, fine and brave, and when we grow up, we're going to be a fireman, riding big engines down the streets." Mr. Watson went to the front office and returned with a small bell which he rang in imitation of a fire engine.

From behind his mother's skirt, Gus watched Mr. Watson with

solemn concentration. At three, Gus still had the large square head which had given him his name, and a stocky body on fat straight legs. He tended to be somewhat serious and did not give very much of himself except to his mother and to Louise. The rest of the world he treated as strangers. When Mr. Watson knelt down to him and reached for his hand, Gus turned from him angrily, clung to his mother's knees.

"That's no way to act," Harriet chided. "Come, darling," she tried to release his grasp, "let's go and sit on the couch."

"Our little fellow's going to be a brave little man," Mr. Watson tried. "We aren't going to make trouble for Mummy and the nice man. We're going to —"

Mr. Watson took hold of Gus's hand and Gus gave a yell. Mr. Watson withdrew his hand, stood up and gazed straight ahead as if he might weep.

Oh dear, dear, dear. Harriet picked Gus up, carried him to the couch. "Gus, Gus," she whispered. Then aloud, "You know how children are. Eddie — you remember, she's my next oldest daughter — do you remember how she carried on about her picture? Mad! I never saw anything like it — and that picture of her, we've laughed till we cried over it."

Mr. Watson, peering through the camera, his head covered by the black hood, said gloomily, "I remember your daughters, Mrs. Gannon, beautiful children they were. But I guess they've forgotten me. It's been many years —"

"Well, I shouldn't repeat it, I guess," Harriet said, "but many's the person who's told me I have the finest-looking children in Clark City. Eddie could be in the movies — people have told me that. And she was valedictorian of her class — I guess you knew that."

Settling herself happily beside Gus on the couch while Mr. Watson made things ready, Harriet gave herself up to the pastime she liked best. "Flo — she has two of her own, but neither of them is as pretty as she was —"

"I haven't seen any of her children," Mr. Watson interrupted her. "I guess they haven't had their pictures taken — "

"They're bright children, Flo's are," Harriet said, "and prettier than most — Connie's the best looking — but there's a strong look

of their father in both of them. You might not recognize Flo —
she's stouter since her second one came, but she's never given me
an unhappy moment in my life."

"Now if we'll just let the little fellow sit there —"

Harriet started in on Louise. "People say Louise is the most
like me —" but when she stood up to move, Gus scowled and
scrambled after her. "Now Gus, you sit there — be a good boy.
For Mother."

Gus grabbed onto her knees and when Mr. Watson peered from
under the black hood, Gus started to cry. "I don't like you," he
said to Mr. Watson through his tears.

Harriet felt herself getting red as she scolded Gus, red and
exhausted. What a lot — what an endless lot a mother had to put
up with. Sometimes you felt like throwing them out the window.

"Sometimes you feel like throwing them out the window," she
said to Mr. Watson.

Mr. Watson smiled wan agreement. Then he brightened with an
idea. "I know what our little fellow wants," he said, vanishing
into the waiting room. When he returned, he had a small package
in his hand that he held out to Gus. "Little fellows all like a piece
of candy, isn't that right, Mrs. Gannon? That's what little fellows
are for."

The ragged, broken package contained menthol cough drops,
which, when Mr. Watson shook them out, showed by a slight fuzz
that they had been in Mr. Watson's pocket. "Have some," said Mr.
Watson. "Take as many as you want."

Gus stopped crying, reached out his hand for one of the cough
drops, put it in his mouth. While he sucked at it, Mr. Watson
smiled victoriously at Harriet. But suddenly Gus's forehead
wrinkled in a frown and he took the cough drop from his mouth
and hurled it at Mr. Watson. "I don't like you," he said, red with
anger. Then he burst into tears and grabbed onto his mother.
"Mommy, I don't like the man."

Mr. Watson turned away, limp now with defeat. Harriet picked
up Gus and tried to quiet him. "There, there — now be a good boy.
Mother will buy you a milk shake if you'll be a good boy." Patting
him, she turned to Mr. Watson. "As I was saying, Mr. Watson,
Louise is the most like me, and I shouldn't say it, but people think

she's a little doll. I guess you knew she's at high school now, and I shouldn't be surprised if we had another valedictorian on our hands. Miss Kirkham says she's a real scholar."

Automatically, his heart not in it at all, Mr. Watson fought for his place in the sun. "If she wants graduation pictures, your girl, I don't think anyone would deny that I've taken graduation pictures for some of the first families in Clark City."

"But of course what I tell her, you're too modest, Louise. You don't appreciate how superior you are, I say. The boys are different now, I say, and you can't just sit back and expect them to take you places. Call them up, ask them to the house. Put some music on the player piano, I say, we'll make some nice punch or buy some ice cream from the drugstore. Eddie, you know, Mr. Watson, always had a house full of boys. I guess no girl in the town had more boys than Eddie had."

Gus, soothed by his mother's voice, sat quietly beside her on the couch, sucking his thumb. Mr. Watson hid himself under the camera's black hood and motioned for Harriet to move aside.

"You stay there, darling," Harriet said. "Mother will just move to the end of the couch — it's too hot to sit so close together. My youngest girl, Mr. Watson, Helen, is going through the awkward stage just now and it's a little hard to tell — but we think in a year or two she'll turn out fine. You know how it is — they grow too fast. She's always been a very affectionate child, but — well, I don't know."

Mr. Watson squeezed the rubber pump and beamed, triumphantly. "Another, Mrs. Gannon, another. Maybe we could get the little fellow to smile."

"Oh dear. We need Louise for that. Gus — Gus — what does Yooweez say? This little piggy went to —"

Gus didn't smile but he took his hand out of his mouth and grabbed for his foot. And he watched Harriet expectantly. Mr. Watson got the picture.

"Fine, splendid," said Mr. Watson, with the resonant voice and taller stature of a man who has just been lifted to self-respect. "Now one more. I never skimp my old customers."

"I wondered — he has such a dear body and it *is* a warm day — we might just take one of him lying on the couch — without his clothes — on his stomach, of course."

"Well ——" Mr. Watson's hand sought the elk's tooth. "We don't generally — that is, *usually* they're a little smaller than your fine boy."

"Oh I know, I know. But after you've had six children, Mr. Watson, you don't get around to these things as soon as you do with the first ones." And she began undressing Gus.

Mr. Watson fussed with his camera, keeping his back to Harriet and Gus. "You had another boy — back East some place to college. I recall seeing a picture of him in the paper — one that I'm afraid must not have done him justice, although I don't mean to disparage the work of a competitor."

"Jack," Harriet said, after the merest pause. "That was Jack — he was at Harvard. He's in New York now — doing research. We decided, Papa, that is, and I, that a year away from school might be best for him — he writes, you know, he has many plans. We're confident, however, that he'll be back in Harvard soon — he has one, maybe two more years." Her fingers stopped their work of untying Gus's shoe; she looked up at Mr. Watson's back. "You knew, I guess, that he would have been the only boy from Clark City ever to have graduated from Harvard."

"My sister sent me a postcard once of Bunker Hill monument. She was a great traveler — always traveled in the best style. A whole week in Atlantic City."

"Well," Harriet said, "well, I don't know. I suppose these kiddies know what's best for them." She kissed Gus's bare back. "It's just that you wonder sometimes."

"Is the little fellow about ready, Mrs. Gannon? No hurry — I like to take plenty of time for each study — but you just tell me when he's ready."

"Ah, he's ready — my big boy's ready." She picked him up and blew kisses on his neck.

Mr. Watson scuttled to the back of his camera and covered his head with the black hood.

"Eddie — that's my next oldest daughter I was telling you about — she's in New York visiting. Papa and I decided it would be a nice opportunity — Jack could introduce her to all the best people. And she's wanted to go for some time."

"Down, Mrs. Gannon, would you put the little fellow *down*."

Harriet stretched Gus out on his stomach once more but this was suddenly a game for Gus: each time she put him down, his fat little body would shake with laughter and he would jump up again.

"No, darling, no," Harriet said. "Down, like the man says."

Gus looked up from his position on his stomach with a betrayed frown at Harriet's siding with the enemy. But just as Mr. Watson reached for the rubber bulb, Gus apparently decided that Harriet was only fooling. Up he jumped, pushed out his stomach, shoved a finger in his navel, a fist in his mouth and let out a deep gurgling laugh.

"Oh my God," gasped Mr. Watson. "I took it!" He pulled his scarlet face out of his camera, saw Gus still laughing and fingering himself, ducked again under cover of the hood.

"My youngest girls," Harriet said, "Louise and Helen, that is — Helen's the one we call Babe — they're the only ones at home now. We bought them Chautauqua tickets. You see some fine things at the Chautauqua, Mr. Watson. Have you been to any of their shows?"

Mr. Watson uncovered his head, took a quick look at Gus, then turned his back. "You don't seem to understand, Mrs. Gannon," he said. "I took the picture when the little fellow was — standing up."

Harriet looked at Gus, patted his bottom thoughtfully. "Maybe we should try another one. Do you think we should?"

"I never skimp my old customers, Mrs. Gannon, and even with prices what they have been since the war, I'll take another if you say so."

"Well, maybe this one would do. He was smiling, Mr. Watson."

"Oh my God," said Mr. Watson, returning to his camera. "*Down*, Mrs. Gannon, let's have the little fellow *down*."

Harriet stretched Gus on his stomach and while he was incapacitated with laughter, Mr. Watson took the picture. Harriet lifted Gus and kissed him loudly on the cheek. "He's been a good boy, hasn't he, Mr. Watson? Mother's proud of her big boy."

Mr. Watson drew a soiled handkerchief from his back pocket and wiped his forehead. "We do our best, Mrs. Gannon. For forty years it's been my policy to try to please my customers."

Harriet was very much pleased indeed. On the way home, past Pioneer Park so that they could look for Babe, she told Frank about what a nice morning it had been ("Gus was as good as gold," she said) and what a nice old friend Mr. Watson was. "I almost feel he's one of the family — he's taken pictures of every one of my babies and of me as a bride. And I'm sure he feels the same about us." And he catches a good likeness, she told Frank. "If your wife wants pictures taken of any of her babies, she couldn't do better than Mr. Watson."

Frank smiled and nodded and said something which might have been, "Very nice — very nice."

"I don't see Babe," Harriet said, as they slowed down for Pioneer Park. The morning session of Chautauqua seemed to be over and only a few stragglers sat on the lawn about the big khaki tent. "She may be home." Harriet squeezed Gus and patted his fat leg. "He's been a dear boy, he has," she said.

Babe was not at home. She was lying on the grass, under a tree, from where she could see the car as it passed, because she suspected they would stop by for her and she wanted to know that they had missed her. Probably they would be worried and if she stayed away long enough, they might even call the police. She could see the headlines: "Beautiful Daughter of Prominent Citizen Missing from Chautauqua Tent," and underneath, "Helen Gannon (Babe to her friends) lovely and gifted daughter of Jack Gannon — " Mother would be weeping into a long chiffon handkerchief, and Dad would be in his library, sadly puffing away at a cigar, and all the kids would be crying because they hadn't been nicer to her.

Babe wiped the tears from her eyes and turned over on her stomach to joggle the sad thoughts from her mind. It was hot, even with the sunlight broken by the leaves of the tree, and her middy and skirt were no outfit for a day like this. But could *she* wear light, transparent gowns that trailed behind her when she walked? Oh dear no — *she* was just a *child,* but Louise, dear grown-up Louise, *she* could have a voile dress the color of lemon sherbet. Dear me! Pooh pooh!

Babe rested her cheek on the cool grass, removed her glasses and tossed them away from her. Her fingers sought the roots of the grass and she rubbed her nails around to fill them with the cool dirt. Her skirt, she knew, was pulled up so that her garter showed, and if anyone saw her, they'd have a fit. But let them. Who cared? Did they have a car with a chauffeur? Did they have a lot of diamonds and a brother in New York? They could all go jump in the lake. Anyone in Pioneer Park at this hour must have been to morning session of Chautauqua and anyone who went to morning session of Chautauqua must be pretty dumb. And if her mother thought she had been to morning session of Chautauqua, her mother must be pretty —

She sat up quickly and put her hands over her eyes to keep her mind from saying the word. But her mind said the word — her mother must be pretty dumb. She dropped her arms, stared miserably at the ground while sweat covered her body. Yes, of course, her mother was dumb, everyone was dumb, everyone but the brilliant Babe Gannon. Everyone was dumb and ugly and repulsive and clumsy as an ox, all except —

She dropped her head against her knees, let the tears come, let her body shudder with sobs. The truth was that only she was vile and it was a mistake that she had ever been born into such a wonderful family who were all ashamed of her and they had a right to be. Eddie herself had said that Babe was repulsive, that it was humiliating to be related to her and that if Mother didn't make Babe wear a brassière, Eddie wouldn't acknowledge Babe on the street. She knew now that she had never been part of them and yet she'd die — she wished she could die — to let them know that the only thing in the world that mattered was to be part of them, to be able to say that they were her sisters and brothers. In this whole blue universe of sun and trees and summer-morning drowsiness, there was none so vile, so abject, so humble as Babe Gannon. Not the smallest insect, not the merest fly.

Then the tears began to subside and she lay back on the ground and wiped her cheeks with her dirt-covered hands. Her big breasts spread out to the sides when she lay down, filling out the middy like water wings. Mother had said Babe was still a child and didn't need a brassière and Eddie had screamed, "Look at her!" Everyone did look at her — the boys at school, the teachers even, the girls in gym when she had to run. There was nothing you could do about them. They just grew. And if she was still a child, she was pretty strange for a child. They should sell her to the circus, to the sideshow, make money off the miracle of the century. Mother had finally bought a brassière and Babe wore it, but it was uncomfortable and she never fastened it.

Well, if Eddie thought she was repulsive, there were things about Eddie she could tell. Lying to Mother and Dad, stealing their mail so they wouldn't know Jack had been kicked out of Harvard. That week Eddie had pretended to be sick so that she could stay home and get the mail every time right from the mailman's hands. And if they thought Jack had quit school to do research, they must be pretty — And if Eddie thought Babe didn't know where she hid Jack's letters, Eddie must be pretty dumb. And if Eddie thought Babe was repulsive, Eddie could go jump in the lake.

Babe felt around on the ground for her glasses, stood up and brushed herself off. She was on a diet and never ate lunch, but she didn't want to cause *too* much of a rumpus at home. She'd stayed away long enough for them to worry but it would be better in the long run if they didn't call the police.

Walking home, dragging her feet along, squinting through her glasses at the glaring light, Babe thought dully of her list, her list that daily changed from long to short and back again, her list of those who could go jump in the lake. Eddie was first today. In fact, it was more and more often a tossup now who should have first place, Eddie or Louise. Louise's position near the top of the list was fixed, but sometimes Eddie outdid Louise for first place. Dear little dainty Louise, teacher's pet, always right, just too too perfect. Well, she wasn't. She was two-faced, a betrayer, a fairwater friend. Or was it weather? The betrayal of Louise burned into Babe, it was a poison, a disease. Her dearest friend, her sister, her more than sister! But Louise had rejected Babe, cast her aside. Dear little Louise was grown up now. My, my! And didn't have time for baby sister. Just too, too busy with all her grown-up friends and boys she sneaked off to meet. Betrayer, sneak, pygmy!

Right up there with the leaders was Mabel Randazzo, who lived down the street a ways and whose father was a — was a — Babe didn't know what he was, but something that ought to make Mabel *proud* to have Babe Gannon for a friend. All their lives they had played together, when Mabel was just a dirty little Italian girl to whom they sometimes gave Babe's cast-off clothes. And now

Mabel, very grand indeed, with those silly little knobs bouncing in front of her, had taken a bath and sat every night holding hands with Ronald what's-his-name at Chautauqua. It was nasty. It shouldn't be allowed. The juvenile court should do something about Mabel Randazzo.

And of course on the list was every boy in her class at school. Every day of her life she told herself that every boy she knew or ever had known could go jump in the lake. Jack, of course, was an exception and Gus, but he didn't count. Even Bill Miller sometimes made the list when she realized that she had never seen him since that Christmas party, that she must mean nothing to him, nothing at all. But most often she counted Bill Miller an exception along with Jack and Gus.

You couldn't put your parents on the list, of course — you wouldn't *want* to. It was just that sometimes she wished her mother would try to understand, would stop referring to her as a baby girl, would not reach out to brush Babe's hair away and make Babe feel like an elephant beside her mother, who was small. If she would just — Oh golly, it was hopeless.

Home stood out in the sunlight like a big yellow cake with white frosting. The car was parked out in front, and the hose with a spray nozzle was watering the grass under one of the white birch trees. Babe stopped on the sidewalk, measuring the distance between herself and the coolness which lay beyond the open door. Her whole body sagged with exhaustion. Why was she always so tired? She brushed hair from her eyes and dragged herself up the stairs, her knees aching with each bend that lifted her to the next step. She pulled open the screen door and staggered through the dark hall and music room into the rose room. She dropped onto one of the love seats, letting her feet hang over the end, and fell into a drowsy half-sleep.

Through the thickness of sleep she heard her mother's voice: "Is that you, dear? I didn't hear you come in."

She forced her eyes to open and groaned and turned over on her side. But she extended so far over the endge of the love seat that she had to sit up to keep from falling on the floor. She rubbed her eyes and yawned and stared at the floor.

"Did you have something to eat?" Her mother sat beside her,

rested an arm on her shoulder. "We had a sandwich and a glass of milk. We didn't know when you'd be back. Shall I fix you something?"

"No," Babe grunted. "I'm on a diet."

"Now Babe — you have to eat something. I'll fix you a nice salad and a glass of milk."

"No."

"You'll only make yourself sick. You're a growing girl and you need your food."

"All right, all right." Everyone was always crabbing at her. "I'll eat some fruit."

She stomped off to the kitchen, taking an apple from the breakfast-room table on the way. As she stood against the sink, chewing on the apple, her eye was caught by the cookie jar, which, she discovered, contained large, fresh oatmeal cookies. She took eight of them, searched in the icebox, and took out three bottles of cream soda. With one arm holding the bottles against her and her hands filled with the cookies and bottle opener, she went out the back door and sat on the lawn to eat her snack.

It must be about three o'clock, she figured — too late for the afternoon session of Chautauqua, but anyway she'd rather die than sit in that hot tent and listen to some old bore talk about the South Pole. Honestly, how people could stand it! And besides, she had other ways, more important ways of filling her afternoons.

She hid the empty soda bottles under a forsythia bush, brushed the crumbs from her skirt, and stole around the house so that she wouldn't have to do a lot of explaining. Then she started down the street, only slightly groggy from her nap, only slightly weak from lack of food.

It was, as a matter of fact, her diet that had suggested these pilgrimages to her mind — the diet plus her having wept solidly through four showings of The White Sister. The Catholic Church, which had been just a lot of voodoo that Mabel Randazzo and other foreigners went in for, became, with the new spirituality induced by starvation and the new understanding awakened by Lillian Gish and Ronald Colman, a haven for the present, a harbor for the future. For she had decided, halfway through her third time at The White Sister, that she would take the veil. And since the first day that she had slipped fearfully through the gothic portal and huddled in a corner lest she be seen, her resolve had grown, taken wing, filled to the rafters the little Western shrine.

As she approached the church, she looked around to see if any spies were watching. She was not ashamed of her mission, far from it, but she had an inner knowledge that God would reveal to her the time and manner of announcing to the world her immolation. And besides, what Eddie would do with a thing like this! Eddie's name flashed out in red lights at the top of the list before Babe had a chance reluctantly to quash the picture. The list was for another part of the day and suffered temporary death in the sacred precincts.

She sat in the rear of the church, off to the side, her eyes closed, her handkerchief covering the top of her head. "Oh Lord," her lips murmured, "forgive me. I have sinned." She had sinned against Eddie, who, she admitted to the Lord, was her ideal. Everything she wanted to be was personified in Eddie. And if she became angered by Eddie, it was only because she realized how far she was from Eddie's perfection.

She had sinned against Mabel Randazzo, who was a poor underprivileged child of ignorant parents. She thanked the Lord for sending Ronald what's-his-name to hold Mabel's hand in Chautauqua.

She had sinned against her mother, who was, she knew, probably more like the Lord's own mother than any woman who had ever been created. And if Mother was always brushing Babe's hair away, it was because Mother was ashamed of her. And she had a right to be. How could Mother be expected to be proud of a monstrosity so unlike herself?

She had sinned against the boys in her class and she humbly begged the Lord's forgiveness. They couldn't help it if they were a loathsome, ignorant, sub-human group. She should pity rather than censure them.

But most of all, she had sinned against Louise, who had once been her dearest friend. Louise had rejected her, as the Lord knew; but why should Louise be expected to want her younger sister tagging along everywhere, especially when the younger sister was someone the whole family was ashamed of? And why should Babe resent Louise for being small? Louise couldn't help it if she was small and pretty and lovable, any more than Babe could help being a big lumbering ox. It was just that it was hard to remember the old days without feeling a kind of homesickness for the way it used to be. Babe prayed fervently that the Lord would make her worthy once more of Louise's friendship.

Then she knelt and told herself and the Lord that she was vile, vile, vile. She read other people's mail, she envied, she slandered, and if the Lord had blasted her with ugliness as punishment, He had done only what was right — she would have done the same in His place.

She knelt for some time, exhausted by her purgation, letting her mind wander from sin to the blissful loveliness of herself in the garb of a sister, administering gentleness, cut off from the world, from her family whom she had renounced. The picture always brought tears to her eyes — part sadness, part peace — tears that cleansed her of hate, of envy. As she left the church, she felt that she had glimpsed a moment of divine wisdom.

But that night when she went to Chautauqua, the old evil Babe was with her once more. When she saw Mabel Randazzo holding hands with Ronald what's-his-name up on the second row, when she saw Louise sitting with her crowd near the front and that Paul person giving her moony looks, the list flashed into being like a devil from the bowels of the earth. Sitting alone near the back of the tent, squinting, biting her nails, keeping herself hidden so that they wouldn't see her unbraided hair, her magazine-coupon lipstick, her eyes without glasses, Babe felt the old sickness, the old poison return. What did it matter that she could hardly see the stage from where she sat? She'd rather die than sit up in the front. If Louise and Mabel were just too *old*, too *sophisticated*, too *wild* to be bothered with her, who cared? They could all go jump in the lake.

When Chautauqua was over, when Nanki Poo and Yum-Yum had been pardoned by the Mikado, Louise tried to escape before Paul could get to her, but there he was, standing in the aisle, waiting. His shirt was open at the neck, his sleeves rolled, his tanned smooth skin and thick hair and loose-jointed posture made him look younger than seventeen.

"It was good, wasn't it?" she said helplessly, foolishly. But what could you say?

He gave her that slow, serious smile that was more a sign of politeness than of amusement. "It certainly was. Say, would you mind if I walked home with you? If there's no one else — "

Why didn't he just walk with her? Why did he ask? He made such an issue — he made everything so important. "I'm sorry, Paul — but I think I saw my little sister — I'd better go with her."

This time he laughed. "She can take care of herself, I bet. I bet she's even gone off and left you." And he took hold of her elbow as if that settled everything.

Outside, his hand dropped and reached for hers but she folded her arms, looked up at the stars as she walked.

"I'm sorry," he murmured. "I didn't — "

"That's all right," she said quickly. "Have you ever seen any Gilbert and Sullivan before?"

"No."

She didn't look at him, but he would be frowning, trying to figure something out. He was bright in school — he got A's in chemistry — but sometimes he seemed so dumb.

They walked on in silence. The sidewalk cut through the middle of Pioneer Park; it was lined with trees and every so often a green bench where a couple sat, not seeming to mind the Chautauqua crowd who talked and watched as they went by, or hummed "The flowers that bloom in the spring, tra-la — " It was a summer night with crickets, a dark warm sky and stars, arc lights that spat, and sounds carrying from all parts of the park. But why go out with a boy if all you do is listen to crickets and other people's voices coming in from the distance? A boy that you couldn't even look at because every look he gave you created a situation.

Then he said, "Louise — " folding his lower lip between thumb and forefinger, frowning — "Louise, look. May I ask you a question? You don't have to answer — that's your privilege. I won't even ask it if you don't want me to."

She wanted to say, "Oh, for heaven's sakes, Paul"; he probably wanted to ask whether she minded his walking on her left side rather than on her right; but she said quietly, "Of course you may ask."

"Look, Louise, do you mind about me?" he asked painfully. "I mean that I haven't anything — that my family isn't — What I mean is, if you do, if you'd rather not see me, I could try to get my paper route changed. It's just that — well, I don't want to bother you."

"You know that's a silly question."

"Oh gosh, Louise — no it isn't." His voice cracked. He spoke lower. "It isn't, Louise. There's nothing wrong with my people. I guess my dad just wasn't the kind of man that ever wanted to do anything for himself. He's always been satisfied with what he has which is nothing. But there's me and my sisters. Anything we ever have, college or anything, I'll have to try to do something about. These jobs — well, they aren't much, but you see how it is — going to school, you have to take what you can get."

"What's the matter with the jobs? If you hadn't delivered our papers, we would never have got to know each other." She had hardly spoken before she knew she had said too much. He reached his hand toward her, his eyes actually moistened. For a moment he didn't speak.

"It's just that I'd like to do more for you," he said huskily.

Why did he do this to her? She could be so annoyed with him that it was hard even to be civil — then he would say something that utterly dissolved her.

She moved farther away from him. "That's silly too," she said.

He already did so much for her that it was embarrassing — she had to hide his presents because Eddie and Babe teased her so much and Mother would get an amused smile on her face. Even Jack, in his letters, asked about Paul's presents. He never came to collect for the paper without bringing her a present, and if she didn't answer the door, he'd leave it anyway. "Would you please give this to Louise?" he'd say. And every occasion or holiday, there was a present — even Halloween, even Lincoln's birthday. Films for her camera, photograph album and scrapbook, perfume that she couldn't use, jewelry she couldn't wear, enough jelly beans to last a year, green carnations, pink rosebuds. Her defense against the family was that she had never once asked Paul inside the house, didn't take him to the Girls' Dance at high school, never sent him so much as a Christmas card. But there he was. He was always there.

"I admire a boy for working." Louise tried to sound forceful. "I think it's — well, *fine*. That's what our country's based on. My grandfather started without *anything*. *He* didn't even have *shoes*."

"Well, I've got shoes. But there's still an awful wide gap between your family and mine. The shoes don't seem to make much difference."

Louise felt the blood of the Gannons rise in her. "Honestly, Paul, I don't think you should complain. You don't know how lucky you are. Think of the Japanese — or the Armenians. You can have anything you want or *be* anything you want if you aren't afraid of work."

"Who's complaining? Who's afraid of work?" His voice shot up in vexation she would never have dreamed him capable of. "Gosh, Louise, you miss the point. I was just saying — well, look at that house. Sure, I'll have one someday, but when? Where'll you be in the meantime? And maybe I'll be able to work my way through State, but I'll sure never see the inside of Harvard."

Louise drew herself up and spoke with quiet, cold distinctness. "You don't have to be nasty, Paul. I happen to love my brother — and I'm proud of him. He's very talented and people should help talented people. He's doing research, and you — you just don't know about writers but we're very proud of him and if you'd rather not see me any more, I certainly — "

"Oh Louise," he groaned. "For gosh sakes, what are you trying to do to me?"

"I think we'd better say good night. Good night, Paul."

She started toward the steps of the house. He reached out his hand and grasped her arm. "Don't be like that," he said hoarsely. "I — I just can't stand it."

She stopped, turned briefly toward him, then away. His voice, the look he gave her, the foolish defensiveness that had carried her along — She wanted to cry, but that would be wrong. There was nothing but to stand with her eyes down like a child. "I'm sorry," she murmured.

"Please, please don't be sorry. It isn't that. It's just that — well, you don't know how you get into a man's blood." His hand still held her arm; he took her other arm. "Louise," he said in a tremulous whisper, "would it be all right — would you mind — if I kissed you?"

"Oh Paul." Her voice was weary and sad. She twisted away from him, went to the step and sat down.

"I've kept myself clean, Louise," he pleaded. "I've never kissed another girl — I'll never want to kiss another girl."

"You don't want to kiss me, really." She let him take her hand. "Then I'd lose you too — you wouldn't like me any more. I guess that's why I'm so awful. I'm always afraid of losing things."

"I think you're the most perfect woman I've ever known," Paul said passionately.

"I dream all the time that Mother or Dad has died and then I wake up crying. Or when I'm trying to study, I start imagining that we're poor and we've lost the house and we need money but there's nothing I can do to earn it. Or that all my friends hate me or that the family is all broken up and we never see each other. I'm always afraid."

"I want to do everything for you. And I *would* do it too. If it was for you, I guess there isn't anything I couldn't do."

She looked at him and she let herself smile, softly, gently, because in spite of all those presents, in spite of anything the family might think, he was nice.

He pressed her hand and looked down at it and said fervently as if in prayer, "I respect you more than any woman I've ever known."

She withdrew her hand and stood up. "Good night, Paul — and thanks for walking me home."

She watched from the porch as he walked down the street, and then she looked up in the sky and watched a cloud pass in front of the North Star. It was like something that had passed through her mind, but when it was gone, the star was there. And a summer breeze ruffled the trees. And from down the street came a boy's whistle.

CHAPTER 2

EDDIE RETURNED the end of August with bobbed hair, presents for everyone, and boxes of new clothes for herself. Two dresses imported from Paris, two more with New York labels; a light flannel bathrobe cut like a man's, turquoise bathing suit and white jersey cape; costume jewelry from B. Altman, sweater with horizontal stripes from Bonwit Teller. It was an adventure for the whole family: while she unpacked, they gathered in Eddie's bedroom and watched quietly, shyly — Clark City subdued before New York.

Eddie had changed with her trip, in just those weeks. She had gained the assurance that traveling was supposed to give one and Harriet hesitated mentioning her own trips East. In Harriet's day it was quite the thing to see the Statue of Liberty and the aquarium and eat a meal in the automat. Harriet had spent half of one exciting afternoon riding on an escalator, but these were not memories to share with Eddie. And when her trips were over, Harriet was always glad to be home — no place in the world looked so good to her as Clark City. But as Eddie unpacked and couldn't remember which drawer had held her nightgowns for some dozen years or more, which her hose, Harriet realized that things were different with Eddie.

And her hair! Louise almost wept when she saw it; Babe swore that she would have short hair before the day was over; Papa was sentimental — not once before in Eddie's life had the lovely black hair been cut; Harriet was worried. "But do really nice girls wear it short back there?"

"Oh, Mother, of *course*," Eddie answered. "Don't be so *provincial*." Eddie added a smile and Harriet smiled in return. It was Eddie's first day home.

That night, Flo and Grant and the two children came to dinner. When Gus heard them arrive, he ran for the little striped blazer Eddie had brought him and threw it at Sammy's feet, then drew back to watch what Sammy would do with it. Sammy scarcely looked at it. He ran up the stairs, shouting, "Hey Eddie, where's my present?"

"Isn't he awful?" Connie inquired of anyone who would listen to her. "Isn't he awful?" she continued to ask throughout the dinner.

Eddie had to repeat for Flo what she had already told the others — the plays she had seen — *Abie's Irish Rose*, Jeanne Eagels in *Rain*, *The Devil's Disciple*, George White's *Scandals*; dinner at the Waldorf, luncheon at Alice Foote MacDougal's; tea dancing at the Plaza; the exciting trips to Greenwich Village — all the fascinating people. She could name the streets — Madison and Park rolled off her tongue as if she had been saying them all her life, and she located every station of her pilgrimage, sometimes having to ponder whether it was Forty-Ninth or Fiftieth.

Flo listened, rapt, leaning on the table, her chin in her hand. When Eddie stopped, Flo sighed. "It's all so far away — another world. It could be another planet. And when you've lived here for so long, you begin to forget that there's life on it."

"What are you complaining about now?" Grant said crossly. He turned to Papa for sympathy. "Women are always complaining."

Flo looked at Grant with no expression, then back to Eddie. "What about Jack?"

Jack was fine; he had a floor in a brownstone house in the East Fifties, seemed to have a lot of friends — she hadn't seen too many of them. Actually she had been in his apartment only a couple of times — she had stayed at the Martha Washington.

"But how *is* he?" Harriet urged. "How does he *look?*"

"Seems to be fine, as far as I know. He looks just the same." And then Eddie went on to describe an amusing experience she'd had trying on dresses in Bergdorf's — how the clerk had been absolutely dumbfounded to discover Eddie wasn't a native New Yorker.

It had gone that way all day — Eddie had told them nothing. And why did she think they had sent her to New York — why but to return with news of Jack?

"How's his research coming, dear?" Harriet asked. And what did it mean, she wanted to ask, *doing research*, and what were his plans and when was he coming home.

Eddie didn't answer immediately. "He doesn't talk much about it," she said finally, keeping her eyes averted. "He doesn't seem to be actually writing. He sees lots of people, he's getting to know New York, of course — "

"I don't get this," Grant said, leaning back in his chair. "If you want my opinion, this research business is a lot of baloney. He's probably doing his research on chorus girls."

"I'm very proud of him," Louise blurted out. "We're just too dumb, too stupid to understand about writers."

"Do you think," Papa asked with an approving nod at Louise, "do you think he's still serious about this writing business?"

"I can answer that," Grant said, "and the answer is no. He's a regular kid who wants to raise a little hell before he settles down in business. So what happens? All the women tell him he's a genius. College, they say. Hawvuhd! He must be a writer, they say. Research! What I say is baloney."

Terrible silence followed this outburst and Harriet felt sick for poor Flo that Grant could be so offensive, in front of the whole family. To save Flo further humiliation, Harriet quickly changed the subject. "Tell me about his friends, dear. Did any of them take you places?"

"Some. Dinner two or three times. Dancing once."

"But who were they? Anyone we'd have heard of?" She had had such hopes for Eddie — even (and why not?) — even the Prince of

Wales. Through Jack's friends it would be arranged. And of course
he would fall head over heels in love with her (there wasn't a boy
in Clark City Eddie couldn't have). Why not?

"Well, there was a boy named Johnny Carton — he went to Harvard too only Jack didn't know him at Harvard. Jack apparently
knows far more Harvard men in New York than he ever knew in
Cambridge."

"Was he nice? Did you — "

"I don't know. He left — early. Oh Mother, don't ask. Get Jack
to tell you about his friends."

What was the use? Eddie had changed, hardened. It was what
happened to women in big cities. Given time, she would be her
old self again and they would draw the whole story out of her.

"If I could express a beautiful thought in beautiful words," Flo
said with misty-eyed intensity, "if I could compose a beautiful
piece of music or paint a lovely picture — " She turned angrily on
Grant. "It may have taken us three generations to produce Jack
but he's better than all the tractors or all the money you'll ever
make."

Grant dropped his toothpick on his plate and held out his hands
to the room in general. "What I'd like to know is," he said, "what's
so bad about being able to make a little money?"

Later in the evening, Tommy Reed dropped by. He wore white
linen knickers, a black sweater, and looked taller each time you
saw him, thinner, more cadaverous, as if he must have a chest
cough.

"I'm worried about you, Tommy," Harriet said, "and I'll bet
your mother is too. I'm afraid they don't take very good care of
you up there in Harrisville — not the same as at home."

Tommy stretched out on a chair, pulled a pipe from his back
pocket. "You know, I worry about myself, Mrs. Gannon." He
chewed the pipe thoughtfully. "It's just that people don't treat me
right, I guess."

Papa chuckled and said, "You could use some of your father's
weight. None of the Reed men were lean. Your grandfather was
a big man."

"Well, it's like I say, Mr. Gannon, they didn't have to face the tough life that a young guy faces nowadays." Tommy raised his eyes in the direction of upstairs. "Where's the beauty? I'd like to get the good word."

Harriet called Eddie and when she appeared, Tommy whistled and said, "Jesus Christ! Excuse me, that is, Mrs. Gannon, but it isn't often in a man's lifetime that — "

"Shut up, Tommy," Eddie said. "Those pants look like gym bloomers."

Tommy stood up, his eyes fixed in exaggerated wonder on Eddie's hair. He placed his hands on her shoulders and turned her around. "My God, Mrs. Gannon, what do you make of this modern generation? Here we have a supposedly nice girl going around without any hair on — trying to usurp man's place in society."

"Eddie says they wear it that way — back in New York," Harriet said, correcting Tommy's provincialism. "I guess it's all right — " she looked to Papa for support. "We'll probably get used to it."

"I guess I'm just not modern enough," Tommy said. "Don't adjust to change. A woman without hair — well, it just seems to me something sweet and lovely is missing. Like a woman without —" Tommy brushed tears from his eyes. "Now Eddie," he said, "before all the Clark City Romeos hear you're back in town — how about a malt? I've got the family car, or if you'd prefer, I could go home and get my motorcycle."

"Well — If anyone calls, Mother, just say I've gone out with one of the neighborhood boys. I'll be back early."

Harriet smiled and said, "Drive carefully, Tommy. And Tommy," she added, "take care of yourself."

On the way to Taylor's ice-cream parlor, Tommy didn't talk about Jack, as he should have, but about how perfectly swell Eddie was looking, how beneficial he thought travel was — broadening and all that — and how he certainly would like to see a bit of the good old country himself someday. Then at Taylor's, he drove around to the back, where it was dark, turned off the lights and motor, leaned over, stretched his arm along the back of the seat.

"You know, Eddie," his voice was low, intimate, "gee, you and I have grown up together — since we were kids. Why I remember when you had pigtails — you know, kid sister and all that. Well, hell, Eddie," he reached for her hand, let a throaty quality come into his voice, "I guess I just never noticed what a hell of an attractive girl you are. Know what I mean?"

Eddie nodded.

He squeezed her hand and continued. "Now, it's like I'm seeing you for the first time — not the crazy kid I used to know but a woman, a lovely woman — "

"Without pigtails."

"Yeah, without — "

Eddie laughed, took back her hand. "Don't be an ass, Tommy. I never had pigtails in my life. And don't look so stupid. That's the most ridiculous line I ever heard."

Tommy reddened, drew back. "I beg your *pardon*. If I've been *offensive* — "

"Are we going to have a malt?" she asked wearily. "I thought that's what we came for."

Tommy stepped out of the car, walked with frigid dignity around to her side. He didn't offer to touch her as she stepped out and they walked into Taylor's.

But sitting across from her, sipping the malted milk through straws, Tommy suddenly grinned. "That *was* pretty bad, wasn't it?"

"Honestly, Tommy, it was terrible. You really should do better."

"It works with most."

Eddie sat back, contemplated him, shook her head. "With most? But why — why bother? Does it have to be every girl? Don't tell me I'm old-fashioned. It just seems such a waste — it doesn't get you anywhere."

"Why you all the time wanna get somewhere? I like it here." He leaned forward, let his knees touch hers. "You know, you really are a hell of an attractive girl."

Eddie took a sip of the malt, smiled wanly. "All right, Tommy. I'm sorry. I shouldn't have said it. Do you want to take me home now?"

They started toward home, then Tommy suggested they might just look in at the Red Barn.

The Red Barn was at the mouth of Clark City Canyon, an old barn of field stone and clapboard, made into a dance hall with a large cement floor out by the river. It was the summer night spot for Clark High, her students and alumni home from college, and was as dear to their hearts as the alma mater itself. Eddie had been there hundreds of times — it was where a boy took a "nice" girl. And the nice girl always said yes to the invitation, out of curiosity to see what other nice girls would be there.

Tommy paid the dollar for admission, held her arm. "Isn't this a hell of a place? I wonder why people come here."

"Probably because glamorous men in white knickers ask them weeks in advance."

"You wanna dance?"

"I suppose we better."

The orchestra was playing "I Cried for You." A little man with a smiling red face was jazzing it up on the banjo; Harry Green, the leader of the band, a dope addict, it was whispered, was very peppy on the piano. And people whom Eddie had known all her life, whose lives and hopes and ambitions were as secret from her as the top left drawer of her dressing table, were dancing the fox-trot as if all the best dreams of man were centered under these old rafters. They smiled and waved automatically, then noticed Eddie's hair, and whispered to their partners who turned around to wave and stare.

"What's the word on your big brother?" Tommy asked.

"I don't like this place. Why did we come?"

"How's the gentleman and scholar? How's Clark City's gift to wisdom and the arts?"

Eddie drew back and looked at him straight on. "He's very well, thank you," she said.

"I guess now that he's in New York, he'll have more time for his art — you know, all those books. Never did understand how a two-bit place like Harvard thought it could hold him, not with all that talent."

"Look, Tommy, if you're being funny, I'm not amused."

"Well, how *is* he? *Tell* me something."

"He's fine."

"Oh hell, Eddie. How many blondes has he got in that apartment?"

Eddie stopped dancing, brushed his hand off her shoulder. "You're not only despicable — you're disgusting! Take me home."

Tommy smiled broadly, pulled her to him, went on dancing. "God, you're terrific, Eddie. Fine old Irish temper, flashing eyes. Anyone ever tell you you're a hell of an attractive girl?"

"Look, Tommy, I'm serious. I don't think I like you very much."

Tommy raised his eyebrows, shrugged, started humming the dance music. Then he spotted Louise and Paul. "Hey, there's your kid sister." And he danced over to them. "My favorite Gannon, dear old Weezie."

Louise and Paul were dancing very straight and far apart. They were both dressed in clothes that looked as if a price tag might still be dangling somewhere, and Paul's hair had been showered in hair oil but it didn't stay down. When they saw Eddie and Tommy, they drew apart quickly; Louise went stiff, Paul went loose.

"You're a sight for sore eyes, Yooweez," Tommy said. "Eddie doesn't like me and I don't want to dance with her any more. You have to dance with me."

"Louise — what on earth are you doing here? Does Mother know you're here?"

Louise turned a sick little smile from Tommy to Paul.

Eddie then recognized Paul. "Oh, you're the paper boy. Paul, isn't it? Paul — well anyway, this is Tommy Reed."

Paul bent almost double reaching for Tommy's hand. "Glad to know you, sir."

Eddie placed her hands on Louise's shoulders, excluding the men from the intimacy of girls' talk. "Why didn't anyone tell me you were coming to this dreary spot? This really is a coincidence." She leaned across to whisper in Louise's ear, "He's improved a *lot*, Louise."

"You girls can gab later. I want to dance with Louise," Tommy said. And to Paul, "Do you mind, old man?"

Paul put two fingers inside his collar, stretched his neck in an eager nod. "No — I mean certainly. That's fine."

Louise held her hand for Tommy to take, then caught Eddie's frown directed at her behind, protruding somewhat in her unrelaxed posture. She blushed hotly, straightened herself, and turned in despair to Tommy. Tommy danced her off in the exaggerated style that would be a college boy's idea of gratifying a high-school girl.

"Well," Eddie said, as if something had just been settled. She smiled graciously.

"You — wouldn't —" Paul's hands were big naked things, seeking cover. He folded his arms and fortified himself with a deep breath. "You wouldn't like — some soda pop, would you?"

"Now don't think you have to do that." Eddie's voice patted him on the head. "Why don't we just sit down and watch?"

"Yes," he said weakly. "That'd be fine."

For a while they watched the dancers, Eddie with a bright smile, Paul with stern concentration. Finally Eddie broke the silence.

"Do you still bring the paper? I've been away — I haven't seen you for a long time."

"Yes," Paul said. And after a pause, "I still do."

They watched the dancers and Eddie caught sight of Louise and Tommy. "Look at Louise! Isn't that funny? She looks scared to death." She waved her hand until Louise looked and then her lips formed the word, "Relax! Relax!"

"That Reed fellow — is he, is he a friend — of yours, or —"

"Oh, you don't have to worry about Tommy," Eddie reassured him with a smile. "He's a friend of my older brother. Mine too, I guess. Certainly not Louise's."

"Oh."

Eddie's smile continued, but she began to be restless, to look more and more pointedly for familiar faces, to squirm on the hard bench.

"I understand — that is, Louise mentioned — you were in the East. Did you — enjoy your trip?"

"You don't really want to know, do you?" Eddie chided. "I certainly wouldn't bore you with that."

Paul reddened. "Oh no, I —" He brushed his hand through his hair, looked at the grease on his hand, bewildered what to do about it. "Really, I —"

"That's all right. I try to make polite conversation myself."
Eddie stood. "If you don't mind, I think I'll go powder my nose.
I'll be right back." She walked away, her eyes still looking over
the couples on the dance floor.

Eddie didn't powder her nose. Once relieved of Paul, she simply
wandered out by the entrance and tried to look as if she were waiting for an escort who was either in the lavatory or out parking a
car. She stood against the wall and glanced at her watch and
peered into space as if he might be striding in from almost any
direction.

No escort appeared, but the Driscoll family did — Howard Sr.,
Howard Jr., and big Mrs. Driscoll in flowered chiffon, huge straw
and velvet hat, and too many diamond rings. The father and son
looked alike, both ugly with brown skin and bad teeth, but lean,
muscular physiques. In Eddie's crowd, Howard Jr. had always
been considered a stuffed shirt; when they all were learning the fox-
trot, he still clung to the two-step. He hadn't gone to Clark City
High but to military academy on the west coast. The fact that his
father was the most prominent lawyer in the region and owned
stock in practically everything helped Howard Jr. some; the fact
that Howard Jr. had been to Stanford and Stanford law school
helped him even more. He was a stuffed shirt, but a shirt for full
dress, the most expensive kind, for tuxedo or even tails.

Since Howard Jr.'s graduation from law school and entrance into
his father's firm, the Howard Driscoll Sr.'s had been making
obvious efforts to help their son's adjustment to Clark City, to
make him happy with a place they had never before considered
worthy of him. Tonight they would have taken him to the City
House for dinner, all of them dressed up, the men in their white
suits, big Mrs. Driscoll in her diamond rings. And then to give
Howard Jr. the chance to see some young people, maybe a pretty
girl or two, Mr. Driscoll would suggest they stop by the Red Barn.
They would all be home by ten and as the Howard Driscoll Sr.'s
climbed into their huge mahogany bed, they would assure each
other that the adjustment was coming along just fine.

Eddie nodded to them, then turned her head away, straining her
eyes for that escort. But even with eyes averted, Eddie was aware
of the scene that would be taking place; it would occur to the
three Driscolls simultaneously that here was a pretty girl, un-

attended; a glance would pass between the two lean men who looked so much alike, and Howard Sr., remembering the needs of young men, would give Howard Jr. the sign that would say go to it, son. She could hear Howard Jr.'s footsteps walking toward her, but she didn't turn until he stopped before her, practically breathing in her face. "Oh," she said. "You startled me."

"Hello, Eddie. I'll save preliminaries for later and get to the main point. If I'm going to beat someone else's time, we'd better get started. Will you?"

"Will I?"

"Will you dance?"

"Oh — I'm awfully sorry, Howard. I'm waiting for someone."

"I rather imagined you were. It hadn't occurred to me that you'd be out alone. Will you dance with me?"

Feeling somehow that he had the advantage of her, as if he had caught her in a lie or something, she went on to explain: "My date — he's — well, I'm waiting for him." Then she saw herself as very foolish, like a silly adolescent, making a situation out of nothing, like — well, like Louise or somebody. "Thanks very much. I'd love to," she said irritably.

The orchestra was, thank heaven, playing a slow number so that if anyone saw them, they wouldn't look *too* old hat. His dancing was not bad — nor was it good. He held her very firmly: the muscular Mr. Driscolls. It was not unpleasant except that there was a kind of arrogance in it, an assertiveness which was presumptuous.

He surprised her by saying, "I love this place."

She was turning her head to give the room a bored glance in preparation for a bored reply, when he continued with, "It's a perfect symbol of the mawkish provincialism, the cultural sterility of the town and state — of the whole country, in fact. It's fascinating to watch, to listen to, to put your finger right on a vein of America."

Now she was confused: he was twisting her about, forcing her to condemn, then magnifying her condemnation all out of proportion so she must reject it and resent the ex-patriate's contempt. He finished her off by taking her into his camp. He said, "The one girl in all of Clark City that I would not expect to see here — the *only* girl — is Eddie Gannon. So you see —" he smiled (his teeth *were* bad but nothing about him wavered: the muscular-smiling Mr. Driscolls) "you see, I'm right in liking this place. It has all the worst and some of the best."

Eddie had said not a word. He had given her a moment of superiority, of irritation, of impressive flattery as if she were a passive little thing simply hanging on a man's words. She was forced, now, to assert herself — after all, this was not the dark ages.

"I'm awfully fond of Clark City — naturally." She smiled her tolerance at him, smiled all the assurance derived from being a third-generation Gannon. "But it isn't a very stimulating place — there's certainly no one very *interesting* around here."

"*Interesting!* My God!" The idea seemed to amuse him. "Imagine trying to discuss Shaw — or Havelock Ellis — with any of these people! Why, I'd be surprised if any of the so-called professors at State had read a word of Darwin or even heard of Freud. I'd be surprised if they can even read. But I'm being cruel. I'm sure they can read."

There was a coziness in this kind of talk although it might be dangerous ground. Could she discuss Shaw? She could mention *The Devil's Disciple,* and *Candida,* and *A Doll's House.* But all she knew of Havelock Ellis was that a nice person couldn't ask for his books in a library; she had never read Darwin; she had heard of Freud but couldn't remember in what connection. And *was* it Shaw who wrote *A Doll's House?* Oh Lord.

Now she hated Howard Driscoll Jr. He was, of course, including her in his contempt — she was part of the stupid, dreary mob, and her father — the only person to blame for her not going to college — was the only person she could not hate for it. And so she hated Howard Driscoll Jr.

"Of course, Mr. Driscoll," she said, too angry to impart the full force of her sarcasm, "you must be patient with us. We're not all so fortunate as you." She would have said more but her voice might not come through.

If Howard was aware of the emotion he had aroused, he gave no indication of that fact. "It's not a question of being fortunate." Then drawing back and looking at her, he said, "Thank God for you. You're the only person in this town I could talk to. I've known that for a long time."

No one ever had said anything more soothing to Eddie's soul. No one ever could say anything that would so flood her with gratitude, bathe her with so sweet a balm.

"Oh, if you only knew," she said despairingly, shy in revealing so much. "If you knew — so much that I've wanted, so little I've got. And I've *really* wanted it. It doesn't pay to be a girl — even now. We're supposedly free, but not for any of the things I want. I should have been the boy."

"Well, I'm glad you're not." He looked at her with a kind of possessive approval. "I like your hair."

"Do you? I think it has ruined my reputation — apparently it makes me a trollop. An old friend of the family tried to make love to me tonight. I guess he thought I was wild."

"It's an aphrodisiac to a man." He looked at her with a half-smile, waiting for her to be shocked.

Eddie had never heard the word, but if he could say it, she could listen. She returned his look. "Oh?" was all she said.

The music stopped and couples broke up, the men to smile blankly and clap, the girls to pull in their stomachs and tug at the backs of their dresses. Then the men in the orchestra, dressed alike in white flannels and blue coats, stood in a row, arms on each others' shoulders, paper hats on their heads, and burst into loud singing. "Yes, we have no bananas," they sang, bending their knees, bobbing up and down in unison.

"Does one dance to this stuff?" Howard asked.

Eddie shrugged as if to say, what can you expect?

"Dear old Clark City," Howard mused. "This is America — this is civilization. And look at that ass in the white knickers. There's young America — her life blood."

Eddie followed his look to where Tommy Reed, over by the orchestra stand was swinging his hips and Louise to the broken rhythm of the song. Eddie *died* for Tommy, was humiliated for Louise, and in sudden panic for herself. What if, now, Tommy came over to claim her?

"But it can be very amusing," Howard continued, "if one just sits back and watches. The microcosm — the little vulgar world. All our values expressed in that song."

The vocal chorus finished, a few squeaks of the saxophone announced intermission. People clapped, voices grew from nothing to a dull rumble, and Eddie caught a glimpse of Louise's worried, searching face and of Tommy's clasped hands waving a handshake to the orchestra. She turned her back on them and started walking off the floor.

"I hate to give you up," Howard said. "You wouldn't like to leave, would you? We could take my parents home and then have the car. We could go someplace."

"You see? It's my hair. It seems to give the wrong impression."

"Oh Christ. Don't talk like a Clark City virgin." He smiled his bad teeth at her. "Do I shock you?"

His attempts to shock her were becoming irritating. She had, after all, been around. She had seen New York. "Don't be stupid," she murmured.

She looked over her shoulder and saw that Louise and Tommy were pulling away from the orchestra — they would be searching her out. On a bench by the wall, where she had left him, was Paul.

She acted hurriedly. "Good night, Howard — awfully nice — thanks." She pulled her hand from his grip, heard him, as she walked away, say that he would phone her.

"Oh hello, Paul. Sorry I was so long. Would you mind if we left now?"

Paul had jumped to his feet at her approach. He listened vacantly to her words.

"Oh I forgot," Eddie laughed. "We didn't come together, did we? Well, if you don't mind — Louise is taken care of and it would be awfully sweet if you'd drive me home. You could come back if you wanted."

"Well, I — sure, but I'd better tell Louise."

"Now Paul, don't be vain. You can tell her when you get back."

Eddie took his arm and was able to get him out before Tommy could reach them. On the way, she smiled at the three Driscolls. Paul, clumsy and worried, turned to give them an unhappy stare. "I hope this is all right, Miss Gannon," he said.

The next morning, Eddie was up earlier than usual so that she could talk to her father before he left for the office. It couldn't wait. She tied the new mannish bathrobe around her and ran a comb through the short black hair.

Her father and mother were at the breakfast table, and Gus, squeezed into his high chair, licked jam from a piece of toast. She closed the door to the kitchen so that Martha wouldn't hear everything, and started right in.

"Dad, I've got to talk to you. I want to leave — I want to go back to New York. I can't stand to stay in this place."

Her father set down his cup, rested his hands on his legs, looked in silence at her, at her mother, at her again.

She held her head high and hurried on. "There's nothing for me here any more. I have no friends — I've nothing to do. The family isn't enough — I'm grown up, Dad."

She shouldn't have said that because now his eyes clouded over with the hurt look that defeated her in any argument. "Have we failed you, Eddie?" He spoke with difficulty. "We've tried, your mother and I, to give you everything —"

"But none of it has been what I wanted. Don't you see? I wanted college — not piano lessons. You've been wonderful but I have to lead my own life — I have to accomplish something on my own. And I can't here. I just die in this place."

"Maybe," her mother suggested, "maybe if she went to New York, she could live with Jack — take care of him. They could take care of each other."

"That isn't what I want. It's a chance to live my own life — not Jack's. I'm tired of taking care of Jack."

Her father frowned and shook his head. "That wouldn't do. It wouldn't be right — a young girl in a single man's apartment."

"You won't have to support *me*," Eddie said. "I'll get a job doing something — I don't know what and I don't much care as long as I get away. And at least you know you can trust me."

"It's not the money, Eddie — you know that."

"Dad — don't you *see?*" Eddie cried desperately. "This isn't just a whim — my whole life is involved." Her eyes filled with tears. "Dad, I'd rather die than have to live the rest of my life in this town. I mean it."

Louise came into the room, her hair hanging down her back like a little girl's. She was white and her eyes were puffy and she spoke to no one.

"Here's Louise," her mother said cheerily. "Did you have a nice time last night, darling?"

Louise sat down, attacked her grapefruit. "Ask Eddie," she said quietly.

Eddie had turned her back to them, and finding no handkerchief in her bathrobe, had reached for a napkin to wipe her eyes. "How should I know?" She sniffed, touched her nose with her wrist. "I certainly don't think much of that boy you were with. I should think even you could do better than that."

Louise didn't raise her eyes from the grapefruit. Her mother came to Paul's defense. "Why I think Paul's a lovely boy. He has a lot of —"

"Dad, could we go into the library?" Eddie interrupted her. "I'd just as soon not have the whole family in on this."

"Of course, Eddie."

In the library, Eddie sat in a leather chair, waited for her father to speak.

"You know how we feel," he said finally. He stood before her, straight, strong as he'd always seemed, but his hair was graying fast and his eyes beseeched her not to hurt him more. "A girl of your background, Eddie — girls like you don't leave home, live alone in big cities. How does that look?" He paused, reached out to stroke the leather of her chair. "If we knew a nice family in New York, people like us who would take you in, with some kind of understanding, of course, we might be able to send you back for a few months — a few piano lessons, see the museums, some concerts. But what would people say if I let my lovely girl go off, running elevators, selling — selling soap, cold cream —"

"What does it matter what people say? What's important? Dad, it isn't eighteen-ninety."

"You're young, Eddie." That solid fact strengthened him. He squared his shoulders. "You don't know the world and I pray to God you never will have to. This is where you belong."

Eddie pressed her hands against her eyes, asked in a muffled voice, "How about State? We could find one of those lovely families for me to live with and I could come home every weekend."

Her father reached out for one of her hands, pressed it in his. "But you don't need that, Eddie," he said gently. "That college business might be right for a boy, but it would destroy everything lovely in you, merely make you unhappy, unfit for the kind of life you should lead. You're complete — ready right now. Stay with us, Eddie."

He squeezed her hand and laid it on her knee. Then he went to the safe, opened it, took something out. He came back to her, stooped over and kissed her forehead. "All I want is your happiness, Eddie. You know that." He laid five one-hundred-dollar bills in her lap, squeezed her hand once more. "Go and buy yourself a nice treat — something you'd like."

After he'd gone, she sat where she was, one hand covering her eyes. She felt hollow, numb. The clock ticked in the hall and would go on ticking until time had really finished her for all and good. As of this moment, everything was over — it was simply a matter of waiting it out, knowing that on the other side of the mountains were all the interesting people, the people who were alive, the people who could have breathed life into her if only she could have reached out to them.

What was the point, where was the meaning? Jack, mounted on a glittering steed of a merry-go-round, was bowing to the applause, reaching out for the gold rings the family tossed him as he swept by. Given the word, just one word from Dad, Eddie could whisper life into the wooden animal and soar off in a clean, straight line. But she must stay where she was, hear the music, see the flash of color and movement, clap her hands and toss the gold rings.

Eddie stared up at the ceiling to stop the tears. Reaching in her lap for something to dry her face, her hand touched the five one-hundred-dollar bills. She folded them, and slipped them into her pocket, pulled out the napkin she found there.

She stood up, dried her face, looked out the window and then at the walls of books. This man's room, this little world of men. She was ready, Dad had said, complete. For what?

Her eyes stopped at the dictionary. She hesitated, then pulled it out, settled herself in a leather chair. A — A as in Arthur — A for *aphrodisiac*. Ah! And then she surveyed the rows of books. Which one would tell her the author of *A Doll's House*?

In three weeks, Mr. and Mrs. Jack Gannon announced the engagement of their daughter, Edna, to Howard Driscoll, Jr.

CHAPTER 3

I⊤ WOULD BE an autumn wedding. And that was nice, Harriet
decided, because one should be busy in the autumn. She was getting too old to care much for her thoughts, and during the autumn
they did so seem to come at one. But a wedding such as this left
no time for questions: it was all affirmation. She and Eddie made
a quick trip to San Francisco to buy Eddie's trousseau at the
White House and City of Paris; there were invitations to address,
teas and luncheons to attend, and arrangements to see to for the
reception. Howard Driscoll, Jr., was, so everyone told her, eminently suitable for Eddie; the ladies of her club said that Eddie
and Howard were made for each other.

And Jack arrived two weeks before the wedding. She had
written, suggesting that he might like to stay at home for a while
— at least until after Christmas — and perhaps do a little work at
the office, just to try it out. But when he arrived at the Clark City
station, his hat on the back of his head, his camel hair coat loose
and open, and his face, eager as a boy's, straining to see who was
meeting him, he brought only two bags. Nothing he'd like better,
he said, than to stick around the little old town, but you know
how it is — you get all tied up.

He was gay and charming — the wedding was a great lark — and he changed all their carefully made plans with a snap of his fingers. Flowers? He insisted that there be not a pink carnation or a lavender sweet pea in the house but all autumn colors — chrysanthemums, even maple leaves — and gardenias for the rose room and dining room table — hundreds of them — low things full of them. Gardenias? Send to the coast for them — they can pack 'em in ice. Eddie's wedding, he said, should be the biggest show on earth, and if old Jeremiah's money had to be unearthed from the ancient recesses of the First National Bank to pay the tariff, at least it would buy a spectacle that the old boy would be proud of. Do it the way Jeremiah himself would have done it: all the best from all over the country — ordered by telegram, packed in ice, delivered by fast express — and all of Clark City invited for a look.

When he wasn't making plans, he was whistling about the house, dressed in white sweater and slacks, and he drove Harriet to town, and he spent a good deal of time in the basement working on a kite for Gus.

Mornings, after Papa had gone to work and the girls to school and Eddie to the beauty parlor or dressmaker's, Jack would come downstairs in his silk dressing gown and ascot scarf, needing a shave, his black hair not quite straight, handsome still, more than ever handsome because this was Jack intimately without the sleekness of his dressed-up good looks. He and Harriet would take coffee into the rose room and talk for an hour or more, relishing the impropriety of just talking when so much was to be done.

"Is Eddie happy?" Jack asked Harriet one morning.

"Eddie happy? Why of course she is. Isn't every bride?"

"But do you think she loves the guy?"

Harriet couldn't take the question seriously. "I don't think you have to worry about that. I think this is a real love match. All the girls get this way — it's a big step for a girl. Someday a girl will be acting this way over you."

"Now Harriet," Jack leaned against her and patted her knee. "Don't start working on me."

She covered his hand with hers, smiled to conceal the true feeling, the worry. "Isn't there someone, Jack? You shouldn't wait too long. A young man ought to settle down with the right girl."

"Look, honey, Pa got her. I'm gonna have to be an old bachelor." Jack stretched, settled his arm on her shoulder. "No, Harriet, you gotta live first — find yourself — see what the world's about. Maybe times have changed — a young fellow nowadays wants more out of life than just a wife and family."

"More? But what else is there?"

Jack laughed, squeezed her, kissed her cheek. "Ah, my sweet Harriet. Don't *you* change. If I could find one like you, I'd marry her tomorrow."

"But no, Jack —" She mustn't let him put her off. "Is it Harvard? Your degree? Is it that?"

For a moment he was sober, searching, then he smiled again. "No, I couldn't go back there now — not with those kids. Why, I'm getting the best education a man can have. Not books but life itself, Mother. You won't regret it. And Dad — it isn't money, is it?"

She shook her head.

"Well then," he beamed, "everything's all right!"

Harriet bit her lip, studied the veins in her hand. "Before I die, Jack, I want to see you settled down — with the right girl —" she smiled at him with moist eyes — "the best in the world — so she'll take care of you right — and be a good mother to my grandchildren."

"Well, look. I'll strike a bargain with you. If you'll promise not to die for a good long time, I'll promise to marry a lovely girl before I give you any grandchildren. How's that?"

That was the way he talked to her — he wouldn't let her be serious or emotional, and sitting there holding her hand, he made her feel like an irresponsible and quite innocent girl — separate from her children, free, younger by years.

"But seriously now, just between the two of us," he said, "what do you think of Howard? Doesn't he strike you as kind of a prune?"

"Jack — that's an awful thing to say!" But in spite of herself she must smile and then because of the smile, she must defend Howard. "I'm sure he's a fine person — you can tell to look at him that he has a good mind. And I've always considered the Driscolls a fine family. They've given Howard all the advantages that money can buy."

Jack grinned at her. "Don't give me that old line." Then he rubbed his forehead and became serious for a moment. "I guess it's just that I expected something better of Eddie."

While they were talking, Tommy Reed appeared, coming in through the kitchen. Tommy had decided to postpone his registration at State until after the wedding. "No use in commuting every day," he said. He moved his portable phonograph and collection of records over to the Gannon music room and spent most of his waking hours draped on the little hard green love seat listening to "Who's Sorry Now."

"Ask Tom what he thinks of Howard," Jack said. "He's an ass, ain't he, Reed? I bet on their honeymoon he shoves Eddie in the upper berth and takes the lower for himself."

Tommy laughed and then shook his head in disgust. "Why did this boy never learn any manners, Mrs. Gannon? He hadn't ought to talk that way in front of a lady."

"He's awful, isn't he, Tommy?" She patted Jack's hand in reprimand. "He says terrible things."

"Ah, come now, Harriet, you love it." Jack placed a loud kiss on her cheek. "Hey Reed, who's the prettiest gal in Clark City? The prettiest gal west of the Rockies — west of the Mississippi, in fact?"

Tommy held out his hands toward Harriet, cocked his head to one side as if to say the answer was obvious.

Harriet felt herself blush at their foolishness. She raised her hand to her nose, then turned to Jack and patted his hand some more.

"Trouble with Reed is," Jack said, "he sits around all day criticizing a fine fellow like Howard when, any way you look at it, Howard could beat the stuffings out of a poopout like Reed."

Tommy folded his arms, lowered his head to scratch it. "There's a lot of truth in what you say, Jack. While a couple of bums like you and me sit around admiring a beautiful woman, Howard's out digging for gilt-edge securities with the sweat of his brow."

"You know what I heard? I heard that the Boy Scouts of America had voted Howard their ideal camper for 1923."

"That's a lie," Tommy said. "The straight dope is that the prohibitionists are running him for President — with full backing of all the Rotary Clubs in every village, town, and hamlet."

"And the mothers of America — you know what I heard? — they're running Howard's picture for Mother's Day instead of Whistler's Mother — to make all the girls of America want to be mothers."

"You boys," Harriet said. "You shouldn't joke about things like that. Howard's fine — and so are you. It isn't in you not to be." She sat up straight, preparing to rise. "I guess I'll leave you now. I've been awfully lazy — I'd better get busy."

"Look, Ma," Jack held her arm. "Why don't you take it easy? Tom and I will do everything that needs to be done. Give us a list and you go upstairs and lie down. You been working too hard."

"Sure, Mrs. Gannon, you go rest. Let Jack and me take care of this wedding. Just a couple of cupids. Anything for the course of true love."

"Oh heavens, I can't rest. If you'd like some little jobs though, you might bring up the tables from the basement to put in Eddie's room for the gifts. And Gus ought to have his hair cut before the wedding and there's a lot of trash in the basement that ought to be burned — you could have a nice bonfire in the back. And there are a few things I need from town — if you're down there with Gus."

Jack stretched and yawned. "Okay, Harriet, you name it. I'll go dress. Tommy can help Martha do up the dishes."

"If you don't mind," Tommy said to Harriet, "I think I'll just rest a little, while I'm waiting. I don't want to overdo."

And so everything should have been quite perfect — all her children home and her second daughter making the best marriage of the year. Should have been — but somehow wasn't.

When, for instance, Jack and Tommy brought Gus back from the barber with all his hair shaved off, Harriet could have wept. Her baby, her darling boy — she was to have been so proud of him — all her friends were to have seen and admired him and said what a fine little fellow he was. And now he didn't even look very bright, like a little prisoner. To Jack and Tommy, it was an immense joke — they roared with laughter whenever they looked at him — called him Cicero because his stomach was too big for

Augustus Caesar. It was a joke, but one that she was not allowed to share. She had to search the town for a little cap that Gus could wear to the wedding.

And Eddie went through the appointments and teas and Howard's nightly calls with a calmness that not only quelled Harriet's excitement but raised (if one permitted) discomforting questions. Papa's eyes followed Eddie, wretched, speaking the thoughts for which he had no words, and at night, lying beside him in bed, Harriet, in kindness to Papa, kept all the wedding plans and problems sealed in the chaos of her mind.

And two nights before the wedding — it was at the dinner table — Jack said to Papa, "Tommy and I can get champagne for you. It won't be cheap but we can get it."

"I don't know, Jack," Papa protested — more, it seemed, against participating in the preparations than against the champagne itself. "Do you think that's right? All those people — a law's a law. If it were just the family."

"Ah Dad, you don't want to be an old fogy," Jack wheedled. "This is a wedding — you gotta have champagne. We want to make it the best wedding anyone in this town has ever seen."

"Of course, Dad," Eddie said, her voice brittle. "We must have a jazz band too — what would a wedding be without that? We might embarrass Jack if we were stuffy and respectable about this. Or am I not to be consulted?"

"Sure, Eddie," Jack said mildly. "We're consulting you."

"Well, I don't want it," she cried, stiffening against the trembling in her body. "I don't want any of your cheap rottenness. There's still a little decency left — a few decent people — And if you don't like it, you don't have to come!" She got up from the table, sobbing, and ran from the room.

In the first moment of surprise, Harriet caught the look of embarrassment and apology on Jack's face, the pain on Papa's.

Jack wiped his mouth on his napkin, spoke in a controlled voice as if he wanted nothing but to be courteous, inoffensive. "If you'll excuse me —" He stood, pushed his chair back in place, walked quietly from the room.

They all waited for her — Papa confused and helpless, Louise trusting, Babe miserable. All she could say was, "Eddie can't help it. We must try not to think about it."

But later that evening, when all the female members of the family had gathered in Eddie's room to watch the damask and lace go into the hope chest, to try on the velvet dresses that had arrived for Louise and Flo, Eddie seemed actually happier than she had all along. For the first time, she seemed to share the excitement that had carried the others for days.

"What will I ever do with all this stuff? I'll have to have a big formal banquet once a week even to begin to get through it all."

"Oh, you'll find a use for everything," Harriet assured her with blessed relief. "The Driscolls, after all, are not accustomed to eating off oilcloth. You'll find you'll need all those things, won't she, Flo?"

"Hm?" Flo murmured absently. She had donned her matron of honor dress and was standing before the mirror trying to create the new trim lines within the rigid confines of her undergarments. "Why does everything have to be flat?" she asked crossly. "Nothing short of an operation is going to make me look the way I ought to in this dress."

"I think it's the most gorgeous dress I've ever seen," Babe said. Babe was leaning against the foot of the bed, resting her chin on her clasped hands, swinging her hips in a wide arc. She chewed gum and watched and listened with wistful intensity.

"I think you have a very nice figure," Harriet asserted, "considering — everything."

"Oh Mother, for heaven's sakes, considering what?" Eddie asked. "Two children is no excuse for letting yourself go. Flo's simply got to diet, that's all."

Flo turned from the mirror and looked disconsolately at Louise. "Well, at least you can wear them, Louise. I'll just try to be inconspicuous like some old aunt while you pretty young things get all the attention. I can remember the time, though —"

"Oh golly," Louise said, "I'm scared to death. I'll probably drop my flowers or stumble or something awful. And this dress makes me look so *old* — twenty at least."

"Don't be a fool," Eddie said. "You'll be the best-looking girl at the whole wedding and no one will even look at anyone else. In fact, I'm not even sure that I like it."

Louise laughed with nervous pleasure and Harriet felt the last tension of the dinner scene vanish. Flo's good nature reasserted

itself to make her wriggle out of her girdle so that she could fully
enjoy herself. But Babe — when Harriet turned her smile to Babe,
she saw Babe's jutting posterior hesitating forlornly in its motion,
her cheek resting against her hand, her gum rolling absently
beneath her tongue.

"Come and sit down, dear," Harriet said, holding out her hand.
"Come on."

Babe straightened up and turned her back to them. "No."

"What's the matter with you?" Eddie asked. "Did someone say
something?"

"Oh, why can't people leave me alone!" Babe hit her hand
against the bed. "Nothing's the matter. If people would just leave
me alone!"

"Come on, Babe — don't be like that," Flo said. "Show me your
dress. What are you going to wear?"

Tears started down Babe's cheeks. "I'm not going to the wedding."

"Of course you are." Harriet went to her, the need for action
excluding new despair. "What's the matter, dear? We couldn't
have the wedding without you."

Babe pulled off her glasses, dropped her sobbing head against
Harriet's shoulder. "No, I'm not, I'm not. I'd just embarrass everybody — you'd all be humiliated and ashamed. I'd rather die than
go."

"Babe — what a thing to say." Harriet gave Babe a troubled
smile, shook her gently. "You know perfectly well we're always
proud of you."

"What *is* she going to wear, Mother?" Eddie asked.

"Well — she has that lovely little georgette party dress." Harriet
looked at their faces and then began justifying herself. "It was a
very expensive dress and at her age — she's changing — I thought
we might wait a while before we buy her a new one —" But she
surrendered to their accusation. "Maybe we should buy her a new
one now."

Eddie put her hands on Babe's shoulders and twisted her away
from Harriet. "Look, Babe, I have a better idea — if you'll just
wipe your eyes and blow your nose —"

Babe broke away, covered her face with her hands. "I'm not

going," she sobbed. "I don't want a new dress. Why can't you leave me alone!"

Eddie went to her closet, reached into the gingham dress bag for the Paris evening dress she had brought from New York. "How about it, Babe, will you wear this? I want you at my wedding."

Babe lifted her head, gazed in worship at the soft blue velvet, the fragile pink bodice, the rosebuds.

"You've never even worn it!" Louise exclaimed.

"How about it, Babe? It won't fit you the same places it fits me, but maybe my bulges will make up for yours."

"You've never even worn it," Babe whispered.

"Well, all the better. You don't want people to think it's an old hand-me-down, do you? Take off your dress and try it."

Babe started to slip off her dress, but more tears came and wholly incapacitated her. She threw herself on the bed and wept into the pillow. "Eddie," she mumbled, "Eddie — I'd give my life for you."

And finally, after days of too much ice cream and cake, too many open-faced sandwiches, too many gallons of fruit punch, too many urns of tea, after crisis and nervous tears and despair, the wedding day itself arrived. Up until the last moment, confusion maintained itself in full force; then suddenly, at ten minutes of four, Harriet was straightening Gus's cap and together they walked down the stairs.

The string quartet was settled in the music room playing "I Love You Truly" and the rose room was filled with men in dark suits and women in beaded dresses. A somber rustle of whispers came from the room and Harriet had to stop for a deep breath or two before she could face it.

The mother of the groom was seated on one of the low, plush chairs, and, when Harriet entered, had to spread her knees for leverage to rise, so that the metal of her garters and the overflow of flesh from her stocking tops were part of the effusiveness of her greeting. "Mrs. Gannon," she said, making a monosyllable of Mrs., "you've excelled yourself, Mrs. Gannon, you've excelled yourself. This lovely old room's a picture, a perfect picture. I told Howard Sr. I knew we could count on you to do it right. I know value,

Mrs. Gannon, I've always had beautiful things and I know you couldn't have got these lovely flowers for a cent under three hundred dollars. I know Howard Jr. is going to be pleased; I'm sure he's going to be very well satisfied."

While Mrs. Driscoll spoke, she held her hand over Harriet's as if to detain her, as if to ordain silence until she had finished. The middle finger of the hand had three diamond rings on it, one with two stones. She wore lavender lace and a huge feather hat and several strings of pearls around her neck and an elaborate beaded bag hanging from her arm. Over the deep crack of her huge bust was a corsage of twelve red roses.

"We want you to know, Mrs. Gannon, Howard Sr. and I," she continued, "that we didn't stand in Howard Jr.'s way one minute when we saw which direction the wind was blowing in. We've approved of your daughter all along, Mrs. Gannon, and we said to ourselves, if she's what he wants, we're very well satisfied. We think they've made a good match — they're very fortunate — both of them."

She spoke the words with such a ring of congratulation that Harriet had to fight down resentment. But she smiled her acceptance of the compliment, withdrawing her hand from Mrs. Driscoll's, and led Gus toward the white candles and screen of gardenias where the Reverend Mr. Atwell would stand.

The two or three minutes before the quartet swept into the "Wedding March" were perhaps the first since Eddie's announcement that Harriet had had a chance to think. It was too late now for planning; the afternoon must proceed on its own momentum. Her maternal responsibilities toward Eddie were suddenly completed — she was as much an observer now as any of the guests. It was not a happy thought.

Her eyes searched the room for faces that would reassure her. These were the friends who went back to her girlhood, women who had witnessed her own marriage, who had brought little crocheted presents when Eddie was a baby. If it was true that people had roots, it was in this room, at such a moment as this, that you knew how deep was their penetration into other lives, other hearts, how intricately, how richly intertwined was their growth. Julia Harkington, Rose Cranfeld, Ruthie Harper (such

a queer little thing now) — to look at them, one would find it difficult to explain how they could mean so much, how they could
mean anything at all. But looking at them, one would have no
way of knowing that Julia and Rose and Ruthie, standing stolidly
on swollen feet, clasping the handkerchiefs that would catch their
tears, were part of a precious abstraction called *my life*.

And Grant, standing opposite, with Connie and Sammy, who
were, thanks be, awed into quietness by the flowers and sad music
and all the people — it could, of course, have been the setting for
a funeral as well as for a wedding (where the Reverend Mr. Atwell
would stand had stood Grampa Gannon's casket and more flowers
than at any other funeral in Clark City). Grant was looking very
solemn, his neck bulging out of a stiff collar that seemed too small
for him, and his children repeating the solemnity, the pink hair,
the scowling foreheads, like three saints in a triptych, all the work
of the same primitive hand. Connie and Sammy were Grama's
sweethearts and she loved them.

As much as her own? As much, for instance, as Gus? His little
wet hand was squeezed in hers, and looking down she could see
only the top of his sailor hat and the projection of his stomach.
Her whole being dissolved in love, poured through her hand into
his. Gus moved a little closer to her so she could feel his body
against hers. Was it fair to expect love like this to be repeated —
for someone else's children?

Down through the open doors into the music room, she caught
a glimpse of Babe, officiating over the musicians, stiff, holding in
her stomach because Eddie's dress was really too tight for her,
trying to maintain her balance on the new high heels. She saw
Babe's flurry of excitement and "I Love You Truly" became the
"Wedding March."

The hats and the dark suits turned toward the music room; from
the dining room, the Reverend Mr. Atwell sailed in like a slow
ship, followed by Howard Driscoll Jr., and Howard Driscoll Sr.,
looking exactly alike, dressed alike, hard and weathered, affable,
solemn, hired pallbearers. In the moment of waiting, Harriet
chilled, her breath tightened.

Then Louise appeared, white and terrified, her bouquet of
gardenias trembling, her eyes desperate with concentration as she

tried to manage the slow hesitation step of the march. Too soon afterwards, Flo, smiling at people she knew, paying no attention whatsoever to the music, gained on Louise with every step until finally she simply stopped in the middle of her progress to allow Louise to regain her lead. Sammy and Connie came to life: "There's Mommy — there's Mommy."

And finally Eddie and Papa. Eddie looked beautiful, beautiful and cool. Her large dark eyes looked non-committally before her, the white skin and high broad cheekbones and wide red mouth were exquisitely without expression. Perhaps that was how brides should look, untouched, unreachable. But there was something about Eddie's look that was a reproach to people of ordinary flesh and blood. Her dress, alternate bands of satin and Valenciennes lace, loose sleeves to the elbow, hemline slightly below the knees, wide trailing veil, was certainly the handsomest and richest that would ever grace the Sunday Society page of the *Clark City Sentinel*.

Papa was pale, tense — you wanted not to see how old he looked, how tired. When they appeared, Mrs. Driscoll reached over her hand and rested it on Harriet's, a gesture of friendliness, no doubt, but so irritating that Harriet wanted to push the hand away, to draw back from any contact with Mrs. Driscoll. Howard Jr. and Howard Sr. stepped forward simultaneously, the same sure, waiting smile on their faces, no impatience because they knew that always they would win. And Papa bringing what was to him probably the most precious thing in his life, guarded, always, and loved, handing it over to two other men, like a contract, a deed to a house, to do with as they liked.

Can you hate the man to whom you are marrying your daughter? For a blind, suffocating moment, Harriet hated all the Driscolls, Mrs. Driscoll, a fat spider who had already reached out to draw her in and was just waiting to pounce on Eddie; the two Howards, possessive and destructive like hangmen.

Then the singing voice of the Reverend Mr. Atwell took over and the "Wedding March" became "Oh Promise Me," and Harriet was thinking, Oh dear, why can't someone *tell* him. The hundreds of weddings he had performed in Clark City had not taken the song out of the Reverend Mr. Atwell's voice; in fact, he seemed to get worse with the years, the quavering more uncontrolled. He was a town fixture, a fine and worthy man and a wedding wouldn't be a wedding without him. But, oh dear. And would his Hallelujah ring out at the end of the service? She had meant to ask him, very tactfully, of course, please to omit the Hallelujah.

And then she was hearing the words and it was her little girl to whom they were being said and to the fine, clean young man who was to be her son-in-law. And though she had vowed that at Eddie's wedding, at least, she would not let herself *go*, when Eddie's clear, pure voice said "I do," she felt her resolution crumbling disastrously, and she raised her eyes to blink away the tears. In the large mirror over the mantel, she could see the whole room reflected — rows of people staring solemnly with no awareness that they were being observed; Babe way in the back, scowling because she couldn't see without her glasses. Beside her was Martha, in Sunday black for the few minutes of the ceremony, Martha red-eyed and lonely, watching another part of her life drift off into maturity. Where, among all the dark suits and beaded dresses and velvet hats was Jack — Harriet searched the mirror for his face. But the Reverend Mr. Atwell was asking for the ring and his round bald head rose and fell at the base of the mirror like a moon over the horizon.

Howard lifted Eddie's veil and kissed her chastely (you could tell he had been raised like a gentleman). There was a moment of silence while Eddie and Howard looked at each other and smiled, while the whole room looked at Eddie and Howard and smiled. Then out it came, the Reverend Mr. Atwell's joyous Hallelujah; the string quartet played a lively wedding march, Howard and Eddie and Flo and Louise swung gaily, happily out between the rows of people, and Julia and Rose and Ruthie, with wonderful contentment, wiped their noses.

Harriet and Gus and Papa and the Driscolls followed the young people into the library where they all kissed and complimented each other and Harriet felt that you couldn't find a nicer family anywhere than the Driscolls. Howard Jr. kissed her and thanked her for everything she had done and for having so beautiful a daughter. Even Papa, standing a little apart, tried to smile. Howard Jr. was a lovely boy.

As they were all straightening themselves to return to the rose room, Eddie went to Papa and clasped her hands behind his neck. "Are you happy about this, Dad?" Her voice was intimate, only for him, as if no one else were in the room. "This is what you wanted, isn't it?"

Papa looked around at the others, at the Driscolls. "Of course, Eddie," he murmured. "I want whatever will make you happy."

Eddie's eyes didn't waver from his face, while he spoke or after. She waited, oblivious, watching. "Have I been a good daughter, Dad?"

Papa frowned slightly, as if bewildered. He gazed at Eddie, at the others, at Eddie again. Then his head began to tremble, and he broke the clasp of her hands, kissing one hand. "Excuse me," he said and rushed from the room.

The wedding took over. People stood in line to meet the in-laws, congratulate the bridegroom, and kiss the bride. People stood in line to inspect and compare and evaluate the wedding gifts. People stood in line to receive a plate of chicken salad, hot rolls, ice cream, three kinds of cake, punch, nuts, olives, and gum drops. The string quartet played "Roses Are Blooming in Picardy" and "Smilin' Through." The autumn afternoon passed through the colors of sunset, felt dimly through lace curtains and damask draperies, into early dark.

A beautiful wedding, people said, and never had they seen a prettier bride and Louise was going to be a real beauty and wasn't Helen turning into a fine-looking girl. And dear old Flo, how they all liked her. And that's a fine little boy you've got. Gus was playing a kind of tag with Sammy and Connie in the front hall, his cap gone, his head a gleaming orb.

But where was Jack? No one had mentioned him and Harriet was straining more and more anxiously to catch a glimpse of him through the crowd. When the line broke up and the bridal party trailed into the dining room for refreshments, Harriet started out to find him.

He was in none of the downstairs rooms and she sent Connie to search upstairs. In the kitchen, she said, "Martha, have you seen Jack?" Martha muttered sourly to herself, and Harriet went out to the back porch to peer into the darkness for the car.

Faintly, from far away, she heard music. It was Tommy's piece, all right, "Who's Sorry Now," that he had been playing on the graphonola. The music came from the basement.

She felt her way down the dark back stairs, through the fruit room into the long dark hall where light showed under the crack of a closed door and the music was loud enough for her to hear the words of the song:

> *Who's sad and blue*
> *And crying too*
> *Just like I cried —*

She stopped for a moment, held back by a fear to which she would not have given words, and then she banished it with a tap on the door. The voices inside became still, there was a loud grunt of someone rising from the floor and a girl's shrill laughter. Then the door opened and Jack frowned into the darkness.

"Friend or foe?" he demanded.

"Oh, there you are!" Harriet made her voice light. "I've looked all over the house for you."

Jack's face brightened into the most welcoming smile anyone had ever given her. He stepped back, threw open the door, opened his arms to her. "This is the happiest moment of my life." He said it simply, he wasn't joking. "No, wait a minute," he said, snapping his fingers in remembrance. "Maybe there was another — when I was a little boy — there was a row of some kind — you took me down town to dinner and to a movie. Out of the whole family, it was me you took. I thought at the time it must be because you loved me best of anyone." He kissed her and with his arm around her, presented her to the room.

"These are my best friends — my dearest best friends." His voice was a little thick. To them he said, "This is the person I love better than anyone else in the world."

His best friends staggered up off the floor and came over to her. Tommy Reed in the sweat shirt and dirty corduroy trousers he had worn that morning to help move furniture. Muriel Hooper with bobbed hair, redder than it used to be, expensive evening dress that was wrinkled and mussed. A second girl who was familiar but unplaceable; she wore a sweater and skirt, too much lipstick, and her hair a huge marcelled halo. Ah, that was it, Harriet remembered, one of the operators at Murleen's Beauty Salon. Jack was in tails. His white tie had been pulled undone and two red lips had been kissed onto his starched front.

"Weren't we just saying," Tommy leaned his elbow on Muriel's shoulder, "weren't we just saying that something was missing to make this party complete? And here she is, by Jesus, this lovely, beautiful — "

"I don't know if you'll remember me, Mrs. Gannon," Muriel Hooper said. "I'm Muriel Hooper. Gee, I've grown up with your kids — why Eddie, I've never admired anyone so much in all my life as I admire Eddie. I consider Eddie one of my dearest, most intimate friends. And this old devil," she indicated Jack by pushing her finger in his stomach, "well, I won't say what I consider about him."

Yes, she remembered Muriel, and nodded her recognition.

The other girl just smiled and said, "I'm happy to meet you."

Harriet could think of nothing to say. How does one respond to this — what are the words of this language? "Well," she faltered, "you seem to be having a little party — "

"A wedding," Tommy corrected. "A wedding. We just gave Jack in marriage to Virginia here."

"You nut!" cried the marcelled girl.

"Well, for heaven's sakes," Muriel exploded, "let's make the bride's mother comfortable. Honestly, Mrs. Gannon, these kids have no manners."

They all searched for something for Harriet to sit on, but there was nothing. The room had been an extra maid's room, then a play room, and now a storage room. There were trunks and boxes and piles of old schoolbooks and Babe's doll house and a pair of skis and Jack's boxing gloves and some moth-eaten bathing suits. They had pulled the mattress of an old brass bed into the middle of the floor — a disreputable thing that she used to bring out when the babies were sick. That was their only piece of furniture. Beside it was the large saucepan she used for putting up fruit. It was half-filled with a liquid, and four cracked kitchen cups and Tommy's phonograph were on the floor beside it. The room was clouded with smoke; cigarette stubs had burned brown spots into the wooden floor. The only incongruous thing in the room was a huge branch of a maple tree with brilliant flame leaves. It leaned against the wall, desolate enough in this atmosphere.

"Hey, we'll drag over a box," Tommy said, inspired. "Come on, Gannon, gimme a hand."

"No, please," Harriet said. "I can't stay. I was just checking up."

"To tell you the truth, Mrs. Gannon," Muriel said, rubbing her back, "I wouldn't mind sharing a box with you myself. You know how it is."

And so they brought a box for Harriet and Muriel to sit upon; Tommy and Jack sat on the mattress with the marcelled girl between them. Jack filled the cups and tried to force his on Harriet — just a teeny little taste — but Harriet shook her head.

"My God, this is life," Jack said, beaming with perfect complacence. "The people you like best in the world, some nice little thing to refresh you, good talk — what more does life have to offer?"

"Now tell the truth, Mrs. Gannon," Tommy urged, "wouldn't you rather be down here with us than upstairs with all those stuffed shirts? And to think I almost went to that wedding." He looked into his cup as if the idea might make him sick.

"Well, I didn't almost go," said the marcelled girl. "I went all through high school with Edna Gannon — for two years we were in the same gym class together. But did I get invited to her wedding? You can bet your life I didn't."

Jack smiled at her, wisely, an old man to a little girl, but his eyes couldn't focus on her. "You shouldn't complain," he said gently. "You should try to understand. We're the rejected down here, the dreamers, the crackpots, the untouchables. All those J. P. Morgans upstairs — why should they be concerned with us? All they're concerned with is respectability — that's what Eddie said. Decency."

"Who the hell are you calling a crackpot?" the marcelled girl cried angrily. "Look at you — just look at him. I don't have to take that from anybody." She tried to rise from the mattress, but Tommy pulled her down.

"How come J. P. Morgan got invited?" Tommy asked. "Didn't know you were acquainted with him. I'd like to meet the gentleman."

"Maybe we ought to go upstairs after all," Muriel said. "I think it'd be exciting to meet him — I've heard so much about him."

Jack started laughing, so hard that he fell back on the mattress and spilled his drink down the front of him.

"How's that darling little boy?" Muriel asked Harriet while the marcelled girl wiped Jack off with Tommy's handkerchief. "Really, I've never seen such attractive men as your sons, Mrs. Gannon."

"Gus is fine," Harriet murmured, rising. "I must get back — I must leave you people."

"Ah, no!" they whined in chorus. Then Tommy suggested, "Maybe we should escort her back to safety."

"No," Harriet heard herself saying. "Don't bother — don't interrupt your little — " She was asking Jack not to come to Eddie's wedding and felt such shame that she couldn't face them, him or his friends.

"Wait a minute, Mother." Jack got to his feet, with rear help from the marcelled girl and Tommy. He walked over to her, kissed her lightly on the forehead. "Thank you, Mother, for coming. I guess I knew you would."

She turned abruptly to leave, but he held her.

"Wait. I want you to do me a favor."

He walked unsteadily over to one of the trunks for a small, leather-bound book.

"My wedding present — for Eddie." He gazed solemnly at the book, flipped its pages. "A young guy, a poet — name of Brooke — who wanted to live. Like Eddie." He handed Harriet the book. "He died young too."

Too tired for more pretense, Harriet accepted the book, stepped quickly from the room. In the darkness of the hall, she waited for her eyes to make out the staircase and heard the party pick up once more. "Who's Sorry Now" and the girl's shrill voice, "Jack — stop it! For heaven's sake!"

If it's a party, Mother, you're invited. Since he was a little boy, that had been Jack's way. Let's have a party, Mother. Let's go down town, Mother, just you and I, and have a beautiful party.

And she had believed in it always, that world of Jack's, as a special glittering place, warm and comfortable. But now she was rejecting it — the fun had gone out of it — like the tea party in *Alice in Wonderland*. The red leaves of a maple tree couldn't conceal the dreariness of that room. And Jack's words and kisses couldn't make her feel at home. Perhaps she hadn't understood those parties at all. Had he been laughing at her — he and his friends?

Upstairs, they would be missing her. The Driscolls would think it odd, her vanishing this way, and Papa would want her there when he gave Eddie and Howard their check, and after a bite of refreshments, they could all look at the presents together and then she must help Eddie dress for the trip. She was losing Eddie. It happened so quickly.

And Jack, her mind asked, had she lost him too?

But that was nonsense, she told her mind.

She crossed the dark hall, felt her way up the stairs, clutching the book to her. Poor little Gus — he was probably starved. No one had paid him a bit of attention. She opened the door at the top of the stairs and stepped into the light.

She could hear the voices in the dining room — Mrs. Driscoll's steady monologue, Flo's admonitions to her children, Howard Sr.'s commendation of the silver service. Hesitating, she opened the book to the flyleaf where Jack had written, "For Eddie, As ever, Jack." She closed the book and hurried toward the dining room to join the others.

CHAPTER 4

W<small>ITH</small> E<small>DDIE</small> <small>MARRIED</small>, Louise, now the oldest at home, moved
from her dark little room on the north to Eddie's sunny corner
room with striped wallpaper and its own bath. The room had been
first occupied by Flo, then Eddie, and when Louise married, Babe
would have her turn at it. It was the pre-marital chamber — the
virgin's sanctum before the advent of the bridegroom, the victim's
temple before the performance of the sacrifice. It was the place
of honor in the house, but, like life and youth and virginity, tran-
sient. Its occupant lost the rights of private citizenship, and, like
a performer called into the ring for a contest, bore an obligation
to succeed.

The movers who came for Eddie's elaborate suite of Grand
Rapids French Provincial moved Louise's bird's-eye maple chest of
drawers and desk and her small brass bed into the new room. The
family gathered to see how Louise arranged things and Louise
wished they would leave because her possessions were as inadequate for the room as she herself felt. The bird's-eye maple chest
and desk seemed scrawny and apologetic after Eddie's florid
dresser and vanity. The brass bed, when against the wall, was lost

in space; jutting at an angle into the room, it was overassertive. Her pictures — a sepia print of Dante catching a glimpse of Beatrice and a Maxfield Parrish Winken, Blinken and Nod — were juvenile and embarrassing. The only real thing about the room was the pile of books on her desk. They were schoolbooks, to be sure — not the poetry and novels Eddie read — but books of any kind were legitimate equipment for this room.

And now it was up to Louise to do as well as Eddie, to make them all proud of her as they had been proud of Eddie. When company came to the house, Louise would hear her mother relating the past triumphs of the older girls as she passed around their tinted graduation or bridal pictures. The climax would come, of course, with how well their husbands were doing. Marriage marked the high point — and the end — of triumph. And then her mother's proud, excited voice would ring out: "Louise (this is Louise here) — well, she's just been a joy all through. There's not a sweeter, grander girl any place — I don't care who she is. And Miss Kirkham (she's at the high school, you know) — Miss Kirkham just goes up over Louise — she says Louise has real talents — she says she wouldn't be surprised if we had another valedictorian on our hands. (Eddie — my daughter Edna — she was head and shoulders above anyone else in her class.) People say Louise is like me — I don't know as I see it. But many people say she's a real beauty — she's gone out with some lovely boys — " Louise would cover her ears with her hands and shrivel inside. Why did her mother do it? What must people think?

And then she would lock herself in her room and pore over her books. School had come easy for Eddie — it had never been work for her. For Louise, it was excruciating, back-breaking labor. She got A's, but despite Miss Kirkham's pronouncements, the A's were reward for constant and painstaking application — not for scholastic talents.

Louise's last two years at Clark City High were a bad imitation of what a girl had a right to expect of high school. After hours of studying, during long nights before exams when she twisted and turned till morning, sick with fear, she told herself it was all wrong, she was being badly, cruelly cheated. High school was supposed to be a long series of successes — boys and student body offices and prom queen and exciting afternoons of getting out the year book. For Jack and Eddie, it had been the heightened animation of acting in a play, with an audience and applause after every act. But for Louise, it was two years of sitting in the audience, alone, on the back row, bolstering herself by speaking of the leading actors as if they were her intimate friends. And at night, after studying, at night, before exams, she would hear her mother's voice saying: "Louise is the quiet type — but they're the ones who sometimes accomplish the most. Just look at President Coolidge! Papa and I have never had an unhappy moment over Louise — we've always been proud — "

Louise's hours of escape, when she could allow herself to believe she was all the things she knew she wasn't, were Paul's gift to her. He waited each day to carry her books home from school, and each day his face lighted in surprise that she granted him this favor. And he talked earnestly of his plans and dreams or told her anecdotes. Weeks in advance he asked her to school dances and brought her presents on every possible occasion.

But then she would hear her mother talking to Flo: "It's quieter at High than it used to be. Louise's friends don't seem to take as much part in the activities as you older children did. I guess they must spend more time at their studies than they used to." And one night Dad asked about Paul's father, who he was, what he did. Paul was none of the things her family would consider "successful"; he was not captain of the football team, nor editor of the paper. Dad had never heard of Paul's father; he kept trying to think if some of his friends didn't have boys her age. The few times when Louise had to ask a boy to a party, the whole family would discuss the possibilities, the son or younger brother who might be willing to escort Louise if Mother or Flo or Eddie just made a little phone call. It never occurred to them that she might ask Paul. She usually asked Dick Bingham with whom she had gone to school since kindergarten. Her mother thought Dick came from a nice family, and Dick was a nice boy, but he had never learned to dance and he talked mostly about guns and pheasants.

Junior year passed dismally. School was a matter of living for weekends and then working so hard that by Sunday nights she would weep tears of exhaustion. And home was different; it wasn't a crowd any more. Babe was impossible to live with — moody and quarrelsome and resentful. Flo still dropped in just about every day; Eddie and Howard came for Sunday dinner. Eddie had very rapidly become Mrs. Howard Driscoll, Jr. She criticized everything about the house and said that Martha should be fired.

Jack's letters arrived every week, wonderful glowing letters describing New York's waterfront at five in the morning or Fifth Avenue in a snowstorm or Times Square with theatres letting out. Vivid exciting letters that told nothing about his life, and when people asked what he was doing, it was hard to know what to say. Somehow, within the family, they didn't seem to speak of Jack so much any more. And Dad seemed to have aged and Mother could find little in the letters to tell the women in the club. He wrote wonderful descriptions of the cheering crowds at a football game in New Haven — but what could you say about that?

And Gus. Gus still cried for Yooweez and sometimes at night when he was unhappy in his own bed, she would sneak him off to her room and tell him stories, or, if she had to study, read aloud her American history. Cinderella's glass slipper or Tom Paine's *Common Sense*, it was all the same to Gus. He liked Yooweez and her interests were his.

In the spring of junior year, when she had to submit a collection of flowers for botany, she would pack Gus and some oranges and candy bars into the Packard (it was 1924 and Dad had finally conceded that a woman might be trusted with a car) and off they would go into the country or up the canyon. And Gus would run through the mud hunting specimens of Indian paintbrush or larkspur or sego lily, and they would sit on a rock and eat their candy bars. She would tell him plots of movies or make up love stories that featured herself as the queen of the campus; or she would tell him what happened at school or describe all her friends to him. His capacity for being interested seemed to be infinite. His chief contribution was the recurrent question, "And then what happened?" Maybe he didn't even listen — she couldn't tell. But they were wonderful days of peace, of escape.

And nights, when spring smells and sounds, the rustle of new leaves, the winds flowing in from the mountains, the awful yearning ache, seemed to reach in through the window to draw her outside, she would take off her glasses and rub her eyes; then she would go to Gus's room, open the door softly. "Gus," she would whisper. "Are you asleep?"

"No," he would whisper back. "I'm not asleep. Are you?"

"Gus — do you want to go someplace? A secret — just the two of us?"

He would scramble out of bed and she would bundle him in his flannel bathrobe and bunny slippers and they would slip down the stairs — he, one step at a time — and out the door, down the street, running, skipping all the way — wanting, seeking — heaven only knew what. In the shadows of Pioneer Park, she would dance an exquisite dance before the crowned heads of Europe, and he would bob up and down in a primitive rhythm of his own. Titania and Puck in an enchanted garden, Miranda and an earthy little Ariel in the spirit-breathed darkness. And then they would lie on the soft new grass and she would name the stars for him and tell him about the lovely, fascinating people who inhabited them — lovely people who never had to study because they knew everything. People who exchanged presents every day — not just on Christmas — and lived happily ever after.

During the summer before senior year, Paul got a job in Yellowstone Park and gave up his paper route.

"And it's a good thing, too," Eddie explained at Sunday dinner. "He's done Louise a lot of damage, hanging around here all the time." Eddie held a piece of roast lamb suspended on her fork and looked across the table to Howard for confirmation. "Haven't I said for a long time, dear, that we ought to do something about Louise? I think it's a good thing."

"Well, I don't know," her mother said. "He's a nice boy and they're both young yet — I doubt if anything will come of it."

"I wouldn't be so sure," Eddie insisted. "With him around, the really right kind of boys will stay away. He may be a nice boy, but for heaven's sakes, Mother, they're *all* nice boys. He has absolutely nothing to *give*."

"I think he's a droop," Babe declared.

Louise dropped her fork to her plate. "Of course *you* would," she said to Babe, her voice trembling. "Just because no boy would ever look at you, you think they're all droops."

Babe's face grew red, but being on the side of the majority, she managed a contemptuous smirk.

"Well, aren't we sweet!" Eddie said. "You should be grateful, Louise, that someone takes an interest in you."

Martha made a special trip in from the kitchen with a plate of bread so that she could say, "It seems to me Louise is a bright enough girl to watch out for her own affairs."

Eddie leaned back in her chair until Martha left the room, then she stood up from the table and closed the door to the kitchen. "Dad, when are you going to get rid of that horrible woman?"

"What's that, Eddie?" he muttered over his food. Dad didn't follow conversations very carefully any more.

After dinner, Louise walked slowly up to her room and locked the door and threw herself on the bed. Breathing into the candle-wick bedspread, she felt hollow, burned out. Maybe what they said was right — maybe, maybe. She couldn't get Babe's expression out of her mind — the embarrassed, red defensiveness. It had been a terrible thing to say to Babe, but why did Babe goad her on? She had made a scene and upset everyone and the thought of Babe made her almost sick.

There was a low tap on the door and Gus's voice calling her. She unlocked the door to let him in and he climbed onto the bed and she told him a story — a story about a lovely princess who hadn't a nerve in her body. No matter what people said to her, she kept her temper and never yelled back at them to hurt people's feelings. And all the right kind of princes flocked around her because she was so agreeable a companion, and she married the one that was *most* right and lived, of course, happily ever after.

And so Louise wrote Paul that it seemed best to call the whole thing off. She thanked him for all the presents he had given her and for the consideration he had shown during their acquaintance-ship. She expressed faith in his future success and wished him luck and signed the letter, "Your sincere well-wisher, Louise Gannon." She wept herself into exhaustion, sealed the letter and sent it off. Paul didn't write after that, but within a week a package arrived from Yellowstone Park. It contained a silver ring with a bear seal, book ends carved like bears, and a satin pillow with Old Faithful hand-tinted on it. There was no card.

In the fall, senior year began, and it looked as if Clark City High would win the football championship, but then a hick school from the country with a lot of farmers on the team beat them 13–6, and everyone felt just terrible. Louise signed up for chemistry, which scared her half to death, and French and English and civics and gym. This would be a hard year, she told herself. As she walked to school that first week and saw the boys in flivvers with "C. H." painted on the doors and "Oh you kid!" and pictures of Barney Google, when she saw the girls, all with bobbed hair now and dresses above their knees and something clever to say to the boys, she told herself, wistfully, that it would be a hard year. It certainly was a good thing Paul wasn't going to be hanging around all the time, not with all the work she had to get done. So she told herself.

But as the days went by, she couldn't help wondering what had happened to him. After all, Clark High was pretty small and if people were around, you did, at least, *see* them. When she sat in her room trying to memorize meaningless formulae, when she stood in the laboratory trying to achieve results that just couldn't seem important, she would wonder so much about Paul that she'd find herself in a dizzy kind of dream. And it hit her that he was the one who was doing the avoiding. Eddie and all of them worrying about how they could keep him away from the fascinating Louise — well, it was only too easy.

Then one day in study hall, she turned suddenly, and there, at the table directly behind her, was Paul. He had been watching her — she caught his eyes for a moment before he dropped them to his book. She started shaking so uncontrollably that she had to ask Miss McCafferty if she might be excused. She hurried out to the hall, rubbed her arms, stretched her head back and took deep breaths. Then she walked slowly to the fountain for a drink of water. On the way back to study hall, she repeated, "This is foolish — this is foolish — this is foolish — " like a child writing the correct spelling of a word on the blackboard. One didn't behave this way, there was no excuse — but Paul was walking toward her.

He stopped in front of her so that there was nothing she could do and he hesitated a moment before he said, "Hello, Louise."

She couldn't just *ignore* him, so she forced a smile and said,

"Hello, Paul." He didn't return the smile and she was trembling again. She clasped her arms tight across her and tried one deep breath. "I hope you had a nice summer."

"It was all right," he said, staring at her without expression.

"I wanted to thank you for the presents," she said. "They were — awfully nice."

He said nothing, just watched until she thought she couldn't stand it any more. "Well" — she made a little laughing sound — "I'd better be getting back."

He reached out his hand and held her wrist. "Louise — could we talk someplace?"

She drew back and said, "Well not *here*, Paul" — like a silly girl to whom improper advances have been made. Blushing at the idea, she only made it worse — "After all, I have to get back — Miss McCafferty — "

"That old battle-axe," he said angrily.

Paul had changed. He wouldn't have said that in the old days, he wouldn't have held her wrist this way. He was older and tanned and his hair was blond from the sun and he didn't seem so loose-jointed. He co-ordinated and was certainly better looking. To fight against all of this, she made herself even more despicable to herself. "You're hurting me, Paul."

"What's happened, Louise?" he pleaded. "What's gone wrong? Can't you just tell me?"

"This is hardly the time or the place — "

"Look — will you go to the prom with me? That's all I ask."

She couldn't look at him — she could scarcely speak. "I'm not going out much this year, Paul. I'm taking an awfully heavy course — "

He was gone. She stood in the corridor, listless, empty. Through the doors at the end of the corridor was study hall. Study hall and her books — she must get back to her chemistry and civics. But she didn't want to go back. She wanted only to walk home, to be with the family, to let them know what she had done.

And so senior year passed, a repetition of junior year, only worse. The work was always there — more than she could possibly get through. She could see that her mother worried about her not going out, but the boys who asked her were always mild little things in English or French who blew on their glasses before they polished them. Better to stay home than have to hear the family's comments on them. Chemistry continued to be baffling and terrifying and she got only a B for her midyear grade so that it seemed impossible she could be valedictorian. The day the grades came out, a letter arrived from Jack and as she watched her mother read it, Louise could think only of that B in chemistry and how she was failing them too.

On a Monday in May, Louise was summoned to the office of Mr. Tobin, the principal, and informed that she was to give the valedictory address at commencement, and that night in the *Clark City Sentinel* was her year-book picture for junior year: "Beautiful and Talented Daughter of — "

The news brought none of the ecstasy that she had counted on — not even the relief. She knew only that she was more tired than she had ever been in her life, too tired to remember how awful it would have been had she lost. She walked home slowly, soberly; not till she caught a glimpse of the house did she feel any excitement at all. Then she thought of Mother and Dad and all of them, and of Gus, and she wanted to cry.

Her mother, when she heard the news, said, "Of course, dear, that's fine. But we knew all along you'd get it." Then she frowned thoughtfully. "You know, I shouldn't be surprised if Papa needs a good tonic. I bet he isn't getting enough iron. I think I'll tell the doctor."

Her father merely squeezed her hand and said, "Good, good," as if she were reporting on something entirely expected, as if she had said, "Dad, I haven't stolen anything this month."

Gus didn't know what valedictorian meant.

That night after dinner, she went to her room and lay on the bed and stared at the ceiling for a long time. Then she thought about the work she should do for tomorrow. With a little sob, she got up quickly, ran out of her room, down the hall, down the steps, outside to the spring night. Passing through the downstairs hall, she had heard her mother's voice speaking over the phone: "Of course we're proud, but we've known it all along. Miss Kirkham says — "

It took a few days for complete realization to sink in but by the end of the week, she knew. She had made it, she hadn't let them down, and for the two weeks left of school, she was free, she had stored up more than enough success to carry her through. The kids at school congratulated her — even those she didn't know very well, the ones who held offices, the cheer leader, the boy who had been voted Clark High's Beau Brummel. And on Friday, the Clark High *Gold and Blue* had that same awful picture of her on the front page and she nearly died of embarrassment.

The *Gold and Blue* was distributed at the end of last class on Friday afternoon. For Louise, it was study hall, so she could read all about herself and know that everyone else was reading about her and looking over their shoulders at her. And all that was exciting — what high school ought to be. The article stated that Mr. Tobin had made the announcement of the honor granted Louise Gannon — whose father was a prominent Clark City businessman; whose sister Florence was Prom Queen at Clark High, vice-president of the student body and lead in the school play; whose brother Jack was senior class president, captain of the tennis team, editor for two years of the *Gold and Blue*; whose sister Edna was Prom Queen, vice-president of the student body and valedictorian of her class. Louise, it stated, had been a member of the French Club, was well liked by her friends, and in her four years at Clark High had maintained a straight A average except for one B in chemistry.

Louise caught the anticlimax, but that didn't matter. She was part of an illustrious group and to be identified with that group, for all Clark High's edification, was victory enough.

But what would people think, seeing her gloat over her own picture as if she were a movie star or something? She turned the page, rattling the paper, to Graham Nye's column, which everyone always read first anyway.

Graham Nye was editor of the *Gold and Blue* — he was good looking and awfully wild and terrifying and one of those who ran the school. His column was called "The Inner Circle" and was supposedly anonymous, but everyone knew that Graham Nye wrote it. His signed editorials were always about the need for more school spirit or more courteous conduct in assemblies. "The Inner Circle" was filled with innuendoes about students and teachers, gossip, criticism, condescension and contempt. Most of it implied — nothing he could be expelled for.

This day's column began: "Those of us who admire real scholarship combined with personality and service to the school are wondering why Jerry Rayburn was recently overlooked. Jerry has not only been year-book editor and an outstanding athlete, but has consistently maintained an A average. Couldn't be, could it, that Clark High is corruptible?"

Louise wondered what it meant. Jerry Rayburn was certainly one of the "Inner Circle," just as wild, just as terrifying and just as important as Graham Nye. Also, he was Graham Nye's best friend.

She went on to the next item: "Who was that redhead we seen parked up the canyon in a car that looked suspiciously like Fred Parker's Franklin? Oops! That was no redhead, that was my —"

Louise lifted her eyes to the first item again, felt herself go cold. She read the words once more and knew what they meant. She sat still, wondering if everyone in the room had read the words too, if they were all staring at her and hating her for trying to horn in where she had no right to be. Waiting for the bell to ring, she sat rigid, her eyes fixed on the paper before her, her mind brooding over what she must do. First thing, of course, she would go in to see Mr. Tobin and withdraw her name. Then, perhaps, she should write a letter to the *Gold and Blue,* explaining that it had all been a mistake and that she realized more than anyone else how inadequate she was for this honor and how perfectly right Jerry Rayburn would be. "Let's all get behind Jerry Rayburn," she would conclude, "and let him know that we're one hundred per cent for him."

When the bell rang, she hurried down to her locker and put her things away. She went in the lavatory and soaked her handkerchief in cold water and held it to her eyes and forehead. She licked her lips, smiled sweetly, and murmured, "Mr. Tobin, I wondered if I could see you for a moment." Then, before she could change her mind, she stepped quickly down the hall to his office.

But Mr. Tobin was busy and rather than be seen waiting in his office, Louise slipped into the hall and willed herself out of the building. Down the street, where a lilac tree cut off the view of the school, Louise stopped to massage her forehead. "Why did it have to be me? Dear God, why me?" Then, lest someone see her lurking there, she stepped back to the sidewalk and hurried home.

All the family cars were out in front and at first Louise simply wondered, and then in terror that something might have happened, she ran up the stairs. "Mother!" she called from the hall.

Her mother and Flo came from the library, disturbed but not tearful.

"Is anything the matter?" Louise stopped still.

"You mean you haven't seen the *Gold and Blue*?" Flo asked. Louise's relief was so great that she put her hand to her forehead and laughed.

"My poor baby," Mother said, her arms about Louise. "I could just kill that nasty boy."

"These young smart alecks," Flo said furiously. "How could they do it — be so cruel? They've no sense of responsibility. They're — they're *inhuman*."

They were crazy but it was wonderful and Louise let the tears come because now it didn't matter who saw.

"You just have a good cry," Mother soothed, patting. "Everything's going to be all right. Papa and Eddie have gone over to see Mr. Tobin and if necessary, we'll wire for Jack to come home."

"Oh Mother!" Louise drew back, wiped her cheek with the back of her hand. "This is so awful! I don't want all this fuss." More tears came and she leaned against her mother's shoulder. "It's all so awful."

Flo handed Louise her handkerchief. "Here Yooweez." Flo's own eyes had filled with tears.

Gus came running in from the kitchen and held his arms wide for Louise to bend down for a resounding wet kiss on her cheek. "Poor Yooweez," he kept saying. And when they took her in the library, Gus sat beside her on the couch, his arms stretched up so that his fingers rested on the back of her neck.

"But how did you know?" Louise asked. "It just came out."

"Miss Kirkham phoned — she was in an awful state — I shouldn't be surprised if she resigned her job."

"We mustn't let her," Flo said. "This is our problem and I think we should handle it."

"It isn't *our* problem — it's *mine*," Louise blurted out. "I mean —

well, it's all fantastic and Miss Kirkham should mind her own business."

"I can't think who this Nye boy could be," Mother said pensively. "He can't be anybody, really, I guess. Papa's never heard the name."

Footsteps sounded on the front porch and Flo went out to open the door for Dad and Eddie. They had brought Miss Kirkham along.

"Everything's all right," Dad's suppressed voice said. "We've checked through their grades and that Nye boy is going to apologize or be expelled from school. I'll see to that."

Eddie appeared in the doorway, hatless and ruffled. "She's here, Dad."

Dad and Miss Kirkham swept past Eddie into the room and Dad kissed Louise's forehead and squeezed her hand. "It's all right, Louise. That — that —" he looked at the others in the room, "that boy behaved like a scoundrel but the facts are against him. If he's a gentleman —"

Miss Kirkham's terrifying guffaw split the air. "He's no gentleman — you can bet your life on that." Miss Kirkham wore a seedy winter coat and oxfords and a brown felt hat that made her look her age, whatever that was, a colorless old maid. But when she ripped off her hat and the flying white hair asserted itself, when she laughed and spoke in the powerful voice that students imitated but always respected, then the ageless toughness of the spinster schoolteacher was revealed and here, you knew, was something to be coped with. "Graham Nye is a growth — a fungus — a slimy thing that doth crawl with legs — but no gentleman."

"What happened, Dad?" Flo asked.

"I'll tell you what happened!" Miss Kirkham took over. "They did it out of spite. Louise is just too much of a lady for that crowd. I think I might say, Mrs. Gannon, I'm not easily shocked, but I could tell you things about that crowd —"

"What did Mr. Tobin say?" Flo interrupted.

"We checked through their grades," Dad said, his face red and throbbing. "That young Rayburn — his father, I found out, is out at the smelter, been a troublemaker all through — this young fellow had a good record, considering everything, but he had a C in — what was it he had a C in, Miss Kirkham?"

"English, Mr. Gannon. My English. He's an illiterate."

"Mr. Tobin," Eddie carried on, "says Louise has been promised A- for this semester in chemistry, so there's no question — absolutely none!"

Dad couldn't stand still; the aged warrior had been aroused, and despite the best advice of the medical profession, he was giving in to his anger. "Tobin," he muttered, "Tobin," as if the principal himself were there before him, "if my children can't win honors on their own, then give them to someone else. If Louise isn't the brightest person in this school, I said, I don't want her to be valedictorian. But I know that she *is* the brightest person in the school, and by God I'm going to see that she gets what she deserves."

Then everyone was talking at once: Mother was telling Dad not to excite himself, Miss Kirkham was repeating some faculty meeting scandal about Graham Nye, and Eddie was trying to give Flo a coherent account of what had happened in Mr. Tobin's office. Gus sank closer to Louise, sucked his finger and stared in bewilderment about the room. Louise heard the confusion, too weary to seek sense.

Dad said, "That young Nye will print an apology in the *Blue and Gold* and I've been thinking I should have Sam Baker print an editorial in the *Sentinel*."

"Oh no, Dad!" Louise groaned. "It'll just cause more trouble — I'll have to go through it all again. Don't you see? They hate me as it is —"

And then they were all talking again — Mother saying how things had changed since the older ones were in school — "I never know these young people's families any more — I can't think what's become of the better class of people"; Flo saying what she'd like to do to Graham Nye and Jerry Rayburn; Miss Kirkham saying it was an honor to be hated by such people as young Nye and Rayburn.

"Well, Yooweez," Eddie gave her a tired smile, "we'll take all the credit, but you did it yourself. If you've got the goods, they can't hurt you."

"The point is," said Flo, "they can."

"Louise, maybe," Eddie smiled again, "because she's such a nice person. But not me. I could have handled those boys on their

---

own level — limb from limb. But then I'm not such a nice person."

Miss Kirkham radiated her complete approval. "When I ever saw a nicer one," she declared, "I'd be hard put to say."

"It's just that I don't want it any more," Louise said quietly. "I don't think I can go through with it."

"Nonsense," boomed Miss Kirkham. "With your talents, that's a lot of nonsense. I've often said, Mrs. Gannon, that your children have some of the finest minds —"

The last two weeks of school were not very happy ones. She had triumphed, of course, but it was a withered triumph of little joy. The following Friday, Graham Nye's column printed an apology: "This column," it said, "made an error when it stated that Jerry Rayburn had the finest personality, the most activities, and the highest grades of any of the competitors for a recent honorary appointment. Apparently another candidate had higher grades." The sneer of Graham Nye's word followed her around, clouded her mind so that she couldn't concentrate in class, projected itself into every pair of eyes that looked at her, into every word spoken to her. That she could be the object of so much hatred from people whom she had quietly admired and envied was bewildering; to be involved, so unknowing and unwilling, in an ugly quarrel filled her with so oppressive a terror that two days before commencement, she fainted at the breakfast table and Mother had to call the doctor. Drugged with sedatives, Louise lay in bed and composed her valedictory address.

The night of commencement, the whole family came to dinner — Flo and Grant and the children, Eddie and Howard. They all brought Louise presents. Mother and Dad gave her a diamond watch and Babe spent every penny she had to buy her a sequin evening bag. Gus had wheedled money from his mother and bought a box of drugstore candy.

After dinner they walked in a procession to the high-school auditorium — just the grownups. Martha stayed at home with the youngsters. It was an early June night, still light at seven-thirty, the trees a sharp naked green, the iris and bridal wreath in full bloom and the air cool and sweet.

Louise walked between Mother and Dad and the three of them

were shy, now — all the nice things had been said and there was only anticipation. Behind them, Grant was teasing Babe, and Eddie and Flo were arguing evolution with Howard.

She felt numb. Her fear seemed to have localized itself about her heart so that she couldn't breathe deeply but there was no fear in her mind. The bromides she had taken seemed to have detached her mind from her body so that she could look down with a kind of ironic gentleness at this poor pathetic creature who couldn't breathe very well. Her hands were damp and felt as if they were a great distance away and it would be difficult to lift them. Graham Nye and Jerry Rayburn were a dull ache in her body, forgotten like the first sharp pain of an operation, present like a drying wound.

In front of the high school, she had to detach herself from the family and for a moment, as she looked back at their protective smiles, fear penetrated the bromides and her mind returned shivering to her body. But as she walked up the steps saying automatic hellos to excited friends, her mind pulled away to its own particular cloud and she was all right again.

The glee club and the class officers and Mr. Tobin and the superintendent of schools and several of the teachers were finding their places on the stage behind the closed velvet curtains. They smiled at her and shook her hand and Mr. Tobin stood with his arm around her and funny, bony Miss Carmichael who taught gym even kissed her. It struck her as surprising and a little ludicrous that everyone was being so nice. She found her place and sat with her hands folded and listened to the strange obscene noises of the band warming up on the other side of the curtain. And after a while — it could have been hours — she heard a sharp tick and the band started playing the procession march from *Die Meistersinger*. The curtains drew apart and out in the vast darkness was a blur of faces and hands, smiling, clapping. Then the senior class of Clark City High, 1925, marched down the aisles with bouncing stride to fill the front rows of the auditorium.

There was prayer, first, then joyous shouting from the glee club, and speeches — words, words, words, and the endless smiling. At a certain point in the program, Louise heard her name called and found herself looking out at all those faces, speaking more words —

big words that her body couldn't hear or feel but her mind could observe with knowing detachment. She spoke of our forefathers and the best hope of man and of how an idea that had inspired a few had caught a whole nation and infused strength and beauty into an organism and achieved its greatness.

"To us in the graduating class of Clark City High," she said earnestly, "the year 1925 offers a great challenge. As we go out to face the world, we must be ever mindful of our obligation. Civilization has reached a peak in our time, in our land. We young people here tonight are the inheritors of a way of life for which our forefathers died. American prosperity, American opportunity were earned by Washington and Lincoln on the bloody fields of battle. *They* made America great; it is up to *us* — we young people of Clark City High — to keep her great."

There was clapping and soon the band was back into *Die Meistersinger* and the graduating class was trooping by to receive diplomas. The girls all wore evening dresses — flat, long-waisted, hemlines at the knees; the boys all had greased hair and carnations in their buttonholes. These were the people she had known and gone to school with all her life — the hope of America — grinning, looking sheepishly into the auditorium when a burst of applause located family or friends.

Those on the stage received theirs last — the glee club and then the class officers and Louise. When Louise reached for hers, a small vigorous area of applause told her that the family was all together out there and they were proud of her. During the school song, for which everyone stood, she found it hard to keep back tears. They'd be singing too — Mother and Flo and Eddie. They had graduated from Clark High too. And now Louise.

> *See our banners proudly waving,*
> *Dear old Gold and Blue,*
> *Emblem of our high endeavor*
> *Loy-al-ty to you.*

Some of the horns in the band cracked on the high notes and the voices raced out ahead of the music. It certainly wasn't very impressive, but still it was hard not to cry. Babe would be next, then Gus, the cycle repeating itself. Clark High was part of the life process — just as much as birth and death.

Afterwards, out in the front hall, everyone was being much kissed and much congratulated. Mother and Dad were so busy shaking hands with people and hearing how proud they must be that they didn't even notice when Louise came up. Flo kissed her and said, "You were just wonderful, darlin'. It was one of the grandest things I ever heard."

Eddie patted Louise's behind. "Little Yooweez. Who would have thought she had it in her."

Babe hugged her and didn't say anything.

Even Howard was nice. He kept standing by her the whole time.

Then Mother noticed her and said, "Come here, dear, and meet these people." And she had to smile and say, "How do you do" and "Thank you very much" over and over again.

Miss Kirkham strode up in the long-sleeved satin evening gown which she must have worn to commencements since the school was founded. "You were splendid, Louise. You know I'm not lavish with my praise, but what you had to say had more sense in it than all the rest of them put together. You have a real talent."

Mother grabbed onto Miss Kirkham and introduced her to everyone who came up. "We consider Miss Kirkham a real friend, we Gannons do," she would explain.

Miss Kirkham said they must all go to the reception in the gymnasium — they were, after all, the stars of the performance. Flo and Eddie excused their way out, but Miss Kirkham wouldn't accept Louise's plea of being tired. "That's a lot of nonsense, Louise. Not till your bones get as old and achy as mine can you use that for an excuse." And she swept them off, Mother, Dad, Babe and Louise, with a vigor that would deny she had ever had an ache in her life.

The gym, dusky with red and purple lights, was crowded and noisy. The young people were dancing to a very loud orchestra and their parents stood awkwardly by the refreshment table drinking lime punch in paper cups. Mr. Tobin and the superintendent of schools and various teachers were being gracious and reassuring to parents, revealing an affability that brought a shock of amazement to the children.

Louise looked hopelessly around the room and would have slipped out had not the eagerness of her parents reminded her that this was their evening. Their pleasure was, after all, the only thing that gave point to any of it. But one more person's beaming congratulations, once more to stand by with a ridiculous grin while teachers and old acquaintances discussed her with Mother and Dad would, she knew, reduce her to hysteria of one kind or another. So she said her throat was dry and wove through the crowd to the punch table.

The lime punch, sweet and flat as it was, tasted wonderfully cool and she had three cups in quick succession. The bromide was wearing off and she felt dull and tired, her head ached, perspiration was on her forehead, her dress stuck to her back. She tried to be inconspicuous by standing behind a dark bulky couple who blocked the way to the punch table. Had she had the strength, she'd have been agonized to appear at a dance without an escort, she'd have simply died of humiliation to appear with her *parents*. But now she was too sick to feel any of that; she only knew that she should feel it.

"Louise —"

She knew, even with her back turned, who it was. She put on a bright smile and looked around in surprise. "Oh Paul — hello."

"I just wanted to say congratulations. You were great."

She gave what was supposed to be a gay little laugh. "Well, hardly that — but you're awfully nice to say so."

Paul had on a new brown suit and yellow tie and the red carnation in his buttonhole. The hope of America. "How about some punch — would you?"

"Thank you very much. I *would* like to try a little." She gazed with wide-eyed interest at the couples on the dance floor. The orchestra was playing "Sleepy Time Gal." "It's good music, isn't it."

"Swell."

She sipped her punch and smiled until her face ached.

Finally he said, "I guess it's all over. High school, I mean."

"Yes, I guess it is."

"It's been great. Hasn't it?" She hesitated and he continued rapidly, "For you, I mean. You've been such a success. You must have a great feeling of contentment."

No other boy she knew would have said it that way, without sarcasm. "Well, I don't know —" She was too tired to pretend any more. It was all so silly. "What about you, Paul? Do you have some plans?"

"Well I — " He was bashful and young. "I got a kind of scholarship — it doesn't mean much. University of Chicago. I guess I'll be going back there."

For no reason she would possibly face up to, his going away struck her as terribly, terribly sad. But she gave a little gasp of delight. "Paul, how wonderful! Why don't you tell people these things? All that talk about *me!*"

Paul sniffed and rubbed his hand along his nose. "It doesn't really mean very much but it — well, makes things possible."

"Why I think it's the most thrilling thing I ever heard — honestly I do."

He shifted and said, "Well, as you know, it's what I wanted."

Yes, she knew. She knew too that she had better leave in a hurry. She looked around for her parents.

"Look, Louise —" Paul spoke with painful embarrassment. "I'm terribly sorry I — can't ask you to dance. I'm — I'm with someone else. I wish I weren't."

She fled. On her way out, she motioned to Babe. In the cool darkness, she leaned against the building and closed her eyes and listened to the muffled music and felt humiliation in every cell of her body.

Mother and Dad and Babe came out immediately, worried that she might be ill.

"I'm all right — just awfully tired."

"Poor baby," Mother said. "You've been under a bad strain — but it was grand, everything was grand."

Dad had apparently taken up the problem of Graham Nye with the entire faculty and administration. "They *all* said Louise was the one for the job. I told Tobin my children get by on their own merits. Tobin, I said, if she didn't deserve it, I wouldn't want her to have it. *But*, I said, if she *did* deserve it, nobody can take it away from her. Not while I'm around."

"I could just kill that Graham Nye," Babe said. "I just despise him."

"Well," Mother mused, "it's all turned out for the best and we should try to forget the unpleasant things. Louise, I heard the grandest compliments for you you ever heard in your life."

And so they walked home, arm in arm, talking pleasantly. And when they arrived, there was a telegram from New York: "Love and congratulations for dear old Weezie. And may her life be just as rich and wonderful as she is sweet. Jack."

And when she finally dragged herself up to the big corner bedroom, she found that Gus had paid her a visit. On her pillow was a bouquet, crushed and brown, of dandelions.

CHAPTER 5

THE FASHIONABLE WINTER RESORT for those of Clark City who could afford it was the stretch of beach that ran from Venice Pier, through Ocean Park and part way to Santa Monica in southern California. The hotel accommodations were far from lavish, with a tendency toward wicker furniture and faded cretonne; the apartments had drawer beds and dark little kitchenettes; the cottages were cracked and raw from the salt wind, and sand grated under the feet in every room. But this was a place for children (and a fashionable resort meant, to Clark City, a place to which you could pack off all the children). Right in the front yard, as it were, was all that sand. Merely suggest to a child that he dig a tunnel to China or mention a shell collection; let him discover for himself the joy of ocean water pulling the sand from under his feet, of making queer noises with kelp, of chasing the little bubbles in the sand when the tide went out. And grownups could sit on the hard green benches and read *Clark City Sentinels* and doze in the sun. Or promenade along the beach and meet quite unexpectedly familiar Clark City faces and be nostalgic together for the hometown.

The summer was quite a different matter. Most of the well-to-do families had cottages in the canyon, and twenty minutes from the heat of the city, they could be in the mountains with the shade of pine and cottonwood and aspen, with the sun-shot mist of the cold mountain stream running over boulders. Or, if their children were old enough not to be a worry, they might board the overnight train to Yellowstone Park and take a conducted coach tour, both an education and a pleasure, through nature's curiosities and beauties. Those who knew a senator or congressman sometimes made a trip to the nation's capitol to dine with the near-great and buy post-cards of historic sites. Some went to New York to take in a play and see the Woolworth building. But the California beaches were not, as a general rule, for the summer. There were so many strangers on the beach and one seldom saw a friend. The children had to be watched — you never knew what evil might be hidden behind the dark glasses of a summer tourist. And the young couples that came to the beaches for Saturday-night dancing and Sunday swimming — well, things went on that children shouldn't see.

But the doctor suggested California. Papa must get away for a complete rest, away from cities and excitement. He must think about nothing; he must leave all worries behind. And low altitude and sea air would be the finest things in the world for him. That blood pressure — we mustn't let it run away from us.

So Harriet wired the Ellison Apartments, closed up the house, and loaned Martha to Flo for a month. She reserved a compartment for herself, Papa, and Gus, a lower berth for Louise and Babe, and in the middle of June, they were off to California.

When they had kissed Eddie and Flo good-bye and the train pulled out of the Clark City station and they were all in the compartment watching through the window the receding slums of the town, Harriet drew a deep breath and said, "Well, this is grand." She rested one hand on Papa's knee and with the other smoothed Gus's hair, and smiled for them all, the smile you would use when starting off for a picnic or a dinner-downtown-and-movies evening, a smile that denied any serious business in life and defied anyone not to be at his Christmas-day best.

Gus could be enthusiastic about the diner: "Is it time to eat yet? When will that man come?" But the others simply stared out the window.

They had, perhaps, caught her own mood. Perhaps they could see beneath her hearty "This is grand" to her vague uneasiness. But of course, they had not been too eager about the trip in the first place. Papa was no invalid, he had insisted, to be packed off to California at the whim of a doctor. You took a vacation when the proper time came for a vacation, not when a doctor told you to. Louise had been agreeable and helpful. "If it's best for Dad, of course we must go"; but she had added, "I'm not just sure what I'll do down there." Babe said it all sounded gruesome to her; she was no child to spend her life on a beach. Only Gus had been ecstatic.

Harriet's own enthusiasm had been forced all through. If Papa was really sick, the best place for him was home, with his own doctor and all the family, his own bed. Babe and Louise should be swimming up the canyon and dancing at the Red Barn so that they could meet the right kind of young men from the best Clark City families. Louise especially. At nineteen (Harriet had been married at nineteen, a mother at twenty) Louise was without direction or purpose or prospect. Her year since she finished high school had been a lonely one — Harriet could see that. Louise had wanted to go up to State but Papa held firm his belief that college ruined a woman. And so Louise had helped around the house and gone to the movies with the family on Saturday nights. With her brilliant mind — it did seem a pity she couldn't meet the right boy.

But doctor's orders. And Harriet had told herself many times that everything would work out for the best. Papa had finally consented to let Louise register for a course or two at summer school — U.S.C., perhaps — provided she take nothing that mattered. They thought maybe a little art appreciation and perhaps some French. And Babe had resigned herself to a summer of swimming and walking along the beach and jumping rope with kelp and the loss of at least two inches around her hips. If things became too deadly dull, she could always go on a new diet. And if they kept an eye on Gus to see that he talked to none of the wrong kind of people — well, perhaps everything might really work out for the best.

She looked out the window at the landscape that was losing its Clark City look and was now just West. "We'll all have a grand summer, I'm sure."

Babe took over the responsibility of Gus. The first day, Dad bought him a swimming suit and a bucket and shovel, and they put him out on the sand and that was all there was to that. He was like an amoeba, self-contained and vegetative in the water, sand, and sun. Babe could lie for hours, daydreaming or watching people, and only occasionally look up to see that a shark or a masked kidnapper hadn't run off with Gus.

Gus was on an allowance of five cents a day; Babe, three dollars a week. Every few days, Babe would make Gus put on his white duck sailor pants and they would take the long walk to Santa Monica village to splurge in Woolworth's. Babe's first purchase had been a canvas shopping bag. Her succeeding purchases gradually filled it with every shade of lipstick and nail polish Woolworth's offered, water-wave combs, mirror, brush, creams and oils, mascara and, eventually, an eyelash curler. The excursions had at first been rare adventure to Gus, but when he learned the basic principle of economy — that a nickel spent on a rubber ball or tin airplane in Woolworth's left no nickel to be spent on an Eskimo pie or salt-water taffy at the beach — he began to be difficult. Since it was essential that he accompany her, because she couldn't go off and leave him alone, Babe would have to part with an extra five cents of her allowance, muttering the while that she loathed children.

Every morning, after a breakfast of toasted hamburger buns and cocoa, she and Gus would cross over to the beach, he with his bucket and shovel, she with her shopping bag of cosmetics, and settle down for the day. While Gus made fortresses and tunnels, she would prop her mirror in the sand and go to work. A new hair-do each day, a new color nail polish. The weekly movie magazine her allowance permitted was her source of inspiration; a little spit and the eyelash curler gave her a momentary illusion that with different coloring and a slightly different-shaped face, she would look not unlike Clara Bow.

Babe's eyes were her best feature — whenever Mother's friends commented on Babe's beauty, it was her eyes they mentioned or her thick chestnut hair. Her worst problem was her figure which was not like a boy's, and in a period when it was stylish to be built like a boy, she looked more like a boy's mother. If she watched herself, she could keep her weight around a hundred-thirty-five, and if she wore a tight enough brassière, she could make herself fairly shapeless. But it was hard work and at sixteen, she was always taken for older than Louise, who was nineteen. Louise didn't even have to wear a brassière under her bathing suit.

An hour or two of concentrated effort would complete her beauty ministrations and then she would sit for a while on the green bench, gazing through dark glasses at the surf. She kept her ears sharp to any comments the passers-by might make on her hair; or, they might, of course, take her for a movie star. A few days had established a nodding acquaintance with some of the tourist-residents of the area, and she watched for them, waited in restless anticipation of their cluttered arrival on the beach, then writhed inwardly at the appraisal she imagined them making of her person. As she made conversation with them about the weather or a movie or an accident, her hand would stray irresistibly to her hair and she would murmur, "Darn my hair! I can't do a thing with it." And they would either say it looked all right — fine, in fact — or, scanning the beach, would say nothing. Sometimes Gus would scowl and say that he thought her hair looked terrible.

Generally she and Gus crossed over to the apartment for lunch — she for her salad and iced tea, he for a peanut butter sandwich and milk. And after lunch they generally took a walk out to the pier to check what was at the movies or stare at the big canvas come-on of the bearded lady, or price the magic tricks and shell ornaments and nasty postcards in the curio shops. Then back to the beach to doze or walk or dig. At five o'clock, she would take a dip in the big breakers, ruining her hair so that it would have to be done all over again the next morning. But she had a theory that the big waves, beating against her body, broke down the fat tissue and would reduce her hip measurement considerably.

Daytime settled into an agreeable pattern of uneventful existence, and though she complained daily about what a nuisance Gus was and swore she'd never have any children of her own, she really, secretly, didn't mind too much.

But nighttime was awful. On her allowance, she could go to three movies a week and the movie magazine took care of a fourth evening. But the other three evenings of the week — oh my gosh! how did people get through them! Mother suggested that she become interested in something — embroidery or stamps or reading or something, but it all sounded just too terrible. Then finally, one day when she and Gus had made the trip to Woolworth's, she was inspired: she purchased a scrapbook and some mucilage, and from then on devoted three nights a week to cutting her favorite stars out of movie magazines and pasting them into the scrapbook.

Louise was no help. Either she studied or read or sometimes went to the movies with Babe or sometimes for a little walk, but Mother didn't like them to be out alone at night or off the direct route to the movies. It was just that she and Louise had nothing much in common. Either they were fighting or else they were polite to each other. But gone was the wonderful intimacy of their childhood; gone too was the resentment of their beginning adolescence. It was strange that sisters could be so far apart; even stranger, perhaps, that after you'd felt so much about a person, you could get to feel almost nothing. Louise, she told everyone, was a simply swell person. But inside herself, she couldn't really see it.

One afternoon, Babe had been brooding over the terrible emptiness of life and watching an awful couple petting — right out where everyone could see. He was kind of hairy and repulsive and he kept bending over to kiss the girl and then he'd rub oil on her thighs and back and tickle her, and she'd slap him — right on the behind. Babe thought it was perfectly terrible, but before long she had endowed the man with the face of Ramon Novarro and was bitterly criticizing the awful, cheap girl. What she could see of the girl was a bit of red bathing suit and fleshy legs that would indicate *at least* forty inches of hip measurement. And when the girl stood, she had a pair that made Babe's look like miniatures. *Honestly!* And that divine, gorgeous-looking man. Babe wouldn't even deign to stare as they left the beach.

But their departure made her quite miserable, and if she had felt lonely before, it was worse now. In the entire world, every girl had some man to do awful, fresh things to her — except Babe Gannon; in the entire world, only she was unloved, despised. The only people in the world that she felt she really could count on were her movie stars. The rest was just one long dreary routine of bratty kids.

She raised up to look for Gus and couldn't see him. She stood and frowned against the light to inspect the length of the beach. Then she spotted him, trudging along the beach, way down by the pier where he would soon be out of sight and if anything happened to him, she, of course, would have to take all the blame. So she groaned and dragged herself along after him, muttering.

By the time she reached him, he was settled in the musty shade of the pier, playing a solitary game of tit-tat-toe in the damp sand. The roar of waves and rattling traffic on the boards overhead made a booming sound that vibrated and echoed like a rumble in a cave. She hated it here — clammy and terrifying, dark, noisy, smelling too much of the sea; the waves beat against the heavy pillars, winding them round with lifeless seaweed, pulling away, then slapping back again.

"Gus, for heaven's sakes," she whined, "why can't you stay out there where you belong. My gosh."

Gus had looked up with a welcoming smile, but changed his expression when she rejected his hospitality. "I'll do what I want to."

"Oh you will, will you? You're just getting a little too smart —"

She started toward him, but he was off with a gleeful shout, running further into the darkness. She chased after him, stopped. "Gus — I'm leaving," she called. She waited until he advanced triumphant into view, then turned and started back to the world of light.

She had taken only a few steps when her eye was caught by a patch of color up where the sand was dry and the pier's ceiling so low that you couldn't walk upright. Something somebody had forgotten — but she'd go take a look. Within a few feet of the object, she stopped dead still, felt an awful knot in her chest as she watched, then ducked her head and ran.

The patch of color was, of course, the red bathing suit — but, oh my gosh! And she looked around guiltily, fearful that people on the beach might discover in her face what she had seen. With elaborate casualness, she planted her feet in the sand, stared out over the water and fumbled with her straps as if she were lost in a daydream. But the daydream that flashed through her mind almost made her dizzy. That awful, awful man — and to think the girl would let him! The picture was not only in her mind but spread to all her senses, filled her body, smothered her breath. Oh my gosh.

Then, with a knowledge that almost sickened her, she knew she would have to go back in. If she died for it, she must look again.

Gus was waiting for her just inside the pier roof and skittered off when she approached. "Gus," she called, "have you seen my dark glasses? I must have dropped them —" And she began a long, careful search for the glasses, which she had left back with the shopping bag. Her attempt to appear unaware forbade her looking even once in the direction of the man and the girl, but knowing they were there and that she was close to them filled her with a trembly, shameful kind of excitement. Finally, when the glasses were nowhere to be found, and Gus had joined her to help search, she said they might as well go back.

Outside, with a feeling of loss and disappointment, she spanked Gus and told him he must never go there again.

But she was soon to withdraw the restriction. At first, she tried to put the image from her mind, to forget all about it. She would be sitting with the family and suddenly think about it and feel loathsome and nasty, cut off from them, isolated like a leper. Then she would close her eyes, count to ten, and concentrate on the latest movie she had seen. At night, before she went to sleep, she concentrated so much on movies that she awoke every morning with a headache.

Later, the change occurred and she found herself struggling to recall the image, to re-create every detail of sight, every quiver of emotion. At the movies, Ramon Novarro — Richard Barthelmess and John Gilbert — they all became the man on the beach — with hair on their shoulders. Then it was she decided she was getting too much sun and should spend the latter part of every afternoon in the shade of the pier. Gus didn't like it too well, but every afternoon about four, she would gather up her shopping bag, Gus his bucket and shovel, and they would change location. And the cold damp gloom beneath the pier became as much a part of her life as her three movies a week and her scrapbook. Separate obsessions, but, in a crazy, confusing way, all interrelated, all one.

The Clark City reunion took place about a month after the Gannons arrived in California. Babe said she wouldn't be caught dead at the thing, but when no one coaxed her, she decided she might as well go — just for a minute — she could always leave.

It had all come about one day when Mother and Dad were

walking along the beach and ran into the Wades from Clark City.
The Wades said how wonderful to see someone from home and
Mother said the beach was much nicer in the winter because you
saw more of your friends, and then Mrs. Wade suggested they
print a notice in the *Los Angeles Times* telling all the people from
Clark City to meet some Sunday afternoon at Venice Pier. Babe
had said, later, she thought it was a gruesome idea, and even Louise
wondered why you bothered to leave home if this was your idea
of a good time. But Mother and Dad had looked kind of hurt so
Louise had kissed them and said she thought it was a lovely idea.
Naturally.

The reunion was at two. Babe spent the morning on the beach,
doing her hair and nails. Her latest purchase had been a bottle of
wave-set, sticky stuff, and in that week's movie magazine she had
found a hair-do on Patsy Ruth Miller that she had never tried. So
she borrowed Mother's manicuring scissors, cut bangs and stuck
them in waves to her forehead, made spit curls up both sides of
her face. Then she curled her lashes and used a little of the
mascara — not too much or Mother would make her wash it off.
Just before they left, she fastened a gold chain around her ankle.

Except for Gus, who didn't think they should allow her outside
the house, no one said too much. Mother merely asked did girls
really wear their hair that way, and Louise said, "Oh Babe!" Well,
it was nobody's business — they wanted to treat her like a child.
She was sixteen and by that time lots of girls had — well, my gosh,
just look at the movies! Walking toward the Penny Arcade, which
had been designated as the meeting place, she chewed her gum
disconsolately and muttered about *some people's families*.

The reunion was just as dreary as she had anticipated. A lot of
old people telling her how much she had grown and how they
never would have known her, a lot of yelling kids. The only surprising thing was how many people were there — people you
wouldn't have expected. The Driscolls, for instance, Howard's
parents, the madame in all her jewels. They kind of apologized for
coming: Mrs. Driscoll said to Mother, "Howard Sr. and I don't
usually frequent these sort of places — especially on Sunday" —
but, Babe noticed, they seemed to have as good a time as anybody
and Mr. Driscoll kept winning kewpie dolls in the shooting gal-
leries. The Thomases were there, and the Isaacsons and the Rays

and the Badgers. And old Gatty Nuttall with her hair dyed red and a Pekingese dog, and Mr. Hinkley, who was principal of the high school in Mother's time, and a Mr. Bishop who had apparently gone to school with Dad. Mother said afterwards, all flushed with excitement, that it was one of the grandest days she could remember — all those people she hadn't seen for years.

For the younger ones, it wasn't so hot — Babe, at any rate, thought it was terrible. She got stuck with Frank Badger, who came about to her shoulder, was at least a year younger, and whenever he got excited, his voice cracked. Louise got that darling Bimbo Thomas, who had on a bow tie and straw hat right on the back of his head and puffed a pipe that he kept tapping every few minutes. On the scenic railway, he grabbed Louise on the long, uphill grade, but Louise threatened to stand up if he didn't let go. Frank was so stupid he didn't do anything — just got so scared his teeth were chattering. Practically.

In the fun house, Bimbo was behind Babe once when her skirt was blown up and right after that he came over and pinched her — actually. She hadn't known he was nasty, but oh my gosh, he was cute.

They went on the dodg'em and down the dragon slide and over-the-falls. They ate hot dogs and candied apples and cotton candy. In the Penny Arcade, Bimbo looked into penny movies that had bathing beauties and called different boys over to look with him. The girls put pennies into the pie-throwing movies and fortune-telling machines. Babe couldn't take her eyes off Bimbo. He looked over a couple of times and grinned to show he knew she was crazy about him.

Along about five, the old ones and the young ones congregated toward the end of the pier so that they could watch the sun go down and say good-bye to those who were leaving and make plans for those who stayed. Louise wasn't paying any attention at all to Bimbo, and finally he came over to Babe and said, "How's little sister?"

Excitement pushed every thought out of Babe's mind, destroyed all control so that she could do nothing except laugh too loudly and bend her shoulders forward to try to look smaller.

Bimbo started to sing, "Say mister, have you met Rosie's sister — "

Babe covered her mouth and shrieked with laughter, bending back and forth, kicking the wooden fence with her shoe. Finally she pressed her hands against her sides and gasped, "Oh — you *nut!*"

He put his hand through her arm in a fatherly gesture, looked around to see that he wasn't being observed, murmured, "You know, I think maybe I've been hanging out with the wrong generation. After all, I'm still a kid at heart."

He was absolutely so smooth, so sophisticated, that she wanted to die. But what can you say? What can you do? The laughter was sounding forced, the muscles of her stomach ached from effort.

Inexplicably, she was pointing to a back tooth, trying to talk with her mouth stretched wide open. " 'ook — my 'ooth. I go' 'affy in i'."

Bimbo hesitated, then bent forward to look at the tooth. "Well — uh — I don't have any toothpicks with me."

This time she pressed her arms against her stomach for the awful, tearing laughter that came from her hot dry throat. "Oh you *fool.*" She shook her head back and forth. "You *crazy fool.*"

Bimbo had withdrawn his hand and was now tapping his pipe against his palm. "Well, guess I better get back over there." He waved his hand in an easterly direction. "See you later."

"Oh sure," she gushed. "So long."

She stood for a moment, humiliated by her awkwardness, by the Patsy Ruth Miller hair-do and the chain around her ankle. She could kill that Bimbo Thomas. He had no right — why did he have to follow her — why couldn't he — The mascara on her lashes stung her eyes.

She moved over to a bench and sank down beside a man with a fishing pole. Frank Badger rushed over and said, "Hey, Helen, you want a frozen custard?"

"No thanks, Frank," she murmured. "No thanks."

Most of the kids her age went off to eat some more, to spend more money on Keno or darts, to find out when the dancing started. Most of the parents were calling it a day and saying long good-byes to people out of the past, people whom they would never see again.

Babe wished they would all leave — and hurry up about it too. She wanted to be left alone — with the sunset and the sea and

all the tired strangers who came down here for one last look at the
water before they started for home. She wanted to cut every tie
that connected her with herself, to obliterate every association that
reminded her she was Babe Gannon. The rushing, swishing water,
far away then close, was of a melancholy to match her own. She
wanted nothing that would remind her.

She watched an old man break up a hot-dog roll and throw the
pieces in the water for the sea gulls to fight over and then eat the
hot dog himself and lick the mustard from his hands. He bent
over the railing and laughed at the silly birds as if he had fooled
them, outwitted them, proven that he was more greedy than they.
And the birds flew up above, hovering over the man and screeching as if they knew it had all been a trick.

Babe wanted to laugh — but then memory cut through her and
she closed her eyes and worked her forehead with her fingers and
sorrow hung over her like one of the nagging, screeching birds.
" 'ook a' my 'ooth," and Bimbo and Frank and all of them were
peering into her mouth. She pulled her hand away to let sea and
sky chase the picture away. What she saw was someone staring
at her.

It was a man, not too old, leaning with his elbows against the
railing and a cigarette between his fingers. But when he caught
her eye, he came over and stood before her and grinned down at
her.

"Hi."

She drew herself up for a deep breath, and turned her head
away, grandly, coldly.

Instead of being terrified or apologetic, the man started to laugh.

Infuriated and a little scared, she gave him a quick look of rage,
and in a freezing voice, said, "I beg your pardon!"

Again the man laughed. "My God," he said. "It must be in
the blood. Maybe they really are aristocrats. Maybe the God-
damn family is even as good as it thinks it is."

Forgetting for a moment that she should avoid all contact with
the creature, she became curious, scornful. "What are you talking about? *Honestly.*"

Before he answered, he took a long drag on his cigarette, blew
the smoke out slowly. With a sneering smile, he said, "Hi, young
Gannon."

The name brought back security, made everything legitimate, brought back self-consciousness. "Oh gosh," she floundered. "I didn't know you were from Clark City. I didn't mean to be rude."

"Don't apologize. I've been talked to that way before. Many times. In that same voice."

"The thing is," she went on to explain, "I didn't notice you at the reunion. You must've come late."

He slouched against the railing, shot his cigarette butt out onto the water. "Tell me this, for Christ's sweet sake: why should anyone from Clark City want to see anyone else from Clark City? Why in hell wouldn't they turn their tails and run in the opposite direction? That town is the stink hole of the universe."

This should have angered her, but he was too cute for anger — even if he was too old. "Then you *weren't* at the reunion."

He didn't answer. He set his jaw firmly and sort of spat out, "How's Eddie?"

Oh my gosh — she knew. "But you've *changed!*" she gasped. "You're Bill Miller."

"Yeah. I guess I have changed." He rubbed his hand in a grating sound along his cheek. "I'm rich."

Then she was confused and flustered and couldn't look at him. He had changed — there seemed to be a little gray in his hair and he'd lost the sloppiness of the old days. But he was still kind of massive — as he'd been when he played football; and when he pushed his hand through his hair and mussed it all up, he still looked like something out of Charlotte Brontë. "But how did you remember *me?*" She tried to sound more amazed than coy. "I mean, who told you who *I* was?"

He snickered at this. "Look — I could spot a Gannon a mile away. I saw your whole family down here — I've been watching 'em."

"Are you really rich?"

He seemed pleased that she had asked, but he answered her offhandedly. "I can't complain. I have a little string of restaurants — root beer, that sort of thing. I could probably buy your family out."

She looked at the old man beside her to see if she could make room for Bill to sit down. But the old man was firmly planted —

even though he'd never, probably, catch a fish at this hour. It was beginning to darken to twilight.

"You better come along with me," Bill said. "I'm a big rich guy. I might even buy you a frozen custard."

Later, when they had eaten their frozen custard and inspected for the hundredth time all the concessions along the pier, Bill suggested they get away from this mob and go sit on the beach where they could really talk. Babe didn't say anything and he took her arm and led her off.

Babe couldn't say anything. Her breathing had stopped and she knew that from the cold cavern inside her, no words would come. Her mind saw a splash of red bathing suit underneath the pier and knew that it was now, now, now! God or Fate or whatever it was had sent Bill along to test her. She knew Bill was evil. And she went along beside him, more fearful that he would see her terror, feel her trembling, perceive her innocence than that she could not withstand the unknown things he might do to her.

But Bill stretched out in the sand — away from her — his hands beneath his head. He looked around at the stars and then said, half mockingly, "This is like — oh hell, it's like you'd been kept after school for breakin' windows and finally the old battle-axe lets you go — free."

And all her tension vanished and warmth returned to her veins because she knew what he meant. She laughed — the laughter came easily — and she rubbed away the goose pimples from her arms. "I know what you mean."

The ocean was quiet — just the gentle splash, far away, and the soft lapping; the lights and noises on the pier didn't include her and Bill — she could see them off in the distance, hear the rattle of the scenic railway and an occasional feminine scream, but she and Bill weren't part of that. Nor were they part of the busy little people from Clark City scurrying around Venice Pier in search of fun. And she wanted to laugh deep down to the darkness inside of her.

"You know" — Bill said in a sort of dreamy, faraway voice — "they didn't give me a very easy time of it in that town." He reached over and took hold of one of her fingers. "I guess I was one of the most unhappy kids Clark City ever produced. My claim to fame."

"I thought you were a hero. My girl friends and I used to nearly die we thought you were so wonderful."

He smiled. "Yeah, I guess I was sort of a hero — in a way. But not really. Always on the outside — never quite good enough." He held her finger so tight that he hurt her. "You know, I went to school with Jack — we were pretty good friends — at school. But he never asked me inside that house. As far as I was concerned, he was it — the clear thing. And Eddie. Jesus. She was the most beautiful woman, the most desirable that any man ever looked at. And cold as ice. Oh God. Gorgeous ice-cold virgin."

She should have been angered by this — slapped him, maybe, or cried out that she wouldn't sit by and hear her family insulted. But his words made her sad — wistful and sad. Because she knew so well what he meant. Jack and Eddie and all of them — so perfect — but Babe, well she'd always been on the outside too.

She drew her knees up and clutched them to her. "I know," she whispered.

"I bawled myself to sleep one night when I was a kid because I wasn't invited to a party at your house. I hated my mother and dad because we weren't rich." He lay quiet for a moment, then lit a cigarette, and inhaled deeply. "I could buy ten of Eddie now."

Babe was startled by the bitterness, the smugness of his tone, because she didn't feel that way at all. But then she saw through him and it was so simple she almost had to laugh. "What a coincidence," she said, "that you happened to be down here today — what with the reunion and all."

"Yeah — I sure wouldn't have come if I'd known about it. Jesus Christ."

"You know," Babe said — maliciously because she had never felt such a sense of power before — "some of us girls noticed you and wondered who that distinguished-looking man was. We thought you must be someone terribly important."

He looked at her sharply. "Oh yeah?"

"Yes. I'm sure everyone noticed you."

He said nothing, but the tight line of his mouth told her she had gone too far and that he wasn't going to take any smartness from a kid.

"I guess I noticed you too," he said finally. "Not because you were so distinguished and successful. You have a very beautiful sister. There's a certain family resemblance."

If she was supposed to feel wounded, she didn't at all, because he had used her own kind of weapon — and he didn't know it and she did. She looked down at his sullen, surly face and saw in it all her own meanness and spite. And as if she were her mother stroking Gus's head, she reached out her hand and brushed the hair off his forehead. He stretched his head back, opened his mouth, and bit her finger.

Then he sat up suddenly and brushed sand from his back. "You better get home. Your parents would have the police out if they knew who you were with."

"I know," she murmured.

But neither of them stood. They listened to the quiet sounds of the ocean and Bill looked up at the stars. And then he looked at her with an uncertain smile as if he had just realized he was not alone. And then the smile broadened to the friendly grin you'd give a stray puppy and he moved closer to her. "You know," he said, "you're not the girl your sister was but I like you better."

"Oh." She pushed herself to her feet.

Bill reached up quickly and grasped her hand. "What's your name? I don't even know that."

She was trembling and her voice could scarcely say the word. "Helen."

Bill watched her with that same smile, let his eyes travel over her body to see that she was trembling. Then his lips parted, he slowly wrapped his arms about her legs and pressed his face between her knees. "Sit down, Helen."

She began to cry, softly — not in fear but in loneliness. It was as if all of life had been deluding her until this moment, allowing her to imagine that she was a safe part of something and then suddenly pushing her out, alone.

She fell back into the sand and felt Bill's hands on her, his rough impatience, his lips breathing against her skin. And through her tears, she heard his hoarse whisper, "This is the least I can do for the Gannons."

CHAPTER 6

I T WAS A HOT AUGUST DAY, too hot, Harriet had thought, for Papa to play golf, but after all the trouble Mr. Driscoll had gone to, Papa didn't think it right to call their game off. Mr. Driscoll had said this was a real opportunity for Papa to meet the influential Los Angeles businessmen because the country club was completely restricted and no one without the very best connections was allowed to play there.

Papa dressed in his white knickers, white shoes and shirt and black bow tie, white cap, and was waiting in front of the apartment house when Mr. Driscoll drove up.

Papa said: "Well, sir, good morning." When he was settled in the car and they were headed back toward town, Papa fidgeted some because he never felt completely relaxed with Mr. Driscoll.

Mr. Driscoll not only looked like his son Howard but he drove a car exactly as Howard did — as if the car were not a machine but a living creature that he had subdued. He explained about the club: "One thing, you can always be sure you won't run into any of the *wrong* kind of people — if you know what I mean."

Papa nodded wisely.

"I've always found," continued Mr. Driscoll, "that you can't be too careful whom you associate with. Every so often, you just should stop a minute and think, Now how would this look to the other fellow. In a town like this, you can't be too careful."

Papa wanted to say something nice about the Clark City golf links, but it occurred to him that Mr. Driscoll might consider him something of a hick so he remained silent.

It turned out that Mr. Driscoll was perfectly right about the club; when Papa saw the imposing Spanish hacienda sprawled across the lawn, he commented that he was sure no one but the very best could *afford* to belong to such a club.

But Mr. Driscoll shook his head sadly. "Unfortunately, some of the wrong ones often have the most money. It's getting so that now you can't judge a man by the amount of money he's made. I think you know what I mean."

Mr. Driscoll had borrowed a set of clubs for Papa and he steered Papa, like the car, around to the first tee. He stood by respectfully while Papa drove his ball halfway down to the green, mumbled a polite word about the straightness of Papa's shot, then put his own drive within six feet of the cup. He took one putt and waited for Papa's three more shots to finish the hole.

It was perfectly clear to Papa that he wasn't the athlete Mr. Driscoll was and he was grateful to Mr. Driscoll for being so patient. Mr. Driscoll would stride down the fairway, hatless, his tanned face tight and intent. Before each shot, he would roll his shoulders to relax, and afterwards, his eye would follow the ball with intent pride. Papa plodded along behind, playing his average game.

They talked little — Mr. Driscoll was not the sort who liked to talk while he was concentrating on something else. And anyway, he was out ahead most of the time.

The heat seemed to grow worse, hanging heavily beneath a gray sky. There was no sun — just the hot, damp air, drawing out sweat to soak the white shirt and paste the white knickers to the insides of his legs. It was no day for hurrying, not a day for talk. And it didn't look as if Papa would have a chance to meet many influential businessmen — the course was drowsy and empty — those men knew when to stay indoors.

He would have liked to say something to his caddy, something friendly, something that would make the boy laugh. The caddy was a fine-looking young fellow, probably about fourteen, just getting his height, tall and blond and sloppy. His shirt was stuffed carelessly into his pants, and his navel squinted through an opening in the shirt where a button was gone. Papa would have liked to make a joke about the navel — he supposed the boy would refer to it as a "belly button" — but he couldn't think of just what he might say, just how to establish the proper relationship. He noticed that the boy whistled when he walked along by himself but stopped when Papa was by. That showed a nice sense of upbringing and so Papa thought he had better forget about the navel. He contented himself with commenting on one of his shots, "Well, I guess that's not too bad for an old man," and giving the boy a friendly smile. But the boy said nothing, did not return the smile.

It occurred to Papa, as he walked heavily down the hot dry grass, that here was a fine opportunity for a boy: a chance to learn the value of a dollar under conditions that could not but make him the right kind of citizen. California had it all over the cities of the East in that respect; it was no accident that the streets of Chicago turned out gangsters while the golf courses of California turned out clean young fellows with blond hair. Outdoors and *work* — a combination that would make real men.

Faith in the value of *work* as a molder of character — work that earned money — was fundamental to Papa's philosophy. But sometimes, bent over his desk in the library at home, Papa would let his mind struggle with the problem that seemed to him the great dilemma of our time: How can a man give to his children all and more than he himself ever had (and so achieve full integrity as a father) without depriving the children of their right to make their own way in life? The measure of a father's success was his ability to give his sons a college education; the measure of a boy's success was his ability to earn his way through college without help. Or better yet, to set up a successful business without going to college. Somewhere along the line, either the father or the son must yield.

Today it pleased his mind to think that here was a boy who now had nothing, but someday he would have everything. Working outside all day would build up his body, keep his mind — elevated. The businessmen who belonged to the club would stand as a model for the boy, keep the goal before his eyes, create the right standards of success. Associating with influential people would be an inspiring opportunity as well as a good practical one. He would no doubt make contacts that would have future rewards, and a word or two from men like these could pave the way for a boy. Papa wanted to say something to the boy — to remind him that it's hard work that does it, to impress upon him how fortunate he was, having this chance to prove himself.

But as he looked at the boy, who walked along either ahead or behind, absent-minded, isolated, scratching himself sometimes, wiping his forehead with his arm, making loud throaty preparations to spit, Papa felt his own inadequacy in getting across to people. So much to say — but most of the time it all went unsaid. It was easier with girls — he could talk easily with Eddie; Jack, however, always had given the impression that he was in a hurry. Boys seemed to feel that you were intruding, preaching.

Papa decided to give it a try anyway. He wanted to do it but also he felt it a kind of duty. That was the American way. He remembered how his own father used to joke with the miners' sons and give them quarters. Some of those boys had grown up to be fine men and taken their place in the mines.

So, when the caddy handed him his mashie, Papa stood as if to rest a moment and catch his breath. "Quite a hot day," he began, removing his cap and wiping the line of sweat from his forehead.

The caddy stared at the heads of the clubs, silent — almost, Papa was afraid, subservient.

"Fine golf course you have here." Papa's eyes swept over the long stretches of grass, dry from the Los Angeles summer. A straight line of eucalyptus trees edged the course, noble trees, though somewhat scraggly. Their odor was faint in the heavy sea-damp air. "I guess you Californians have a lot to be proud of," Papa continued, playing on the boy's pride of ownership and belonging. "I'm not a native — I come from east of here."

The boy looked up, expressionless, unfriendly, but Papa waited for the boy's "Where from?" that would break down his barrier of silence and they could be friends. But the boy turned his eyes away and muttered, "Yeah, I guess you do. Sir."

Papa hesitated, uncertain. Then he smiled faintly and replaced his cap. "Well — I guess we better be getting along."

After the first nine holes, Mr. Driscoll suggested they take a breather. "After all, we're on vacation — no sense in pushing it."

Papa sank down gratefully on the hard bench. Certainly if Mr. Driscoll had been pushing it, he bore none of the signs. The sweat on his face and arms merely added a glisten to smooth muscles and sharp edges of bone; the fine animal vigor rippled through him undiminished.

"Young Howard and I used to play a good deal of tennis," Mr. Driscoll said. "Nothing like a real sweat to tone up the old body."

Papa took the handkerchief from his back pocket and ran it along the inside of his collar. "I guess you're right," he said, making a grieved search of the sky for the hidden sun that was doing this awful thing to them.

"Been great companions, Howard and I have — great friends always," Mr. Driscoll mused. "More like brothers."

Papa took the two cigars from his shirt pocket and gave one to Mr. Driscoll. That was how fathers and sons should be, he supposed, companions, sharing things together — only sometimes it was difficult. And Mr. Driscoll was deserving of a good deal of praise, Papa was sure, that he had managed it.

"From the time Howard was a boy," Mr. Driscoll continued, "I took him along on hunting trips — always treated him as an equal — talked things over. I don't suppose he ever had a problem we didn't talk over together. Even now. Even — " He stopped abruptly, laughed, clamped his hot hand on Papa's knee.

"Well," said Papa, drawing pensively on the cigar, "that's a fine thing."

"By the way, how's your boy? What's he doing now?"

Papa had to think that over for a minute. He didn't know exactly how to answer and he wished Mr. Driscoll hadn't asked. It was difficult to discuss Jack with business associates or friends because sometimes they didn't understand.

"Jack," he said finally, "is in the East."

"In business?"

"Well —" Papa said, "you knew he went to Harvard?"

Mr. Driscoll nodded.

"He's now — oh, just looking around. Sizing things up. I guess you might say he's learning how they do things in New York." Papa chuckled weakly.

"Well, that's not a bad thing for a young fellow," Mr. Driscoll encouraged him. "Let him look around — sow a few wild oats if he wants — I guess we had our share of that too. But let me tell you something. I think you'd make a big mistake not to take him into your business at home, help him out a little, let him take over after a while. We shouldn't hang on to these things too long, Mr. Gannon — give the younger boys a chance. And" — he put a hand on Papa's shoulder — "I don't think you'd regret it. Let me tell you, one of the happiest days of my life was the day Howard moved into my office. I felt that that day was what I'd waited for all my life." His voice was strong and keen with pride. "Yes sir."

"Yes," Papa murmured. "I suppose you're right."

Mr. Driscoll stood up, put one foot on the bench, and leaned his elbow on his knee. "Here's how I look at it, Mr. Gannon," he said. "This country belongs to the young people — the real Americans. This is a young people's civilization, the highest the world has ever known, the richest. We don't want Europe — Europe's through. We don't want any of the backward civilization of Asia. What we want is America just as she is, without any of the poison of the outside world. And we want our young people to be free — free to develop the great resources of our country and of our natural inheritance."

They were Papa's thoughts too, but being a lawyer, Mr. Driscoll put them more forcefully. It occurred to Papa that Mr. Driscoll rather looked and sounded like a Boy Scout leader or a director of games; his fine, healthy physique was certainly representative of the youthful spirit of America. The spirit of fair play and sportsmanship. Papa had read some place that the lessons a boy learned on the field of sport were the best preparation he could have for adult life.

"I agree with that one hundred per cent," Papa said. "And," he added, "Calvin Coolidge is the right man for the job."

"And," Mr. Driscoll repeated, "Calvin Coolidge is the right man for the job."

The second nine holes were more agony than pleasure for Papa, and he would have liked to sit them out or call it a day and go home. He'd had too much heat, too much walking — too much for an old man. His head was throbbing and his back was tired and the sweat had not toned up his body so much as drained it of energy. He was tired.

But Mr. Driscoll struck out, fresh and glowing, and Papa followed.

He tried to raise his spirits by thinking more about the caddy and Mr. Driscoll's fine words and he wished the caddy had been near enough to hear them and absorb their inspiration. Hearing a successful man like Mr. Driscoll speak such high principles could have a great influence on a young fellow.

It was Jack rather than the caddy, however, who filled his thoughts, and brooding over Jack threw him off his game so that he became more depressed than ever. Somehow, somewhere, he had failed, and his feeling of inadequacy, of guilt twisted him inside. Should he have gone on hunting trips with Jack? Taken up tennis? Jack had never confided in him — their talks had been unsatisfactory, embarrassing. The truth was that he and Jack never had been friends, equals, never had shared anything, and the realization — now that it was too late — left Papa sad and empty. All these years, Papa had failed to grasp this richness that could have been his; somehow, his back had been slightly turned. And if Jack had been cheated, was not the real loser Papa himself?

Perhaps there was nothing really wrong with the boy (Flo said that none of them was willing to give him half a chance); it might be easier if there *were* something wrong — then they could all get behind him and help him out. He just didn't seem to have a proper sense of values, he had lost sight of the proper goals. Or maybe it wasn't that so much as that he took those goals for granted — money, position; he forgot it's hard work that does it. And to Papa, there was something weak, shameful, un-American about a man who could forget that it's hard work that does it.

Jack was spoiled. Why this young boy — the caddy here — with

half of Jack's opportunities, he'd be well on the way to success —
in a bank, perhaps, with all the big men interested in his career.
Jack had never learned the value of a dollar. Perhaps if he had
had to *earn* the money to go to Harvard — delivering ice, cutting
lawns, carrying golf clubs around in the hot sun — earn and save
— then it would all have been a different story. Harvard degree,
a few books written while he was still in college (if that's what he
wanted) and ready to settle down in business after he was graduated.

And then the day would come when Papa would be ready to
step out and let Jack move in. It had happened to Papa when he
was a young man and the cycle would repeat itself, permanence
and order, no change really. The business would go on, asserting
their immortality, and death, when it came, would not be an end
but a completion. And when your friends on the golf course asked,
"What about your boy?" you could feel warm with pride and
security, and answer, "Well, sir, my son — "

Right now the thing was to finish the golf game so that he could
get home and lie down in the dark coolness of the Ellison Apartments. Eighteen holes of golf was for the younger men; nine
would have been just about enough. There seemed to be wind to
rustle the top leaves of the eucalyptus trees but none to breathe
coolness into the day. Back home in Clark City, gray heat like
this was prelude to storm; but summer rain, they said, was un-
heard of in southern California.

Mr. Driscoll's shirt was soaked through and almost transparent
so that you could see the dark pattern of hair on his chest. But
right up to the last, he was fresh and buoyant, and complaining
that he had gone two points over par. Although Papa was well
over a hundred, he couldn't feel too disturbed so long as the game
was finished.

As they walked over toward the caddy house to leave their
clubs, Papa thought about what he might say to his caddy — something the boy would remember one day when the going was
tough, or just something friendly that would indicate Papa accepted him as an equal. And he wondered how much he should
tip the boy. In Clark City, thirty-five cents was enough for nine
holes, seventy-five, generous for eighteen. But because Papa had

taken a special interest in this boy, he thought he might give him a whole dollar, thirty three and a third per cent more than his usual tip. At that rate, if the boy saved his money, he would have enough, in a few years, to help pay his tuition in college.

While Mr. Driscoll checked in the clubs, Papa stepped around the caddy shack to wait where it was cooler. He was thinking what a difference it might have made in Jack's life to have earned his Harvard tuition as a caddy, when he observed that the boys had drawn some pictures on the shack. Papa looked closer to inspect this boyish fancy. One picture was a golfer, dressed not unlike Papa, cigar in his mouth, swinging at a ball. But the man's pants were around his ankles and it was not a golf club he held in his hands.

Papa drew back, startled, and hurried around to join Mr. Driscoll. Their two caddies were waiting at a respectful distance; the clean young blond who had caddied for Papa observed Papa's agitation and a smirk spread over his face. Papa looked quickly away.

"How about a nice cold shower now?" Mr. Driscoll demanded. "I'd like to show you around the club house — maybe run into somebody."

Papa was confused and unhappy — as if someone had gone out of his way to be cruel and insulting. And he didn't want to stand beside Mr. Driscoll in a cold shower. If he could just make it home to the dark apartment, to his world of women —

"I'm sorry — I'm afraid I should get back," he said. "Too bad to drag you away though."

Mr. Driscoll gave him a sharp look. "Not at all," he said. "Let's be going."

Papa handed the caddy a dollar without looking at him. As he and Mr. Driscoll walked away, he heard, beneath Mr. Driscoll's explanatory voice, the voice of his caddy. "A buck," it said. "One lousy buck!"

Papa was quiet on the way home. He was too tired to think and there seemed nothing more to say. He watched the palm trees and real-estate offices that lined the boulevard. And nodded whenever Mr. Driscoll made a remark.

"Great country," Mr. Driscoll would say; or, "California's got a great future — this will be the money-making center of America."

Papa wondered a little about the future, turned the question over in his mind. What would it be like? Better, probably, better and better. With the remarkable progress in science and America's inexhaustible wealth, the future seemed to stretch ahead ever more golden, with the sharp strong light of opportunity shining brighter and brighter.

And suddenly Papa thought about Gus and almost with shock realized that it was my *sons*, not my *son*. The future, of course, belonged to Gus. Give Gus another ten years and he'd be facing the problems of a man; twenty years and Gus might be settled down in business, thinking about his own children. The cycle repeating itself.

Papa wanted desperately to do something for Gus, to make up for Jack, to help out the future. Poor little Gus had just been allowed to grow — no one giving a thought to him — it had all gone to Jack. And Papa felt shame at the neglect, at the mistake he had almost repeated. He and Gus would be friends, great friends. They would share everything, talk things over, any problem that came up.

As they drew nearer to the beach, Papa said, "I wonder if you'd drop me off in Santa Monica. A few things I want to do."

Mr. Driscoll hesitated. "Wouldn't it be better to postpone them? I think we should get you home."

"It's all right," Papa said. "Just a little tired, that's all."

"Well, look here: you do what you have to do and I'll wait for you. That's too long a walk."

Papa was slightly annoyed by Mr. Driscoll's solicitude, and he said firmly, "I'll get home all right."

So Mr. Driscoll dropped him at the town of Santa Monica, and asked once more if he couldn't wait. Papa thanked him for the pleasant day, slammed the door, and waved him good-bye. He watched Mr. Driscoll drive away, then free and happy, he started out to find a sports shop. Old Gus. Papa could picture him on the beach, thinning out now, brown and scrawny like a little monkey. He and Gus would be great friends.

When the bespectacled young clerk came up, Papa said, "I

want to buy a tennis racket — the best one you've got in the store."
"For yourself?" the young man asked.
"For my son," Papa said. "It's a present for my son."

Later that night — it was getting on toward twelve — Harriet
sat on the hard couch, under a lamp, trying to keep her mind on
the story she was reading in the *Journal*. She could hear Papa's
loud breathing from the bedroom and every so often Gus mumbled in his sleep. Then Louise got out of bed, the drawer bed in
the dining room, reached for her kimono, and came yawning into
the room.
"Go to bed, Mother," she said. "You know she's all right. Sitting
up worrying won't do any good."
Harriet dropped the magazine, grateful that there was someone
she could talk to. "I'm sure she's all right — I just can't sleep."
She tried to sound as if not being able to sleep were an amusing
foible. "It would be the same with any of you. Many's the night
I've sat up waiting for Eddie."
"Well, if parents are going to be so silly, they shouldn't expect
any sympathy."
Harriet and Louise smiled at each other and Harriet tried to
think of something to say, but fear was so obviously in the room
that it couldn't be ignored.
"It's not so much what might have happened to her," Harriet
said, clutching the magazine in a tight roll. "I'm *sure* she must be
all right. It's just the not knowing."
"Don't think about it. Tomorrow you must make her tell you.
You can scare Babe into anything." Louise stood up, walked to
the window, and looked down. "What do you suppose ever got
into Dad to buy Gus that tennis racket?" she asked brightly. "It
seems a queer kind of present."
"Oh, heavens, I don't know. Men do some awfully strange things
sometimes. And that's one more thing to pack." But remembering Papa's excitement over the present, tired and sick as he was,
Harriet added guiltily, "I guess it'll be a fine thing for Gus to
have."
"It's a beautiful racket."
Then Harriet felt a kind of panic. Certainly Papa looked ill and

here was Babe off every night, no one knew where. Her eyes filled with tears and she pinched her lip. "We should never have come," she said bitterly. "Right from the first it seemed a crazy notion to me. But what could I do? I've known all along something terrible would happen — "

"Stop it, Mother!" Louise came over and kissed Harriet's forehead. "Go to bed, Mother," she said gently. "Everything will be all right."

"Of course." Harriet's fingers pressed into her cheeks. "I'm being foolish." She squeezed Louise's shoulder, then stood up. "I'll get ready for bed."

Undressing in the bathroom, she kept telling herself that Louise was right and she was foolish. It was a game Babe was playing — she was probably sitting on the beach with some girl friend, knowing they would be worried and for that reason staying out all the later. Babe was merely being perverse — and she would have to stop it. And Harriet must get control of herself.

But who sent the flowers, the two dozen long-stemmed roses? Certainly not Frank Badger, as Babe had said. Babe would be perfectly capable of sending flowers to herself — if she had the money. And she would be perfectly capable of sitting in a movie every night of her life — if she had the money. But why was she always so late coming home? Why did she carry on so whenever Louise wanted to accompany her? And what had changed her disposition, making her tense and irritable? Where was Babe's old apathy? However simple the answer might turn out to be, however innocent the explanation, Babe was unquestionably leading some kind of double life.

But everything would be all right — because it must — and she mustn't let herself be foolish.

She turned off the bathroom light and padded into the living room, rubbing lotion into her hands. Louise was on the couch with her knees clasped to her.

"Good night, dear," Harriet said. "You go to bed too." Louise nodded quietly and Harriet felt great tenderness for Louise. "Louise — " she wanted to say something, to tell Louise how precious she was to them, but she only smiled. "Good night, dear."

It was almost two before Babe came in. Harriet looked at the phosphorescent face of the alarm clock when she heard the door open and shut and she listened for all the sounds that would tell her Babe was safe in bed. Papa was breathing easily, they were all here together, night was half over and tomorrow everything would be all right. Some of the tension left Harriet's body and she drifted into light sleep.

Shortly after four, she was awakened by a strange sound from Papa, a raspy, throaty breathing that was not a sound of sleep. She turned on the light and screamed for Louise. Louise rushed in, looked at Papa, then at Harriet.

"I'll call Mr. Driscoll — he'll know a doctor." Louise put on bedroom slippers and a coat and ran out into the night to find a phone.

Gus stumbled into the room, whimpering; Babe stood in the doorway, white and silent. Harriet crushed Gus to her and gave way utterly to her grief. "I knew this would happen," she sobbed. "I knew it would happen."

When Louise returned, there was nothing for them to do but wait. And in that horrible, endless eternity, Babe sat off by herself, quiet, frozen.

And of course, by the time Mr. Driscoll and the doctor arrived, it was too late. Without ever gaining consciousness so that he might know they were all there together, Papa had died.

CHAPTER 7

In the fall, Gus entered the first grade at the Lincoln School. Harriet bought him a woolen sailor suit at the Golden Rule and corduroy knickers and a knitted helmet that came down over his ears. Martha dragged the cases of empty fruit jars from the basement and filled the house with the smell of Concord grapes and chili sauce. And the nights grew cool and the leaves began to turn.

It had all happened before, year after year. The world could crack — and break apart — but except for distant rumbling, the prospect would not alter much. The same processes would sustain the same appearances and one would have to search very diligently indeed to find that life was any different. The same grate fires, the drowsy afternoons, the rose taffeta hangings in the bedroom, the couch, the *Delineator*, the waiting for the still house to break into noise with the slam of a door and then Gus climbing the steps to find her; the milk spilled, the crumbs of Martha's oatmeal cookies ground into the pattern of the oriental rug.

Sometimes, at first, it was hard to concentrate on the stories in the magazine — words blurred and lost their meaning — and for a while she worked at an afghan, counting stitches as if order and design could be re-established with a crochet hook. Papa's death was a disorganization on which she had not counted; he had been the thread, perhaps, that held all the little squares together, but so unobtrusive that she had forgotten how essential he was to the whole. She had forgotten so much during those years; it took his death to remind her how much. Somewhere along the way, he had ceased being Jack and become Papa. His friends who knew him and remembered him mourned someone very different from the Papa of her and the kiddies. She tried to remember Papa as he was before they were married, but the person she remembered wasn't Papa at all.

The same thing must have happened to her, of course, the loss of personality, of identity, the submersion of self so that he must often have looked at her and wondered who she was, where she came from, perhaps felt cheated. She had become Mother — not wife, not Harriet. The children had taken all that. And for years, her only means of communication with Papa was through the children. Had there suddenly been no children, she and Papa would have been strangers, cut off from each other, with no language to reach across.

The mood lasted for days, while the fires burned softly in the grate and the big house creaked a little and groaned in its emptiness. If she felt sad, it was the sadness of futility and waste. She and Papa had simply lapsed into taking each other for granted, because it was easier that way, because their love had been diverted toward other objects. She realized with guilt, with melancholy affection for Papa, that had it been Gus, for example, who had died, or Jack or Louise, she would have been prostrate with grief. But this was something different. She would merely have liked another chance.

She was not so sure now, as she would have been a few months before, that the children must come first. First in importance, perhaps, but not first in consideration, because if you gave yourself entirely to your children, they resented you for it and ran from you. Wanting some good for your children built up in them a desire for the precise opposite. That's how it seemed.

The thought of Babe was so painful to Harriet that her whole being rebelled against it, connived to keep it hidden. Someday, she told herself, she would think about Babe. Someday they must discuss Babe. But not now. Tomorrow or the next day or the next, but not now. Babe's scrawled note had instructed them to consider her as dead, and Eddie had announced that she would. Bill Miller, Eddie said, was scum and had obviously married Babe only to insinuate himself into a social class infinitely beyond him. But Eddie was harsh and Babe was not dead. She was still part of the family and whether they liked it or not, so was Bill Miller. And soon they must all think about it and discuss it. Sometime, soon.

The important thing now was to get back to normal, without bitterness, without unhappiness — if possible. It meant adjustment to a shrinking pattern, what with Babe gone and Papa gone, Jack in New York, Flo and Eddie married and Louise working all day in the library at Clark City High. It meant a quiet, empty house and the daily recognition of the passage of time and the coming on of age. If she hadn't had Gus — But she put that thought from her mind because she did have Gus and he needed her and that was a reason for living.

There were other things too, of course, that carried one along. Fall meant the rebirth of Sewing Club, which followed an inverted cycle of death in the spring and resurrection in the fall. There were the weekly letters to Jack, Saturday shopping with Louise, and all the family in for Sunday dinner. And before you knew it, Thanksgiving would be here, and then time to get ready for Christmas. Introspection was not a weakness of Harriet's generation; before too many days had passed, Papa had slipped over into the realm of legend, and life seemed actually to have settled back to normal.

Perhaps Harriet herself might have postponed consideration of Babe until she was fortified to face it — but Sewing Club, she was to discover, was impatient for news, and it struck her that the first meeting of the year was called somewhat earlier than usual.

Flo talked her into going. "It will be the best thing in the world for you, Mother. You must start going out sometime. This'll be the easiest way."

And so Flo called for her and they drove together to Orpha Graves's.

When Orpha met them at the door, her round circle of a face lengthened to a sad oval. She gave Harriet a resounding kiss and ushered her into the sudden stillness of the living room. "Here she is, girls," she announced to the other members. "Here's Harriet."

Charlotte Cranfeld pushed herself up from the depths of the overstuffed couch, listing dangerously on her way to Harriet.

"I think she looks quite well," said Ruthie Harper cheerily.

Charlotte and Julia Harkington frowned a reprimand at Ruthie. "She looks as well as can be expected, Ruthie," said Charlotte gravely. "But she certainly shows what she's been through."

"You've aged ten years, Harriet," Julia said, in full tribute. "Easy that — at least ten. I don't think I'd have recognized you on the street."

Charlotte seated Harriet on the couch as if she were a fragile vase and found a less comfortable place for herself.

"Well, we'll all wait on Harriet today," said Orpha. "We'll all take care of her."

While Orpha slipped off to the kitchen to see to the lunch, Nettie Sewall bit her lip and sighed. "I never thought we'd see the day that half our group would be widows. Sometimes I think it's just as well we don't know what lies ahead."

The ladies had embarked now, but Flo, being younger, did not intend that they should indulge themselves. "How's Ama, Mrs. Harkington?" she asked. "I haven't seen her in years."

"Ama's just fine, Florence," Julia Harkington answered with gloomy pleasure at Flo's interest. "And say, let me tell you, she thought a lot of your father. She always used to say, 'Mr. Gannon is the most distinguished man in Clark City.' And I think she was quite a favorite with him too."

"Well," said Dorothy Meacham, "I never saw such flowers in my life as were at Jack Gannon's funeral."

And so they discussed Papa and the funeral and what a wonderful way it was to die, and by the time Orpha had the luncheon on the table, there was not a dry eye in the room, and Harriet had to excuse herself before she could sit down to her meal.

Approval of Orpha's scalloped halibut and whipped gelatin salad lightened the mood and permitted a change of subject. Children and food, food and children — until finally Charlotte Cranfeld edged up to the main topic of the day. "You must find it pretty lonely sometimes, Harriet, what with that big house and just two left. But once the young ones start going, there's no stopping them."

Ruthie Harper looked up with her undirected stare. "I sometimes think it's a terrible thing," she said. "Once they start going, there's no stopping them. But," she added wistfully, "my Dorothea never seems to meet any young men. I sometimes wonder if it isn't better for them to meet a young man — providing he's well fixed — and go off and marry him. I don't know."

Orpha started rolls, jelly, and olives around the table. "Nettie Miller was telling me about her boy," she added offhandedly. "She says he's made a big success. In California."

Now it was Harriet's turn. Better to catch the ball and toss it quickly to someone else than allow it to drop at your feet. "He's done very well."

"Isn't that grand," beamed Julia Harkington. "It just goes to show some of the wild ones turn out the best. When is Helen going to be sick?"

She asked the question in apparent innocence, but the silence that followed indicated that she had fooled no one.

Finally Flo asked, "Just what do you mean, Mrs. Harkington?"

Julia's neck grew red and she looked around the table, flustered. "Well — sick. You know. I understood — "

"Babe has been married hardly two months," Flo said quietly.

"Well now really, Florence," Julia said, "I'm just saying what I heard. Ama told me — "

"Maybe you shouldn't listen to what Ama tells you, Mrs. Harkington." Flo faced Julia's agonized retreat with perfect calm. "I suppose some people feel we should have had a large wedding, within a week or two of Dad's death. Personally, I don't feel that way." Julia started to protest, but Flo, smiling at Orpha, said, "May I have another roll, Mrs. Graves? They're perfectly delicious."

Later, when Flo was driving Harriet home, she let anger break through the calm. "Mother, if that old cat ever opens her mouth again, I believe honestly that I'll kill her. I was so angry today that I felt sick — I really was dizzy."

"Julia's all right — you mustn't let her upset you." Remembering Julia's red face, her awkward, stammering defeat, Harriet felt a little sorry for her. "Julia's really a good friend — she'd do anything in the world for my family."

"And Ama — that prying, foul-tongued little slut! If I ever run into her — well, I wouldn't trust myself."

Harriet smiled. "Flo, you amaze me sometimes. Poor Ama's probably never had a beau in her life and so she just has to talk about other people's beaus. God wasn't very good to Ama, I'm afraid."

Flo heaved a tired sigh. "Well, I can't worry about that. I'm just sorry I insisted on your going, that's all. But who would have thought it would be so gruesome?"

"Why, I had a lovely time, Flo. It was nice to be with those ladies again." Harriet looked out at the familiar street in the late afternoon shadow — schoolboys on bicycles, Mr. Hazen burning a pile of leaves in the gutter. "It's nice to be with old friends. I guess I'm just about as queer as they are. And sometimes I think it's a good thing to talk things over — you feel so much better afterwards."

"Well, at least we've taken a stand on Babe and maybe that's a good thing."

Harriet felt herself quivering on the edge of sadness. "You know Flo, when I think about Babe, I feel a hundred years old." She looked down at her hands, rubbed her fingers against her palms. "Maybe if Babe had been able to talk to somebody — I feel as if I never knew her. There are certain things you can't imagine a child of yours would ever do."

As Flo drove up before the house, Harriet said, "Maybe I should have Nettie and Charlie Miller in for dinner some evening. I don't know as they've ever been in my house."

"I think that would be nice," Flo said. "Sometime soon — before winter comes."

The Benefit Ball was to be a big occasion that year (Bigger and Better than ever, the *Sentinel* announced) because the Charity Hospital needed a new wing. Harriet read about it with momentary nostalgia and quickly suppressed memories. She wished that some nice young man would invite Louise to go, but as for herself, that sort of thing was over now. It was probably the first time Harriet had ever missed a Benefit Ball — except for the year when she was too far along with Eddie to appear in an evening gown. The first year they were started — it was just after Flo was born — she and Papa had gone and he had made her buy the most expensive gown in Clark City, an elegant thing it was, all beadwork, and an egret for her hair. The City House Hotel had just been built and its ballroom with mahogany woodwork and red damask walls was the handsomest thing between Denver and San Francisco. A colored man stood at the door to help the ladies from their coaches and the Wades had a supper party before, with champagne. And Grandpa Gannon lit the men's cigars with a twenty-dollar bill.

Well, that was over and done with and she would send in a check as her contribution to the Hospital and perhaps she and Gus could have dinner downtown and go to an early movie. When she received an engraved card asking her to be a patroness, she knew she must refuse, but nonetheless, she wept with gratitude.

Eddie thought she should go. This was the *only* thing Clark City did that one needn't blush over and Eddie seemed to think it a great compliment that Harriet had been asked as a patroness. "They're asking *nobody* who isn't *somebody*." Howard's parents had, of course, been asked.

Flo said, "I think you should go, Mother. I remember the first ones I went to — how I loved it because the older people were there. It was — oh, it was *dignified,* it was historic. You represent something — you have to be there."

Louise said, "Of course you must go, Mother. After all, you're young, you're beautiful. You'll be the best-looking woman there. You must go and have a wonderful time."

Flo and Grant would take her and once there, she would sit in the patrons' box with people she knew well and everyone would be glad to see her — all the young people whom she had known since they were born would rush up to greet her and everyone would really appreciate and respect her effort to be there.

Well, Harriet said, if they really thought she should, if they really thought it was her duty —

She felt like Cinderella rescued from the kitchen, like Lazarus raised from the dead.

Two weeks before the Ball, the word spread about Joe Wilson. Joe Wilson was currently from Los Angeles, but according to Joe Wilson, he was a citizen of the world. Joe Wilson had sold himself to the affiliated ladies' clubs of Clark City as a new force in the American way of life, a dynamic force, he said. If the Benefit Ball wanted to make money for a hospital wing, what they needed was a promoter. He could triple, easily, the net return of the most profitable Benefit Ball on record, so that the small fee he would accept needn't even concern them. His qualifications seemed to be excellent — he had been a newspaper man, was a member of the American Legion, and had recently "promoted" a marathon dance in Cleveland. Would he run off with all the funds — as in the movies — the ladies wanted to know. Apparently not — at least the telegrams their husbands sent out checked that he never had done so before. With excited reluctance, Mabel Lathrop, chairman of this year's Ball, sent off the telegram that opened up Clark City to the new dynamism.

Joe Wilson turned out to be exactly what he had said he was, a live wire. His first day in town, without consulting Mabel Lathrop, he canceled the reservation at the City House Hotel and hired instead the Golden Crescent Ballroom. When Mabel heard the news, she took three aspirin and called her committee together to face Joe Wilson. Joe Wilson, a dark, curly-haired man with a large cameo ring, said, "Ladies, ladies, you mustn't excite yourselves. Now how would they do it in New York, in Chicago, in Detroit? If they were building a hospital for litt-le children, would they hire the Ritz Hotel which holds five hundred people or Madison Square Garden which holds ten thousand? I'm asking you."

Joe himself announced the change in a full-page *Sentinel* advertisement which he persuaded the local brewer to sponsor. The advertisement said that the Benefit Ball would be held in the West's most beautiful and spacious dance palace, the Golden Crescent Ballroom. The price of admission would be *not* four dollars per couple, as in former years, but one dollar and a half for ladies, two dollars for gents. And it reminded all people interested in charity that when they were hot and irritable from dancing, Stebbins's *Stebbo,* the near-beer with a kick, really hit the spot.

Joe lined up several local concerns to sponsor sandwich-board trucks that drove up and down the streets blaring out loud phonograph music and announcing in violent red script that the place to meet your friends was Clark City's biggest super-spectacular Benefit Ball. The ladies' ready-to-wear departments of Clark City's stores did such a booming business that Joe convinced them they should, as a mark of gratitude, sponsor refreshments, tickets, and paid advertising.

The night of the Ball, Louise and Gus followed Harriet into her room, and Louise stretched out on the bed; Gus emptied the gold lace bag of jewelry onto the couch and arranged the jewelry in rows.

"I wish you were coming too," Harriet said, undoing a curling kid. "I hate to see you miss something like this."

"It doesn't matter." Louise had her palms over her eyes and Harriet couldn't see her expression. "There are worse things than staying home."

"You're too particular. Girls get that way. You're too fussy."

"Refusing to go with David Young doesn't mean I'm particular, for heaven's sakes. It just means I'm not blind."

"But you never meet *other* boys if you just stay home." Harriet frizzed her hair with the comb. "I don't see what's so bad about David Young."

"Well — let's not talk about it."

Gus had paused in his work to watch for a sign of Louise's feelings. "Do you wish you were going?" he asked tentatively.

Louise flung one arm away from her eyes and looked over toward Gus. "I'd rather stay home with you."

Gus returned happily to his diamonds. "What shall we do?"

"Well," Louise thought for a moment, "maybe we could make some fudge."

Harriet finished her hair and coated her face and arms and neck with powder. She was slipping into her black velvet dress when they heard the front door open and Flo's yoo-hoo. Harriet stood before the mirror, fastening snaps and smoothing the dress over her hips. "I don't think my figure's so bad — for an old lady," she commented to her image.

Flo was gorgeously dressed in turquoise lace and an evening wrap with white fox collar. Flo had been the last of the girls to submit to bobbed hair, but she kept her hair in such full marcel that she looked little different from her high-school pictures when her hair was all blown up with rats. In fact, nothing about Flo had changed very much except her weight; she had rounded, lost any sharp edges, but none of the trappings of the jazz age could disguise her contemporaneousness with "A Long Long Way to Tipperary" and Liberty Bond drives and "Smilin' Through."

She was panting a little from the climb up the stairs, but she gave them her warm smile, gasping, "Oh my," and said, "Ah — you look just lovely, Mother."

They all turned to survey Flo, and Harriet said, "Oh Flo, take off your coat, let us see." And when Flo had removed her coat and turned around for them and held out her arms, Harriet said, "You've never looked better in your life. Has she, Louise?"

"It's a beautiful dress," Louise said.

Grant followed into the room, scowling somewhat, and no word of greeting. Something about the tight fit of his tuxedo and his red face suggested sausages to Harriet, and to make up for the disloyal thought, she said, "And Grant looks very handsome."

Grant settled his fat buttocks onto the couch, grunting, pushing aside Gus's pattern of jewels. Gus looked up in surprise, and the look Flo gave Grant suggested so much dislike that Harriet wondered whether she should be giving some thought to Flo's and Grant's relationship. Perhaps she should, in a day or so.

"Gus — bring me my jewels. Earrings first."

And while she put on Papa's gifts, they watched silently. And when she was all finished, they surveyed her, cocking their heads. Louise rose from the bed to tug at the hemline of Harriet's dress; Flo smoothed powder on her forehead. Then they drew back to look again.

"Mother — just a little lipstick — it would do wonders," Flo said.

"Oh lands no!" Harriet blushed at the idea.

"It would, Mother — no one need even know you have it on," Louise said.

Flo searched through her evening bag for a lipstick. "We'll just put a little — now just stand still."

Harriet started to move away, but Louise held her. Then the three of them were struggling and laughing and Gus jumped up to watch, giggling shrilly.

Grant muttered, "Trying to make her look like a chippy."

"Now there!" Flo said. "Look at yourself. You're ten years younger."

"Oh my lands," Harriet said. "What crazy children." She hurried to her dressing table to wipe the nasty stuff away, but she secretly had to admire what a little color did for her and so she rubbed very lightly.

Louise ran downstairs and returned with a corsage box.

"What's that?" Harriet said. "Where did that come from?"

Louise handed her the box, and while Harriet opened it, she looked at their faces. Under the green tissue paper was an orchid. She picked up the card. "Have fun!" it said, and was signed, "Flo, Eddie, Louise, and Gus."

Harriet's eyes filled with tears and she had to turn away. "You spoil me," she said. She thought about Papa and all of them and the tears simply ruined her face. "You shouldn't do these things — you — you're spoiling me."

Joe Wilson's Greater Benefit Ball, as it had come to be called, seemed to be in full swing when Grant drove up to let the ladies out, and the Golden Crescent Ballroom was lighted as if for a capacity Saturday night. Waiting for Grant to park the car, Harriet glanced uneasily at the glittering domed edifice, listened to the chorus of male voices that shattered the night with "Oh how I *wish — I was* in Pe-*o*-ria, Pe-*o*-ria, to-*night!*"

"Have you ever been here before, Flo?" Harriet asked in a small voice. For years the Golden Crescent Ballroom had represented in a vague way the world of unknown people who were somehow not the *right* people. Standing here with Flo, two women alone by the ticket office, she wondered if they looked like bad women.

"No — I never have. Helen Adamson's maid comes here every Saturday night — she's says it's lovely — the cat's pajamas, or some such thing."

Harriet smiled ruefully and took Flo's arm. "Well, I hear that Mr. Wilson says it's much finer than anything in New York or

Chicago. They should make a lot of money for the hospital."

Grant came puffing along the sidewalk and for the first time that evening, smiled and addressed himself directly to them. "What? No pick-ups? Business falling off?"

Flo ignored him, but because he spoke Harriet's own guilty thought, she had to say something. "Grant, what a way to talk."

Once inside, with their coats checked and familiar faces to nod to and her orchid to give her confidence, Harriet felt better. "Now, I don't want you two to bother about me," she told Flo. "If we can just find the patrons' box and get me settled, I'll be fine."

The ballroom was so big and crowded that it was impossible to see anything. Flo asked the ticket taker where the patrons' box was.

"The what?"

"The patrons' box," she explained. "The stand or platform where the patrons are to sit."

"I don't know what you're talking about, lady," he said. "If you want a folding chair, you'll find one inside."

Flo gave him a blistering look and squeezed Harriet's hand protectively. "Probably one of Joe Wilson's *gangsters*," she muttered. "I'll find someone who knows what's going on."

Flo returned in a moment with Mabel Lathrop, whose face was flushed and damp and her red taffeta dress streaked down the back.

"Oh, Mrs. Gannon, you were an angel to come," she said breathlessly, "but something awful has happened."

"Awful?" Harriet asked.

"Well, not really, I guess. This is for charity — we *do* need a new hospital wing." Mabel searched Harriet's face rather desperately. "Mr. Wilson has taken over the patrons' box."

"Oh? Well —"

Mabel wiped perspiration from her forehead. "We worked all day on it — even Harry came down to help and it was just like at the City House. Then when we arrived tonight, there — in the patrons' box — was an automobile. Mr. Wilson said it was a surprise — he's going to raffle it off."

Harriet smiled uncertainly, trying not to yield to despair. It was a little thing, really — but, oh, she could at this moment have been safe in a movie with Louise and Gus. "Well, Mabel — "

"It's a beautiful car," Mabel added weakly. "It's a Lincoln."

The beautiful Lincoln, black and shining, was just visible above the heads of the dancers. Mabel Lathrop found Harriet a folding chair against the wall and from where she sat, Harriet could see the corner of the velvet-draped patrons' box and the large basket of white chrysanthemums and the tail light of the beautiful Lincoln. The younger people crowded close, to gaze enraptured at the car. Certainly, Harriet had to admit, the patrons would not have elicited such admiration.

She forced a smile of eager interest to her face so that anyone observing her would not pity her for the lonely old woman she was. Not that people *would* be observing her: she was surely not so conspicuous as she felt, and the young couples doing the Charleston were attracting all the attention. The girls must become frightfully overheated — but according to the advertisements, that needn't worry them, she guessed.

It was hard to keep in mind that this was the Benefit Ball, even that it was Clark City. All these people — who were they? Where did they come from? Had this sort of thing been going on every Saturday night in the Golden Crescent Ballroom? After living her whole life here, sure that she knew the town because she *was* the town, she now had to realize that things had been going on of which she had been wholly unaware. The Ballroom itself was so incongruous a part of the Clark City she knew that she was amazed at her having accepted its existence for so long without ever knowing or questioning its significance.

Every now and then, she saw someone she knew — the Wades, the Harkingtons, a friend of Flo's, someone out of Louise's graduating class at Clark High; sometimes they saw her and came over to speak. But mostly she watched from the folding chair, creasing her handkerchief, wondering whether the orchid might seem ostentatious. It was a victory of love and loyalty that restrained her from removing the orchid and dropping it under her chair.

A blare of trumpets wrought silence for Mr. Joe Wilson's announcement that this "be-yew-tiful" Lincoln, "the finest flower of the genius of that great American, Henry Ford," was to be raffled off at one dollar the chance. Mr. Wilson's oratory ripped from his throat as he proclaimed that no longer need one be a John Jacob

Astor to own a "be-yew-tiful" Lincoln: "Just as any full-blooded American can rise to be President of these United States, so, for only one dollar, can any full-blooded American be the owner of a be-yew-tiful Lincoln. It's all a matter of chance, folks, a turn of the wheel." He announced, slyly, that certain lovely little ladies would mix with the crowd to give Clark City the opportunity to acquire this monument to progress for only one dollar. "And remember, folks," he concluded, "it's all for charity."

Then the music started up again — "Sleepy time gal — you're turning night into day — " and a golden spotlight flashed onto the Lincoln in the patrons' box, and from her folding chair at the side of the dance floor, Harriet watched the young people press around the patrons' box.

Flo came to sit out a dance with her while Grant went outside for a cigarette. Harriet was self-conscious. She wanted not to appear as ill at ease as she felt; she wanted to show that she was having a lovely time. Her discomfort left her dumb.

"The ventilation is bad in here," Flo said. "You're lucky not to be in the middle of all that mob."

"It's just fine here," Harriet said brightly. "I'm very comfortable."

"I saw the Driscolls — they asked about you. They're going to try to find you. Just wait till you see *her*."

"Now Flo — "

"I know, Mother, but she does have the worst taste."

A blonde girl in black satin shorts, white blouse, man's top hat, black stockings on her long legs, slithered up, whining, "Chances, chances on the beautiful motorcar. Only one dollar."

She stopped by Harriet, close, so that Harriet had to turn her eyes from the tight satin that fitted like a bathing suit.

"It's for charity, madame," the girl reproved her.

Harriet quickly opened her purse and handed the girl a five-dollar bill.

"Thank you, madame," the girl chanted, counting out five tickets. "It will be greatly appreciated, I'm sure."

Flo smiled and patted Harriet's hand. "Poor Mother. Don't be shocked. It's the way things are."

"Shocked? I'm not shocked." But Harriet felt her face go red. She dabbed at her nose with her handkerchief. "I just wondered who she is. Do you suppose she's a Clark City girl?"

"Of course — they all are. There are other things going on too, I suppose, that might surprise you."

Then Flo was gone and Harriet was alone, creasing her handkerchief. She shouldn't have come, she shouldn't have come. Like some of those women you saw in California — down at the beach with little dogs — they didn't know when their time was up. Here she was, wearing lipstick and an orchid, thinking that she could have a lovely time, that people would be glad to see her. But no one was glad to see a solitary old woman. If Papa were here — but she mustn't think of that. The warm, enveloping kind of security that he had provided hovered for an instant in the thought of him and then vanished, leaving her chilled and desolate.

The long-legged girls in black shorts passed back and forth, singing, "Chances? Chances on the beautiful motorcar?"

Eddie's party didn't arrive until after eleven and they created something of a flurry. Claire O'Neil had taken sixteen of them to dinner at the country club for her out-of-town guests, and they arrived together with sixteen times the assurance that each would have had as an individual. In the vast room, the knowledge spread, by insidious magic, that here were sixteen who knew where they stood in the universe; and all the hundreds of less knowing souls turned to stare.

Harriet watched for Eddie, wanting to catch her attention, then wondering whether Eddie would be ashamed to introduce her to her friends.

Eddie and Flo came over together and sat down on either side of her. Eddie wore a short metal-cloth dress, low waisted, cut low in front and back, and a chiffon scarf draped over her shoulders. She fanned herself with the end of the scarf.

"What a ghastly affair this is," she said. "Poor Mother, you must be bored to tears."

"Oh, I'm having a lovely time. It's interesting to watch the young people. How was your dinner?"

"It was fine." She looked across Harriet to Flo. "Don't you think it's amazing that a man like David Hagen would marry such a dowdy little woman? Living in New York — with all that money —but I guess she just has no taste."

"Who are the Hagens, dear?" Harriet asked.

"Claire's guests. He's terribly important — awfully rich. I found him very attractive."

"Oh Eddie, he weighs three hundred pounds," Flo said. "And I'll bet he pinches."

"He knows important people, though. You can talk to him."

Harriet felt easy now, sitting here between her girls, and she hoped that everyone would look and see that she was not alone, not just someone's old grandmother.

But Eddie was squirming, looking over her shoulder. Of course you couldn't expect the young people to sit on the sidelines; they should be enjoying themselves.

Then Eddie got a malicious grin on her face and bent across Harriet to speak to Flo. "Look — leaning against the wall."

Harriet saw a woman in a raincoat and old felt hat. She was leaning sideways, resting one shoulder against the wall. She held a cigarette between her fingers.

"Oh heavens!" Flo said. "What do you suppose is the idea of that? I'm surprised they let her in."

"She thinks she's Iris March. Look at her. Isn't it killing?"

"Eddie — she never read a book in her life."

"Who is it?" Harriet asked. The woman blew a long breath of smoke straight up and flicked ashes onto the dance floor. Harriet never had seen a woman smoke and she found it embarrassing. "Who is she?"

"It's dear old Muriel — but she thinks she's Iris March. I'll bet anything that hat is green. Watch her — isn't it horrible?"

"Oh Eddie," Flo had to laugh, but she turned away. "Don't be mean."

Eddie stood up, made a little motion of her shoulders — knowing full well that she was cute and attractive — and oh, she was! — and held out her hand to Flo. "Come on Flo — we better get going before Iris Hooper seduces our husbands. Virtue can't compete with *that*."

"Are you all right, Mother?" Flo asked.

"Of course I am. You run along and have a good time."

Eddie wrinkled her nose at Harriet and waved a finger. "Have fun."

She watched them vanish into the crowd, pleased and happy

that for a few moments, at least, people had seen they were hers, that she shared in the aura that was theirs, the aura of success.

Then she was horrified to see Muriel Hooper walking toward her. Muriel's hands were plunged deep in the pockets of her raincoat, and Harriet couldn't tell whether Muriel was angry or happy. But when Muriel came closer, she held out her hand, and certainly there was no question of her genuine pleasure.

"This is the only nice thing that's happened to me all evening," Muriel said. "Really, the only one. May I just sit here a minute?"

"Oh please do. How are you, Muriel?"

Muriel sat down, none too certain, and, Harriet was afraid, there was an odor of alcohol on her breath. "Oh, I'm fine, Mrs. Gannon — a little blotto, if you'll excuse the expression — but fine and dandy."

"Are your parents here? I haven't seen them."

"I guess so — but I haven't seen them either, and I don't want to. But I'm really glad to see you — I *really* am."

Harriet smiled and looked down at her hands. Muriel's hat *was* green — whatever that meant. And her skin was very white and lifeless.

"You know, Mrs. Gannon," Muriel continued, "when I see how that Wilson fellow has cheapened the Benefit Ball, I could just heave. I didn't like it much in the old days, but it had something. I don't know, it had something. But just look at that!" She waved her arm toward the mass of Clark City youth dancing cheek to cheek to "Brown Eyes, Why are you Blue." "Scum," Muriel said. "Scum."

"Well — I don't know, Muriel. Maybe this is best. I'm sure they've made more money than we ever made in the old days. Our trouble was we never realized how many people there were in Clark City. We thought we knew everyone."

"Well, just thank God you don't. Thank God for that. Because if you want to know what they're like, just look at them. Like pigs, waiting for that bloody car to be raffled off. Honestly, Mrs. Gannon, every time I look at that bloody Lincoln, I could just heave."

Muriel looked as if she might actually be sick; her eyes stared unfocused and every so often, she covered a belch with her finger-tips.

"That reminds me," she said suddenly, "Tommy's going to be very disappointed he missed you. He really is."

"Ah, Tommy. I miss Tommy too — we never see him any more. Is he here?"

"Well — in body but not in spirit, or maybe vice versa. He had a little accident on the way in — matter of fact, he never got in."

"You give my love to Tommy. Tell him I think of him."

"Let me tell you, he certainly thinks a lot of you. We all do, Mrs. Gannon. And do you know why?" Muriel turned to gaze sleepily at Harriet, her head swaying. "It's because you're a lady — an honest to God lady. I mean it, Mrs. Gannon," she said, slapping her knee. "Everything else is crap. They can take this Benefit Ball and their Joe Wilson and they can — "

"I'm afraid the old Benefit Ball is finished now, Muriel. They could never go back to it after this. Progress — "

"They can take their progress and their Joe Wilson and they can — Listen, Mrs. Gannon," Muriel bent over her, breathing in her face, "do you know what Tommy and I have said — many times? The two people in this town we'd choose to be like are you and Mr. Gannon — " Muriel's eyes filled with tears. "He was a gentleman."

"Thank you, Muriel." Perhaps Muriel didn't know what she was saying, but Harriet accepted the tribute hungrily, gratefully. "I've always felt as if Tommy were one of my own." She looked at the sad bleary-eyed girl in the green felt hat. "You too," and she squeezed Muriel's hand.

Muriel took out a handkerchief and blew her nose loudly. "Well, I better go look for Tommy. He really is an awful person, Mrs. Gannon. He really is."

"Thank you for coming over, Muriel. I might have — I was beginning to feel sorry for myself. You were sweet to come."

Muriel pulled her hat further down on her head, thrust her hands into her pockets, staggered moodily toward the door.

And the girls in the satin shorts cried out, "Chances? Chances on the beautiful motorcar?"

Driving home, Grant passed the City House Hotel, which was dark except for one light and seemed to have shrunk in size. The square wooden pillars needed a coat of paint and the old white sign across the front should have been in lights, Harriet realized, lights, perhaps, that blinked on and off. It had been there so long, so familiar a part of Center Street that Harriet hadn't noticed before how shabby it was. In the clear autumn night, it looked like a set for a Western movie, one of those movies that people laughed at nowadays. Not a real building — just a front, and if you walked through the door, you'd see only Western sky.

Flo and Grant were silent because they were tired and Harriet because no words could say what she felt. Tomorrow, Flo would drop in and they would talk over the evening, who was there, what they had worn. Tomorrow, everything would settle back into order, things to see to around the house, and there was Thanksgiving to start thinking about and then Christmas.

Louise had left the hall light on, but the house was a huge, black outline against the night.

"Will you be all right?" Flo asked. "Do you want me to go in with you?"

"No thanks, dear." Harriet kissed Flo's cheek. "I had a lovely time and thanks for everything."

"Grant'll walk you to the door. Good night, Mother. I'll see you tomorrow."

Harriet unlocked the front door and thanked Grant and made her way upstairs, turning on one light, turning off another. In her own room, she stood before the mirror to unpin the crushed orchid from her dress and she hung her coat in the closet. The house was still, so still that one could hardly think that it contained a living being. Harriet listened and suddenly was frightened. She rushed from her room, down the hall to Gus's room. Then she stopped. His even breathing and mumbling when he turned over restored peace and certainty and order. She stood by his bed until her eyes could see through the dark to his blond head on the rumpled pillow, his scrawny little body sprawled across the bed. She let her hand rest lightly against his cool forehead and she stood there for minutes.

Then she bent to kiss his cheek and whisper good night.

Part Three

CHAPTER 1

ONE SATURDAY AFTERNOON, late in October of 1929, Gus Gannon and his mother took the streetcar downtown and went to a movie. But before the movie, they went to Fisher's for lunch and Gus ordered a hot roast beef sandwich and a chocolate nut sundae, because that was what he always ordered when he went to Fisher's. The movie — or talkie, rather — was called *Gold Diggers of Broadway* and was an All-Talking Vitaphone smash hit in color with Winnie Lightner starred as chief Gold Digger. On the way out, Mother said she didn't think much of the picture, but Gus rather liked it — he got kind of a kick out of Winnie Lightner who wasn't much to look at but was quite a comedian.

It was about four o'clock when they came out, blinking into the sun, for although it was October, it was hot for October, more like summer. The way he felt coming out of that theatre was this: it's a hot day but you can tell it's fall by the sweaters and skirts the schoolgirls wear and by the Saturday-afternoon something that lets you know that Saturday afternoon is a holiday and not just one more lazy day of summer. A kind of excitement in the air that tells you things are happening.

Mother asked did he want to stop in Fisher's again for some caramels and he said sure. But before they reached Fisher's, Mother said she was anxious to read the headlines and so they stopped by a dirty-looking kid and read the headlines. PANTAGES JURY LOCKED UP FOR NIGHT, the headlines read.

"What's all this about Pantages?" Gus asked.

"That isn't what I was looking for," Mother said, scanning the paper. "I wanted to see what they say about the stock market."

"Well, what'd this Pantages do?" Gus insisted.

Mother turned from the paper and thought for a minute. "Well," she said, as if she'd rather he hadn't mentioned it, "he got into trouble over a young girl. It's called criminal attack."

Gus thought that over while Mother searched the paper some more. Criminal attack suggested machine guns and brass knuckles and policemen's clubs — he had seen it many time in the pictures. That it should happen to a young girl seemed too bad and Pantages seemed like a pretty black character.

"Does that mean there won't be no more Pantages theatres?" Gus asked.

"*Any* more," Mother corrected him. "Does that mean there won't be *any* more Pantages theatres. I guess it does."

They started to walk away when the dirty-looking kid said, "Hey, lady, wha'd'ya think this is? A free public library?"

Mother got red in the face and fumbled through her purse for a nickel to buy the paper, even though they'd have another just like it at home. Gus didn't think much of that kid.

Not until they were in Fisher's buying the caramels did Gus remember about the stock market. "Hey, how about the stock market?" he asked.

"It didn't say very much," she answered, reaching for change. "President Hoover says everything's fine again. He says business is on a good sound basis."

That's how Gus remembered things. He remembered all about the feeling of the day and about that poor girl getting beat up, but the stock-market crash was just something that went along with something more important.

Along the same line: one morning he was lying in bed having a nice dream (he was thirteen, then, and in this dream, he'd just been made captain of the soccer team, but then he remembered he had promised to drop in after school each day to run the family business, and so how could he accept?); well, he was feeling a little sad but really pretty good about this dream when his mother's voice broke in and wakened him to a dark, gray morning, no heat in the radiator, get up and close the window, turn on the light, shiver out of your warm pajamas and into your cold B.V.D.'s. Then look out the window at the dirty March morning and realize that your dream had made you feel good about something that wasn't true at all. Winter with the starch gone out of it, the dirty laundry of winter. And school would be like any other day.

Dressed, he staggered sleepily downstairs to the breakfast room where Mother had his orange juice and mush and cocoa all ready for him. He didn't like to look at his mother on a morning like this and he acted disagreeable because the thought of his having dragged her out of bed to get his breakfast gave him a hollow feeling that he just couldn't stand. Ever since they had had to let Martha go, he'd felt that way when he saw his mother do the heavy housework, and especially on mornings like this, it got so bad he couldn't look at her.

Then he noticed a newspaper, an extra the *Sentinel* must have printed during the night. The headline said, ROOSEVELT DE-CLARES BANK HOLIDAY.

Gus nodded toward the paper. "Good or bad?"

"I don't know, dear," Mother answered. "I hope it's good."

What he remembered about the crash was old man Pantages beating up that girl; the bank holiday was the sweetness of that dream, how it had felt to be the sole support of his family.

Another thing about memory. Was it actually true that the olden days were better or did they just seem better because of something that memory added to or subtracted from the actual happening? Thinking back on when he was a kid, Gus couldn't remember that anything ever went wrong — with him or anyone else. The unpleasant memories of his childhood he could count on one hand. Like his mother's scream that wakened them in the night when Dad died. Like being scolded and sent upstairs for swinging on Sammy once when Sammy had been teasing him. Like having to go to Sunday school when Sunday school was murder.

But the good memories — there were hundreds of them! A little thing like sitting on the curb of a hot summer morning and letting the cold mountain water rush over your feet in the gutter. Thinking about that, Gus could feel again the weight of the sun on his back, the icy water crawling up his leg, the slight motion of heavy air with the smell of roses or marigolds, and hear the lazy chattering of birds. Just thinking about it could give Gus a tickling in his throat and bring on an exquisite stretch.

Or, walking along the beach with Dad to buy a bathing suit. The bathing suit was what made that memory so special because it was a two-piece bathing suit, white top, black trunks. For a moment in the darkness of the store Gus had had a terrible premonition that Dad wouldn't care for the two-piece suits and would buy a regular one-piece suit like the other kids had, a navy-blue one that would droop at the crotch when wet. But Dad bought the two-piece suit, and when they walked out of the store, the silver arms of the salt-water taffy machines were twirling, orange juice was shooting through a long glass tube, hamburgers were sizzling, and the air was sunlight washed by sea.

When he was a kid, he used to look at all the grownups in the family and think, Oh boy, it must be great. That motorcycle in the garage, for instance. He couldn't remember ever having seen Jack ride the thing, but when he was a kid, he used to go out and take a look at it and think, Oh boy, what it must be to grow up and tear all over town on a motorcycle. On a spring night to hop on a motorcycle and go meet Tommy Reed and race through the night and worry the folks half to death. Oh delicious thought!

The parties they used to have — with the old player piano pumping away and girls swinging dance programs on their wrists and the boys looking so old with their stiff collars and slicked hair. He had built up an idea of *party* in his mind that the real thing, when it came along, couldn't even approximate. There was always such a feeling of tension about the old parties — girls crying, boys slamming doors, engagements made and broken — as if they had saved all their romantic troubles to settle to the tune of "Oh Harold, Oh Harold," and "Dirty Hands, Dirty Face." By the time Gus was old enough to be invited to a party — a dancing party, that is, not a birthday party — parties had become so dull that he and Buddy Sawyer locked themselves in the lavatory and pitched pennies until time for the ice cream.

Eddie's wedding, he just barely remembered. Would there ever be such another? Would men ever be as hard to figure and scary as he had viewed them through Louise's eyes? Would women ever be as rich and beautiful and dangerous as Jack's women through his mother's eyes? Would Clark High football games be as exciting, New York plays as spectacular, Christmases as rich, love as world-shaking, snows as deep, summers as hot as in the legends of family history? And was it memory that did all that — or had times really changed?

Being so much younger than all the rest of them had had a lot to do with it, of course: he'd lived so many grown-up lives before he was old enough to know what it was all about. He'd had a kind of funny perspective on things. Flo, for instance. He knew she was his sister and he called her Flo, but she was never his sister the way Louise was his sister. Flo was Sam's mother and when Gus played with Sam, Sam could always have his way because he'd say, "I'll tell Mother," and scare Gus into agreement. And yet Gus followed her life, knew all about it, knew when she fought with Grant or had trouble with Sam or Connie. It would be the same thing as this: supposing one day when Gus went over to play with Buddy Sawyer, Mrs. Sawyer said, "Gus, I want to talk to you," and sat him down and told him all about her and Mr. Sawyer. Maybe it was no wonder that grownups always seemed kind of fabulous to Gus.

There was another thing. Anything bad that happens to somebody you love is a lot worse than anything bad that happens to you. Or anything good is a lot better. And so if your first look at life is through that somebody else's eyes, the whole thing is going to be exaggerated. For instance: Gus had never cared one way or the other whether he got to be valedictorian when he grew up, but he could work up a real sweat thinking how Louise almost didn't get to be valedictorian. And instead of seeing right off that the reason he could work up a sweat was his feeling for Louise, he just naturally assumed that to be valedictorian was better in the olden days than now.

Gus and his mother worked that one out together. And yet he often wondered whether his mother didn't *really* think the old days were better. At the dinner table, they often talked about the past. When they had finished eating and everyone was too lazy — or too tired — to clear off the dishes or even turn on the light, someone would say, "Oh me. Oh for the good old days and dear old Martha." (If Jack said it, it went: "Oh for the good old days before Roosevelt took over." Why Roosevelt? On the day of the crash and the Pantages incident, it was Hoover who was President.)

Then someone would say, "Remember when — " and then everyone would be saying "Remember when — " And in the half-light, Mother would look almost young again and Louise would laugh and lose that sort of gray look she got from working in the Clark High library, and Jack would sparkle so that you didn't notice how bald he was getting, how puffy.

One night, Mother happened to look over at Gus and stopped in the middle of what she was saying. "It wasn't *all* wonderful, Gus," she told him. "It seems so — looking back on it — because we remember the good things and forget the bad. I used to have *plenty* of sleepless nights."

"Harriet, that's a lie," Jack said. "Gus, don't listen to your mother when she talks that way. She never had a sleepless night in her life. *Everything* was wonderful. 'Bliss was it in that dawn to be alive, But to be young was very heaven.' Mr. Wordsworth said that in 1926."

"Well — that's not so long ago," Gus said. "Even *I* can remember that far back."

"Ah — it was centuries ago." Jack got the brooding look on his face that always preceded a Roosevelt outburst. The moment of melancholy. "Those were days of infinite possibility, of delirious freedom. Park Avenue at five o'clock with the sun going down and five o'clock haze sort of soft and rosy. You could stand there with a million cars and people going by and yet feel a complete individual. Behind some door was adventure, some particular adventure, just for you. You just had to reach out an arm — and pluck it."

That sounded wonderful to Gus. "Well, what did you do?" he wanted to know.

But Jack's moment was over. "That's what this man Roosevelt has destroyed — the thing I can never forgive him for. Economic theories — what do they matter? Money's nothing! But freedom is everything — and that's what he's destroyed. He's making us all slaves of the state!"

It was funny to hear Jack talk about Roosevelt. Gus couldn't quite figure it. And it was particularly funny to hear Jack say that money was nothing. Every night it was something different. Gus couldn't figure it out at all.

Always after Jack had spoken his mind on Roosevelt, he would have to leave and go down to Tommy's, get away from it all. Tommy had an apartment downtown and except for meals, Jack spent almost all of his time there — in fact, he helped pay the rent and he usually slept there.

He would sigh and throw his napkin on the table (Mother always folded it afterwards and slipped it in the napkin ring), and then he would say: "Harriet, you look tired, you work too much. Why don't you just *leave* the dishes?"

And he would kiss her and tell her how pretty she was and you could see her face light up and know, whether you liked it or not, that Jack did her more good than all of the rest of you put together. She would finger the shiny cuff of his suit and say, "Poor Jack. How's the suit fund coming?"

"Twenty-one bucks and thirty-eight cents. Think I'll make it before the pants split out?" Then he would kiss her again and say, "Prettiest gal I ever saw."

After Jack had gone, Gus and Louise would send Harriet to bed and do the dishes themselves.

That afternoon haze that Jack talked about — Gus knew what he meant, because his own memories, if they went far enough back, were always lighted with a peculiarly wonderful light. Not necessarily sun: Fox and Geese on a winter night had that sparkling blue light of stars and night shadows on the snow.

But the more recent memories seemed to have a lot of gray in them, winter days of slush, the cold gray house when the furnace wasn't working right and he or Mother or Louise would have to go down every few minutes to nurse the fire. Nights when the furnace would go on the blink and the pipes would freeze and in the morning they would huddle around the kitchen stove, trying to joke about it and yet Gus would get all tied up inside when he saw how tired and desperate his mother looked. All because they couldn't afford to pay a man to care for the furnace properly.

They were, of course, as his mother kept reminding them, among the lucky ones. Look at the Wades — Mr. Wade had, almost overnight, become an old man and Mrs. Wade had to take in boarders and sell cakes so that they could live. A man Dad used to know in San Francisco jumped from a hotel window. And look at the Driscolls! When they first felt the pinch and Mrs. Driscoll discovered he had been using half his money to support his secretary, she went down to his office with a kitchen knife in her purse. Luckily she didn't kill the secretary. They packed Mrs. Driscoll off to California and Mr. Driscoll divorced her and everyone (except Mother) felt very sorry for Mr. Driscoll. They said everyone should have known such an athletic man couldn't be happy with that awful woman. Mr. Driscoll never married his secretary, however.

For a while, right after the crash, dividends kept coming in and Jack stayed on in New York. Then there was nothing except Dad's insurance, which was just about enough to keep them fed and pay the taxes on the house. Jack came home to see what had gone wrong with the business and after the bank took over, they let him stay on because they had all thought so much of Dad. It was a blessing, everyone said, that Louise had found a job before the crash, because she never would have found one after. She turned over most of her salary to Mother and that paid for coal. Jack asked if they could manage without any help — economic help, that is — from him because he was being paid a starvation wage and he felt obligated to help Tommy out. Mother said of course they could. When Gus heard about that, he was just scared Mother would give Jack an allowance or something, and it was hard to remember that you should love your brother as yourself.

Gus tried in 1932 to find a job but there just weren't any jobs for a twelve-year-old punk. Any job a kid could get paid for, a grown man with a family could do just as well. If he'd had a paper route *before* the crash, the way Louise had her job, then everything might have been okay. He'd have earned enough, he figured, to pay a man to keep the darned furnace going. Delivery boys nobody wanted. A friend of Eddie's owned a gas station and Gus tried there to see if he couldn't wash windows and check tires. But this guy's father-in-law had that job. The only job he could finally find was kind of humorous. Old lady Hansen paid him two dollars a week to come three times a day and take care of her furnace. Here he couldn't even keep their own furnace going and he was being paid to keep someone else's going. But she had a little bitty furnace and it seemed to Gus that even a bucket of water wouldn't put her fire out.

When he got his first week's pay, he brought it home to Mother, but she wouldn't take it. In fact, she started to cry and hugged him and made him feel like a stupe. Finally they compromised and each took a dollar. With a dollar a week, he felt pretty rich, but a dollar a week didn't go too far buying clothes, even in those days. It helped out some to have Sam's outgrown clothes. That left a little for movies or miniature golf now and then.

For three years, just about, Gus had been keeping old lady Hansen's fire going. Also, in the summer of '33, he was taken on at that gas station because the guy's father-in-law had acquired rheumatism from working outside in the cold so much and when summer business picked up, he couldn't move around very fast. Ted Webster (the guy) said he couldn't afford another grown man, but he'd pay Gus a dollar a day to help out. And so during the summer, he was rich, though a little tired, and he turned over five dollars a week to Mother. And after that he could always count on a little work at the gas station. Whenever the cold got too bad for the father-in-law, Ted Webster gave Gus a ring.

There was one other thing about all this. The house. With a smaller place where all of Louise's salary didn't have to go for coal, they wouldn't have to worry so much about money and Mother wouldn't have to work so darned hard. Flo and Louise and Gus decided they better sell it. Jack said it was like selling a member of the family — like betraying someone you loved just because things were a little tough. Just wait a year or so, he would say, till Roosevelt was out of office, and everything would be all right again, and they could find another Martha.

But it was Eddie, probably, who, more than anyone else made them hang on to the old place. Of course, sell it, she said. It was so hopelessly old-fashioned, so Victorian. Even if they could afford to keep it, the whole thing would have to be entirely done over. As far as she was concerned, she would just as soon have her money out of it right now.

After Eddie's proclamation, Mother and Louise and Gus sat in the old rose room on the little plush love seats, which, it was true, were wearing out. And they all, he supposed, were thinking that maybe what Jack said wasn't so silly after all. Mother did phone a couple of real-estate offices, but there was no market and so they just went on as before.

It was as if Gus's life had a sharp dividing line down the middle of it; there was the early part, the lighted, memory part when no one seemed to worry about anything; and there were the last few years when everyone seemed to worry about everything.

That wasn't wholly true, of course. He was growing up the way any kid grows up — school, sports, hiking or fishing up the canyon. And homework. He and Sammy had been good friends, done a lot of things together. They'd played cowboy and they'd gone camping with the Scouts and they'd swiped cigarettes and they'd peeked in the Reeds' basement window to watch the maid undress. Of course, when Sammy's voice started to change and he was suddenly a whole head taller than Gus, he kind of dropped Gus. He'd make a point of calling Gus "Uncle" around the bigger guys to make them laugh, and he went with an older crowd who considered Gus a baby.

Louise was one of the best things. He could talk over anything with Louise — even, you know, things you couldn't talk over with your Mother. He'd look at Louise and think she was the prettiest, sweetest thing he ever saw and wonder why some wonderful guy wasn't smart enough to see what a catch she'd be. But he was beginning to think that most guys were oafs and as he got a little older and began learning a few things, he wasn't so concerned about Louise's being single. In fact, he didn't even like to think about Louise and that wonderful guy; he didn't like to think about it at all.

The depression, perhaps, was in part responsible for the friendship between Louise and Gus, because when things were bad, they sort of banded together as a protectorate for their mother. Eddie was outside of it; Jack was outside of it — he was always seeking protectorates for himself; Babe they never even heard from; and Flo, though willing, had a different set of problems, a more pressing set of loyalties. Mother was always saying that hardship made people band together. Maybe. The depression wasn't all bad, he guessed. There would be things about it you'd remember afterwards.

Like his birthday, the birthday when he would be fifteen.

Gus hadn't given it very much thought. It was another birthday; if anyone wanted to help him pay for some shoes, that was fine; if anyone wanted to contribute four bits to his stamp collection, that was fine. But there was to be no fuss about it. The day came in the middle of the week, and though Mother had suggested having the whole family in for dinner, Gus wouldn't let her go to that much work.

A couple of nights before the day, he came in from fixing old lady Hansen's furnace and Mother and Louise must not have heard him, because they were talking about him and didn't stop as he walked up the stairs. So he just sat down on the stairs to listen. It was nice to hear them talk about him, he got real pleasure from it.

"I don't know what to get him," Louise was saying. "I thought maybe a shirt or pajamas, but everyone always gives him something *useful*. I wish I could think of something he'd get some fun out of."

Ah, good old Louise, he thought.

"What about some nice stamps?" Mother asked. "He always seems to like stamps."

No, no, Gus frowned. Women never seemed to get the point about stamps: they just picked out the prettiest ones as if they were picking out a hat.

"Well, I don't know," Louise answered. "He has such queer taste in stamps — he never likes the things I like."

"How about a nice book?"

Gus held his breath on that. Sure, a book was nice, but —

"He never seems to have time for reading. Of course it might be a good idea to encourage him."

Gus relaxed a little. He didn't think she'd buy him a book — he felt almost positive she wouldn't.

"You know what we *really* should get him?" Pause while Mother would give an inquiring look. "A razor."

"Oh Louise."

"Mother, he's no baby — you've got to face that whether you like it or not. And he *needs* to shave. That peach down can't stay there indefinitely."

Then both women laughed.

They weren't making fun of him, Gus knew, but that laughter was the most painfully embarrassing thing that had ever happened to him. He was hot all over and he felt as if the breath had been kicked out of him. Sure, he knew the fuzz was there, but somehow he thought they might not know; somehow he didn't want them to know. He knew that probably it was time he shaved, but he didn't like to think about it.

"Maybe we should let Jack give him a razor," Louise said. "It might embarrass him if either of us did."

Gus tiptoed quietly up the stairs and made it to his room and into bed without their seeing him.

And he lay there, troubled about being troubled.

What the heck had got into him? A year ago, when there wasn't a hair on his face, he had locked himself in the bathroom one day and shaved with Jack's razor, upper lip and all. And when Sammy first sprouted a few red gold hairs on his body which he displayed proudly to Gus, Gus had hated his own hairless body and hated Sammy for being so condescending. "What a man!" Sammy would say if Gus undressed before him in the bath house. "Oh boy, what a man!"

And now when all that was changed, Gus didn't feel very happy about it. Now when he really needed to shave, he didn't want to. And the worst thing of all was how he just couldn't stand having people know what had happened to him and laughing about it together.

Gus felt all hot again. What the heck got into a kid? He must be screwy.

Well, he received the razor. When he came home from school that day, there were packages from Flo and Eddie: pajamas from Flo, shirt and tie from Eddie. He phoned the girls and said the presents sure were swell. Sammy dropped by just before dinner with an orange necktie covered with little black dollar signs. It was hard to know what to say about it, but Gus thanked him. Sam ran the back of his hand along Gus's cheek and grinned.

They had all the special food and a birthday cake with fifteen candles. Then the presents came out and Gus felt himself get red in the face when he saw the little box Jack handed him.

Mother's present was a ten-dollar bill and a note saying she hoped he would always be as happy as he had made her. He couldn't even thank her. He just looked at the note. He couldn't even smile at her.

Louise's present was in a box, and when he removed the lid, he saw three ordinary postage stamps torn off letters. He looked up wondering what it was about.

"Look again!" Mother said.

Underneath were three dollar bills.

Then he caught on: she meant he was to buy his own stamps. He rubbed his nose with the back of his hand. "Gee, Louise." He tried a laugh that sort of broke in the middle. "That's swell."

And then Jack's little box. "I wonder what this could be," Gus said, keeping his eyes down because he knew his mother and Louise were smiling. "Gee." Almost before he had raised the lid, he exclaimed, "Oh boy, a razor."

And then he looked again.

"What is it, dear?" Mother asked. "Show us."

It was a razor all right, but — well —

"Jack, what have you done?" Mother exclaimed. "It looks like gold!"

"Not solid," Jack said. He jumped up laughing, and went around to kiss her. "Don't worry, Mother, I didn't steal it."

"Oh Jack!" Louise said. "Who would have thought a razor could be beautiful!"

"It should be," Jack said triumphantly. "It cost twenty-eight dollars. My whole suit fund!"

Gus felt kind of sick and Mother and Louise must've too.

Jack looked at them all, surprised and hurt. "Ah, don't be like that," he said. "Don't spoil the fun." He reached over and mussed up Gus's hair. "Nothing's too good for old Gus."

Remembering that, some day, how would it seem? Would they just remember the beautiful present and say, "Remember when Jack gave Gus the gold razor?" Or would they remember the other things about that night, the things they felt and thought? Would it be one of those shining, clear memories that were so easy to pick out of the past, or would it be one of those things they would rather not even remember?

Later that night, when Gus returned from fixing old lady Hansen's furnace, he took the gold razor and locked himself in the bathroom and removed all his clothes and lathered his face until it looked like peaches in whipped cream. Then he stood before the mirror to get the effect.

He kind of had to laugh.

He took the razor and with exquisite care cleaned off one little patch of cream. Then he stood back to get the effect once more. The fuzz was gone.

He touched his fingers to the thick cream, then to his tongue. He scowled. It sure was a pain what a man had to go through, all this shaving business. But he caught his eye in the mirror and had to smile.

"The hell with you, Sammy," he murmured. "The hell with you."

CHAPTER 2

Louise and Gus had speculated for a long time on just what went on in Tommy Reed's apartment. Gus had read a *Fu Manchu* story when he was a kid and because there was a kind of mystery about the apartment, he conjured up a picture of oriental splendor — golden hangings, satin couches, slant-eyed girls, and a faint odor of opium in the air. But when he told Louise, it all sounded a little silly, and they decided that it wasn't too probable.

Gus's next suggestion was that maybe it was a Ku Klux Klan headquarters. He couldn't rid himself of the idea that they must dress in costume and act out rituals, like Shriners or Masons or something. Otherwise, why was it secret? Why had they never invited the family down for ice cream or root beer some Sunday afternoon?

Louise was the first to see inside the apartment, one hot night in the summer of 1935. She and Frank Davis had driven up the canyon to cool off a little and he had been describing a business trip he'd taken to Pocatello and Idaho Falls. He had told her how many cases of soap he sold in each town he visited and some of the favorable comments his accounts had made about the company's new soap flakes.

Noticing suddenly that she was rather quiet, he said, "Maybe you'd like to stop in at that Barn place. I'm not much of a dancer — but, well, I'll try anything."

"No thanks, Frank. Don't worry about me — I'm enjoying the ride."

"How about a movie? There's always something to see at the movies."

"I don't think so. Isn't it a little hot for that? Besides, I'm just fine."

"Well," Frank said, working hard at the idea. "Let's see." Then he remembered something. "A fellow who eats breakfast down at the Owl — we talk together sometimes. He invited me up to his apartment — told me to drop around any time. If you'd just hold the wheel a minute — "

While Louise guided the car, Frank searched through his wallet until he found a ragged paper napkin with faint pencil markings on it. "Yeah — here it is," he said, straining his eyes. Then he took over the driving and smiled pleasantly. "How about that?"

"I guess so, Frank. If you want to."

Frank Davis was their roomer. He paid twenty dollars a month for Martha's old room and bath in the basement, and in the three months since he arrived, he had always used the back door and behaved like a perfect gentleman. To advertise in the paper for a stranger to come and live in your house had seemed like inviting disaster — particularly if the stranger should turn out to be a man; but after the first night when Frank moved in and they heard his radio turned on to Amos 'n' Andy, they felt he must be all right.

Mother's sickness had come in March and though the doctor assured them it was a heart condition of age and did not mean, if she were careful, immediate danger, it did mean, of course, that Mother could not take care of the house. Louise quit her job, Jack offered to contribute twenty-five dollars a month, and they decided to advertise for a roomer. The power company had begun paying a small dividend, and so, economically, the family came out just about the same as with Louise's salary. They put the house up for sale, but their only offer was eight thousand dollars from a mortician.

Frank Davis was a newcomer to Clark City, only recently trans-
ferred there to sell soap to the intermountain west. He was a solid,
square man with a fine head of brown hair and what Mother called
an honest face. The family liked him because he was quiet and
presentable; as long as it was Frank, a roomer didn't, somehow,
seem such an unmentionable necessity.

From the first moment that Eddie heard of Frank's knocking
on the kitchen door to offer Louise samples of soap, she made a
great thing of what she called Louise's secret passion.

"It's like a movie — or a story in a woman's magazine," Eddie
said. "They can sneak out to the back porch and spoon by the
refrigerator; and he can admire her hands, so lovely because she
washes the dishes with his soap flakes. Mother — you'd better keep
your eyes open."

Louise was not greatly amused by Eddie's little joke and had
no intention of encouraging it. The first three times Frank asked
her out, she refused him; Frank said he was sorry and would she
mind if he tried again sometime. Gus became angry and told
Louise she was letting Eddie run her life for her, and so the
fourth time Frank asked her, she accepted.

Eddie responded. "Oh Louise, you're not *really* going out with
him, are you?"

. "Why not? What's the matter with him?"

"But he's so dreary. He'll talk about soap all evening. And
what will people think — a roomer? Personally, I'd rather stay
home with a good book."

"Well," Gus broke in, "it's a good thing he didn't ask you then.
You find yourself a good book and Louise can go out with Frank."

They had dinner at the City House, that first night, and then
went to the midget auto races. Frank bought her some peanuts,
and beween races, tried to talk to her about library work, which,
he thought, must be very interesting. When that proved a dead
end, he switched to his own work.

"In my line, the fun comes from the problems you have to meet.
Selling's a great game," he mused, cracking a peanut shell. "The
fun of it comes in convincing your buyer that you have a superior,
cleaner-washing soap than the other fellow has. It's the human
equation you're dealing with more than just your product. You

have to handle *people*." He tossed the peanuts into his mouth and chewed thoughtfully.

After that, he asked her out often and whenever he was on the road, he sent picture postcards from Boise or Evanston or Ogden to let her know how business was coming along. When they went out together, it was usually to dinner and a movie. Or dinner and a walk through the park. He frequently asked her to go swimming up the canyon — with a bite of dinner afterwards. Then this night, he took her, in desperation, to Tommy Reed's apartment.

Louise didn't realize until Tommy opened the door that it was Tommy's apartment. Tommy regarded them blankly for a minute, then murmured, "My God."

Frank held out his hand. "Hello, Reed. We just thought we'd drop by. Hope we aren't breaking in on a party."

"Oh hell, no," Tommy said, not taking his eyes off Louise. Suddenly he turned, saw Frank's outstretched hand, shook it vigorously, said, "Come on in."

Several people were in the room — two girls who might have been sisters or twins or the same girl that faulty focusing made appear two instead of one — they had the same pale sweaters that buttoned down the back, the same cheap permanent, the same saddle shoes and string of pearls. A red-faced, strong-jawed man of about forty-five surveyed Louise from a couch, and a dyed redhead of indeterminate age and paunchy body and no clothes beneath the black dress wound a phonograph, blinking from the smoke of the cigarette between her lips.

Tommy wiped his palms on the seat of his pants and said, "Hey, Jack, we got company."

Jack looked through an open doorway, frowned, then beamed with recognition. "Yooweez!" he cried, reached for a towel, stumbled over crashing bottles, cursed, appeared once more with outstretched arms. "Hey, this is wonderful."

"Hello, Jack," Louise said. "I'm sorry — but this is what comes of Frank's talking to strangers in drugstores."

"Sorry? Hell, I'm tickled to death. Tommy, fix these folks a drink — and look, you gotta meet these people."

The girls in the sweaters were named Phyllis and Carol and

they gave her the same smirk, the same mumbled acknowledgment. The man was Joe. He grunted his way off the couch, came over and took possession of her elbow in his damp hand, said with a leer of sophistication, "Hey, Jackie, why don't you move over and let me crawl in?"

"You remember Muriel." Jack indicated the redhead. "Muriel Hooper — great friend of Eddie's."

"Oh yes. I'm sure I do. It's nice to see you again."

Muriel just stared, biting her lip. Then she said, "Oh Christ, what a sweet little thing!" and clasped Louise against her great soft breasts and kissed her. "I've known that little thing since she was a kid," she tried to explain, but had to turn away.

"Here your drinks, fellas." Tommy handed Louise and Frank highballs. "It's all we got. It ain't lemonade, Weezie."

"I'll try to remember, Tommy."

Frank put on his friendly, conversational smile. "Didn't know you were a friend of this Reed fellow," he said to Jack. "We eat breakfast together sometimes. At the Owl."

"Not friend," Jack said. "Acquaintance." He watched Louise as she tasted her drink. He grinned. "God, this is fine. Isn't this fine, Tommy?" He went to her and kissed her. "Look around. What do you think of our place?"

Louise glanced at the jazz-plaster walls and wrought-iron chandelier hanging from the center of the ceiling, at the broken-down couch, the cot with Navaho blanket, the bookcase. Over the cot was a large, unframed reproduction of a painting — a nude stretched on a couch with colored maid and black cat in attendance.

What did she think? This was Gus's den of oriental splendor, his hideout of exotic mysteries. Its odor was not of opium but of human bodies, too warm on a summer night. And Muriel Hooper was its slant-eyed goddess.

"You don't like it," Jack said, "do you?" His smile was gone; petulance succeeded. "You're right — I don't like it either. This is no way for a white man to live." Indignation, now, brought color to his cheeks. "But what can you expect? What happens to standards of living when you've got a socialist — a red — running the country?"

"Now Jack. It could be nice — it needs, well maybe just a woman's touch."

"Come here," he said. "I want you to see this." He led her to the painting of the nude. "Isn't she wonderful? She's mine — I had her in New York. Manet's 'Olympia.' No sense of shame, has she? Thumbing her nose at Victorian prudes. Just a healthy awareness of life's possibilities."

"I'm afraid she's a hussy."

Jack looked at Louise, must have decided she was joking, smiled dreamily at Olympia. "You'd have liked my place in New York, Louise. Did Eddie ever tell you about it? It was really nice. The way a man could live before we came to this — this — Maybe if things get back to normal — if people in this country catch on — "

"But I like it, Jack. Really I do."

Jack gave her a sad smile, squeezed her arm. "You're a very sweet and understanding girl, Weezie. I better have a drink."

Louise watched him stumble toward the kitchen and tried to think what it was she understood. Age was doing a queer thing to Jack, making him want to dwell on his grievances, argue his prejudices. Or maybe it was alcohol. Younger, he would never have admitted that anything could go wrong. Maybe it was Roosevelt.

She felt a breath on her neck and turned quickly to find Joe behind her, studying Olympia over her shoulder.

"I always like a nice picture," he said, with a modest shrug of the shoulders. "I've always been a sucker for art. Not the modern stuff, I don't go for that, but Leonardo da Vinci, Whistler's Mother, both great."

"Oh? Well, I like art too."

Joe put his arm around her waist and gave her a little squeeze. "You know you're all right," he said. He was perspiring and Louise held her glass to her mouth so that she could breathe the odor of cheap whiskey. "You're really all right. There aren't many women you can discuss a good book or a picture with. You know, sometimes you wake up and find some old bag layin' there (know what I mean?) and you think now what'n the Christ am I gonna say to her? If you started talkin' about a good book or a picture, she'd think you was off your nut. No sir. A woman's gotta have more'n a wide rear axle to interest me."

Louise nodded into her whiskey, and said, "Why don't we move over by the window? Doesn't it seem warm to you?"

Joe winked at her — indicating that he knew there was something naughty beneath her suggestion — squeezed her, and as they walked to the window, let his hand slide, casually, downward.

"Oh, books," Louise said brightly, twisting away from him and kneeling to investigate the contents of the bookshelf beneath the window. Copies of *Time, New Republic,* and *Western Stories* were scattered among *An American Tragedy, Sanctuary, Penrod and Sam,* Bartlett's *Quotations, Fanny Hill.* But mostly there were games — Monopoly, Pit, Rook, Pollyanna, stacks of jigsaw puzzles and trick games — rings to pull apart and put together again, skill games to get the silver balls in the right holes.

"You like literature too — as well as art?" Louise asked, looking up at him.

"Do I like literature!" Joe knelt beside her. "Say, did you ever read that book *Green Mansions? There* is a really beautiful book. Such scenery. The author of that *Green Mansions* has a really great gift of description."

Joe began edging closer and Louise was preparing to rise, like football players shifting before the great lunge. But Muriel Hooper stopped the play. "Honey, would you like to go to the little girls' room with me?"

It struck Louise as an odd favor Muriel was conferring, but she accepted gratefully, backing away from Joe.

"Hurry, honey," he said. "I got a lot more things to talk about."

She followed Muriel through the tiny bedroom with its brass bed and ancient dresser. Blankets were pulled up to cover the pillows, soiled underwear had been kicked under the bed. In the mirror frame were many snapshots — different girls, alone, in pairs, or being genially embraced by Tommy or Jack. One girl had been caught with her back to the camera, nude. On the dresser were a hairbrush, men's garters, dirty glasses — gray from time, coffee can which served as ash tray, and *Collected Poems* by T. S. Eliot.

Muriel locked the bathroom door, and then turned in fury. "That crook," she exploded, "that fourflusher! Honestly honey, when he started in that line of his, I just saw red."

"Who? Did Frank — "

"Joe. That crook. He's never read *Green Mansions* in his life.

Just ask him the name of the little girl in the book — that Rima — just ask him and watch him wriggle. The crook used the same line on me, and old trusting Muriel, she fell for it, hook, line, and sinker. Jesus Christ. I even went out and bought the book and read it myself." Muriel looked in the mirror and poked angrily at her red hair. "He's cheap, honey. He's not your type at all, and I just don't like to see you get mixed up with his kind."

Louise couldn't restrain a smile. "Oh Joe's all right, I guess, but he's strenuous. I'm glad you rescued me."

"That's just what I'm saying," Muriel explained, trying to be patient. "All that talk about pretty pictures and that God-damn book, you start thinking, Oh Joe's all right, he's different from the others. Here's an intellectual. And in no time flat, he's got you flat — and I mean on your back."

"Well — I'll try to keep away from him. Thanks for watching out for me."

Muriel's chalk face broke into a misty smile. She spread her hands on Louise's hips. "If you just knew what I think of your family — I guess there isn't anything in the world I wouldn't do for your mother or her kids. Why, when I think about that little Mrs. Gannon and all those kids — Oh Christ!" Tears were pouring down her cheeks and she fumbled in the neck of her dress for a handkerchief that wasn't there.

"Here," Louise handed Muriel hers.

"Thanks honey." Muriel heaved a great sigh, the soft hills and valleys of her body rolling gently with the motion. Under the tight black dress, her navel was like a small dark well in the mound of her belly. "God, I make a mess of mysef." She studied her face in the mirror while she dried her cheeks and returned the handkerchief.

"Shall we go back?"

Muriel was about to unlock the door, then looked around the room. "Oh hell, as long as we're here — " She sauntered over to the toilet and sat down. "How are you and this Frank getting along?"

Now it was Louise's turn to concentrate on the mirror. "Oh, he's just a friend. He's our roomer."

"He seems like a real gentleman." Once more Muriel sighed.

"But I always think they are. By the way, if you ever get in trouble with one of these gentlemen, you know who to come to."

This, Louise supposed, was as intimate as one woman ever could become with another. That it was with Muriel Hooper Louise was sharing this intimacy was cause for laughter as well as despair.

Louise turned to Muriel and tried to smile her acceptance of the guardianship. "I'll remember."

Muriel winked and flushed the toilet.

Louise unlocked the door and was reaching for the handle when Muriel turned her around, pressed her hands against Louise's breasts, kissed her warmly on the mouth. Louise was at the moment only surprised. Muriel opened the door, murmuring, "God, you're a sweet little thing."

Back in the living room, Jack and one of the Carol-Phyllis girls were dancing, a new couple had arrived and were on the couch talking to Joe, while Tommy and the other girl were mixing drinks in the kitchen. Frank stood by the bedroom door, with a full drink, waiting for Louise.

He took her arm and led her over to the bookcase. "Do you want to go?" he whispered. "Maybe I shouldn't have brought you here. I didn't know it was this sort of thing."

"Do you want to go?" she whispered back. "It's very confusing, isn't it." She could feel Muriel's hands like crawling things on her body and she felt surrounded, unclean. But through the whiskey she had been drinking, Frank's face looked much nicer than usual, and she felt very well disposed toward Frank. "Frank, you have an honest face."

Frank grinned a little uncertainly, and took a long gulp of his drink. "I hope you like honest faces," he said.

Frank must have felt a little fuzzy too because it wasn't like him to make a retort clever. "Frank, I do." She took his glass from him and stood it on the bookcase. "Why don't you dance with me? You never have."

And then Frank outdid himself. "You've never asked me," he said, and led her stiffly but adequately to the sad, sweet music.

Love is well worth the waiting for
When it comes knocking at your door —

Over and over again.

"Do you want another drink?" Frank whispered.

"No. That one was plenty — too much."

"It's the heat. You wouldn't feel it if it weren't for the heat. Do you want to go?"

"Yes."

Then Jack took her and gave Carol to Frank. "Carol says you're cute, Frank. Now take it easy there."

"But we're leaving, Jack. We really must."

"Ah no — you can't leave. You just got here. We haven't even talked. Come on, Louise. We gotta talk." Jack seated her on the cot and himself beside her, her hand clasped in his. "This is just so damned nice," he said.

"Jack," Louise said, "tell me about Muriel." Muriel and Joe, on the couch opposite, were quietly, obliviously necking. "I remember her at a Christmas party we had — years ago. I thought she was pretty. I even remember her dress. Orange velvet."

Jack leaned forward to watch Muriel and Joe. "She's pretty horrible now, isn't she?"

"Why didn't she marry? Didn't anyone ask her?"

"Well," Jack said, "I guess no one ever had to. Muriel is a very giving girl. Even when we were kids, in grade school — "

"What?"

"Oh, Muriel's not so bad." Jack took a long swallow of his drink. "She's practically supported Tommy for the last six years. I wouldn't be surprised if he broke down and married her some day, out of sheer gratitude."

It seemed sad to Louise that Tommy might feel under such an obligation to Muriel. Tommy was dancing with one of the high-school girls and he didn't look any older than she. Tommy had ceased to be affected by passage of time. While Muriel had rapidly deteriorated, Tommy had never gone beyond eighteen or twenty. His blond eyebrows were perhaps a little bushier, his hair a little thinner, but he was skinny and wore yellow cords and bow ties and liked trick handshakes and the latest dance records. He was dancing very close to the girl and his hand on her back was underneath the sweater so that you could see a row of her flesh where the sweater was pulled up. Muriel's money might buy something a little more substantial than Tommy, but Tommy's sweetness shouldn't be sacrificed to that great spongy woman.

"How about you, Yooweez?" Jack asked. "You gonna marry the soap king here?"

"Oh, I don't know. Maybe I'll stay single — keep my freedom, like Muriel."

"God forbid," Jack said. "That's no life for you — you oughta marry, have kids. How about Frank? Know anything about his family? Decent people — any money?"

Louise laughed. "How about you? Do you think you'll ever marry?"

"Me? Sure. When the right girl comes along." He leaned against her and spoke in a low voice. "But take Phyllis and Carol here: they're nice enough kids, but I couldn't be serious about them. They're kind of brainless — wouldn't know which side of a baby was *up*. I'd like a more mature woman — at least twenty-five."

"Oh. Mature. And you want a family."

"Of course. I have to have a family. It's up to Gus and me to keep the name alive. Hell, I'm gonna have five sons and name 'em all Jack so it'll just keep going on and on."

"So what will just keep going on and on, Jack?"

Jack drew away, scrutinized her as if she had uttered a sacrilege or a stupidity. "Now look, Louise," he said, being gentle, patient. "We're the upper ten per cent — the people who *should* have children. We'd know how to raise 'em — we'd give 'em the right advantages. But it's the lower classes who have all the children. That's what's wrong with the world today — that's how a man like Roosevelt gets elected. But my five sons'll change all that."

He put his drink on the floor, felt his pockets for cigarettes. Quickly, before he had a chance to explain politics to her, she said, "Jack, why has Eddie never had any children?"

Jack snorted. "You want my honest opinion?" He forgot the cigarette hunt, took up his glass. "What I really think? I think Howard's waiting for the stork."

"Now Jack. But why hasn't she? Do you see Eddie much any more?"

"You wanta know why? I'll tell you. Eddie's scared. Eddie's the most scared person I ever saw in my life. That's why."

"Oh come now. She's the only one of the girls who isn't scared. We're all afraid of Eddie."

"Now wait a minute. You asked me something else." He held his glass against his forehead, closed his eyes in concentration. "I got it. Do I see much of Eddie? No I don't. And that's too bad — for Eddie." He leaned back to watch the effect of his statement on Louise. "I could do a lot for Eddie," he said cannily. "That crowd — they're all hypocrites, all afraid to be what they are. They don't know what it is to be free, real honest-to-God people —"

"Free like Muriel Hooper? Real like Carol and Phyllis?"

She had sat forward and couldn't see his face. When he made no answer, she turned.

"Well, listen to the little missionary," Jack sneered. He was white with anger. "Listen to the little purity league. Just who the hell are you, for Christ's sake, to criticize these people?" His fist was clenched, as if he were restraining himself from slapping her.

"But Jack, you yourself — " Oh, what was the use! She felt anger, frustration swelling in her chest. She stood up. "I'll go."

He grasped her hand. "You're angry! Aw, come on, Weezie, don't be like that!" He pulled her back beside him. "Look, maybe I shouldn't have said that, but I was *surprised* at you, really *disappointed*. The one person in the world I'd expect to be tolerant, to hate sham and hypocrisy is *you*. Gosh, Weezie, I feel as if you've *failed* me."

"I couldn't be more brokenhearted," she said, trying to control her trembling. "Now I must go."

But he wouldn't release her hand. "Now you're mad. What's got into you? I'm really surprised the way you're acting."

She felt an almost overpowering urge to scream, to beat him with her fists.

The phonograph record ended and the whining voice of Tommy's girl said, "My gosh, I'm hot." Louise turned to see her remove her sweater and toss it in the corner.

"Oh Phyllis, you awful," shrieked the other one with Frank.

"What's awful? I've got a bra on. If I was in a bathing suit, I wouldn't have half as much on."

And so Carol, who wore a slip, took off both sweater and skirt, and she presented herself to Frank for the next dance. Frank's arms dropped, his face reddened. "Come on, come on," said the girl.

"Don't pay any attention," Jack said. "They're just a couple of kids. You want a drink?"

"No thanks."

"Sure? You aren't still mad, are you? Look — don't go now. I'll just fix myself one."

Jack went off to the kitchen, followed by Joe. That left Louise and Muriel, facing each other. Louise stood and hurried to the window. She'd had too much and the thought of Muriel's soft, alcoholic lips made her almost nauseated. The night, through the window, looked clean and fresh. Escapist though she might be, she longed to run away from these honest-to-God real people, into the hypocrisy of the night.

The music ended, and in the moment it took Carol to lift the phonograph needle from the record, Frank escaped to Louise. "If you don't mind, I think we better be off. I'd like to get an early start tomorrow."

"Don't let him kid you, honey," Muriel called from the couch. "That's a chiseler's excuse if I ever heard one. He'll be back for that little chippy."

Frank's jaw tightened. "Look," he muttered, "this is my business." He held out his hand. "Come on, Louise."

Outraged, Muriel tried to push herself up. "Who do you think you're talking to, for Christ's sake? I'll mind any business — "

Her voice brought Joe and Jack from the kitchen. Joe came over and gave her a hard slap on the cheek. Muriel looked around in surprise, then crumpled on the couch, sobbing.

"Come on, Louise." Frank grabbed her arm.

"She'll be all right," Jack said. "Don't give it a thought. Gee, it was swell of you kids to drop in. Come any time. We're always here."

As they left, Joe and Carol were cuddled on the couch — talking art or good books, no doubt; the new couple, whom Louise had not met, were stretched on the cot in the dinette playing Pollyanna; Tommy and Phyllis had disappeared into the bedroom; Muriel, weeping brokenly was bent over on the cot.

"Thanks Jack," Louise said. "We had a lovely time."

Outside, on the pavement before the apartment house, Louise stopped suddenly. "Do you mind if we just stand here a minute — and breathe?" She leaned her head back, stretched her arms to the sky. "Why must reality be so smoky?"

"Good idea," Frank said, unbuttoning his jacket. "Pretty warm in there."

"Warm and — Ah, Frank," she said, "I think soap's a lovely business to be in."

"It's interesting, all right. Particularly my end of it, the selling end."

She looked at him, a little deflated, and he gave her a warm friendly smile. "Maybe we should go now," she said.

In the car, she leaned limp against the cushion, allowed herself to feel as drained as she was. It was all so sordid, but Jack was right, who was she to criticize. But after all, Jack himself — and she was all tangled up again. Remembering Muriel's startled expression before her face collapsed in tears, Louise could forget the repulsiveness and realize only the tragic waste. "Do you suppose she knew?"

"What's that?" Frank said.

"Muriel — when he slapped her — I wonder if she saw herself, at that moment, as she really is."

"It's hard to say." Frank puzzled over the question. "But chances are, I think, that by morning, she'll have forgotten it all."

"Oh Frank — " He was as bad as Jack. She pushed her hand through her hair — Or was there something wrong with her? "Is that what your human equation makes of this?"

Frank smiled. "I haven't a lot of use for sympathy, Louise. That may sound hard to you, but I haven't found that sympathy accomplishes very much in the world. That woman — Muriel, she doesn't need sympathy. She needs a doctor and a psychiatrist."

"Well — I'm sure that's a very lofty attitude to take," she said indignantly, "but we're not all capable of such objectivity. You should be a scientist, Frank. Selling's not worthy of you."

He snickered. "I guess I had that coming to me. I talk too much." Then serious: "My point is, I guess, that we save our sympathy for where it's needed. That crowd tonight, they all feel so sorry for themselves they don't need *our* sympathy." He rubbed his cheek, watched her sideways. "I don't mean to run this into the ground. It's just that — well, my father was an alcoholic. Sure it was sad. But what he did to my mother was a lot sadder."

Louise cringed with shame. Dear God, why wouldn't she learn. Jack was perfectly right — she was a hollow little shell. She mumbled, "I'm sorry."

"Hey, now, don't say that. I just don't express myself very well. Since high school, when I debated, I've always tended to sound pompous. I have to work on that."

"Ah Frank," she smiled. "Don't work on that. We have need of people like you — to put people like me in their place."

"Now see what you're doing? You're pretending to be at fault, but you're actually criticizing me. No man is a match for any woman."

Louise laughed. Like the product he sold, Frank had a cleansing effect. "Are you really leaving town tomorrow?"

"Yup. I'm going to Evanston — have to get an early start." His brow creased with interest. "You know, that Wyoming country is very fascinating in its way — some great old characters I do business with. Have you ever seen it?"

"No Frank. I never have."

"I've often thought if I could write, there are some great stories around there — you run into them every day. I'd like to take you along some time — you'd know what to do with that material."

"I would? I can just barely write my name."

And Frank told her about an old coot who had been a miner, a trapper, an Alaska pioneer, and now he ran a little store — and you'd be amazed at the size of the orders he put in.

He drew up in front of the house. (Then he would park the car in the back and go down the back stairway to his basement room.) He walked her up the steps to the porch, swinging her hand in his. "Well, Louise, thanks a lot. As always, I'm indebted to you."

It seemed a strange comment on the evening and she laughed. One had to learn how to take Frank. "Can you really say that — tonight?"

"Oh sure. There's no one you can't learn something from. I had a very interesting time."

"The human equation."

"Now don't needle me." He gripped her hand. "Good night, Louise."

He had never tried to kiss her — he was waiting, she knew, for her sign. As the family had discovered, Frank was a gentleman. But what kind of a sign does one make to a gentleman?

"Good night, Frank." She shook his hand, and as he departed, she leaned against the screen to watch him. "Oh Frank —" She stopped him at the bottom of the steps. "Will you send me a post-card from Evanston — let me know how things are going?"

He hesitated, almost as if he would return. "Sure thing. And Louise," he added, "I'll be back in a couple of days."

CHAPTER 3

During the summer of 1935, Ted Webster's father-in-law found some kind of accounting job and Ted took Gus on as regular help at the gas station. It was about time, too. The old man wasn't much good any more, and Gus figured he'd worked long enough on a kid's salary. Ted paid Gus just what he'd paid his father-in-law, and he got about four times as much work for the money.

The summer went pretty fast, because it followed a routine of work with nothing special to interrupt it. On a free night, Gus generally went to a show with Bud Sawyer or out for a coke or sometimes they just walked along Center Street to see what was up and maybe whistle at a high-school girl. If his mother felt like it, he sometimes took her for a ride after dinner although she said it was tempting fate to drive a car before he was sixteen. They'd drive along Center Street to see the lights in the stores or through the residential districts to see if anyone was building a new house. Or sometimes up the canyon to feel the cool air flowing down between the mountains and hear the dark hidden gurgling of the river. Those canyon rides were the one thing that made the job turn a little sour. Boy, he'd think, to be free again and take a sleeping bag and some fishing tackle far up the river where the pines began, and spend about a week just forgetting everything he ever thought about before.

"Bud," he'd say, "how about lying under the stars in a sleeping bag — just you and the mountains and the stars? And get up in the morning and wash your face in the river and make coffee over a wood fire. How about that?"

"That's okay," Bud would say. "But why be alone in that sleeping bag? Why not have Ginger Rogers or Claudette Colbert?"

"Okay," Gus would say. "Ginger Rogers for you, Claudette Colbert for me."

That was a line they had. Actually, they'd have run a mile from Ginger Rogers or Claudette Colbert in a sleeping bag — or even from Shirley Kimball, whom they'd known in the ninth grade at school. They weren't so much at girls, neither he nor Bud, and that summer they hardly got near a girl. And so they developed this line of talk to sort of bolster each other up.

In the fall, they started in at Clark High, green and scared. First day of school, Bud dropped by, all dressed up the way he thought a guy in high school ought to dress — baggy pants, loud sweater, and a hat with a turned-back brim. He looked so funny that Gus had to laugh. Bud still hadn't grown much and there wasn't a hair on his rosy face. It released the tension a little to be able to laugh at Bud, but when they arrived before the massive portals of Clark City High, Gus began to wonder whether he wasn't making a bad mistake to be seen with a character like Bud.

"Hey Bud," he whispered, "can't you ditch that hat?" Gus himself was flawlessly dressed in cords and sweat shirt. Also, Gus was almost six feet tall and had to shave twice a month.

"What'll I do with it?" Bud squeaked. He was a little pale.

"Take it to the principal's office and tell him you found it. Give it to the lost and found."

Bud removed the hat and held it before him as if it were a dead rat. When he returned from the principal's office, they both relaxed some and set out in search of their home room advisors.

High school, after you were used to it, wasn't too much different from junior high, only more of it. You went to classes and in nice weather you sat out on the lawn to eat your lunch and you beefed about teachers and speculated about girls. Some things were different. Like ROTC. Like the guys all smoking cigarettes at John's Coke Shoppe. Like the stories some of the guys related in the lockers or showers.

The main thing that was different about classes was that suddenly you were given a little choice in what you studied, as if you cared about it or knew what you wanted to be. Gus just sort of automatically drifted toward sciences. He'd be a doctor, he guessed. It wasn't that he was so crazy about sciences, but it just made sense to him to take sciences. If you were going to have to earn a living, languages and literature were useless. But sciences — even during the worst of the depression, they said, a good scientist could find a job. The literature was all right if you had time for it. *As You Like It* and *Tale of Two Cities,* he got a big kick out of, and the memory passage from *Macbeth* he practiced before a mirror: "Is this a dagger which I see before me, [clutching his comb] The handle toward my hand?" He'd always found a certain amount of pleasure in reading; he and Louise used to read together, *Treasure Island, Swiss Family Robinson,* even the Oz books. But the way the world was shaping up today, there wasn't time for that sort of thing, and particularly the way his own life was shaping up, there wasn't time.

Gus was no whiz — like Jack and Eddie and Louise; he just managed to maintain a pretty steady B average. He liked sports all right but wasn't good enough to make the teams and he wasn't the type to run for offices and he sure wouldn't ever win a popularity contest. Sam went around with all the big shots — he was a big shot himself in a social way, but Gus was going to be one of those on the outside and as a matter of fact, it didn't occur to him to want to be anything else.

Now that Gus was in high school and had grown a few inches, he and Sam were friends again. They weren't in the same crowd and so it was a distant kind of friendship — as if they were good friends who lived in different cities. But every so often Sam would stop by the gas station to smoke a cigarette and shoot the breeze.

"How's the oil business?" he'd say. Their line was that Gus was the owner of this corner lot which was covered with oil wells.

"Only fifteen hundred barrels so far," Gus would say. "Wells must be clogged."

"Christ, Gannon," Sam would say, "what I can't understand is how a guy with all your dough can dress like such a slob."

This wasn't a slur on Gus's clothes but an invitation for Gus to comment on Sam's. Maybe it was a red bow tie or some two-toned shoes or a big sheep's-wool coat. For one short period, it had been spats. Gus would look him over carefully and shake his head sadly. "Guess I just don't have what it takes."

That always pleased Sam, made him very happy. He'd reach for his cigarettes. "Smoke?" he'd offer.

"No thanks."

And then Sam would blow up. "What? You mean you still don't know how to smoke? For Christ's sake, Gannon, when are you going to grow up? Here — take one."

One day Sam made the mistake of adding, "It'll put hair on your chest." But Sam only made that mistake once, because Gus came back with the obvious reply, "It hasn't on yours." And this was a sore spot with Sam. The fine pink hairs on Sam's chest would hardly be visible even with a microscope. For several weeks, Sam had shaved his chest every day trying to stimulate the growth, but it remained as pink and hairless as a baby's. And so the day this came up about hair on the chest, Sam became un-happy and didn't stay very long.

But usually he'd switch from cigarettes to women.

"How's your sex life?" he'd say.

You could make any answer to that, it didn't matter which. "Thriving — " "So-so — " "Don't have time for much else — " The question was purely rhetorical and sometimes Sam didn't even wait for an answer.

"Boy," he'd say, "what a hot little number I was out with last Saturday." (They were always hot or smooth or both.) "Jeez, she couldn't keep her hands off me — honest to God. I never saw such a hungry woman. Honest to God."

Sam always protested overmuch when discussing his love ex-periences, because he was fully aware of Gus's scepticism. Some-times he'd stop in the middle of his narration and say, "God damn you, Gannon. You don't believe a word I'm saying."

"Sure I do. Sure, Sam."

"And you still think I'm a virgin!"

"Oh hell no, Sam. How could I think that?"

"Now look," Sam would plead with him, "by all that's holy, I tell you I've had it. And not once but twice. I'll tell you her name — go in and telephone her. She'll prove it."

"I believe you, Sam. You were eight when it happened, weren't you, Sam?"

When Sam drove off to call for one of those smooth numbers, Gus would try to keep busy because he didn't like to sit and think about what Sam had said. Sam was a great bull artist, but Gus believed most of it anyway, because certainly necking was common practice and plenty of guys by the time they were seniors had tried the real thing. But just sitting around thinking about it tightened you up inside until you felt as if you'd burst and finally you'd have to step outside and walk around a little until you got rid of the idea.

The amount of time a guy of his age devoted to thinking about sex seemed to Gus way out of proportion to what he gave to the other processes of life: there wasn't an hour, hardly a minute that somewhere in the back of your mind some tickling little idea wasn't carrying on and everything you saw or heard could be twisted into a meaning that would start the blood pounding through you. If people could see what went on in other people's minds — just during an ordinary conversation! — boy, oh boy!

One thing that worried Gus about all this was his attitude toward the girls he knew — girls at school. When some of the fellows talked about this or that sexy little number, Gus always agreed, put on the same easy leer the rest of them had, but personally, he couldn't see it. The women of his mental orgies — and oh God, his dreams — were fat-thighed honky-tonk sirens out of a western movie. Janet Folger, who was considered quite a number, was to Gus just the homely little girl who in the second grade wet her pants one day when the teacher wouldn't let her go to the lavatory. Sure, he agreed, she was built, but he just couldn't forget that day in the second grade. He just couldn't see how certain girls who were, without breasts, such a pain in the neck, were suddenly, with breasts, such hot stuff.

From the day when Sammy, then ten or eleven, first explained the facts of life to him, Gus had regarded sex from a distance as something strangers might engage in but not anyone he knew. When Sammy provided indisputable evidence of his own parents' guilt, evidence gleaned from eavesdropping and searching through his father's drawers, Gus was merely confirmed in his opinion that Sammy was something of a worm, which was only to be expected if Sam's father was that kind of a man.

His own birth, Gus's instincts told him, was not so much a miracle of God's intervention as of his mother's overpowering will to reproduce. In her he saw none of the cold delicacy of the Virgin Mother, shrouded in pale blue, but the warm fertility of self-conceived, self-imposed gestation. Dad, in his mind, was not a man at all, in the way other men were men, but a dark separate figure presiding at the table, bent over his desk. And what did they do when they were in bed together? They made plans for these children Mother had created and they worried together over the ones who were out late.

That took care of Mother, and as he grew older, he never saw the necessity of accepting any other explanation. But there was Louise and a feeling he couldn't understand at all — perhaps a kind of jealousy, though that seemed a little ridiculous. He wanted to see Louise go out with men, he wanted her to be the most popular girl in town. But as she and Frank fell into the rut of two or three nights a week, Gus began to feel cool toward Frank and uncomfortable around Louise. One night when he saw Frank kissing Louise, Gus went to bed, wretchedly betrayed. Frank was taking her from him and Gus felt friendless and alone.

But Gus was not friendless and scarcely ever alone. Maintaining almost constant riot in his brain were the honky-tonk girls, wide-bottomed, full-breasted, with delicious white skin. They were certainly not the sort of girls you could introduce to the family and their behavior sometimes made Gus burn with embarrassment and desire. One of them, a floozy blonde with slightly drooping buttocks and pouting lips, seemed to hang around the gas station a lot. Gus liked to be busy the whole time because that seemed to be the only method of keeping her away.

All in his mind. He was a great guy in his mind — nothing could stop him. But put him face to face with any of the girls at school and watch him clam up like a stupe. Put him on a dance floor and watch him get red in the face if a girl's body touched his. He talked big with the boys, he listened to Sam as if Sam's experiences were his own, but when Sam drove off, Gus would start thinking and worrying and if business was slow, Gus would just about go nuts.

His mother would say: "Gus, why don't you ask some nice girl to a picture show sometime? And don't they have dances at school any more? You and Buddy are getting to be a pair of old bachelors."

Like nature and the vacuum, Mother, he knew, abhorred a bachelor. If there was a bachelor around, it meant some nice girl was missing what God had created her for and Mother didn't like to see that kind of waste.

Well, he tried it once. He asked a girl to go to the Founders' Day picnic in the spring of that first year. Buddy asked three different girls and they all said they were busy — Buddy was still kind of short; so Gus arranged to go along with Sam and Buddy went gloomily to a movie.

Gus's date was Shirley Kimball. She had been in his grade at the Lincoln School and the ninth-grade boys figured she was hot stuff because she developed prematurely and wore lipstick. Also, she had entered the Lincoln School when she was in the eighth grade and so the boys had none of the unfortunate memories of her which deglamorized the girls they had known since kindergarten. Shirley Kimball appeared to them, brand new, with full-blown indications of her womanhood, and all the guys in the eighth grade had stiff necks from gawking.

The picnic was at a camp ground way up the canyon and started at five in the afternoon. The ride up wasn't too bad because they could talk about the classes they were taking and reminisce about Lincoln. Sam's girl was a vivacious little brunette, vice-president of the student body, and she was easy to talk to because she was the kind of girl who made a point of knowing everyone in the school. She had had many offices.

Shirley Kimball, through the eyes of his high-school sophistication, didn't seem quite the menace that the Lincoln boys had considered her. She still had a figure you might turn around to look at but sort of thick ankles and faded blond hair that looked as if it could stand a shampoo. But she talked quite a lot and didn't seem to mind what an oaf he was.

The picnic was okay, better than he'd expected, and he felt glad about coming because a lot of people were friendly and old Miss Kirkham said she could tell he was a Gannon because of his marvelous brown eyes, which he didn't mind too much. They played a little softball, ate hot dogs, pop, and ice cream, sang "Old Black Joe" and "I've Been Working on the Railroad" and such around the fire.

Shirley would say: "Oh golly, it's a wonderful night"; or, "Oh golly, I'm making a pig of myself"; or, "Oh golly, I love to sing around the fire." There wasn't much you could say to any of that, so Gus would put a stupid grin on his face and sing twice as loud to cover up the fact that he wasn't much of a conversationalist.

Then the ride down. He might have known it would be that way with old Sam driving, but he kind of had the idea girls didn't like to neck in front of other girls — reputation and that sort of thing. Well, he was wrong. As Sam drove down the canyon, Sam's girl wasn't exactly in his lap, but his driving might have been safer if she had been. It was funny to see a student-body officer caring so little about public opinion.

Gus, personally, sat as far from Shirley Kimball as he could and told her some interesting facts from astronomy — light-years and such. Shirley had clammed up though and let him do all the talking; she didn't seem to be much interested in facts about the stars.

Finally, halfway down, Sam slowed the car, pulled off the road to a stop under a clump of trees.

"Hey, what's the matter?" Gus asked nervously. "Anything wrong? You want me to take a look? You've got a first-rate mechanic back here."

Sam snickered. "What a joker," he said. "He makes me promise ahead of time that I'll find a cozy spot to park and then pretends the car's busted. What a jerk."

"Oh, Arthur!" Shirley Kimball said, and that "Oh Arthur" meant that Gus was a cooked goose.

"You better call me Gus," he said huskily, out of the quaking depths of his inwards.

"Call him Uncle," Sam muttered and from the warm darkness of the front seat came the purring laughter of the vice-president of the student body.

Shirley Kimball slid over close to him and lifted her lips to his ear. "Uncle," she whispered, and then twirled her tongue in his ear.

Gus wasn't so scared after that.

All wrapped up there with Shirley Kimball, he found that the time went pretty fast. She liked to have him kiss her and didn't seem to mind too much about his hands. What was astronomy to this, he wondered. What was an astral body a million light-years away compared to one Shirley Kimball in the back seat of a car? And when Sam showed signs of restlessness in the front seat, Gus heard himself saying, "What's the rush? Where's the fire?"

At three A.M., Gus stood with Shirley Kimball on the front porch of her house and with wonderful passion, kissed her good night. "I hope you don't think I do this with all the boys," Shirley murmured plaintively. "Oh gosh no," Gus protested. "I wouldn't think a thing like *that!*"

As a matter of fact, he hadn't thought much of anything. The only ideas which had crossed his mind were that it was sure easy once you got the hang of it, and that a girl should always shampoo her hair before she went out with a fellow.

Sauntering back to the waiting car, Gus had the feeling that here was the beginning of a new era. He was one of the boys, now, an initiate, one of the club. With intoxicating worldliness, he wiped the lipstick from his mouth, a little flamboyantly so that Sam and his sleepy girl would not fail to observe the gesture. As of tonight girls would cease to be girls: they would be henceforth *women*.

But it didn't work out exactly that way. By the time Sam had got rid of his girl, he and Gus were too sleepy to brag very much. And waking up in the morning, Gus realized that the red-lipped handkerchief, his ensign of victory, must be destroyed. His mother's eyes followed him even when she wasn't in the room, and Louise, he knew with terrible certainty, was as fully acquainted with the events of the evening as if she had been there.

"Did you have a good time?" she asked — with a little too much brightness, too much innocence.

"Not bad," he growled.

"How was Shirley?" she pressed him.

"Not bad — if you like that type."

Louise grinned and for a moment he hated her and her God-damn sense of humor.

"How do *you* like that type?" she heckled him.

Gus shoved food into his mouth and didn't answer.

"Did you ask her for another date?" she badgered him.

Gus wiped his mouth on his napkin, rose from the table. "No," he grunted, and stalked out of the room.

It wasn't shame or regret — but they made it so God-damn embarrassing for a guy. Like the shaving. Like his voice changing. Oh hell.

And so when he asked Shirley Kimball to go out with him, he tried to keep it secret and somehow the kissing wasn't so much fun if it couldn't be public to let the world know what a great guy he was. And he was still scared to death of all the girls at Clark High *except* Shirley Kimball and in their terrifying presences, he shut up like a stupe.

The secret dates with Shirley continued at long intervals for about a year and when he finally gave up calling her, it was not from dissatisfaction with the kind of evening she gave him. As a matter of fact, he had come to depend on Shirley and he was grateful to her for delivering him from the saloon girls. But he could not escape the idea that Shirley must be a secret from the family. His identification of sex with a real living person had not made sex acceptable; it had merely, with cunning perverseness, made the real person unacceptable. And then Jack, not Shirley, put an end to Gus's pursuit of the double life.

Jack had been away one weekend, a fact of no consequence because he so often stayed at Tommy's. At noon on Monday, Gus had come home for lunch (creamed tuna fish on toast, he remembered, and the October sun casting shadows on the ragged curtains of the breakfast room; the cold clear October day and Louise stirring the creamed tuna fish in the double boiler and his mother sitting at the table in her bathrobe, waiting). While they were eating, the front door opened and slammed shut and Jack's voice called "Mother" and it seemed to Gus as if time had slipped out of groove and the voice calling from the hall belonged to the twenty-year-old boy with his motorcycle parked in the gutter. But it was the 1937 Jack who appeared, his fleshy face beaming with excitement and the thin strands of black hair blown awry by the October wind.

He had someone with him — a woman with a great deal of long, knotted hair, bleached the color of butter. She was, as they were all to assure each other, handsome, but in a way that would make Clark City inhabitants squirm with discomfort. There was more of her than Clark City would consider quite proper, voluptuous, Police Gazette proportions that her handsomely tailored suit did nothing to conceal. And her face was made up in a way that would set Clark City to mumbling, "Hollywood."

Gus glanced quickly at his mother and Louise, and half stood with a clumsy push at his chair. Mother's hand clutched at the neck of her bathrobe, and she gave Jack the lighted smile that seemed reserved for him. "Well, this is a surprise," she said. "Where have you come from?"

Jack stooped to touch her cheek with a kiss. Then he kissed her neck. "Honeymoon, Mother, we've been on our honeymoon."

Gus looked instantly at his mother to catch the quiver of change, but there was none — only the same smile, frozen in an uncertainty of words.

"But —" Louise said after a slight pause, "you haven't introduced us."

Jack wound his fingers around the soft arm of the blond woman. "This is Frances," he said, letting his eyes take her in. "She's beautiful, isn't she." He kissed her lips.

Gus and Louise exchanged a quick glance.

With soft moaning laughter, Frances pushed Jack away and reached out a manicured hand toward Mother. "I don't think we have to be introduced," she said. "Jack told me I'd feel like you were my own mother. He was right."

Mother looked at the red nails of Frances's hand and at the knotted knuckles of her own. Without taking Frances's hand, she reached up and kissed her cheek. "I hope you'll feel that way," she whispered.

"And this here's Yooweez — she's our little sweetheart," Jack said, "and that squirt there is Gus."

Louise hesitated and then held out her hand; blushing fiercely, Gus rubbed his hand on his trouser leg and held it out.

"This is so damned wonderful," Frances said. "I never had a family — and I'm the person who would have liked one."

"Well, you'll sure have enough family now," Gus muttered, and when Frances flashed him a big smile, wondered why he never learned to keep his trap shut.

"Are you a Clark City girl?" Mother asked, leaning forward, clasping her hands tight in her lap.

"Pittsburgh. Pittsburgh P-a. And if you've never been there, I wouldn't let it worry me. I'm going to like it here. I've been on the road for Lady Juliet Cosmetics — selling, demonstrating. Last Wednesday was the first time I've ever checked in at Clark City."

"What you might call a whirlwind romance," Louise said with a terribly friendly smile — as if she thought whirlwind romances were the only thing. "In town one day, married the next."

"Oh, not really such a whirlwind." Frances reached for Jack's hand. "We'd known each other five whole days before we were married. Five wonderful days."

Gus was about to say, well how could you have been on a honeymoon then, when some blessed angel shut him up. Oh my God! They must have been married just that morning. He was going to take a vow of silence. Oh my God!

And it was funny — while Gus and Louise and Mother were playing a desperate game of let's-not-look-at-each-other, neither Jack nor Frances were aware of anything, just chewing each other up with their eyes.

Mother came back quickest, probably from long training with situations. "Have you had something to eat?" she asked eagerly. "Louise — isn't there some tuna fish? We could fix a salad."

"It'll just take a minute — " Louise muttered.

"What I'd really like — " Frances stretched and set in motion the whole upper half of her body, "what I'd really like is a bath. God, I need a bath."

"But of course you would," Mother said. "Why didn't we think? Here, I'll show you — "

Jack reached out his hand. "I'll show her, Mother. It'll be a pleasure."

"Louise will fix you a bite to eat," Mother said. "Whenever you're ready — "

The idea of Jack's escorting Frances to her bath filled Gus with strange, warm excitement and mixed in with the idea was the image of Frances's full moving breasts and the conviction that somewhere he had seen her before. He was lost in this warm comfortable dream and ignoring utterly the creamed tuna fish on toast — Jack taking this perfectly strange woman into the bathroom and here they were, pretending it was all perfectly ordinary.

He looked at his mother, called back to the October noon by the silence. She was not eating either. With one arthritic hand, she was rubbing the misshapen joints of the other, and when he looked at her face, he saw that she was embarrassed, shy, and he remembered where it was he had seen Frances before. She was the blond honky-tonk girl who tormented him at the gas station — the same ripe flesh that he had clutched at so many times, the same straw hair that he had tasted in his teeth. Mother tried to smile, but it was a sad attempt. And Gus was filled with self-disgust that shot through his brain and clouded his eyes. Jack was no worse than he — they both groveled in the same dirt. And there was Shirley. He and Jack were just alike.

He couldn't stand it another minute, all of them trying to think of something to say, avoiding each other's eyes. He should have forseen this and found some way to protect her from it. None of them, except Mother, had ever been fooled by Jack; they were all dedicated, really, to her bright belief — it was part of the structure of their lives, one of the things that made them a family. And here they sat, wanting someone to say something that would actualize Jack's marriage, lay it away as established fact. He couldn't stand it.

Gus rose abruptly from the table.

"Your lunch, Gus," Mother said, and he knew that already she had accepted Frances and was defending Jack. "You haven't finished."

"I'm not hungry," Gus mumbled. He left the house.

And he didn't call Shirley Kimball after that. He worked two or three nights a week and what with studies, he didn't have too much free time. Sometimes he and Bud Sawyer would take in a show or drop by for a coke at John's. But neither he nor Bud was much at girls.

Senior year was like the rest of them — the gas station, studies, and on weekends when he wasn't working, skiing up Clark City Canyon, at a place called Snow Valley, which looked like his idea of Switzerland or the Tyrol, and which, according to all the Clark City people who had been abroad, was really much finer than either. In March of that year, Hitler moved into Austria, but Eddie, who had traveled in Europe during the summer of '37, said that there was not too much cause for worry because communism was the real danger, and much as she hated Hitler, you had to admit that the Austrians *did* speak the German language and that Vienna *was* in the hands of the Jews. Eddie said that if anyone in Clark City had the imagination or sense to build a Tyrolean village at Snow Valley, why nothing in Europe could touch it.

The real worry that year was disposal of the house. The time was past when you could be sentimental about it, and though Jack wandered quietly through the big rooms feeling sad and bitter about the end of an era, neither Roosevelt nor the WPA could be wholly blamed for the fact that there was no one in the family who could or would take the responsibility of the place. Louise seemed every year to have become smaller, more contained — she would be a little pinched woman like Grama Gannon. At night, when the dishes were done, she and Frank would sit on the front porch making plans, probably, for a future that seemed never to arrive. Louise had given up wearing cosmetics; she wore her hair in a tight little bun on her neck. And Mother wept at night over the terrible thing she was doing to Louise.

But no one wanted a big old house — and why should they, Eddie asked, when it would take a small fortune to make the place habitable. Mr. Mason, the mortician, dropped by, looked lovingly at the oak paneling, at the rooms that could be closed off with sliding doors or opened into one vast assembly hall, offered ten thousand dollars — cash. Two months later, in March, he returned with a yardstick, measured the rose room and had a plumber in to give an estimate on some changes in the basement, measured the garage for length and width, and stood outside in the gray slush, pinching his lips. Then he came in, removing his rubbers first, and in Dad's library, gazing possessively at Dad's books, at the plaster bust of Ben Franklin and the tinted photograph of Mother, he made his final offer of twelve thousand dollars. It would take time — a day or two, Louise told him, to get the consent of the others. But there was really no question.

Mr. Mason wanted to take over on June first, and since he was, in a manner of speaking, a friend of the family (he had taken care of Dad's funeral and his father had taken care of Grandfather Gannon's) Louise looked around until she found a two-bedroom brick bungalow with finished basement, renting at forty-five a month. The final move took place the last days of May — the year of Gus's graduation from Clark City High. All mixed up with moving was the whole business of commencement. Commencement, they called it: a beginning rather than an end. Well, maybe it was.

And moving, too, they kept telling each other, was the beginning of a life that would be easier for all of them — easier and therefore better. It would make a new woman of Mother, they said, and now Louise could marry Frank and Gus could go to college. From twenty rooms to five (plus finished basement) would make all the difference in the world.

Then how explain the choking, physical agony that accompanied the joyous occasion? Why must re-birth be so painful? As Gus dismantled Dad's library, packing books in cartons, the empty dust-lined shelves gaped in unnatural nakedness, and Gus finally had to remove Grandfather Gannon's scowling portrait from over the mantel and place it face-against the wall. No invader of a tomb, no desecrator of a temple or destroyer of ancient beauty was ever more nostalgic for the object of his lust or more aware of the frowning disapproval of the deities. Grandfather, Ben Franklin, the rows of stiff-collared men at the factory, Mother with egrets and bird of paradise — wrapping them in newspaper, packing them in cartons, Gus knew the emptiness, the mechanical motion of the man who has rejected God.

And the books themselves — Gus was helpless before them. Among the unread, calf-bound sets, were the fingered, underlined volumes that Dad had studied, bent over a desk in a dark memory of Gus's childhood. *Every Man A King, Work and Win, Man: Master of his Fate, A Business Man's Religion,* and the limp-leather editions of Elbert Hubbard. Gus opened *Health and Wealth*: "I hold these truths to be self-evident . . . That happiness is only attainable through useful effort . . . That the possession of wealth can never make a man exempt from useful manual labor." Gus read the underlined words and Dad's note beside them — "Show Jack." What do you do with such a thing? No one wanted it any more, the five-room house had little space for books, and yet you don't make trash of another man's Bibles. He held the book and then replaced it on the shelf. Let someone else decide.

The afternoon before the trucks were to arrive, Flo and Eddie were to come down and after four, Jack and Frances, to help with the packing and decide about the distribution of goods. The house was beginning to appear stripped — the furniture in the bare rooms looked uncomfortably out of place, the love seats and plush chairs were, after more than thirty years, uprooted and looked, Gus thought, kind of expectant and scared — like mice in cages waiting to see what you'll do with them. Gus himself was so damned tired that he was drained of emotion and maybe a little out of his head. Crouching, waiting animals he saw.

But not so Flo. When she arrived, she could see things for what they were and watching her eyes fill with tears, Gus felt for a moment the old queasy, clutching emptiness. He rubbed his arm across his sweaty forehead. "Wanna buy some old junk? We got plenty."

Flo gave him a halfhearted snicker, a halfhearted smile. "Ah, to be young. You can say that."

She pretended to be joking but she wasn't and it struck him as very odd that she should think he didn't know what it was all about. And Flo ceased to be pathetic and he felt all tired again and Flo looked like a woman's-club president, lost in a big museum. "The exhibits are straight ahead and to your right," he said.

Flo didn't know what he was talking about and his mind did a queer act of dissociation: Flo was this lost matron, no more his sister, part of the family, than the plush love seats were part of the rose room. Confused, suspicious because he was younger and spoke a different language, she stood helpless, a moment, and waiting like the mice. Then she said, "How's Mother?"

"The doc says she better be quiet. She's pretending this is all a party. She'll be glad to see you. She says it's nice to have the family all together."

Flo bit her lip and looked away. The mention of Mother brought everything back: Flo was his sister and Sam's mother and though she was looking sort of old, you could tell she had once been pretty. Gus rubbed his hands on the seat of his jeans. "I better get to work."

Flo went upstairs to see Mother (the doctor had said not more than one or two in her room at a time — better not excite her) and Gus wandered back to the dining room to help Louise and Eddie pack dishes.

"Was that Flo?" Eddie asked.

"Yeah." She knew it was Flo but Eddie was tense and precise and always made conversation when the others were too relaxed or too tired to bother. She could wrap two or three dishes to every one of Louise's and manage to look cool and well-groomed at the same time. She was a good-looking girl, all right, and Gus was always proud to say she was his sister, because she hadn't let herself go the way some do, and she drove big cars and gave the idea that no one else was quite so good as she. Her black hair had quite a lot of gray in it now and there was a tense look about her face but anyone would take her for years younger than poor old Louise. Of course Eddie had never had any children and Howard and his old man had never exactly starved for lack of dough.

"Yeah — that was Flo," Gus said. "How the cartons holding out?"

"Plenty of cartons," Eddie said, "but, oh Gus, a glass of water."

Louise stopped her work, looked at Eddie. Gus said, "Sure. How about you, Yooweez?"

"I'll get some later," Louise answered. She added, "Gus is, of course, the one who should be waited on. He's been working like a dog."

"You know, it really is silly for us to be doing this," Eddie said. "Professional packers could do it better — quicker."

"Sure," said Gus, "but Louise and I are the only professional packers I know who do it for free. I'll get that water."

Jack arrived by way of the back door, carrying two pies with thick meringue tops. "Fran turned out these confections. She'll be down later with the rest of the dinner. How's Mother?"

"She has to take it quiet," Gus said. "That's pretty darned nice of Fran. We thought we might just open some cans."

Jack set the pies on the kitchen table, looked around the room. "Well, this at least looks the same. If Martha were here, it'd look normal. You pretty pooped?"

"Sort of. It's funny you saying that about Martha. I can hardly remember her."

"You're young," Jack said quietly. "This, of course, can't mean so much to you. Let's go and see Mother."

In the downstairs hall, Jack stopped before the grandfather clock, stared for what seemed a long time at the gold and silver face, at the ornate jerking hands. "When I was a kid," he said, "the sun and moon used to change automatically every twelve hours or some such thing. I must ask Mother what has gone wrong."

Mother was propped up in bed, wearing a pale satin bed jacket and a touch of rouge on her cheeks. "Ah — my two boys." She held out her hands to them. "This is nice."

Jack stooped to kiss her. "Prettiest darned gal I ever saw. How do you do it? The rest of us grow old but never you."

She patted his sleeve in a flurry of gratitude. "My Jack."

Flo heaved herself from her chair. "I'm ashamed of myself. I'm letting the others do all the work."

"No cause for alarm," Gus said. "There's plenty left."

"Don't hurry off," Mother said. "It's been so long since I've had you all together. Sit down — " she motioned with her hand — "let's have a nice little visit."

Flo caught Gus's look. "I'll be back. I've been lazy — lazy."

"This room — " Jack sat on the bed, pressing Mother's hand between his — "it hasn't changed — it's like you, Mother — 'but thy eternal summer shall not fade — ' How have we others failed? What's the matter with us?"

"Hey Ma," Gus said, "you oughta see the progress we're making. Slick as a whistle. Pretty soon we — "

But she didn't want to be distracted. "I think I have the finest bunch of children in the whole world. I'm proud of you."

"You and Dad," Jack went on, "was there ever anything quite like you? You never forgot there's a thing called the good life — you never forgot self-respect. The *supreme* importance of self-respect. We others — I'm afraid we drift. Money — somehow it seems so important nowadays." He paused, looked around the room. "Those old draperies — the taffeta would crumble to dust if you touched them."

"Times have changed," Mother said. "Things are different now.

No one in Clark City has a finer family than mine — people *tell* me so."

"Times haven't changed, my sweet pretty Harriet. It's people who have changed — we've lost sight of beauty and poetry."

Oh my God, Gus thought. "Well, I don't care about all that," he said desperately. My God, they'd both be in tears in a minute. "More important than that, Fran is cooking dinner for us. You oughta see the pies she sent down."

"If people come from nice homes," Mother floundered, "isn't that the main thing? It's women with jobs — how can they make a good home?"

Jack patted her hand and kissed her as if she were a sweet child. "What happened to the clock, Mother? The sun and moon used to change by some special kind of magic — "

"Maybe a spring broke," Gus said.

"At certain hours," Jack ignored him, "the heavens would revolve, the chimes would strike, and the morning stars sang together. Where will you put the clock in the new house — the little brick bungalow?"

Mother's deep eyes met his, troubled, surprised. "Would you like to have it? Would you like it, Jack? Grampa Gannon gave it to Papa and me for our first anniversary. He sent all the way to Philadelphia for it."

Jack kissed her neck. "I'd love to have it, Mother."

"Well. How about a little rest now?" Gus rubbed his hands together. "Gosh — this is like Grand Central Station — drive a guy nuts. Come on, Jack."

"You run along — I'll stay here with Mother for a while. We've much to talk over, we two."

Gus wanted to take a poke at Jack — he and Mother would be bawling in a few minutes and Mother'd be sick for a couple of weeks after. But sicker, maybe, if Gus said anything. So Gus turned and had to content himself with, "This isn't a party, you know. There're a couple of things to be done." Walking down the stairs, he could hear Jack purr, "Gus is such a kid — he doesn't grasp the full significance." And Mother excused Gus by saying how hard he'd worked.

In the downstairs hall, Gus came upon a peculiar thing. Piled up in the hall was all the junk they were disposing of, stuff to give to the Salvation Army or the Ladies Aid at church: the old phonograph records and rolls for the player piano, outdated text-books and piles of clothes, vases won at bridge parties, baskets from Dad's funeral, old toys and boxing gloves and ancient enema equipment. Puffing over this assortment, selecting certain items for a separate pile, was Flo's pudgy, red-haired husband, Grant. Red of face and sweating with exertion, he stopped only momentarily to glance at Gus, and then, without explanation, returned to his labors.

"Need some help there, Grant?" Gus inquired.

Grant, his eyes unswerving, spoke with hostility. "These darned fool women would give away the roof over your head if you'd let them." In Grant's little pile, salvaged from female improvidence, were a stack of old *National Geographics,* an antique, broken electric heater, some discarded galoshes that had belonged to Louise, and a single massive candlestick from which gilt had been chipped to reveal the plaster beneath. "It wouldn't hurt any of them to have to earn some of the money that paid for this stuff."

"Yeah, Grant, I guess you're right," Gus said and escaped into the dining room where Louise and Eddie were still at work. He motioned with his thumb toward the hall and they both nodded.

"We had a *scene,*" Eddie whispered, delighted.

"Where's Flo?" Gus returned the whisper.

"She's working at the kitchen shelves — in dignified silence."

"Well," Gus said, in normal voice, slouching against the built-in china cabinet, "we've disposed of the clock. Jack has consented to take it. In the old days, he says, it used to sing as well as chime. But I'm too young to grasp all that."

Louise smiled. "Your real trouble, Gus, is that you haven't an artist's soul. Youth you might recover from" — she brushed hair from her eyes — "we all do. But I've noticed a certain insensitivity in you — "

"Personally," Gus interrupted, "I think Roosevelt's to blame. It's neither youth nor insensitivity but Roosevelt that's to blame."

"Is that true about the clock, Gus?" Eddie asked, her voice taut. She was not playing their game. "Did Mother really say he could have it?"

"Sure," Gus said, looking at her curiously.

For a moment there was silence. Louise and Gus watched Eddie, who knew she was being watched and her white face showed nothing.

"You hadn't thought you might consent to take it, had you, Eddie?" Louise asked.

Eddie laughed, formally, graciously. "It's hardly that. But where will he put it? He hasn't the right house for it — it isn't for Jack's scale of living."

"But it is for yours," Louise said.

"Well, as a matter of fact, I think it is. But that isn't the real point. I see no reason why Frances should have Mother's beautiful things. She's — well, you know what she is."

"You figure Howard would appreciate Mother's beautiful things more than Frances would," Gus said. "Is that it, Eddie?"

"As a matter of fact, I do," she cried angrily. "Howard's family is so far above ours — he's had things that make all of you look like — like shanty Irish."

"Yeah," Gus mused. "I always figured they were lovely people. I wonder what happened to that secretary Howard's mother stabbed?"

"What other things, Eddie, had you thought might fit in with your standard of living?" Louise asked. "There's the grand piano — there's the coffee service and Mother's bedroom set — "

"Well, why shouldn't I have them?" Eddie screamed. "I have as much right to them as you have. You make me sick, Louise, whining around, a nasty little martyr, as if you owned the whole house."

"What else, Eddie?" Louise asked. "We mustn't overlook anything. There's Mother flat silver, there's the rose-room furniture — or is that below your standard of living? There's the Rosenthal —"

Eddie had a Rosenthal cup in her hand. She stood up, smashed the cup to the floor. "Stop that!" she screamed. "Stop it, stop it, stop it." Then she sank sobbing to her chair. "You've always hated me — both of you," she choked. "You've never let me be part of the family — you've turned Mother against me — "

Flo rushed in from the kitchen, Grant slouched in from the hall. "What's the matter?" Flo asked.

No one said anything. Gus and Louise turned to look at Flo. Eddie wept, a small, uncontrolled figure in black.

By eleven o'clock, people were in bed, people had gone home and until morning, when the vans arrived, all operations had ceased. Frances, enormously pregnant, had padded around in bedroom slippers and slacks, feeding them hugely and well; Eddie had called Howard to pick her up, departed before Frances arrived; Grant had piled his treasures in the back of his car and come back for more. During dinner, Jack recalled the past, evoked Dad and Babe for them, grew misty-eyed over Christmases past; and afterwards, when Gus went for her tray, Mother in the darkening room had held his hand quietly. But by eleven o'clock, it was all over and Gus was on the street, walking through the dark spring night.

It was a kind of quest he was on, a giant hunger had drawn him out, a hunger for who knows what or where. He was young, they said — and, how right they were, he didn't understand. Sweaty, unshaven and tired, he knew only what he was escaping — the dissolution, the divergence and decay. But where to turn? Out of the mother group had been spawned the separate little fighting units, all whirling away to spawn more little fighting units. And Gus was left behind, alone in the tidewater, too young to understand.

Perhaps it was true, what Eddie had said — that they had always hated her. Surely something had happened to him and to Louise (to Louise, whom one would have thought incapable of inflicting pain) that they would bait another human being until they broke her down. The image of Eddie stripped and flayed was a haunting, sickening soreness in his mind. He turned cringing from it. But where could he turn — to what, to whom?

Down the streets of the quiet town he walked, through the darkly shimmering park, past the courthouse, past Harkington's and the Golden Rule and the City House Hotel. But these monuments to the Pioneer Spirit, to Industry and Enterprise and the American Way, had nothing to say to him. The night, full of silence and sound, full of whispered promise, had nothing to say to him. The sky washed with stars, close, intimate, had nothing to say.

Moving from a large house to a small house was supposed to solve every problem. But Mother was still bedridden and who but Louise to care for her, who but Gus to help with the expenses.

"I'm a poor, broken-down old wreck of a woman," Mother would say with a mournful smile. "Turning to stone," she would say, and at night, after dinner, in the dusk of her bedroom, she would hold out her arms to Louise and Gus, "It's wicked — I don't know why things had to turn out so badly for you."

"Now none of that, Mother," Louise would answer her. "Just be glad of the chance to live like a lady."

"Hey look, Ma," Gus would say, "if you think you can get any sympathy out of Louise and me, you got another think coming. If you want sympathy, you've come to the wrong couple of guys."

As summer passed into fall, it became clear that not yet could Louise think of marriage, not yet could Gus leave for school. Frank came by every evening, said a few words to Mother, and sat in the living room with Louise until eleven-thirty. Some nights they played Monopoly, and when Frank got the idea they should be improving themselves, they read *David Copperfield* to each other, aloud. He sent flowers to Mother and brought Whitman's

Samplers to Louise and Mother would cry and say it was wicked what she was doing to poor Frank.

Gus thought about trying to find some better kind of job, but full time at the gas station paid about as well as anything for a kid just out of high school — and then there was the waiting. They all talked about college as if somehow, within a few weeks, he could make it — this was temporary, he would shortly be off to college, Louise would marry, Mother would be well. It was merely a matter of waiting.

And so, on the surface of things, life found its new routine and the restlessness beneath boiled along at a quiet pace without too much danger of eruption. They joked about the little house, about stumbling over each other, and Mother recalled the day when their antiquated old Pierce Arrow was the most dashing car in Clark City. "I could have named every family in the town who owned a car. It's different now, I guess."

Working shifts at the gas station, sitting home with Mother — and sometimes, at night, when Mother was tired, shuffling through the leaves of the deserted sidewalks — the crisp nights, the smell of wood fires. At John's, he'd have a coke and watch the younger kids. Put a nickel in the juke box. Downtown, he'd have a malt at Fisher's and look at pictures outside movie houses. All the crowd he knew was off at State or Boulder or Utah or Stanford. Funny how empty the town seemed — no one except his friends had left it.

The best time of all was when he was sitting in Mother's bedroom, slouched on the foot of the bed, talking or dozing in the rocking chair. Then there was no question about the waiting, the restlessness was gone, everything was justified. They talked over many things — most of it familiar — the same phrases, even repeated. Of Papa's courtship and Eddie's successes in high school, of Clark City when it was a frontier town and Miss Kirkham's prophecies for Jack's future.

"People have always thought I had an easy time of it," she would complain. "Even Papa, I believe, thought I had it pretty slick. But Grama Gannon, who was a hard-working little peasant woman from the old country, used to say it was a miracle how I could keep you children looking so neat — and better dressed than anyone in the whole town. And she used to say there wasn't a better housekeeper in the state." She would purse her lips and frown off into space over this, then brightening, she would describe the dresses she had made for Flo and Eddie, the dancing costumes for Louise. "People thought I had sent to San Francisco for them — they didn't *dream* that I could do such a thing myself. No one thought I ever turned a hand."

She talked as if she were starved for talk, as if all her life she had been refused a hearer. And Gus listened quietly, sometimes hearing, sometimes with his mind on other things. Through the rich fabric ran the question, the doubt, and then the answer. Burning within her, forcing the talk, was the need for justification; trapped in her stiffening body, she tried to convince herself of her past utility.

"But you're a *nice gal*, Mama," Gus said over and over again, "and we love you dearly. I don't care if the house had been a pigpen. It was awful nice having you in it."

But she wouldn't get the point at all and would try to convince him that he could never be happy in a house that was a pigpen. "I hope you get a girl who's a good housekeeper, Gus. You couldn't be happy with any other kind."

And she recalled every word that Papa had ever said which would indicate that she had been a good wife. "All the heaven I ever want, he used to say, all the heaven I ever want is you and these kiddies. I don't believe I ever gave him cause to be ashamed — either of his house or of his family. No matter what it cost me in time and effort, I always had things looking right — so that he could be proud."

"Has it ever occurred to you, Ma, that maybe he was in love with you?" Gus asked. "And maybe he loved us too?"

But she didn't listen very carefully. "He didn't half guess the work I went to — but, well — I believe he had everything he wanted in this world. I believe he did."

And there was Babe. Gus tried to keep her off Babe because she usually ended in tears, but there was no holding it back. "I've prayed," she said, "I've prayed night after night for some kind of guidance. It's the tragedy of my life to have failed her. Maybe if I hadn't had her teeth straightened — braces on the teeth can do awful things to girls at certain ages. A girl brought up in the kind of family she was, with the brothers and sisters and nice home —

Maybe I didn't invite enough boys around. She was shy with boys — "

"Maybe we hadn't ought to worry about Babe, Mother. She's probably the happiest one of the lot. She's rich, anyway."

"Maybe if I'd taken her to a specialist — perhaps it was her glands — she developed awfully young — "

Gus wrote Babe a card explaining about Mother's condition, but they never heard from her.

Mother seemed shy when it came to discussing Gus himself. The past she could talk over endlessly — what a dear little boy he had been — but she seemed reluctant to learn too much about the present or future. His plans to study medicine she said were a fine thing, but she had little curiosity and Gus's enthusiasm was hard to sustain. She had ceased inquiring about his life away from her and appeared absent-minded when he told her anything that happened at the gas station. She worried only that he didn't know any girls — he was eighteen and not too young to start thinking about settling down. She wanted to know what all his friends were doing, but did not, somehow, wish to cross over into his own life. And perhaps that was all for the best. The long hours with her passed in hazy, impersonal tranquility — drugged hours of utter peace.

Her bedroom, during that autumn, became for all of them the bourn to which all travelers returned. The cleavage between cell and cell was almost complete, but to the central nucleus they all clung. They slouched on the bed, in the rocking chair, on the dressing-table bench — and talked and talked and talked.

That autumn, Flo's Connie started going with a boy whom Flo considered quite pathological and Flo, haggard and red-eyed, brought the daily installments to Mother.

"He hardly even speaks to me — and he treats Grant like the scum of the earth. Last night when I told them to come home early, he just turned and without a word, slammed the door in my face."

"She's probably told him how you feel about him," Mother said.

"Oh, I've no doubt of it. They plot behind my back and she sneaks out to meet him. Connie and I haven't spoken to each other for three days now — and I've had such terrible gas that I'm afraid I'm getting ulcers."

"Well — that's how it goes," Mother said. "They're going to choose their own friends. Mine all did."

"Oh heavens, Mother, you never had anything like this. Connie has no sense of responsibility — she won't listen to a thing I say. She acts as if I'm her worst enemy. It's the war scare — it's affecting the entire younger population."

"You think I don't know about all this? You think my children all had a sense of responsibility?" (Gus would hear about this later.)

"I've given my whole life to that child." Flo's mouth trembled. "It doesn't make you feel very good to find they don't care a hang about you — "

Later, when Eddie heard that day's report, she would repeat that Connie's boy friend was not half so pathological as Flo herself. "Flo's marriage has obviously been a complete failure — no woman could find any satisfaction with that man. And so she has poured all her love into her children, tying them to herself, making it impossible for either of them to make an emotional adjustment to life."

"Oh, come on now, Eddie," Gus grinned. "It's not so bad as all that. I don't know about Connie, but Sam's making out okay. I wouldn't say he's tied to his mother."

"You wouldn't say it because — well, I won't say it either."

"Go ahead. What's on your mind?"

"Well, just because you're tied to Mother the same way. Any number of my friends have spoken about it — it's clearly an Oedipus complex."

"Oh for Christ's sake."

Even Mother bridled. "Why don't you tell your friends to mind their own business?" She reached out a protective hand toward Gus. Eddie smiled coolly — their response had proved that she was right. "I've been watching it for a long time. I was interested to see whether you'd be able to break away and leave for college. Obviously you couldn't. You can't accept adult responsibilities."

Gus wanted to yell at her — why didn't she open her purse and help Mother a little? how would she like to pay his tuition. But with Mother there, he could say nothing.

"So that's it," he tried to keep his voice steady. "And how do you explain the fact that Louise has never married?"

"Oh Louise," she said victoriously, "poor Louise is just a frustrated old maid. She's repressed all natural outlets and you can see what it's done to her. Dreary as Frank is, it'd be better for her to marry him than go on *this* way. But I seriously doubt that she ever will marry now — she'd be unwilling to accept sexual responsibility."

The only answer to that was a four-letter word which he couldn't say because Mother was already confused and shocked. But Gus had cooled down somewhat. "Say Eddie," he spoke with mock seriousness, "you been spending some afternoons in the public library? Sounds like you been reading that guy Freud."

"No — I haven't *read* him. I've read reviews, of course. One doesn't have to have *read* Freud to understand what he was talking about."

All that talk bothered Gus because it forced him to think, and Clark City's theory was that you weren't supposed to think until you were well along in college and not even then if you went in for fraternities. Thinking made you old before your time and somehow there was something un-American in that.

Well, he was forced to ask himself, was he tied to his mother or was he not? The answer was obviously yes — and so was Eddie tied to Mother and so was he tied to Eddie and so on and so forth — and up till now, that fact had struck them all as rather agreeable, but as of now, it was evil. And did his being tied to his mother "frustrate" and "inhibit" him? Perhaps — certainly it affected his behavior. In the lack of a very definite moral code, Gus could gauge right and wrong according to the effect certain actions had upon his mother and the family group: anything that hurt his mother was wrong, anything that contributed to her well-being was right. It was wrong for Babe to leave home, it was wrong for Jack to fall so short of expectations, it was wrong for Eddie to say Gus had an Oedipus complex. It was right, on the other hand, for Louise to be valedictorian at high school, for Eddie to be the smartest-looking woman in Clark City, for Frances to cook them a good dinner on moving day. It was right for Gus to marry and have many children, but it was wrong for Gus to have any definite knowledge of how the children were to be created. Staying out of college to work must be right; repeating to Eddie the obvious reason *why* he stayed out of college was clearly wrong. If he were not tied to his mother, perhaps none of these distinctions would exist and he might now be in college raising hell with the rest of them. As to whether or not he'd be able to make "an emotional adjustment to life," he couldn't exactly say. But sometimes, thinking about Jack and the girls, it seemed to him that he'd probably do as well as they.

His mother and the family, it occurred to Gus, served the same function as Sunday school must have in the days when people went to Sunday school, or perhaps as various kinds of patriotism when people were patriotic. And maybe that function was a bad one, but where were you without it? You were supposed to be a social animal living in society, but no one followed the rules of any society — or maybe the rules were so conflicting, you got lost in the maze.

For instance: Eddie came storming into Mother one day about a strike at Clark City's flour mills. "Those organizers should all be arrested and transported to Russia," she exclaimed.

"Maybe the men weren't getting enough to eat, Eddie," Gus suggested. It sounded so obvious that he felt a little silly mentioning it.

"Well, let them get other jobs," she said indignantly. "No one's forcing them to work for the flour mill. Those picketers ought to be arrested — it's just the same as stealing to try to prevent a man from doing business in his own flour mill on his own property. Let them go someplace else if they don't like it."

"Maybe there's no place else to go," he said tentatively. "Maybe they can't get other jobs."

"That's nonsense. If they can't, it's their own fault."

"What about the depression?" Mother asked. Actually, she was probably on Eddie's side but certain memories were fresh in her mind. "I knew some fine men who lost their jobs — poor Mr. Olson — "

"No *good* men were without work," Eddie asserted. "That was all Roosevelt propaganda. Howard has statistics to *prove* that plenty of companies were in need of the right kind of men during the depression. There are never enough *good* men for the jobs."

Gus whistled at that. He was not the one to question Howard's statistics, but memories were fresh in his mind too. "What do you mean by *good* men? The sons of bank presidents?"

This angered Eddie. "You talk like a communist yourself, Gus. There should be a thorough investigation of our school systems — and I know plenty of important people who are going to see to it — to weed out radicalism. What I mean by a good man is a man with ambition and initiative. If he has those qualities, he can *be* a bank president — no matter whose son he is."

Oh my gosh — he hadn't heard that old line for a long time, but here it was, in its same old clothes, passing for as good as new. And Eddie — not yet forty — was tagging along beside it. "Maybe times have changed since you were a girl, Eddie — that opportunity business. Maybe it isn't so important that everyone gets to be a bank president as that everyone gets fed. How about that?"

"It isn't times that have changed, Gus, it isn't the times. It's merely the thinking of impractical schoolteachers and irresponsible youngsters that have changed. And now the situation is growing dangerous — time is running out. If the world's to be saved, our class must assert itself — we must take the control away from the radicals."

"What do you mean by 'our class,' Eddie? I'm a working man, you know — day laborer."

"If you don't know what I mean," she said earnestly and in all seriousness, "if you've forgotten, why that's the most tragic thing that can have happened to you."

Gus felt embarrassed, as if he'd been scolded for saying something shocking or crass. Mother looked worried — thinking, probably, not that he could really be serious but that Clark High was doubtless in foreign pay. He girded himself for one more try. "All I'm saying, I guess, is that a man has a right to eat, and if his employer doesn't give him enough, he ought to be able to do something about it."

"I'd be the first to agree," Eddie cried, exasperated. "What he can do about it is quit and get a *better* job — where he'll have a chance to grow and make something of himself."

So where were you? He and Eddie were following different rules, that was all, and it occurred to him that the greatest problem that could face a kid of his age and time, the only problem, maybe, was the discovery of rules, or the choice of rules — if choice were offered you.

He mentioned that to Eddie one tense afternoon, while radios were waiting, waiting to speak the news of a flight to Munich. "What do you do?" he pleaded. "Sure, war's awful — I don't want to go to war. But if you make pacts, if you make agreements, you stick by them. And you don't stand by while a big guy beats up on a little guy. My gosh, you've got to believe in something."

"Well, yes, you do," Eddie said, "but you've got to understand things too. If you'd traveled — particularly in Germany — you'd realize that things aren't so simple as you're trying to make them. As much as I hate Hitler, when you realize that historically his movement was a protest against radicalism of the worst kind, then you must recognize that in a way, we're on the same side."

"Speak for yourself, baby," Gus shouted, then patted Mother's hand to keep her calm. "I ain't on his side."

Mother told him to be more careful of his language and Eddie said she wouldn't even talk to him if he was going to become excited. "You're childish, Gus, and there's no discussing with you at all. Of course he's done some terrible things, but sometimes it's necessary to do terrible things in the interest of a greater good."

She had him there. She was right that he was young and he couldn't discuss things. Again it was a question of the rules. Which did you choose? For the time being, he'd stick by his own oversimplification that one person can't go around saying he's better than everyone else and go bashing everyone's head in. "Well," he mumbled, "just count me out."

"*There* is a typical American argument — you simply withdraw from the facts. If you'd ever *been* there — "

"I know," Gus said, out of patience again, "tell us about Old Heidelberg — "

And so the fall wore on — Flo getting ulcers over Connie's pathological boy friend, Eddie talking more and more about "our class." As Mother lay crippled in her bed, they talked away the days, the weeks. The same restlessness had them all, but it twisted them about in different ways. During the waiting, life went on, of course. Frances gave birth to a fine boy the end of August; by November, she was announcing her new pregnancy.

When Thanksgiving came, Flo said she wished they could all come to her house — but that was obviously impossible. Frances phoned that she was going to cook them a turkey, but Louise said no. Louise stuffed a chicken, invited Frank to dinner. They prepared a nice tray for Mother; Louise and Frank and Gus had a silent dinner in the dining room.

And then Christmas lay ahead — something they all dreaded, a day they'd have liked to pass by in sleep. There seemed no longer any reason for Christmas — that's how they all felt — all, except, of course, Mother. Thanksgiving was hardly over before she began making plans. The whole family must come — the children, the grandchildren, the in-laws. But Mother, there isn't room — where will we put them all? It would be fun, she said, all of them together in that little house — more fun, really, than in the old rambling mountain of a house. It was terrible work for Louise, she knew, but this one favor — she'd never ask another —

Louise and Gus stood by the bed, hearing her talk, listening to the plans, unable to say anything or look at each other because the same thought was in both their minds. And somewhere, the same thought was in Mother's mind, although she hadn't yet recognized it.

Louise phoned the family. Flo was delighted but poor old Louise — what a lot of work! Flo would do the nut and date pudding.

Eddie hesitated. "Are the others coming?"

"Flo's crowd is. I haven't talked to Frances."

"Well, I guess we can make it."

"Don't put yourself out, Eddie — "

"No — it's all right. We'll be there."

Frances gave a joyous exclamation. "Oh God, how wonderful! I was so damned scared we wouldn't have Christmas together this year and it just wouldn't be Christmas without the family. What can I bring?"

"Nothing Frances — just Jack number three and Jack number four."

"Oh, the boys'd come whether I did or not. But I can cook the turkey. You won't believe it, Louise, but I honest to God can. I cooked one for us on Thanksgiving and it was edible, Louise, I swear it was."

Frank appreciated the invitation — "But Louise, I'd like very much to do something for your family. I wonder if they would all have dinner with me at the City House."

"Oh Frank — we couldn't."

"I'm sorry, Louise, I forgot. And anyway, they'd rather have a home-cooked meal, I guess."

Gus went about the business of Christmas shopping without much lightness of heart. Clark City was all decked out, as usual, and loudspeakers blasted carols from street corners and Salvation Army Santa Clauses shivered in the snow. Crowds cussed each other squeezing into elevators, the same old after shave lotions decked every counter, the same old eau de cologne and flower-shaped soap.

And what to buy, for God's sake? What for Mother? The only thing she needed was new hands, a whole new set of joints, new arteries, a new heart. And for Louise, ten years of life to live over again — ten shining years smelling of Elizabeth Arden and Germaine Monteil. Flo could use a new husband and Eddie some hormone magic. For Jack, some kind of gut injection. He wandered along the streets, through the stores. And in a book department he found what he wanted. Three new books of cartoons had appeared for Christmas trade. He bought all three for Mother, one each, assorted selection, for the others. He'd make them laugh, by God. He'd make them laugh till their bellies ached.

Gus bought a tree although they had decided not to bother with one this year. He carried it into the kitchen one night while Louise was cooking dinner. "They had these damned things at the gas station," he apologized. "I don't know where we'll put it."

"Oh, it's a lovely one." Louise dried her hands on her apron. "We'll find a place."

They moved the couch and put one chair in the dining room. The dark scrubby tree in a corner of the dimly lit living room was about as cheerful as a February day, and he mumbled about the asses who cut down perfectly good trees for some outworn foolishness.

"A few lights will help it out," Louise assured him. "We'll decorate it tonight."

But Gus ate his hamburger patties and baked potato in gloomy dejection, bitter about the tree and himself, and after he had dried the dishes, he wandered into Mother's room, sat in the rocking chair with his eyes closed.

"Tired, dear?" she asked gently.

"Yeah — I guess I am, sort of."

"You mustn't let yourself get tired," she said, her voice as soothing as the soft light of the little lamp on her night table. "Working outside so much, you mustn't allow your resistance to fall."

When Frank came, Louise called Gus to come help with the tree, but he muttered that he was going to bed. "Gotta keep my resistance up," he said. He stood by his mother's bed, gazing at her small thin face while she clutched at two of his fingers. He drew a long breath. "You put up a good fight, Ma." He smiled wryly. Then he bent to kiss her forehead. "Good night, Ma."

The day before Christmas, Gus had to work till five. Five o'clock was as dark as night and as cold, by gosh, as the twenty-fourth of December. But try as he would, he couldn't feel sour. He strode through the snow feeling like a kid and blew out steam pretending it was cigarette smoke. Hell, it was Christmas.

Frank's car was there already, and through the window of the ridiculous little house, he could see the tree lights and a grate fire. Gus stood on the porch stamping his feet. "We three kings of orient are — "

Louise threw open the door. "It's Santa Claus," she cried over her shoulder. She drew Gus's head down and kissed him. "Merry Christmas and welcome."

"Hey Frank," Gus said. "Who's this Santa Claus guy? Louise two-timing you?"

It wasn't the sort of question Frank would have an answer for so he merely grinned and sipped from the cup he held.

"You two boozing again?" Gus asked, sniffing.

"We have some for you," Louise said. "It's Tom and Jerry. We're having a party and you're our guests. Frank, our guests have arrived."

Frank set his drink down and went to the kitchen to fix a drink for Gus. Louise swept across the room and stood before the fire. She had on her best dress — the little black velvet dress with the lace collar, and she had let her hair down and tied a ribbon in it. She swayed from her hips, smiling. "Merry Christmas, Gus."

He watched her. Gosh, it had been a long time — She — He smiled at her. "Merry Christmas, Louise."

He took off his rubbers and coat. "How's Mother?"

"Oh fine but she's been perfectly terrible — I had to call the doctor to give her a sedative. She's been calling out to me every two minutes all day."

"Hell, Louise, it's Christmas."

Frank appeared with the drink. "Here you are, Gus."

"Ah — to our guests," Louise cried. "On this rare Christmas Eve occasion, may I give you — our guests."

"To me!" Gus sipped his drink. "Mm. The wassail."

"What's a wassail, Gus? Frank, what's a wassail?"

"It's a small animal, isn't it, Frank?"

"Quite small. We used to hunt wassail in Wyoming."

"I want a wassail coat for Christmas." Louise sat on the couch, on her knees, like a child. "I shall be good every day of the year if only I may have a wassail coat."

"What do you want for Christmas, Frank?"

"Me? I want Louise." He sipped his drink. "Wassail coat or no wassail coat."

"Say," Gus said, slapping his thigh at the idea. "Why don't you two get married?"

"He's never asked me," Louise said. Then she held out her finger with the ring on it which Frank had given her three years before. "Look — isn't it sweet?"

"Enough — cut out the sentiment. What else happened today besides Ma's ants?"

"Oh wonderful news, Gus," Louise drained her glass. "Eddie isn't coming tomorrow."

"Oh?" He couldn't tell whether she was joking. "How come?"

"She phoned that Howard couldn't endure Frances and so they had decided they wouldn't come. They're spending Christmas with Howard's father and friends whom they can endure."

"Oh."

"Frank, I want some more of the lovely wassail — and look at our guests — you're neglecting them."

"Does Mother know?"

"Yes."

"How about some wassail?" Frank asked. "Straight from Wyoming."

"Sure. I'll go have a look at Ma for a minute."

She was lying with her eyes closed in the dimly lit room, breathing evenly as if in sleep. He watched her for a moment and she opened her eyes.

"Gus," she said weakly. "I'm glad you're here — I've been trying to keep awake. That awful Louise — she had them drug me — "

"Well, Ma, if you're not going to behave, what can we do? We just gotta give you a micky." He kissed her.

"I have terrible children." She patted his hand. "Terrible — terrible — "

"And now you're just trying to keep awake to spite us. How about that?"

"Close the door, Gus." She drew a deep breath and rubbed her eyes. "In the drawer — bring me the boxes and paper."

There were five small boxes and a roll of silver paper and some pink ribbon.

"Where'd you get all this stuff? What's been going on here?"

"Never mind — just do as I say. And bring me another pillow."

He propped her up — she'd lost enough weight so that he could have carried her all over the house. "Now what tomfoolery are you up to?"

"Help me wrap these, Gus. That Louise," she moaned, "she had them drug me before my presents were wrapped. She's been just terrible to me all day."

Gus unrolled the silver paper and cut a piece the size of one of the boxes. He started to wrap it, but Mother took the box and with her stiff fingers tried to wrap it herself. Gus couldn't watch — he turned away to cut more paper. Then he heard a whimpering, broken sobs and he turned to see the tears on her cheeks. "I can't do it, Gus," she wept. "I can't do it."

In a kind of panic, he took her in his arms, rocked her back and forth as if she were a baby. "Of course you can, of course you can. It's the drug, Mother — you could do it fine without the drug. It's all Louise's fault, Mother. You could do it fine, fine — "
He kissed the tears from her cheeks and held her. Then he laid her back on the pillow. "I'll do 'em — they won't look as good as yours but — well, you know what they say — it's the sediment — it's the sediment that — You're okay, aren't you, Mother?"

Without opening her eyes, she patted his hand.

He wrapped the boxes, making clumsy bows with the pink ribbon — talking talking — "This pink sure is pretty — I get kind of tired of red and green — that's all you see is red and green — maybe some blue — but not near enough pink — " Talking like a fool, a desperate stream of nonsense.

"Gus," she interrupted him. "Did they tell you about Eddie?"

"Eddie?" He didn't know what to say. "Eddie? Oh sure. Hey Ma, look at this for a professional job."

"Would you mind, Gus — would you mind taking her box tonight? I want her to have it on Christmas."

"Mind? Heck no. I kind of like to walk through the snow at night. It's very beautiful at night — "

Gus wrote the cards — only the name of each child. The boxes had been piled in order, oldest to youngest.

"We must send Babe's," she murmured. "Maybe Mrs. Miller knows where."

"Sure, Ma, we'll find out. Don't give it a thought."

The boxes were wrapped and placed in a row on the dresser.

"That's the business, Ma. And now you better go to sleep." He arranged the pillows and waited for her to open her eyes. But finally he turned off the light. "Good night, Mother — and Merry Christmas."

He made his way to the bathroom and locked the door. In the darkness he wept.

Christmas morning, by five o'clock, Gus was awake. Vague excitement kept his muscles tight, and broke through the cloudiness of mind whenever he hovered on a doze; and yet he was reluctant to have the day begin. A play was to be acted out with no stage or setting, without anyone's knowing his lines, with only a dream memory to pull the strings of action. Excitement out of the past was keeping him awake and then the past was deserting him.

Thinking of the day ahead took his mind off himself and he must have dozed, because when next he looked at his watch, it was quarter to seven. He got up and padded into the furnace room to stir up the fire. He stretched and yawned. Might as well dress — shave later, just before the crowd came for dinner. He gazed through the midget basement window at the gray snow still locked in night.

He climbed the stairs softly and went out the kitchen door, around to the front for the paper. A hell of a morning, cold and dreary, with no tracks of Santa's reindeer in the week-old snow. Back to the kitchen, he turned on the light, put coffee on the stove. WESTERN REPUBLICS SIGN ALLIANCE TO PRESERVE SECURITY, said the headline of the newspaper. And a merry Christmas to you, Gus muttered. DICTATORS' POLICIES ASSAILED BY POPE. FDR PLEDGES SELF TO WORK FOR PEACE. "President Roosevelt promised the world in a Christmas eve message tonight that he would do everything in his power to hasten the day when war shall be no more. The chief executive, who will spend Christmas day with four generations of Roosevelts, spoke at a brilliant tree-lighting — "

Louise appeared through the swinging door from the dining room. She was in her bathrobe, yawning and rubbing her eyes. "The smell of the coffee woke me. What time is it?"

"Getting on seven-thirty."

"It isn't snowing, is it?"

"Nope."

"What a pity."

She sat at the kitchen table opposite him. Why didn't she say it? What were they waiting for? She cupped her chin in her hand and tried to read the paper upside down. "Anything in the paper?" she asked.

"Quite a lot. Is Mother awake?"

"I don't know. Probably. I'll go take a look. I hope we can keep her quiet today — we must."

Not until Louise had started out of the kitchen did she bring it out. "By the way — merry Christmas."

"Thanks. Same to you."

Mother was very much awake and he could hear her excited voice talking to Louise. It made him smile. He stood up and went to her room. "Hey, it's the middle of the night," he said from the doorway. "Why don't we all go back to bed."

"Oh lands," Mother said. "I've been awake since five o'clock. I couldn't go back to sleep. Gus, come here."

He went to her and kissed her. "Merry Christmas, Ma."

"Merry Christmas, darling. I hope it'll be the best you've ever had."

"Now Mother — " Louise began.

"I know — I'll be good. I'll do everything you say, but don't call that doctor — Gus, don't let her call the doctor. That's the meanest thing I ever heard of."

"Listen, Ma, if you don't take it easy, we won't call no doctor. I'll just bash your head in myself."

"I'll be good — I won't get excited. Oh dear," she wailed, "I've got the worst children in the world. Louise, come and let me kiss you. Merry Christmas, darling."

"Merry Christmas, Mother."

"Now what shall we do?" Mother asked. "What's first on the program?"

"Well — " Gus and Louise looked at each other. What *was* first? They could give each other one present and then in about five hours the rest of the family would arrive. How did they fill Christmas morning in the old days?

"Maybe we should have breakfast first," Louise suggested.

"Sure — breakfast first," Gus chimed in.

"Or maybe I should dress first," Louise corrected herself.

"Yeah — you better dress first. I'll see to breakfast."

While Gus was squeezing oranges, Mother called to him. "Gus, have you turned the Christmas tree lights on?"

"No, Ma," he yelled.

"Well, turn them on. They should be on."

He marched into the living room with a half-squeezed orange in his hand. "They're on now, Ma," he yelled. He stopped to survey the tree. It looked nice in a stunted sort of way, nothing special, but nice. Piled beneath it — spread out to look like something — were his and Louise's packages. Hers were done in gold paper and blue paper and shiny black. He had achieved a uniform simplicity by doing all of his in white tissue. They didn't make much of a showing. "Looks swell, Ma."

Gus arranged all their breakfasts on one tray and carried it to Mother's room.

"Oh this is grand," she said. "It's like a party."

"Now listen, Ma, no ants."

She pursed her lips with her fingers and giggled. "The way you talk to me. It's perfectly terrible."

Louise joined them, looking trim and neat and scrubbed —

maybe too much so — with her hair in a tight little knot.

"Hey, Weezy, you know what?" Gus asked. "I liked your hair last night. I liked it fine."

"Did you Gus? I'm glad."

"You oughta do it that way more often."

"Oh — " she made a little gesture with her hands. "Do you suppose we should wait for the others before we open our presents?"

"Oh no," Mother said. "You've forgotten. We open ours now — just the family — before the others come. Don't you remember — the stairs?"

"Louise don't remember nothin'. Eat your breakfast, you two."

Louise, when they were finished, carried the tray out to the kitchen, and Gus went to the living room for his presents. It was funny that the room should be so quiet and so orderly and so empty, and it was funny to have a fir tree in the corner of your living room, all decked out in meaningless shiny objects.

"Had you noticed," Louise asked, "how all your packages are the same size and shape? It looks, almost, as if you were giving the same thing to everyone in the family."

"No. I hadn't noticed."

Louise gave her present to Mother first — all done up in blue paper and a loose silver bow so that Mother could open it herself. It was a crocheted bed jacket, soft woolly pink thing.

"Louise made it herself," Gus explained before Mother had it out of the box.

"Oh, you dear thing — it's lovely, lovely — I used to do that kind of work myself — "

Gus shoved his package at her. "Try this for size."

She dropped the jacket reluctantly. "Now it's you who are trying to get me excited. And then Louise will be scolding me."

She seemed to like the cartoon books okay. "Ah — they'll make me laugh," she said, and, "These pictures I can look at without straining my eyes." But her hands reached for the soft bed jacket.

"They're a wonderful present, Gus," Louise said. "Something the whole family can enjoy."

Yeah — he began to sweat a little — why hadn't he thought of that? At least for Louise. Oh my God.

"On the dresser," Mother said, "hand them to me, Gus. They have your names."

Gus reached for two of the small boxes he had wrapped last night. "Here, Mother."

He gave her the boxes and she looked at the names. With a wavering smile but no word, she handed them the boxes.

Gus had the wrapping off his quickly, but he couldn't look away from his mother's face. Then he opened the box. Tears stung his eyes. "No, Mother — "

"What is it?" Louise asked. She tore at the paper and lifted from her box the gold and amethyst necklace which had been Dad's gift to Mother when Louise was born. She looked at the necklace, shocked, surprised, as if she didn't recognize it. Then tears started down her face and she was sobbing, "Mother, Mother — "

Gus darted from the room. He just couldn't stand it. It was Louise pouring out the tears she had never shed — for Mother, for herself, for all of them.

"You mustn't do this, Mother," she went on in the terrible choked voice. "They're yours — you must keep them — wear them — they're too beautiful — and Dad — "

"No, baby," Mother whispered. "No, baby."

It was a nightmarish sort of day, that twenty-fifth of December, nightmarish in the sense that you participated in all that happened and yet were detached from yourself and from events, and a whole separate set of emotions interpreted the scene. The participating part of you felt gratitude for the old ties of love and comfort; the detached part was fully aware that the old ties did not exist, and that here were strangers behaving in prescribed fashions.

When Gus handed Louise the cartoon book, the dream began — a hideous, ludicrous thing. In his dream world he had bought cartoon books for everyone in the family and as each member arrived, he reached for a cartoon book under the tree. Somewhere, in the back of his mind, he knew that there had been a reason, but in the progressive scene, there was no reason, no sense to it at all. "How wonderful — a cartoon book!" — the phrase kept repeating itself throughout the day.

At nine-thirty, Frank arrived with alabaster lamps for Louise and presents for everyone in the family. As Gus unwrapped the shirt and tie, thanking Frank, truly grateful to Frank, an agonized struggle was going on in that other region: there were not enough cartoon books — he counted them over — he was always one short and it was too late and here was Frank and a cartoon book for everyone in the house except Frank.

Then there was Jack, looking at the cuff links from Frank, and because he had no present for Frank, asking Frank all about business — all about soap. Jack did not realize that Frank could be happy without discussing soap, and Frank, at the risk of boring the others, would satisfy Jack's curiosity. Throughout the endlessly tedious talk was Frances's deep voice saying, "How's Mother?" "This is for Mother." "Can Mother eat turkey?" Wincing at her use of the word, Gus yet watched her hungrily — the luscious thighs and full breasts. The baby lay on a blanket on the floor, tiny and ugly, still glistening and red from the warm wetness of Fran's body.

Flo and her crowd arrived, as sparkling and fresh as the Christmas tree — all of them in new ties and scarfs and glittering rhinestone clips. Connie wore the beaver coat which was Flo's tacit attempt to bribe her from the pathological boy friend, and they were polite to each other because they both knew that later in the day, Connie would be exchanging gifts with the undesirable suitor.

Sam smoked a pipe and wore yellow and red Argyle socks. If it had been a dream, Sam would have been the symbol of Gus's desire to go to college — a desire as unattainable and remote as Sam's appearance. And Gus felt himself drawn farther and farther away, wistful, silent with admiration.

Grant was pink and raw from the cold, embarrassingly genial. He breathed whiskey and kissed all the women and carried a fifth in his coat pocket. Sam, whom Gus had decided to worship, watched his father with a contempt which struck Gus as the most remarkable thing he had witnessed in a long time. Sam finally pushed himself up from the chair, tapped his pipe against the fireplace, and took the bottle from Grant. "The rest of us could use a little of this," he said and went off to the kitchen to mix drinks.

Mother's voice was part of the dream — perhaps the part nearest to reality, because it was warm with genuine excitement. But the excitement would get out of hand and there was Louise to keep the room from crowding, to insist on little rests. And throughout the dream were little square boxes, and out of the boxes came old jewelry, diamonds and sapphires and pearls in ancient settings, jewels that glistened like the tree and caused, just the sight of them, an intense inner pain, like a witch's charm setting fire to the heart.

Eddie telephoned and her voice was like a real voice breaking through the rim of sleep. "Tell Mother I'm thrilled to death with the watch — and completely surprised. If I can break away, I'll try to get in to see her later on." The observing part of his consciousness was saying don't come, don't come, don't come; but he heard his voice say, "Mother'll be glad to see you."

And then they were all sitting in the living room, holding glasses in their hands, sipping what struck Gus as a vile liquid, and staring, all of them, at a little foetus of a baby in the center of the floor.

"He looks like Jack," Flo said; and Connie, "He looks like Jack." "He has Fran's nose," Louise said. "But Jack's eyes," said Flo. The truth, hidden from all of them, was that he looked like nothing at all — nothing human, that is.

Gus looked around the circle at the strangers gathered together and tried to make himself believe that they had once known each other, that these people were the same as those who figured in memories of other Christmases. The names — Flo Jack Louise Grant — designated something so entirely different from their former meaning that semantic truth was being utterly violated. Why not different names for different periods of one's life? Jack should now be Harry; Flo, Ethel; Louise, Ada. Grant had no right to a name any more. They sat around the room, drinking whiskey, all of them, in order that they might have something to say to each other.

Mother's voice called from her bedroom (the door was shut, she was supposed to be resting before dinner). She wanted to know what linens and dishes and glasses were on the table. "That Italian thing, Mother," Louise said. "Sort of beige — "

"But we use the damask for Christmas," Mother said in distress.

"The table isn't really large enough — "

"But Christmas, Louise — and the Bohemian glasses. Oh dear — couldn't I get up and help?"

And so the curious spectacle of the tiny dining room bustling with too many women — Flo, Louise, Fran, and Connie — removing all the silver and glasses and plates, bumping into each other, exchanging the Italian thing for damask, the Sunday goblets for the colored Bohemian glass, the crystal pickle and cranberry dishes for silver. All for Mother — who was slowly dying in the other room and wouldn't see the table. Meanwhile, the men's glasses were refilled, with stronger drinks this time. Jack, it turned out, had also come fortified with a bottle.

During dinner, and as they crowded in the kitchen to do the dishes afterwards, the talk continued — unrelated, disjointed. Fran was telling Louise about a hair rinse that would do wonders. "A pretty little thing like you shouldn't let yourself go. You don't have to *dye* your hair. Just restore its natural color." Connie was asking Gus about his work at the gas station: "I should think it would be intensely interesting — to mix with all kinds of people and really *see* life — far more interesting than college." Sam wandered back to the kitchen because the men in the living room, he said, were all asleep. He poured himself a drink and smoked his pipe while the others worked.

As Connie hung up her dishcloth, she managed to look at her watch. "Oh heavens — I had no idea it was so late — three o'clock. Time to go, Mother." Flo quite noticeably drew herself in and everyone felt the tension. The pathological boy friend.

Flo's crowd searched around for coats; Fran sat on Jack's lap and patted his cheeks to waken him, while his hand slowly raised and stroked her buttocks. Frank stood with his hands in his pockets, smiling amiably, and Louise, tired and tense, her arms folded, obviously wished they would all leave. One by one, they trailed into Mother's bedroom to kiss her good-bye and tell her it was the grandest Christmas they had ever had. Sam said, "Give me a ring sometime, Gus. We'll do the town." And they departed, bearing away Gus's cartoon books, Dad's gifts to Mother.

Gus and Louise and Frank were left standing in the living room. The others had gone off to their separate lives, and Gus felt it was terribly important Louise and Frank should too. "Why don't you get married?" he said, but it was no joke now.

"We intend to, Gus. We will."

"But now — right away. You mustn't wait any longer."

Louise looked at Frank, then went over to Gus and kissed him. Gus smiled wearily at them. "I think I'll lie down for a while. Sort of tired — too much boozing." He dragged himself away, down the kitchen stairs to his room in the basement.

And he must have slept for more than an hour. When he woke, it was dark and his mother was calling him. He rushed upstairs to her room. "You all right, Mother?"

"Of course — I'm fine. Sit on the bed, Gus."

He sat down, kind of dizzy from waking too fast. She took his hand. "Was it a good Christmas, Gus?"

"Swell, Ma — best ever."

"Louise and Frank have gone — the house is empty now."

"Well, that's good. Louise has worked hard."

"Don't you want to go someplace, Gus? Out with some of the young people? I'd be fine alone."

"No, Ma. I don't want to go any place. I haven't any place to go."

She said nothing for a while. She stroked his hand and bit her lip in thought. "Gus," she said finally, "I want you to do something. I've been thinking about it all day. Please Gus — "

"Sure, Ma, anything you say."

"I want to see the Christmas tree. Do you think you could carry me? Please Gus — it won't tire me — I've rested all afternoon."

He ought to protest but there had been too much of that. "Okay, Ma. If you want me to."

He carried her into the living room. She was light to carry, but he was trembling all over when he laid her down on the couch. He put some coal on the fire.

They said nothing — watched the tree, listened to the whispering noises of the fire. It was five o'clock of a cold, gray day.

Mother reached for his hand. "I've always hated to see Christmas end, Gus. Since I was a child."

"Sure, Ma, I know," he said. "But there'll be others."

CHAPTER 5

THE STATE UNIVERSITY was located in Harrisville, forty miles from Clark City, in a green productive valley surrounded by purple mountains that kept their snow well into the month of June. The University itself climbed up the mountain to a Doric temple which served as administration building — these were the "stately pillars" of the school anthem, " — stately pillars crown thy glory, Drive us onward to victory, Dear old State." The second line, the rhyming *victory* with *thy glory*, had been an innovation of a cheer leader in the nineteen-twenties, a cheer leader who was unfortunately not a major in English. Old President Bradbury wrote the original song back in the eighties — "stately pillars crown thy glory, Emblem of traditions hoary, Dear old State." It was after the football game with the University of Wyoming in 1922 that the cheer leader decided something must be done about the old song.

Gus checked his bag at the station and climbed the winding road to the Administration Building where, outside the Dean of Women's office, were listed the rooms for rent. He had talked with the Dean of Women herself, a massive powerful woman with a deep voice, who, because she was single, always felt called upon to reassure her freshman girls that there wasn't much she didn't know about men. Dean Braithwaite had given Gus a few addresses where he might work for his rent, and with a hard handshake, told him to come to her if he ever got into trouble.

Outside, with the addresses in his pocket, Gus leaned against one of the stately pillars and had a look at the college and town below. He felt good, keyed up. It was the day before registration and so not enough people were around to make him feel lonely or shy, but enough for a feeling of promise. Winding down the hill to the town were the other buildings of the University — the medieval tower of the Liberal Arts Building, the square yellow box that housed physical science. State had never allowed itself to be bothered by the trivia of uniformity or order, and with as little concern for central planning as was shown in the buildings themselves, pine trees and formal circles of flowers interrupted the beautifully smooth sweep of lawn; and the winding road cut through the sharp green like a river seen from a distance. At the bottom, a straight horizontal, was Harrisville's Main Street, a row of two-story buildings pressed together in compactness that made Clark City seem, by comparison, a city indeed. Gus could see the hotel and the bank, Penney's and the one movie theatre and gas stations at either end of the town, which then petered off into motels, auto courts, steam-heated cabins. Across Main Street, in neat square blocks, were the streets of neat square houses where people who wanted the culture and refinement of a college community had established themselves. It was nice to look at, there was an amusing kind of pretentiousness about it, and Gus had to admit that the old boy who first envisaged a Greek temple on the side of Harrisville's mountain had really had an eye for a vista.

Ambling down the road toward town, Gus discovered that he was grinning and he stopped for a minute to breathe in the sky and trees and to glance sidelong at a very fresh piece of womanhood panting up the hill. This was it, by God — how Adam must have felt being born full-grown, starting in on life with no trailings from the past, but knowing, somehow, and expecting. The past, that moment, was a suitcase full of clothes checked at the railroad station — and here, in the present, were the lovely curves of lawn and that lovely girl. To have a future made from such ingredients as these — ah bliss! He started walking once again.

With no trouble, he found a room. Mrs. Wood lived in one of the respectable houses and rented the entire second floor to male students. "Not for money," she told Gus. She was a tall, nervous woman, gray-haired — apparently she was going to be a talker. "I feel it as an obligation — I feel that I have something to *give*. Now that my daughters are married, I feel I should share my home with fine young men — I'm very careful whom I take in. I feel that I can provide the atmosphere that nice boys would find in their own homes." And she told Gus about her daughters and their college degrees, and her sons-in-law and their college degrees.

Gus's room was in the basement, small and pretty dark but there was a desk lamp. He could work off his rent by taking care of the furnace, cutting the lawn, shoveling snow in the winter, and helping one morning a week in cleaning the second-floor rooms. It wasn't too bad. The basement room and the furnace-tending seemed more like the past than the future he had been creating, but with this much help, he'd be able to swing a year, at least, without taking a real job. When Mrs. Wood finally pulled herself away, he tested the bed, turned the desk lamp on and off a couple of times, and drew his initials in the dust on the dresser. This is it, he muttered. This is it.

His success in settling himself had been so rapid that Gus now found a whole afternoon and evening ahead of him, free, nothing to do. First, the bag at the station, of course, then see the town. And tonight? Oh hell, he might even take in a movie.

He carried the bag the three blocks from the station, puffing and sweating and worrying that he might have to get his suit cleaned now. But a taxi — no. He stopped to wipe his forehead and remove his coat. Not too bad.

Back in his room, he hung his best suit behind the curtain in the corner, put shirts and underwear in drawers; and dusting the dresser top with his arm, he arranged his mother's picture, his shaving equipment and hair brush. His collegiate dictionary he placed on the desk. Home, by gosh; neat, not gaudy.

Now the town. With lightness of heart that a little whistling helped along, he strode down the street to the crossing where the bank and the hotel indicated the business center. He had a choice: one block to the left, one to the right — that was Harrisville. He decided to do both — do the town up brown. Right first — Hotel Romney, Hirshfield's shoe store, Brown's drugstore, Miss Harper's knitting and gift shoppe, Safeway Market, Standard gasoline. Left — First National Bank, liquor store, Woolworth's, Betty-Jane beauty salon, Penney's, Mode o'Day, movie, Golden Pheasant ice-cream restaurant, Crystal Palace market, Shell Oil. He had done the town.

By five o'clock, he had done the town enough times that he figured he could really find his way around okay. He slouched into the Golden Pheasant, dropped down on the hard bench in a booth, ordered the meat loaf, and wondered how, a few hours ago, everything could have semed so right. Admit it — the town was a dump, his room was cold and cheerless and the old dame was a bloodsucker to expect so much work for such a hole. The girls drinking sodas at the fountain, laughing too loud, talking too loud, were pretty, all right, but what good was it going to do him? Where would the money come from? And anyway, he was an oaf with girls.

Admit it — he was homesick, he was lonely, he felt damned sorry for himself. And that made no sense because you can't be homesick if you have no home, you can't pity yourself for getting the thing you've always thought you wanted. He'd be a doctor, by gosh — no halfway measures, no shilly-shallying around with what you *should* do or *shouldn't* do — he wanted something clear cut. A rich doctor. That way, he could both show the world and cut off doubt.

Tonight he was tired — too many things were too fresh in his mind — he was trying to begin the future a day too early. He was still sore from the cutting away. He had stayed at Flo's after everything was over. Louise and Frank were married, Gus continued at the gas station until fall. But where should Gus go to college? It was like a game the family was playing; on no recent issue had there been such a ruffling of the clan. Jack said Harvard, of course — certainly it had been the greatest experience of *his* life — it would be of inestimable value to Gus both socially and intellectually. And did Gus realize that Ralph Waldo Emerson had also studied at Harvard?

Eddie said Gus should go to Stanford — that Jack himself was evidence enough of Harvard's decline. "Look at Howard," she said. "Look what Stanford did for him." Howard, crinkling his eyes, sucking on his pipe, talked man to man about "the farm," "the peninsula," "the city." Merely listening to Howard seemed to bestow on Gus the privilege of belonging to the fellowship.

Sam said that if it was tail Gus was after, he better go to State and Grant said that the whole business of college education was a damned foolish expense. Louise offered to loan him the money she inherited from Mother; Louise didn't specify the university.

The interesting thing about this game was that at no time was there any question where he should go. State was the only place he had a chance of getting through on his money, but it was one of those self-evident facts, which, if people chose to ignore, you chose to ignore too. When Gus finally announced that he had decided on State, Jack seemed to think he was failing the family and to Eddie he was worth only a shrug of the shoulders.

The good-byes had been affectionate, all of them, with an invitation to return. Clark City had ceased to be home. Henceforth, he would always be a guest.

The girls at the fountain talked too loud and laughed, frisked their bodies around to allow everyone to see the jeweled pins each wore over her left nipple. The dessert with the dinner was apple sauce and cookies. Let the past have today. Start out the future tomorrow.

He paid his check and stepped out into the cool September evening, dark early now, into the hushed, deserted Main Street of Harrisville. The good respectable people of Harrisville had planted their firm cultured bottoms on oak chairs around oak tables in all the respectable square dining rooms, and in the entire world, only one person — Arthur Gannon (better known to his friends as Gus) — only one person was stepping out into the night air, free — free as the night itself, unencumbered as the breeze, stepping out into the night air for what adventure? what chance encounter? He surveyed the empty street. The lights of the movie marquee beckoned with a Betty Grable leg show — but there comes a time, Gus mused, there comes a time in every man's life, when the shadow is no substitute for the substance. The drugstore with its Cokes and sodas, its magazines and strange rubber implements, was, to the maturing man, kid's stuff. To Gus at nineteen, deserted by his youth, but not fully at home in age, only one possibility offered itself: he better buy a copy of *Time* and read about the horrible state of the world — poor Poland, unhappy Czechoslovakia. Somehow, the mere process of reading about catastrophe and doom brought a comfortable feeling of alliance with adult responsibility. Propped up in his iron bed in Mrs. Wood's basement, his mother's picture looking down on him from the past, Gus frowned and scratched and belched his way toward the future.

The succeeding days were not so hard to fill as the first had been, nor was he permitted much time for loneliness. On registration day, he had been awed by numbers, fearful of his own ignorance, shamed by his unsophistication. But all the same, there was something kind of wonderful about it. Never had he seen so many richly ripe young women, so many obviously potent young men. These were no longer the grown-up kids of high school, but young adults, ready and eager to get down to the real business of life. His year out of school, his separateness from his own age group, allowed him to watch the wonderful phenomenon with exciting detachment: the lines of students waiting for registration books, waiting for faculty permissions, waiting for a cashier's receipt, filled Gus with blissfully uncomfortable longing. He hadn't known college would be like this.

Then he was picked up by the processes of college — the chem labs and biology labs and the God-awful grammar of the German language and the weekly English themes. He was picked up by the surprising friendliness of everyone — the students who talked to him in class, the second-floor males at Mrs. Wood's. It was apparently legitimate to talk to anybody you wanted to. If you didn't talk to them, they talked to you. The time passed so quickly that a month could be gone without your even knowing it. The days were shorter, the nights darker. By five o'clock, when labs were finished, and you pushed out of the hot smelly chem building into the sharp, fogged air, it was so dark that the whole University lighted up in comforting assurance of continued activity. At night, when he needed to stretch after too much studying, those lights were just about the friendliest things he knew.

He met a girl that fall, over the Thanksgiving weekend, to be exact, named Leslie Crane. Why Leslie? Because her father had wanted a boy instead. "He says the gods, or whatever it is, are against him: his wife bears girls, his cows bear bulls." She laughed at the crude joke, watching closely to see whether Gus laughed. He didn't. He asked instead how many girls there were. "Five girls," she told him. "Eight bulls."

He saw her first in the library, the night before Thanksgiving, when a bored attendant female scowled at the poor remnant of students who didn't know enough to go off somewhere and be thankful. Gus was searching the card catalogue for material on his English research paper on socialized medicine; Leslie Crane was perched on a stool, poring over cards, writing down references. Suddenly she lifted her head, pulled off her horn-rimmed glasses, and asked, "Have you a cigarette?"

"No — I'm sorry. I don't smoke."

"You should try it sometime," she barked and returned to her work.

In surprise, Gus laughed. The girl looked at him, appraised him, seemed to ponder a decision. "My name is Leslie Crane," she said.

"Why Leslie?" he asked — and they talked for a moment of girls and bulls.

She was a thin girl with straight hair to her shoulders, bangs, and a narrow face. She wore a shapeless box of a skirt and a dark green sweater that barely indicated her small breasts. Her fingers were ink-stained and she was utterly without make-up. She had an almost bluish pallor — particularly at her temples where the veins showed through.

"Why are you staying around this dreary mausoleum?" she asked.

"Well, I — oh, I had some work I thought I better get caught up on. How about you?"

"Me? I loathe my family. I spend as little time with them as I possibly can."

Presuming this to be a joke, Gus smiled, but Leslie Crane was not smiling. She yawned and rubbed her eyes, folded her glasses. "Well, since you haven't a cigarette, you might offer to buy me a cup of coffee."

Gus glanced at the clock, then blushed for doing so. "Oh sure," he fumbled. "I — I wish you would."

Leslie Crane was unlike anyone he had ever seen before. Like other girls faced with his silence, she talked incessantly, but the talk was different, she told him things that Gus had always figured you kept silent about. Her father, she said, was a complete animal, of a low order, who ranched and conceived daughters and treated all women as if they were created only for man's physical relief and domestic slavery. Her mother and sisters she could only despise because they fitted in with her father's idea of them. Leslie herself was her father's favorite because she never bothered to conceal her loathing from him — he fawned over her in a repulsive way and slapped her once when she shuddered at his touch, but it was she whom he allowed to go to college while all the other girls would marry beasts after their father's own image.

All this she told him as they walked down the hill toward Main Street. Over coffee in the White Spot Hamburger Cafe, she asked him suddenly, "How would you describe me? What type would you say I am?"

The question put Gus into agonies of embarrassment. This was not his line at all. "Well — uh," he muttered, searching desperately, "I should think you might be the — the *intellectual type.*"

She was amused and pleased by his answer. She sat back, chewed on her glasses. "You're the nicest person I've ever met. It's really wonderful luck. Generally nice people don't like me or I never seem to meet them or something. I don't know."

"Well, maybe I'm not so nice. Maybe you're jumping to conclusions."

She frowned at this. "You mean you *don't* like me!"

"I didn't say that."

Reassured, she leaned forward and rested her hand on his and confided that because he was so nice, she wanted him to know about her childhood. When she was seven, she said, she had very much wanted a doll for Christmas — she had seen it in the Sears Roebuck catalogue and specified to her mother that that doll was all in the world she wanted or would accept for Christmas. But on Christmas morning, there was no doll — only a book and an old one at that, with her mother's signature and a date many years earlier. Disappointment set her into a terrible tantrum and she hurled the book across the room and screamed that she hated her mother. But Christmas night, after she was in bed, her mother came to her with the book and read a few lines. "'They looking back, all th' Eastern side beheld of Paradise, so late thir happie seat' — I can still hear her voice and still see the amazing magic picture that the words built in my mind — " Leslie Crane's staring eyes filled with tears as she talked. "We read the whole book together — I was only seven. And I was the one she shared it with. Out of all of us, I was the one." Then she added, "I still have the book."

As he walked home with her, Leslie asked what he was studying. For the first time that evening, Gus had an answer and he felt his manhood return. "I'm going to be a doctor," he announced.

"Oh."

"I'm studying chemistry. Chemistry and biology."

"Isn't everyone?" she asked.

"Well — I don't know. For pre-med — "

"Science bores me," Leslie Crane said. "It bores me to distraction. But I suppose it's necessary. If we're to do a satisfactory job of destroying each other."

When he told her good night, she said she supposed that he was all tied up for Thanksgiving dinner tomorrow. He lied that he was. She smiled. "Well maybe another cup of coffee sometime." She held out an ink-stained hand, and as he pressed it, he was surprised how small it was, how brittle and fragile the bones felt.

The following weekend, Gus asked a girl for a date. He couldn't have rightly said why, suddenly, without thinking, he asked Carol Simpson in his English class to go to the Saturday night dance at the Union Building, but ask her he did and take her he did. Carol was short and round and very friendly. She lived in the freshman dormitory, an easy walk from the Union Building, so that the whole evening needn't cost him more than a buck, and to Arthur Gannon, Carol Simpson suddenly seemed eminently worth a buck. Her head just came to his chin and she wore perfume behind her ears, and at the end of each dance, she squeezed his hand — just before she started rattling on. What she rattled on about was mostly sororities — she was in mortal dread that she might not be rushed a sorority and every time she passed a sorority girl, she got a demure look on her face and said a shy hello. Then she whimpered against Gus's lapel about what kind of an impression she had made. "Oh Art — do you think they'll rush me? I could just die I'm so scared." Sure, he'd say, sure they will. It was kind of boring, but sort of nice, and every time he reassured her, she squeezed his hand. He held her hand all the way home and wondered whether he might try to kiss her. She didn't seem the type who'd kiss a guy the first night, and yet he *had* paid a buck and he better get all he could, so under the last tree before the lighted steps of Carlton Hall, he grabbed her and planted one sort of crosswise on her lips. She was soft and yielding, whimpering a little and beating her little fist against his shoulder. God, it was great, and on the way home, stretching his arm to grasp at tree branches, he resolved that, cost him what sacrifice it might, he would devote one buck a week to *women*.

Leslie Crane he saw a couple of times, only to say hello to. She had a strange trick of letting her eyes rest on him a few seconds too long and it made him feel like a traitor, as if he had let her down some way. What was it? Where was the obligation? She had mentioned a cup of coffee; he didn't particularly care for coffee. He didn't particularly care for Leslie Crane. So why in hell should he feel like a culprit? He put her out of his mind.

And Christmas came. Flo asked him down for the holidays, but Christmas night he told her that if you wanted pre-med, there was a lot of extra work. Sam leered knowingly, Flo looked troubled, Gus took the eight o'clock train back to Harrisville. Riding the smoky local, he stared gloomily into the night and tried to forget the day and hated himself for wanting to forget it. At his feet were the Christmas presents, in a large carton — with love to Gus. He had seen them all — eager with questions — the whole family had dropped in Flo's for morning eggnog. Grant made the eggnog, then Sam spiked it with an extra fifth and they were all a little high. And terribly attractive. Gus, in admiration, couldn't but wish that people at State could see the quality whence he sprung — how different from the grimy drudge living in Mrs. Wood's basement. And so friendly and so loving — Jack with his arm around Eddie, Louise talking with great animation and frequent sips of eggnog to Howard, Grant making mild passes at Frances. Then, for one moment, remembering Mother, Gus saw the whole falseness of the picture, the cocktail-party animation — they were all strangers to each other — the importance of the eggnog to the festive scene. As they began to leave, all of them trying to settle on dinner nights for Gus, it occurred to him that if you wanted pre-med, there was a lot of extra work. He told them all he'd call, but that night he took the eight o'clock train. And on the train, jogging along through the darkness, he gave in to dull, empty pain. He couldn't think it through; he knew only that they had shut him out and his own guilt was his inability to pretend he didn't know.

The holidays were a gloomy business, but with the beginning of the new quarter, Harrisville and State opened their arms to Gus and welcomed him home. Registration day was a party, a convention. Plenty of the girls standing in lines knew him by name and weren't ashamed to say hello. He made a date with Carol Simpson for the next Union Building dance, and even Dean Braithwaite remembered him and asked why he hadn't been in to see her. It was really great, and that night, a couple of the second-floor boys at Mrs. Wood's asked him along for a glass of beer. The only place in Harrisville you could get beer was way the hell across the railroad tracks in a grimy little place called the Comet Inn, but walking into that smoky room filled with college guys was enough in itself to make Gus a little intoxicated. Here was the life — he was in!

A couple of weeks later, on a Monday morning when Gus was shaving, Mrs. Wood called down that there were some young gentlemen to see him. Gus dried his face, slipped into a shirt, sprinted up the steps. In the living room were three strange guys, all kind of sallow from the early hour and inhaling deeply on cigarettes. One of them stood up, gave Gus a firm handshake, said, "Gannon, my name's Riley. I'd like you to be acquainted with old Jackson here and this other sleepy-looking guy is Spide Hamilton. Come on, Spide, pick it up."

All the guys grinned hugely at this introduction, and old Jackson and Spide Hamilton gave him firm handshakes and Riley put his arm around Gus's shoulder. "We just thought we'd drop by and give you a lift to school," Riley said. "Any time you're ready."

None of this made any sense. They weren't like the thugs in movies who drop by to take the hero for a ride, and if they were going to haze him, duck him in a pond or something, it was funny Gus had never heard of such goings on at State. He muttered, "Oh sure," and dashed downstairs to finish dressing.

When he returned, the three were dozing in their chairs but jumped up amiably to escort him to the car. Then outside, something else peculiar happened. Another car drove up with three different guys in it. One of them he recognized as Pemerton in his chem class. The original three stopped, glared at the newcomers as if ready for a fight. Pemerton got out of the car, said, "Gannon, I'd like to speak to you."

Riley grabbed Gus's arm. "All right, Pemerton," Riley said. "We've got him now. You run along."

Pemerton then turned to Gus to see whether Gus would be a man or a mouse and Gus didn't know what the hell was going on but he decided he better be a man. "I'll just see what he wants," Gus said and deserted the Riley triumvirate for the Pemerton.

Pemerton, glowing with victory, threw a strong arm around Gus's shoulder and led him to car number two. "A couple of guys I want you to meet," Pemerton said. "Flanding — this is the earliest he's been up in ten years and this is Kimbrough. Fellows, I'd like you to know Art Gannon."

Flanding and Kimbrough grabbed Gus's hand and Pemerton pummeled him on the back. "Hey," Pemerton said, "we wanted to give you a lift to school but old Flanding here, he gets buried in the hay and lets these other jerks beat us to it. How about dinner tonight?"

Dinner? "Well, sure —"

"That's great — pick you up after chem lab."

Flanding and Kimbrough said, "Good to know you, Art — see you later." With an extra, hearty pat, Pemerton released him, and Gus returned to the scowling Riley men.

Riley helped him into the car, and the others followed gloomily. They seemed not so much angered as hurt and, Jesus, Gus didn't know what he should have done.

Riley asked solemnly, "Where's your first class, Gannon?"

"It's English — but not until ten o'clock."

Old Jackson and Spide Hamilton shot Riley a sour look at this piece of information, but Riley seemed heartened. "That's great — we'll take you over to the house — let you look around."

Gus woke up. This was that rush week Carol Simpson had been having hemorrhages over and these guys must be fraternity men and he must be what is known as a "rushee." But why? He didn't know anything about this stuff — it was distinctly not his line. The non-fraternity men at State were called "barbarians" or "barbs," and if ever he saw a guy whom the name fitted, it was himself. This was Sam's world, the world of the big talk and the right clothes and the proper sneer; and in Sam's world, Gus had always been somewhat of a barbarian.

They pulled up in front of "the house," and Gus noticed other groups of three or four entering. The house was a big ramshackle frame affair, pretty much the worse for wear. Mission couches of leather and oak gave out at the seams and overstuffed mohair chairs sprawled limply about the room. An upright piano at one end was carved with so many initials and Greek letters that all substance seemed to have been removed, as from a termite-eaten house. Over the mantel was a large piece of calendar oil painting, a writhing nude male bound to a rock with a beady-eyed eagle hovering over him, and in the turbulent sky, three Greek letters shining with sparkling halos.

Immediately on his entrance, Gus was surrounded by jovial young men, eager to shake his hand.

"This is Art Gannon, fellas," Riley said. "Real name's Gus but they call him Art."

Gus had no chance to correct this error because his hand was passing from one to another and they were sure glad to meet him and they'd sure heard a lot about him.

What had they heard, Gus wondered, but they were sweeping him on to see the rest of the house.

In a corner of the dining room, four fellows, unshaven and in bedroom slippers, were playing bridge. They all stood up to welcome Gus and offer him a hand in the game.

"Well, gee — I'm afraid I don't know how to play."

"Sure you do!" said one of them. "Here, take my place."

Riley saved him by insisting that he see the rest of the house first. In the "game room" downstairs, a billiard game was under way and everyone was shoving a stick at Gus.

"Well, gosh — I guess I never tried this before," Gus demurred.

"Sure you have," they all said, and with half a dozen guys watching, Gus tried to make one ball hit another. His stick, of course, didn't even touch the first ball but slid along the table beside it. After a moment of silence, Riley said, "Hell, it's too early in the morning for this kind of crap," and all the others chimed in, "Sure it is."

Then Gus was whisked away to look at scrapbooks of distinguished brothers, to play a swift set of Ping-pong, to see the shower and can and sleeping rooms. One particular bunk caught Riley's attention, and he put his arm around Gus and said huskily, "That's where old Sam used to rest the body."

"Oh my gosh," Gus said, catching on. "Is this the club he was in?"

"*Fraternity*," Riley muttered. "Yeah — old Sam. We never had a better boy. And he sure thought a lot of you. You know, Sam was my big brother and I just hoped — well, it's been a real ambition of mine to fill the place in your life that he filled in mine. I guess I kind of like your family, Art — "

Riley's voice broke with emotion, but Gus was far too curious to pay much attention. "Well, what did you say the name of your club — or fraternity, rather — is?"

Riley looked at him as if he were a square. "Gamma Chi Gamma," he said coldly. Then he forced a smile. "The Gams — you've heard of us."

"Oh, sure I have," Gus declared. "Sure I have."

By ten o'clock, when he had to leave for English, Gus was the most confused boy at State. Yesterday, he'd never seen any of these guys, never even heard of the Gams; today they were pouring out their love and it seemed that the only thing in the world they cared about was that he should announce himself their brother. When he had to tell Riley that he couldn't, because of Pemerton, eat *all* his meals at the Gam house, Riley had called over a handsome athletic type named Morrison, who turned out to be Gamma Chi Gamma president, and who, along with Riley, closeted Gus in an upstairs room to extract the promise that Gus would make no statement to the Pemerton crowd without first consulting him, Morrison, in person. Gus made the promise easily. "But what's the name of Pemerton's crowd?" Gus asked.

Morrison smiled grandly. "Beta Alpha Tau. No reason you should ever have heard of them."

The Taus, as they called themselves, seemed to feel as strongly about Gus as the Gams and it was hard to tell which group really cared the most. They sang to him — one group about the purity of its sweetheart, the other about her loyalty ("The True Blue Girl of Beta Alpha Tau"). They took him to class every morning, fed him meat and potatoes twice a day, and before Wednesday rolled around, taught him poker, bridge, and the first rudiments of billiards. Whichever group had fed him the evening meat and potatoes would take him to the Comet for a beer after legal rushing hours were over. Here, all the fraternities did their illegal rushing together, vying which could pour most beer down the throats of its rushees. Riley indicated one night that a back stairway of the Comet led to other pleasures, but when Gus showed no interest, Riley said he might have known a relation of a clean-living fellow like Sam wouldn't go in for that kind of stuff. And actually, he said, it was the Taus who kept the joint in business.

By Saturday, you had to decide which group you wanted to claim kin with and those you didn't choose for brothers became mortal enemies. This seemed kind of sad to Gus because he'd never in his life met so many nice guys and he'd gladly have given up the closer relation of brotherhood with either group if he could remain friends with both. Gus didn't really have any preference. It turned out that he'd seen more of the Taus around — met them in classes — but after a few high-pressured days, that didn't seem to matter. On Friday night, Morrison and Riley took Gus to the upstairs room, locked the door, and Riley, with tears in his eyes, confided that the one thing Sam had ever hoped for was that Gus should be a Gam. "He thinks an awful lot of you, kid," Riley said, flicking away a tear with one finger, "and I'd hate to see the disappointment — the *heartbreak* you could cause him."

Morrison put a hairy hand on Gus's shoulder, saying, "Think of old Sam, kid."

The thought of old Sam at this moment was sort of incongruous and it struck Gus as highly improbable that Sam would care one way or another. But it was nice to think of old Sam — after all, he and Sam had been pretty good friends for a long time, and it was nice to think this mattered to Sam. Good old Sam.

And then the next morning, before he left the house, a telegram arrived from Tommy Reed. "You join Gamma Chi Gamma," it said, "or I'll beat the tar out of you. Fraternally yours, T. Reed."

What could he do? In a warm rosy glow, he headed for the Gamma Chi Gamma house.

Twenty-five other freshman boys headed for the Gamma Chi Gamma house that morning, and in a solemn circle, swore that they would try to prove themselves worthy of the honor being bestowed upon them. While the active brothers sang the Gam anthem ("True to the Chapter Eternal"), Morrison, the president, pinned pledge buttons on the new flock. Then much shouting and back-slapping sealed the pact. They were in.

Riley couldn't, at first, find words. Gazing into Gus's eyes, grasping his hand, he finally murmured, "There's only one thing that can ever make me happier than I am right now, Art. That's the day when I can slip you the grip of brotherhood."

Spide Hamilton groaned, "Jesus Christ, what a week. Who wants a beer?"

About half the guys headed for the Comet. Gus stuck with the gang that condescended to watch the Tau True Blue Girl Parade. All the sororities took their new pledges around to the Tau house for a sort of beauty contest to select that year's True Blue Girl of Beta Alpha Tau. Cheap publicity for the Taus, the Gams said, but it was a chance to get a look at the new crop of females.

While the onlookers shivered in the snow, the new pledges giggled their way across the Tau porch to the whistles and catcalls of appreciative Taus. Carol Simpson, bedecked in Hawaiian leis and corsages, was so aglow with happiness that her fat little cheeks looked ready to pop. It was a wonderful show: all of State's freshest, most beautiful girls on radiant exhibit for her most ready men. Jesus, Gus murmured. Jesus.

And he remembered that in the excitement of the week, he had failed to settle for Saturday night with Carol, and boy, did he have some steam to let off. Little Carol looked good enough to eat, and he was just the guy to start chewing.

"Wait a minute, you guys," he said and broke away to find Carol.

He spotted Carol, but he was spotted by Leslie Crane.

She said hello and settled her eyes on him and stopped him cold.

"What are you doing at this shindig?" he asked, not really looking at her.

"What are you?"

"Well — I just pledged Gamma Chi Gamma — I just dropped around." Sudden embarrassment made him forget the pride he should feel as a Gam pledge.

"Congratulations."

"Thanks. Very much. I wouldn't think this was your line."

"I wouldn't think it was yours."

Gus felt the old heat around the collar and said, "Well, I guess I'll try to push through this mob."

But still she looked at him. "I suppose you're all tied up for tonight."

Gus's mind took a wild leap toward Carol, scrambled for something to say. Before the words came, he had waited too long for a lie. "As a matter of fact," he said, "I'm not."

"We're having a dance for our new pledges tonight — it'll be dreary, deadly, dull. But if you'd like to give it a try — We could talk about medicine."

"Gee, are you in a sorority?" He couldn't conceal his amazement. "Well — it sounds wonderful."

She let her smile lick his eyes, his lips. Then she turned away. "You were going someplace. Don't let me keep you."

Gus started forward, then remembered that he didn't have to see Carol after all. He headed back toward his fellow pledges, weaving through the mob, wondering for a confused moment how this strange day had come about. Someone else was pulling the strings, it was someone else's show. In the pressing crowd of students, he was pushed one way and then another, but somehow there seemed to be direction.

TIME WORKED GREAT WONDERS in bringing the unfamiliar world of Gamma Chi Gamma into the focus of reality. Within a matter of days, the courting period was over and the ubiquitous radiance of friendship vanished in the January fog. Gus's education in bridge, poker, and billiards came to an abrupt halt; Riley's affection subsided into the most casual notice. And if all the Taus ceased recognizing him, so too did many of the Gams. Gus was, to be sure, only a pledge, but he began to wonder if there wasn't something about this brotherhood business that could be turned on and off. The Gams were, after all, human.

But Leslie Crane — well, sometimes he wondered. She was never entirely real to him; the more he knew her, the less real she became. The first night, the night of the sorority dance, she had surprised him by being beautiful — beautiful in a scarlet Russian blouse and full black skirt, leopard belt and enormous gold earrings. So dramatic were her clothes that her pale face and limp blond hair retreated into abstractness, fragility. In the incongruous setting of effusive sorority girls and callow college boys, she was cool, detached perfection, eliciting reverence from the girls, nervous discomfort from the boys. Gus could feel his hand tremble on her shoulder when he first started dancing and he struggled for conversation to distract her attention. Anyone could see that she was the best-looking girl at the party — but she was different, her hair, her clothes, everything — and he would gladly have exchanged her distinction for the comfortable ordinariness of Carol Simpson.

Afterwards, though, she was someone else again, pulling her earrings off because they pinched her ears and saying please couldn't they ditch the couple they'd come with — she'd walk, she'd gladly walk — she never got enough of snow — but couldn't they please have a cup of coffee in beautiful solitude and just talk — away from people, people, people! On the way down town, she danced along like a child, kicking the humps of snow from fenders and running boards, sliding like a tomboy down icy inclines. Gus laughed at her but looked around to see whether they were observed before he took a running slide himself. This still wasn't the way people behaved.

She wanted to go to the White Spot rather than the Golden Pheasant, which was much nicer. When she had lit her cigarette and ordered her coffee, she asked him if he knew why she had wanted to come here. No, he said.

"It's because," she said, bending forward to confide, "it's because this is the first place you ever brought me. And do you remember? I said it was wonderful luck. And now here we are again."

He reached for her hand before he had a chance to apologize for the neglect of weeks or feel embarrassed by her confession. "But why?" he asked. "Why is it such luck? Tonight — my gosh, you could have had any guy in the place. Why me?"

"Do you want to know something?" They were leaning toward each other, hands clasped, conspirators. "I've never had a beau. That's a terrible thing for a girl to say, but I never have — a nice one. Boys don't like me — nice people never do. And when I look at you, I — I just can't think how it happened."

Ah, it was warm, it was good. "Am I your beau?" he asked.

Leslie withdrew her hands, pressed them between her knees, looked at the ceiling. "Now I've said too much, haven't I? Before I've even got you, I'm going about losing you."

"Tell me something," he said, viewing her with the benign smile of a parent. "How come you joined a sorority? I just can't get used to the idea."

"Isn't it foolish? But it was so miraculous that any group should want me, I lost my head. And they were badgered into it — they didn't want me at all."

"What does that mean?"

"A prominent alum — Doesn't this bore you?" She picked up her coffee and looked at him over the rim of the cup. "It bores me. But — well, she was my high-school English teacher — she wrote them that they had to take me in."

"Is that so — out of the ordinary?"

"No, of course not. If you *knew* those country schools. You find your friends where you can. I was the only person who had ever read a book. Why shouldn't she be nice to me?"

"No — that isn't what I meant — "

"Let's talk about something else." She took a new cigarette, lit it from the old one.

"What kind of a sorority girl do you make? I think it's funny."

Leslie laughed. "You're being rude. I'm a very fine sorority girl. During rushing, I put on my best clothes and look inscrutable. It scares the little girls. And they all pledge because they worship me. Then I've done my bit and can stay away till the next rush week."

"I believe you."

"Do you? Oh. Well, then I must tell you the rest. Afterwards, they don't like me. They don't like me at all."

Walking home, he held her hand — rather desperately because only through the pressure of his hand could he assure her that he was her friend — she could have him if she wanted him. Out of the strange depths of his feeling, there were no words to penetrate and efface her loneliness, to shield her from the pain that must always come to her.

On the front porch of her rooming house, he kissed her forehead and said, "Leslie, I'm your beau."

Leslie didn't care for Union Building dances or for movies or for Ġam parties; she liked coffee and cigarettes and Gus, and if she could have all three simultaneously, she would ask for no more.

Evenings, they worked in the library until it closed at ten, then walked to the White Spot for coffee, then back to Leslie's rooming house, and Gus finally turned in about midnight.

Leslie's rooming house was not in the cultured part of town. She paid only eight dollars a month for the room, and culture, in Harrisville, came at a higher rate. The house was a tiny, gabled gingerbread structure with cracked yellow paint, and it stood on a drab little street across from the University's heating plant. Leslie took particular pains to justify her living there, tossing off its cheapness as of no consideration at all. It was so quiet, she would say, separated as it was from the nauseating antics of the students; or it was honest and unpretentious — how could Gus endure, she would ask, the hypocrisy of his neighborhood. One night she explained that the real reason for her living here was its freedom from adolescent restriction — she could have people in her room, men, any time she wished. And so they omitted the White Spot from their evening routine and went directly to her room, where, on a hot plate in the corner, stood a perennially full pot of coffee.

The room was tiny — hardly larger than Gus's — and had a slanted ceiling so that only in the very center could a tall man stand upright. Leslie had tried to make it look like an apartment by dropping the springs and mattress to the floor and covering them with monk's cloth, using the dressing table as a desk and concealing in the curtained corner any signs of intimate femininity. To the slanted wall she had pinned magazine reproductions of a Picasso absinthe drinker, a Braque still life, and over the desk Picasso's "Guernica." Lined along the floor at the foot of the bed were her books — a few dollar reprints, a few Modern Library editions, and a twelve-fifty Proust.

"Well?" she said, the first night, watching coldly for his reaction.

"My gosh, Les," he said, jacking up his enthusiasm. "What have you done in here? It's terrif — absolutely terrif."

Then she was shy and turned from him to conceal sudden tears. "It's the first thing I've ever had that was really my own."

She wanted him to come to dinner, immediately, the first Saturday after he saw the room. She would cook the meal on the electric plate. He must come. And so on Saturday, he trudged through the snow to the little yellow house and at six o'clock, rang the door bell. He had never met Leslie's landlady, and he put on his especially agreeable smile to impress her with the fact that he was a clean young man. The landlady did not wish to be impressed. She scowled at him and when he asked for Leslie, she turned to call over her shoulder.

"Oh, don't bother," Gus said. "I'll just go on up."

She put her hands on her hips, leaned forward, with her jaw thrust out. "Oh no you don't." It was a respectable house she ran and if Miss Crane didn't wish to abide by the rules, she could pack up and leave. Gus didn't need to think his night visits had gone unnoticed. She had a good mind to telephone the University and report them both.

Gus could feel his face redden. "But you have it all wrong," he stammered. "It's — well, it's like an apartment — we're fixing supper. We — we drink coffee."

The landlady grunted sceptically, but was apparently reassured by his embarrassment. She moved to the side so that he could come in if he would. But as he started up the stairs, she reminded him that she ran a respectable home and she was going to have a talk with Miss Crane.

He tapped on Leslie's door.

"Oh Arthur — come in." She was kneeling on the floor, trying to chop up a small square of ice with a nail file. "My God, Arthur, how do people do this?"

"Let me try."

"What I need is a man around the house." She rose to her feet and reached for a chipped porcelain pitcher on her desk. "It has to go in here. Would something else be better? I have a can opener — "

"Let's try the can opener."

He jabbed at the ice and succeeded in breaking it in two. "Try that for size."

The ice dropped into the pitcher. Leslie looked admiringly from the pitcher to Gus. "Arthur — you did it! Ah — what a piece of work is a man!" She swished the ice around.

Gus sat on the bed, leaning back on his elbows. "Hey, Les," he said, "you sure it's okay my being here? The landlady, I mean."

"Of course!" She gave him a surprised look. "Why shouldn't it be?" As she filled two cheese glasses from her pitcher, she continued airily, "You don't think I'd live in a place like this, do you, if I were going to have my every move dictated? I simply stated my terms — I have absolute freedom or I don't take the room!" She handed Gus a glass. "Why?" she asked sharply.

"Why? Oh, I just wondered." Gus sipped his drink, avoiding her eyes. "What's this stuff?"

"It's a Martini," she said. "A very *dry* Martini." She watched Gus pick up her notebook and skim through the first pages. "Arthur, look at me. Do you know what I think? I think you're shocked. You're saying to yourself that no nice girl would ask a man to her room. You're classifying me in your mind. You're trying to figure out — "

"Oh for Christ's sake, stop it!"

Leslie was silent for a moment, then murmured, "Sorry." She turned, took from behind the curtain in the corner a small can which she began struggling to open. Gus flipped through the notebook, absently gazing at scrawled class notes. One page caught his eye, the whole page covered with variations of a signature in Leslie's hand. "Leslie Gannon — Leslie Crane Gannon — Leslie C. Gannon — Mrs. Arthur Gannon — Crane Gannon — Leslie Gannon — " Gus flipped the pages, resentment shutting out the other words. He tossed the book aside and had another taste of his drink. "God — what's in this thing?"

Leslie turned, with the stricken look she was capable of. In her sweater and skirt, her face colorless, her hair neatly brushed in page-boy square, she was a confused, wounded child. "You don't like it?" Then she bethought her of the unopened can in her hand. "Here," she said, brightening, handing Gus the can and can opener, "try it with caviar. You know — I had to send for the caviar — there wasn't a place in Harrisville that carried it. I had to send all the way to San Francisco — " She watched him for signs of approval, then dropped to the floor and pressed her face against his knees. "Oh Arthur," she whispered.

They became rather tight on the Martinis and Leslie's dinner was not one to counteract alcoholic effects. After the caviar — so violently repulsive to Gus that he could scarcely force it down — they had a pale green soup made of turtle, square slippery cubes of which Gus swallowed whole in gloomy memory of a pair of tiny turtles Jack had once sent him from Florida. For dessert, they had some slightly burned little pancakes rolled up and soaked in alcohol and orange. They were almost palatable and Gus praised them highly because Leslie had made them herself, devoting all of Saturday afternoon to the job.

"It was a fine dinner," Gus droned from the misty depths of his consciousness. "A superb culinary achievement."

Cuddled cozily against him, Leslie read him poems by a guy named Campion and a guy named Hopkins and a guy named Pound. Gus didn't understand a word she read and the sound of her voice made him a little sleepy, but he had a wonderfully whole feeling with her there beside him.

At midnight, he said he had better leave. Leslie wouldn't hear of it: she said that if he didn't like those other poets, she would read him some Eliot. For another hour, she read to him, curled against him like a purring kitten. At one o'clock, with thoughts of Sunday studying and a clamoring stomach to give him resolution, he stood up and put on his coat. "I gotta go now."

"You can't go." Leslie hurried to the door and stood with her back against it. "I won't let you go."

He stood before her, grinning at the disheveled blurred little girl with the pink tip of tongue between her parted lips. Then he felt her hands sliding up his chest, her arms encircling his neck, and her thin strong body pressing against his. Her lips were hot and sought frantically to enclose his and the trembling of her body passed over to him.

Dizzily, he stumbled backwards, and breathless, tore his face away. He couldn't think — this had never happened to him before — and his hands, of their own volition, absorbed her hungrily. "Shall I stay?" he muttered. "Do you want me to?"

Leslie pushed him away and reached up a hand to smooth her hair. She was flushed but regarded him coolly. "Of course you can't stay," she said. "The landlady — " she shrugged, "well, after all — "

Gus watched her dumbly while she straightened herself. She stopped suddenly, looked at him and smiled. Then she kissed his cheek, patted his shoulder, gave him a little shove through the door. "Arthur — I adore you," he heard her whisper as he staggered down the stairs.

The next morning, slipped under Mrs. Wood's front door, were three pages of Leslie's small handwriting, explaining that she was neither offended nor surprised by anything that had happened. "You were right in wanting to stay," she wrote, "and I was wrong, wrong, wrong — as I seem always to be. Who knows why we do these things, my darling, what instinct of puritanism forbids us — says the everlasting no to our innermost compulsions? I wanted you, God knows, I want you. But it wasn't puritanism because I am absolutely yours, however you want me. It's up to you to say. But let it not be cheap or sordid — let it be the whole of us — "

On Sunday afternoon, when he dropped by her house, no one answered to his ringing. He started down the street and suddenly, for no reason, looked back at the house. Watching him, from the upstairs window, was the face of Leslie Crane. That night Gus phoned Carol Simpson and took her to a movie. Standing under the last tree before the lighted steps of Carlton Hall, kissing Carol good night, it seemed to Gus that sanity had returned.

For more than two weeks, Gus made a point of avoiding any place where Leslie might be; he studied in his room rather than at the library, and twice when Mrs. Wood called him to speak to a young lady on the telephone, he called back that he was unable to come to the phone. January passed into February, the white snows into gray slush, and Gus remembered that the one thing in life he wanted, by gosh, was to be a doctor, a rich doctor. He settled down with fervor to zoology and chemistry.

On February fourteenth, when Gus returned at five-thirty to check Mrs. Wood's furnace, Mrs. Wood met him with a sly look on her rocky old face and a cake box in her hands. "Oh my," she said. "Someone hasn't forgotten *you*. Someone remembers what day *this* is."

Gus took the box with him downstairs — to the infinite but unavoidable disappointment of Mrs. Woods — and left it on his bed while he stoked the furnace. When he returned to the room, he stared at the box, thinking that the only way to cope with it really was to toss it in the fire. But, what the hell, maybe it contained a time bomb or some baby rabbits. (No, this was Valentine's day.) A live, bleeding heart. He pulled off the string, and the heart inside was cake and chocolate, decorated with sugar doves and pink roses. The card said, "This, at least, you can't reject. All my love. L."

"Very sweet," he muttered. "Sweet and sad. Very chawmin,'" and he went to the Gam house for a hearty meal of roast pork, mashed potato, and apple pie, and listened to a description of a circumcision that one of the guys had watched. Walking home afterwards, he thought dispassionately of Leslie Crane and had to tell himself, finally, that he didn't know what the hell ailed her.

At ten-thirty that same night, he heard a knock on the basement door. He was startled at first, but by the time he reached the door, he knew who it would be. Hatless, shivering, she stood watching him, saying not a word. He couldn't ask her in, and there was nothing else to say unless she began first.

"Thanks for the cake," he said finally. "Very pretty."

"I didn't come here for that." She paused. "Are you going to ask me in?"

"Well — no, I'm afraid I can't. My landlady isn't so broad-minded as yours."

Leslie smiled, more in contempt than amusement, but Gus felt in wonderful command of the situation and didn't falter. "I assure you," she said, "that the last thing in the world I'd want would be to jeopardize your reputation. And if it's your virtue — well, that's safe with me too."

"Yeah. I'm sure." He hesitated, then moved aside. "Come in."

He led her through the dark furnace room to the lighted rectangle of his doorway. He closed the door quietly behind them, leaned against it, waiting.

Leslie looked around, removed her coat and dropped it on the bed. "Well, this *is* delightful. Mr. Arthur Gannon, with his un-erring instinct for the elegant — "

"Drop the light touch," he snapped. "Is that what you came for?"

Her small white hand shot up to the back of her neck. Her head leaned forward so that her hair covered her face. "No," she shook her head. "No. It isn't."

Gus was feeling less sure of himself. There was something a little ridiculous in his barking at her and his hands wanted to touch her shoulders, her hair; he wanted to hold her quietly and tell her that everything would turn out fine.

"I've no right," she said, "to ask for an explanation." She kept her voice low, her eyes averted. "But I do ask it. There was never any reason why you should have liked me, but I thought you did. I've been waiting for you — where were you? I've watched for you."

Gus clamped his teeth on his lip and remained silent.

"I've been every night to the library," she continued. "I was there tonight — hoping you'd come. Perhaps I misunderstood from the beginning — but now I don't understand. What have I done wrong?"

"There have been some things that I didn't understand either," Gus said in a choked voice. "I guess I don't understand your terms."

"That's because you won't understand," she cried passionately. "You accept nothing but your own perfection — you demand your own strength in everyone you know — "

"That's not true," he said. "I demand nothing — only that people be honest with me."

"*Only* that — *only* honesty. Only the most difficult thing in the world."

Gus watched the tense working of her fingers, the curve of head, white neck, slender shoulders. "Okay," he mumbled. "Okay. Maybe now I understand a little better."

"Oh, Arthur," she came to him and put her arms around his neck. "Don't talk to me like an Old Testament prophet. Be humane with me. Be Christian."

This was a little too much and he tried to draw his head back to show that he was capable of an ironical smile himself. But she held him close and pressed her wet cheek against his. She held him in a kiss until he yielded to her softness and his hands touched her shoulders. Then she held his hands against her breasts and groaned softly at their pressure. Limp in his arms, she seemed to await him, and Gus, without thinking, sought her.

"No, Arthur," she groaned, pushing him off, "not here, not now. Sometime — I promise you. Darling, not this way — "

She backed away and as Gus stood glaring at her, panting, he was sickened with disgust. But Leslie started to laugh. "Prithee why so pale, fond lover, prithee why so pale. Really — "

"Why don't you leave?"

The surprise on her face seemed real. She turned slowly and

reached for her coat. "Please be patient with me, Arthur — try to be patient." She put on her coat, straightened her hair. From the mirror, her eyes dropped to his mother's portrait. "Is this your mother?"

"Yes."

She studied the photograph. "The atrocious taste of the twenties. It was all vulgar, wasn't it? I like your room, Arthur, I really do. I didn't mean to imply — " She broke off bitterly. "Why are we going on this way? There are so many things you don't know about me — but I want you to know, I want you to understand me. Just — please be patient." She looked around the room as if to check that she had everything. "You received my valentine."

"Yes."

She patted her pockets, buttoned her coat, stood before him for good-bye, then turned away. "Must I go, Arthur? Please ask me to stay. If we could talk, I could tell you all about me."

Gus said nothing.

Looking quickly about the room, she spotted a photograph album in with his books. "Ah," she said, reaching for the album and seating herself happily on the bed. She lifted the cover, gazed for a moment, burst into loud laughter.

Gus's first thought was that Mrs. Wood surely would hear; then seeing the cause of her mirth, he was angry that she would try to turn the evening into a joke.

"It's you, isn't it?" she said.

"It's me."

"But you're so big. How old were you? Can't you hear your mother's friends cooing over that lovely body? How old, Arthur?"

"About three, I think."

"Hadn't they put clothes on you by then? It looks like you — the face, that is. May I have it, Arthur? Please — I want it."

"No."

"Please. *Please.*"

Gus took the album and replaced it with the books. "I'll go and have another taken, same pose, just for you."

"For a valentine? Ah, I'd love it." She lay back on the bed. "You aren't mad at me any more, are you? This is the happiest moment of my life."

Was he mad at her? He didn't know. He looked down at her, thinking that he must hate her, and yet could he hate her and want her too?

He went to her, pulled her coat open, and dropped down beside her. Without tenderness, he drew her toward him, kissed her, pulled at her skirt. She struggled but he was the stronger. Then she sobbed and scratched at his face. "Don't be disgusting," she cried. "Don't be repulsive." She tore away from him and stood up, gasping in her tears. "Let me out of here. *Let me out of here!*"

And was it all over? No. The next morning a long letter awaited him, pleading for patience, for understanding. "That abler soule," she wrote, "Defects of lonelinesse controules." Could she see him — "Give not a windy night a rainy morrow" — at the White Spot? They could start from the beginning — forgetting all the past? "Yet, love and hate mee too — Love mee, that I may die the gentler way; Hate mee, because thy love is too great for mee."

The war was much with them that spring, an uneasy presence hovering in the background of all their days. Through the dying season of March, the world waited, watched to see where the invincible Wehrmacht would strike. The map of Germany was liquid ink, waiting to spread its black shadow over a steadily widening area of Europe. The radio news commentator came into his own, analyzing strength and defeat for the great American public, paralyzed with waiting.

At the Gam house, the news broadcasts drew the boys from all corners of the house to stand in silent contemplation of a pipe bowl or spots on the rug while Kaltenborn, Swing, Pearson fought Europe's war. At the end of the fifteen minutes, when the person nearest the radio switched to music, one of the boys might emit a rolling, thunderous belch, or one might utter constructive criticism of the broadcaster. But the war itself — what was there to say? They had agreed long ago that Hitler was a son of a bitch — but what else? In its early stages, the war had only one hero who could catch the imagination of the young: like an eager football coach, Winston Churchill could instill hope of an intercepted pass, a last-minute fumble, or faith in under-dog determination and team spirit. Old Winnie. Those were solemn but comforting moments when the strokes of Big Ben (were they really Big Ben?) announced the voice from London. Old Coach Winnie.

The boys at the Gam house seemed suspended, waiting for a signal to action, waiting for the word that would interpret murder, oppression, destruction.

The word can come from unexpected sources. At State, a middle-aged assistant professor of English named Douglas was the first to violate the official University admonition to *wait*. In April, the day after the fall of Denmark, Douglas appeared in his class in nineteenth-century literature and instead of discussing the essays of Charles Lamb, he told his students that Harrisville and State were asleep and that it would be of supreme benefit to the community if one of Hitler's bombs could drop precisely in the middle of the University campus as a kind of alarm clock. He spoke of moral obligation, of human obligation — even of common sense. It was, he said, our war. Very pale, his voice trembling, he concluded: "You, ladies and gentlemen, have a right to your own choice. As for me, I prefer loss of life to loss of freedom."

Some of the A students applauded. The rest of the class sat immobile while Assistant Professor Douglas grabbed his coat, pushed a trembling hand through his thin hair, and dashed from the room.

There were reverberations. The editor of State's newspaper, the *State News*, did some research and printed a map showing that the precise middle of the University campus was the Administration Building, and, to be really precise, the wing of the Administration Building in which the President's office was located. A reporter for the *State News* was dispatched to Assistant Professor Douglas to inquire whether he had been aware of the precise middle of the University when he had expressed a wish for one of Hitler's bombs. Assistant Professor Douglas had replied, No. He was, he said, rather speaking symbolically than expressing an actual wish. In an editorial discussing the problem, the editor of the *State News* inquired: "From whom *can* we expect clarity and directness of expression if not from an Assistant Professor of English? One might wish that before Professor Douglas had set out to create havoc and suspicion among the students, he had checked his facts and paid more careful attention to his verbal expression."

By evening, word of Professor Douglas's Declaration of War

had penetrated even the walls of the Gam house which had produced no student of nineteenth-century literature since well before
the First World War. The after-dinner bull session that convened
in Spide Hamilton's room found Professor Douglas, first of all,
unqualified to speak.

"What does he know about the war, for Christ's sake?" Spide
demanded of the assembled intellectuals. "He reads poetry."

"How old is he?" asked a little guy named Rogers. "How old's
this Douglas?"

"Forty?" Gus said. "Forty-five?"

"That lets *him* out," Rogers said triumphantly. "He's too old to
fight."

"The straight dope as I hear it," said Morrison, in the author-
itative voice he had developed as prexy of Gamma Chi Gamma, "is
that this guy Douglas has a kid about thirteen years old. He figures
that if the United States gets in soon enough, the war'll be over
before his kid's old enough to fight. That seems to be the straight
dope."

"Well, there's one other possibility," Gus said. "Could be he
believes what he said in class — about how it's our war."

"That's a lotta bull!" answered Spide Hamilton.

The boys pondered this for a moment; then moving to leave,
Rogers said, "Well, you guys, see you in the trenches."

"Trenches, hell," said Morrison. "Any guy who's sucker enough
to fight from the trenches deserves all he gets. The smart boys
will head for the navy — pick up a little of that brass."

"Sounds okay, Morrison," Gus grinned. "You just show us how."

"I got a better idea." Spide flicked his cigarette butt at the
wastebasket. "We drop down and see Big Bertha at the Comet and
hundred to one, they'll have to reject us."

"Jesus, that's wonderful!" Rogers said. "But make it Friday, will
you, Spide? I gotta study tonight."

Walking toward the library, Gus sought in his own vast emptiness for some definite life-line of belief. He was willing to grant
sincerity to Professor Douglas, but what about Douglas's ideas?
The one conviction that screamed its truth through Gus's whole
being was that war was evil, war destroyed, and that from evil and
destruction came no good. The answering voices wavered unsurely.
Fascism is evil. But can you destroy evil with evil? The peace

and freedom of the entire world are involved. But are they? What about the protecting oceans? Gus had heard someone say that evil carries within it the seeds of its own destruction; why not sit back and wait for fascism to work itself out, to consume itself, or be consumed in the seething hatred it had created?

The lights were on in the University buildings, in dormitories, library, Union Building, laboratories. And perched on the hill, the Administration Building was aglow, its stately pillars mysteriously shadowed by eternal and hidden lights. And behind the University, the mountains were dark against a dark sky and it was difficult to believe that these stars were shared by others, so compact and tight was the little world of Harrisville on which they shone.

Gus breathed more freely. After all, why worry? The name currently applied to men like Douglas was *alarmist*. Douglas was an *alarmist* and self-searching was a grim and morbid pursuit.

Later, when he was walking home with Leslie, it was she who first mentioned Douglas.

"He's an ass, of course. He hasn't the slightest notion what went on in the mind of a man like Keats. But unfortunately he's a dangerous ass."

"What? Why's that dangerous?"

"Arthur — must you?" Her voice was thin with irritation. "He's a warmonger. He's twisting young people's emotions and worse than that, their minds. He's dangerous, that's all."

Leslie had on numerous occasions announced herself a pacifist and so why discuss Douglas? Gus knew her feelings. "Well," he dismissed him, "don't let it worry you. He's probably done no harm — and every guy has a right to his own opinion."

"That's the trouble with you and your kind — you refuse to face issues. You cry over Hitler's fascism and then tolerate the fascism of a man like Douglas. Anyone who brings us nearer to war is doing harm."

What did she mean, Douglas was a fascist? But Gus didn't really want to know. He tried again to turn the conversation. "What do you mean *my kind?*" he asked with attempted gaiety. "Let's talk about me for a while."

"Your kind," she said, "is the great lethargic bourgeoisie."

"Thanks."

"You're angry now. I'm sorry — but you asked me. You want me to be honest — "

"What's your kind?"

"Mine?" Her voice warmed with delicious sadness. "My kind can't really be classified — we're alone — not a group. We're the seekers, eternally restless — "

"Not lethargic."

"No — of course not. The damned — what was it Huysmans said — 'Pity the Christian who doubts, the sceptic who would believe.' "

"Yeah. Well, what are you going to do about Douglas? You and your unlethargic doves of peace."

"You'll see." She hugged her books to her in a kind of ecstasy. "I don't know yet — but you'll see."

Leslie was not long without a plan. The following week she announced to Gus that she was organizing a peace rally and his job was to solicit the participation of all the fraternities and sororities.

"The hell you say!" Gus exploded. "You do your own soliciting. I'm having no part of this."

"You're content," she said with heavy sarcasm, "to sit back in your smug security and let a man like Douglas draw us into war." She reached for cigarettes from the top of her desk and lit a match. "Well, sit back then. I don't need you."

"Maybe he's right, for hell sakes," said Gus, resting on his elbows on her bed. "Maybe it is our war."

"Not our war — yours, maybe, but not ours. A war to protect British imperialism and American fascism is not my war."

"Oh. So that makes Douglas a fascist." Gus stroked his chin in mock seriousness. "You know, I didn't know that's why the war was being fought. I thought it was to protect one way of life against another way of life."

"Another? No. The same. Neither side is worth fighting for — only an idiot or a hypocrite could think so."

"Oh come now," Gus said. "What about the Jews — Poland — "

"What about India?" she screamed. "What about our own Negroes?"

"Maybe freedom is worth fighting for," he said, quietly.

"Freedom to starve — freedom to be beaten up in a picket line — "

"Freedom to *protest* these things."

"Don't be a child!" She rubbed out her cigarette in the ash tray and folded her arms to control her trembling. "You speak from your blind little middle-class world, blind and ignorant. It's time you grew up, Arthur Gannon."

"Okay." Gus raised himself from the couch, reached for his coat.

"Where are you going?" she asked.

"I'm going out to grow up. I'm afraid I'm making it a little stuffy in here."

Leslie grabbed his arms, her tense white face blank with terror. "Don't leave me, Arthur. Whatever I said, I'm sorry — I didn't mean it. But don't go. You'll never come back!"

He twisted away from her. "It's no use, Les." He put his hand on the door knob. "We've been seeing each other because we supposedly got pleasure out of it. But apparently we don't — so what's the percentage?"

Sobbing, she held to him, pressed her body against him, her wet cheek against his, tried to kiss him with wet trembling lips.

He pushed her off. "So long, Les. You'll want to get to work on that peace rally."

The peace rally was a failure, a miserable failure. Gus watched it from a distance, writhed in embarrassment at the pathetic, ridiculous spectacle, learned to know when people were talking about it by the queer looks they flashed at him. First the announcement appeared in the *State News,* inviting all those interested in organizing a Peace Rally to attend a meeting in the Union Building. Then the printed card arrived at the Gam house *urging* all those interested in preserving TRUE DEMOCRACY to gather on the Union Building steps Friday morning at eleven to protest U.S. involvement in an IMPERIALIST WAR. The card was tacked to the bulletin board with the notation from one of the brothers: RAH RAH.

What character was behind *this*, the boys wondered. If Douglas's plea for the country's entrance into the war struck the brothers as a device to save his own and his kid's necks, a rally designed to keep the country *out* of war must be the work of (*a*) a crackpot; (*b*) a Red; (*c*) a fascist. Most of them decided they better show up just for laughs.

Gus had promised himself that he wouldn't, he couldn't go. But on Friday, as eleven came around, he found that he couldn't stay away. He crossed the campus from the library to the Union Building, where a large crowd had gathered. He stood apart, leaning against a tree, hoping he could be unobserved. At eleven, Leslie appeared through the door of the Union Building, carrying a sign, and was followed by six or eight others with signs. The signs were crudely printed in red paint. FREEDOM AT HOME FIRST, Leslie's read, and the others, LET WALL STREET FIGHT ITS OWN WARS; BRITAIN'S IMPERIALISM IS BRITAIN'S AFFAIR, NOT OURS. A crude caricature of a bespectacled professor holding a volume of Keats bore the label, BACK TO THE IVORY TOWER.

The assembled mob cheered, whistled, cat-called as the sign bearers proceeded from the building. It was a sad little group — the unhealthy, the acned, the bespectacled and underfed. Leslie, in her sweater and skirt, horn-rimmed glasses, and no make-up, was one of them, grimly serious and bitter. Some of the others were embarrassed by the ovation and grinned sheepishly.

Leslie stepped forward and held up a hand for silence. The crowed roared — boys shouted offers of dates — one above the rest shouted he'd try a little of that freedom in her home any time, and another yelled, "Where's Gannon?" The girls in Leslie's sorority turned away, abashed; the girls in rival sororities remained in glee. Gus, numb with agony, watched, listened.

When Leslie found that her audience had no intention of being silent, she consulted with her cohorts, then stepped forward to gesture with her arms that all lovers of TRUE DEMOCRACY step forward, join the group on the steps. More cheers, whistles — the joker shouting, "Freedom at home — not here." Only one student answered the call — a Tau who ran up the steps, kissed Leslie's cheek to the cheers and boos of the audience. Leslie consulted once more with the harassed little group. They looked out at the mob, they consulted, they lined up in single file, and with Leslie leading, started marching down the steps. It was minutes before the crowd allowed them passage — and then, as far as the crowd was concerned, the show was over. The parade of eight sign bearers proceeded along the walks of the campus, followed by two children and one barking dog.

For the rest of that day, Gus found he couldn't concentrate so well — his mind wandered from zoology and chemistry to matters quite irrelevant to the career of a rich doctor. He decided to try a walk — a little of that bracing April air to clear the brain. He found himself, by late afternoon, trudging drearily through the Harrisville cemetery, thinking no thoughts of mortality but torn apart by the memory of the lonely girl, jeered at, ridiculed for her futile determination.

By dinnertime, he knew he couldn't face the boys at the Gam house. Chapter dinner on Friday night and they'd all be there. He stopped at a hamburger wagon at the edge of town for a couple of hamburgers and a glass of milk. And after his meal, he went to the library to make up the time he'd lost that afternoon.

He hadn't been to the library for a couple of weeks — nor had he answered the letters that had arrived almost daily. But tonight, if she were there, he wanted to be there. He thought of something he'd said — about how people went together just for the pleasure of it. Well, he was wrong.

But she didn't appear. And Gus couldn't study because he kept thinking of her alone in her room, and the thought of her not even coming to the library made him wretched beyond any possibility of distraction. Had she eaten? And what bitter, unhappy fight was she waging? Or was she exhausted and spent?

At ten o'clock, when the library closed, he looked in every possible room where she might be. He stood outside for a few minutes on the chance that she might drop by for him. The library darkened behind him and the night seemed colder. He buttoned his collar and started down the hill.

It occurred to him that at ten o'clock on a Friday night, the Gam house would be deserted and he might pick up the news before he crawled into his basement at Mrs. Wood's. Or, if just a few of the guys were around, that would be okay too. He wouldn't mind having a little talk with someone.

The Gam house was dark upstairs, dim with half-lights downstairs. Gus took off his coat, turned on the radio, dropped gloomily into an overstuffed chair. It was a hell of an ugly room and the old geezer over the mantel had every right to get that constipated look on his face, eagle or no eagle.

The radio poured out loud music, and somewhere in the house aroused life, for Gus heard the creaking of stairs and Spide Hamilton appeared, shirtless, in dirty cords and run-down loafers. A thick mat of blond hair grew in wild profusion in the open spaces of his undershirt, and only the shaved squatness of his face was a fire break to the tangled growth on his head. He peered with squinty eyes into the dim room, muttered, "Jesus, Gannon, what you doing here?"

"What are *you* doing here? This is Friday."

Spide shuffled over to the radio, folded his arms, pulled at the hair of his armpits. "Christ," he said, embarrassed, "I'm studying." Then in rapid apology, "My grades haven't been so hot — my old man figured I better do something about 'em." He listened to the agonized whine of the Goodman clarinet, and squinted unhappily at the clock. "I been at it for almost an hour. What do you say — don't you think that's it?"

"Well," Gus sighed, "have you finished your work?"

"Oh hell no. I could never do that." Spide straddled a straight chair and leaned his chin on the back. "How about it, Gannon? How about you and me getting us a beer — a couple of beers? We wouldn't need to tell a soul. We could be back here and I could be hard at work before any of the fellows get back. How about that?"

Gus grinned and yawned. "I don't know, Spide. I'm kind of tired — I been working too. And anyway, if we went to the Comet, we'd see the whole damn fraternity. It's Friday — you know that."

Spide scratched his head, regarded Gus with a sly, speculative look. "You know what we *could* do," he moved his hand to his chin, "I got a friend name of Bertha — Big Bertha, they call her — rents the upstairs of the Comet. We might just drop in there for a beer or two — she wouldn't tell a soul. And matter of fact, Gannon, I'd like to have you meet her — I'd like you to tell me your impression. Some people might criticize her — well, you know how people are — but I think you'd see that she has a lot of character."

"Yeah. Guess I would. What do you mean, character?"

"Well, you know how it is," Spide explained. "After you've been around a little — know what I mean? — you get a little tired of these God-damn sorority teasers. Hot pants? Sure — but they don't want a man, they want a husband. No sense in fooling around with that kind of stuff. But Bertha — she's got character, see. She's realistic."

"Well, honest, Spide, I'd like to meet her; but tonight — ah, I'm pooped."

"You know, Gannon, I'd like to introduce you to Bertha personally. She's an old friend of mine — some people might be surprised to hear me say that, but she's got *character*. If I put in a word, she'd treat you right. And if you didn't like her, she could introduce you to her associates — "

"Have they got character too, Spide?"

"Hey — for Christ's sake, Gannon, what are you pulling?"

"Nothing, Spide, not a damn thing. I'm pooped, no good."

"But a couple of little beers," Spide pleaded, "little short beers. Hell, I been *working*."

"Some other time. You go study. I'd like to meet your friends — but not tonight."

Spide pulled himself from the chair, squinted sadly at the clock, turned his grieved, puckered face on Gus. "Now remember that, kid. And that's no bull about those — well, ladies. They could do a lot for you. Hell, they could make a man out of you."

Gus stood in front of the Golden Pheasant restaurant, stamping his feet in the snow, feeling like a Salvation Army Santa Claus — and by gosh, if she didn't come along pretty soon, he might try to pick up a little cash all to be donated to one Arthur Gannon, who was at the mercy of the elements, a victim of slow starvation, a sufferer of the tortures of the damnationed. A loudspeaker atop the First National Bank sang of the little town of Bethlehem and it occurred to Gus that Bethlehem at that moment was probably a darn sight warmer than Harrisville. And why, he wondered, were mortals so set on a white Christmas when Christ himself had had the wisdom to be born practically in the tropics.

Somehow it gave Gus particular pleasure to gripe a little because he felt really too good, too gay. It was a kind of victory over all unhappiness to be able to recognize it, face up to it, and say the hell with it! Ah, where was that young lady? He had an important message for her.

When she appeared, there was snow on her hair, packages in her arms, and a scowl on her face that made him laugh.

"Hey — you supposed to be cheery." He reached out a hand and mussed her hair. "'Tis the season to be jolly."

"And a merry one to you too," Leslie said ruefully. "It's all wrong — the awful commercialism. Arthur, what's happened to *Christmas?*"

"What's happened to you? I am a seething mass of starvation. Come on." He took her arm and pushed her through the door of the Golden Pheasant. "Gosh, Les," he whispered, "don't you ever comb your hair? What'll people think?"

Leslie reached a hand to smooth out her hair, then shook her head. "I will not be badgered into good humor. Is there a booth empty?"

Students had pretty well deserted Harrisville for the Christmas holidays, but lady shoppers filled the Golden Pheasant with a babel of tongues, with an abundance of flesh that overhung the small wicker chairs and tortured itself into the restricted confines of booths.

"A crowd of women is sure a crowd, ain't it?" he said. He squeezed her arm. "Nothing personal, baby — you're more of a female than a woman. Look — with a good plunge through center, we might make that booth."

Seated, Leslie rubbed her eyes with the palms of her hands, leaned back with a tired sigh. "Have you ever thought about religion, Arthur? Maybe if we were Catholics, it would all be better."

"You mean if we were Catholics we wouldn't be so hungry? What do you want to eat?"

"Christmas, I mean. Can we afford a club sandwich? And coffee. I think the Catholics must have an entirely different attitude."

"Tamale for me. Smothered with chili because it's Christmas. You figure the Catholics don't get tired when they shop? Could be."

"No, no — "

The waitress came, took the order and padded off.

"Look, baby," Gus leaned across the table, "listen to me."

"I think the Catholics must remember what Christmas is really *about* — " she paused to light a cigarette — "crèches and things — while the rest of us are simply at the mercy of the National Association of Manufacturers — and *Advertising*. We don't worship the birth of a Christ child, but the birth of Business, Free Enterprise."

"Listen, baby, listen to me." He reached for her free hand.

"Well?"

"I'm in love."

Leslie lifted her head, then turned her eyes from his, her face reddened. "Arthur, I'm blushing!" She withdrew her hand and held it against her cheek. "Who's the lucky girl?"

"You do think she's lucky, don't you," he said earnestly. "That's the main thing."

She looked into her lap so that her hair concealed her face. "My mother used always to say that the luckiest thing a girl can have is the love of a good man. But Arthur — " she shook her head, "you do so take a girl by surprise."

"I just found out," he said solemnly. "I thought you ought to know."

"Well — yes — thank you. I'm glad you told me." She forced herself to look at him. "Where were we? What were we saying?"

"You were talking about the Catholics."

"Oh yes. Doesn't it strike you that we're all wrong? About Christmas, I mean?"

Gus squeezed her hand. "Baby."

"Oh Arthur."

They munched at food, shy and silent like long-separated friends who have so much to say, they know not where to begin.

"I'm not so hungry as I was," Leslie muttered.

"You better eat though. You need energy — this cold weather —"

But over Leslie's second cup of coffee and cigarette, the words came out.

"First of all," Gus said, "I'm not going home for Christmas — Clark City, I mean. We can have it together now. And you know — the damnedest thing — since I've decided that, I've felt so much better. Do you suppose it could mean anything? Growing up, maybe?"

"Oh?" Leslie studied a fingernail, scratched it with her thumb. "What about all those sisters? Will they allow that?"

"Ah, Les." But Gus's pleading look changed quickly to new excitement. "You're going to meet one of those sisters. Louise —

golly, she's really a person. Honest to God! And it has nothing to do with our being related. She's coming up the day before Christmas. She — she wants to see me. And you too — I've told her all about you."

"What have you told her? What have you said about me?"

"Oh — everything. And you know something? She's scared to meet you — she thinks you're so learned. She didn't ever get to college and she's scared of you. I told her not to be."

"Will she like me?" she asked. "What will she think of me?"

"She'll think you're swell. And Louise — " Gus looked down, his voice low, "well — I have a kind of sacred feeling about her, I guess. We were close — I guess I got to know her — she's unselfish, absolutely. Selfless in a way that you never see. Her feelings aren't just personal — ever, but always out of people or in relation to people. She's shy and yet really the most social person I've ever seen."

"Arthur," Leslie leaned back, blew smoke just above his head, "why do you like me? Or why do you think you do?" She paused only to flick ashes in her saucer. "I'm not any of the things you admire in women. You belong in the times when men were gods and women were slaves. You do! You hate to grant personality or individuality to women. Mice — mousy little appendages to men — "

"Oh gosh no," he said. "Louise isn't mousy — you don't understand. She's very positive, really. She has individuality — "

"Did I say she hasn't? How could I? I haven't met her." Leslie began squirming into her coat. "I'm sure she's everything you say."

Gus watched her, miserable. "Where are you going now?" he asked finally.

"Do you have to know?" She gave him a faint smile. "Anyway, you're due back at work."

Gus's holiday job was with the post office and he had used it as his excuse for staying away from Clark City. He needed the money, of course: there was a price, he found, for brotherhood. For the use of the secret grip, the whispered Latin mottoes, the oaths of virtue and loyalty till death, there was a fifty-dollar initiation fee. For the use of the Gam chapter house — rickety, to be sure, but dear to the hearts of the boys — a house assessment of fifty dollars. Then after the bonds of brotherhood were sealed, sworn to, and wept over, there were monthly local dues and semi-annual national dues to keep brotherhood alive. Brotherhood was a fragile thing, he found, that drew its strength from dollars. And in the fall, he had moved to the Gam house for room and meals — not much more costly, really, than eating out during his year at Mrs. Wood's, but it all took money. When Eddie had called, and Flo and Louise and Frances, to invite him to Clark City for the holidays, it was simple and clear cut: sorry and thanks — but the job.

Then Louise wrote that she would come to Harrisville — could he see her, just for lunch, perhaps — or any time he could get away — "but Christmas, Gus, you can't just ignore it."

On the twenty-fourth of December, Gus watched for the eleven-fifty-five train from Clark City, and tried to conceal from himself the fact that the job had been only the most acceptable reason — one of several. When he saw Louise being helped from the train, looking around her, expectant, apprehensive, so small — tiny, really — and her hands reaching to her hat to set it right, he felt a rush of guilt and affection.

"Gosh, Weezy, it was swell of you to come." They kissed — a family custom, of no significance, for arrival and departure. "It means — well, so much."

She was paying no attention at all. Excited with the strange town, secure, now, in his presence, she was indulging her curiosity. "Think of it, Gus — you live here all the time, this is all ordinary to you, and I've never even seen it — I haven't been able to picture any of your life here — "

"Not much to see," Gus muttered.

"That doesn't matter. It's just that — well, the strangeness of the town cut me out — I couldn't pry into your life, any more. Now I'm back in."

"Welcome," he smiled.

"It's small, isn't it?" They were in sight of Main Street. "But you can tell it's a University town. You can feel the difference, can't you?"

"No."

"Oh but you can — you've forgotten Clark City. This seems so — refined."

"Baloney, Weezie."

"You're used to it. It's just what I've been saying — we don't even *see* the same things. We're still in different towns. I'm in Harrisville — the center of culture in our whole state. I feel — humble. Oh Gus, will I meet that girl?"

"Yeah — she's coming for lunch."

"I'm scared. Is her name really Leslie?"

Gus rubbed his forehead. "Yeah, it's Leslie." Should he tell Louise about the bulls? Better not. "Leslie Crane. Nothing to be scared of." He gave her his best big-brotherly smile. "You'll raise my stock a hundred per cent."

At the First National Bank, Louise stopped him so that she could get her bearings. "Is that State up there? It has to be, doesn't it? I feel as if I'm watching a movie."

"It's State. Real too."

"This, you know, is the first trip I've had since California — the summer Dad died. Yesterday, I was so excited, my stomach got all tied up in knots." She took a deep breath, looking around her to take it all in. "I feel just fine now."

"How's everyone?" he asked, steering her toward the Golden Pheasant. "Frank? You look fine."

"Frank's fine — he sent you his love. Frank's very nice, Gus."

"And the family?"

"Fine, I guess. Eddie's turned Anglophile — violently. I think she wishes she were a British nurse. Connie seems to be engaged."

"Did Flo pick him?"

"It seems to be all right. His family has money. Fran's pregnant again."

"Good God. Don't they ever do anything but — "

"Apparently not. I like Fran — she wears well, I guess. But I drive her nearly crazy. She wants to roll up her sleeves and do me over — into a cigarette girl for a night club or something. Whenever she looks at me, she gets a creative frown on her face."

Gus snorted. "This here is where we eat. Leslie's never on time."

Gus jammed his hands into his pockets, looked over hunched

shoulders into passing faces. Louise folded her hands, cast an appreciative glance at the architecture of the Golden Pheasant.

"Maybe we better go in," Gus said. "It gets crowded."

Settled in a booth, they told the waitress they wouldn't order quite yet, they were expecting someone.

Gus rubbed his eyes, muttering, "Ever hear from Babe, Louise?"

"No — I write her at Christmas and on her birthday but she doesn't answer. She hates me, of course — I'm not sure just why." She spoke calmly, lightly. "I told her you were registered for the draft. It would be hard for her to imagine your being grown up. Mrs. Miller says they have a new Cadillac. Flo heard that at her club."

"You look like Mother, Weezy. Or maybe not look like her so much as seem like her. I could be talking to her right now."

"Why wouldn't you come for Christmas, Gus?" Louise stretched her napkin across her knuckles. "I couldn't help thinking what Mother — "

"My job, Louise — I couldn't get away."

"Of course."

Gus looked at the clock and frowned toward the door. "We better order." He made an angry gesture to a waitress, and with a deprecating shrug, explained, "She's always late."

Louise took a sip of water. "Don't worry, Gus. I'd love to see her but — you know how it is — things come up."

"What's that about Eddie?" He asked quickly, scanning the menu. "Going British on us?" He gave his order and looked at Louise for hers. As the waitress moved away, he said, "How do you figure that — the British angle?"

Louise laughed softly. "It's good to see you, Gus — we haven't talked — oh and I've missed it." She leaned her elbows on the table, pressed her fingers against her temples. "Eddie — What is it, Gus, the awful emptiness? Jack told me once it was fear."

"Fear! Eddie? What the hell's she afraid of?"

"It doesn't make sense, does it. But I think he was right. Herself — she's afraid of herself."

Gus scratched his head, gave her a quizzical look. "I always figured you were a little scared — for no damn reason at all, and Babe — why has she carried on this way? I've kind of thought she was afraid of something."

"It's Eddie — we've always been afraid of her, always had to be something we weren't so that we could be as good as Eddie. But Eddie's was something different." She leaned back, fingered her silver. "With her it's almost — well, fear of survival. She never had a chance to prove that she could have created her world — she was just born into it. She never had a chance to prove herself. And so she's had to pretend — it's her only hope — that her world was safe and secure and eternal. And anything that has threatened it has been evil. And the greatest evil of all is change itself."

"You pretty bitter about Eddie?"

"Oh — I don't think so." She balanced her spoon on her knife blade. "It's over now anyway. I've given up caring that I'm the ugly duckling — and now I just watch. She's the one who's still being torn apart."

"Ugly duckling, hell. Damn you, Weezie, when you talk like that — " He grinned. "Look Weezie, I'm gonna beat you. Now tell me about the British business."

"It's protection — Eddie's always seeking protection. England's to protect her against Hitler — Hitler was fine as long as he protected her against communism. Whenever anything threatens what Eddie is or might become, she's in a panic — she has to deny it or destroy it. Well — you know, Gus, the depression just didn't exist."

"Yeah. I heard that one. It's all very strange, isn't it."

"Maybe not so strange. I think she got it from Dad. They both wanted a wilderness to conquer. But Grandfather had all the fun of that and Dad never quite believed in his own manhood."

"Do you think we're worth saving, Weezie? Do you think we oughta survive?"

"I don't think Eddie cares about *self*-survival — she's essentially too scared to think herself worth saving. It's class survival. If Eddie couldn't be rich — if she can't be first family, she'd rather not survive."

Gus took up his sandwich, bit into it thoughtfully. "Do you believe all that?" he asked, chewing, taking a swallow of milk. "Do you believe it — or have you just not had anyone to talk to?"

Louise, with her head back, her fingers at her throat, worked at his question. Then catching his grin, she relaxed into laughter and leaned toward him. "Merry Christmas, Gus."

"Hey, don't stop. This is fascinating. What about Jack? What do you make of him?"

"What do *you* make of him?"

"Oh Jack — " Gus thought a moment. "He's dead. He died the day of the crash."

"Did he? No — he just never grew up. That's why women like him — he appeals to the mother in them."

"He's a hell of an active child. Such spawning."

They looked at each other and laughed. "Gosh, this is nice," Gus said, feeling suddenly all easy inside. "Do you know what it's like right now? It's like we were having lunch in Clark City — day before Christmas. We step outside, walk home through the snow — and there they all are — Dad in the library — Mother upstairs putting on her diamonds — Tom and Jack sprawled on the floor playing records — Eddie in the hall in that gray squirrel coat — you and Babe and I decorating the tree — "

"That's what it's like," Louise murmured. She smiled with tight lips. "That's what it's like."

"Weezie," Gus's eyes dropped, he was embarrassed, "how come you haven't a family? You oughta have, you and Frank."

"We're trying, Gus. Maybe I waited too long — but we'll have one anyway. It takes awhile before you admit you're ready to adopt."

"Look. Keep trying."

"We will."

They were almost finished with lunch and no sign of Leslie. They both recalled themselves to that fact and looked about, Gus muttering an apology, Louise explaining away the absence. Then they ordered mince pie à la mode, and Louise inquired about his studies. When Leslie finally appeared, they were almost finished and Gus's irritation turned all to gratitude that she hadn't failed him.

"I'm sorry we didn't wait." He stood awkwardly in the booth. "But work — Well, look, this is Leslie, this is Louise."

"Hello, Leslie," Louise held out her hand, "I'm really very happy to — to meet you — "

Leslie gave her a quick, sidelong smile, touched her hand and slid in beside Gus. "I'll just have time for coffee. I'm meeting someone."

"Oh?" Gus said — and before he could stop himself, he had asked, "Who?"

Leslie smiled, hunted through her purse for a cigarette. "Cigarette?" she offered the package to Louise.

"No thank you. If you don't mind," Louise added quickly. "I'm afraid I don't smoke."

Leslie looked wonderful — Gus in a quick glance took her in — all in black, heavy gold chains around the high neck of her dress. Her lips were plastered heavily with lipstick, her skin white, the straight haircut and bangs giving her the look of a child. A child who had seen too much, Gus thought. And whom was she meeting?

"This is a great treat for me," Louise said, filling in the silence. "Clark City — well, I guess it isn't what you'd call very cultured, is it, Gus?"

Gus studied the criss-cross pattern a fork could make on the table cloth. "No — I guess it isn't."

"I was just saying to Gus," Louise struggled on, "that you can certainly feel the difference in a college town — the minute you step off the train. But maybe you're used to it — maybe you don't feel it either. To me, it's the center of — "

"Louise thinks this here town is cultured," Gus interrupted her. He tried with a grin to turn the conversation into a joke. "First time old Harrisville has ever been accused of that."

"No — I don't think you're being fair," Louise insisted earnestly. "There's a certain refinement — there can't help but be. This is where the really worthwhile people would congregate. My older brother — Jack, that is," she explained to Leslie, "went to Harvard. Perhaps Gus mentioned it. Jack has always said that there's just something different about Massachusetts — "

What was Leslie thinking, Gus wondered. That Louise was mousy? Boring? That Gus liked women without personality — appendages, as she called them? He couldn't look at Louise's serious face — he wished he couldn't hear her words which elaborated on Jack's reactions to Harvard. Louise was doing all the work — painful work for her too if she must resort to Jack. But oh Jesus, let her stop!

Leslie smoked, sipped coffee, and when Louise concluded that she felt about Harrisville as Jack must have felt about Massachusetts, Leslie turned to Gus and asked, "Why do they call you Gus? You never told me."

"Why Gus," Louise scolded, smiling at the chance to discuss with Leslie the boy they both loved. "You shouldn't keep that a secret. When he was a little boy, Leslie — "

"Leslie couldn't possibly be interested," Gus snapped. There was instant silence and Gus caught the nervous quiver of Louise's forehead, the agonized apology of her eyes. "Look," he said, trying to be jovial, "I don't get my two favorite women together to hear them discuss me as a baby. I was a cute kid," he said to Leslie. "Let's leave it at that."

Leslie, with her head against the back of the booth, turned to Gus so that her cheek touched the leather upholstery. "I ran into Professor Douglas. He looked at me and actually grew quite pale before he turned away." She smiled, almost demure. "They say he takes nembutal every night to put him to sleep — he had his wife with him today — I shouldn't be surprised if it were true."

"Professor Douglas," Gus began (Louise had sat forward to catch Leslie's words, her eyes questioning, her hands clasped in an attitude of interest)— but how explain a course in nineteenth-century literature, a peace rally, a crude joke? "Well — it's a long story," he finished lamely.

"Are you staying in Harrisville?" Leslie asked Louise. "Maybe Arthur could bring you to my apartment for cocktails."

"That's terribly sweet — but I can't really. I must get back this afternoon."

What was Leslie pulling? She knew damn well Louise wasn't staying. And apartment, hell! "It's Christmas Eve," he said. "Remember?"

Leslie looked at her watch, quickly finished her coffee and snuffed out her cigarette. "I must run. I hate to break up a party — but I do have a date."

"You just got here," Gus said.

"I know." She stood up, her coat around her shoulders. "But you wouldn't want me to be late. Good-bye," she said to Louise.

"You were sweet to come," Louise said warmly. "I've looked forward to this very very much."

Leslie smiled, reached for her bag, and was gone.

Gus hadn't stood. He twisted his napkin, then dropped it to the table and reached for his glass. With concentration, they collected themselves to leave, Gus paid the check, and having spoken no word, they were once more outside, facing each other on the sidewalk. Christmas shoppers passed them, glared at the obstruction they made. From the loudspeaker on the bank, carolers sang, "Peace on earth, Good will to men, Peace on —"

"Well, Weezie — I hate to leave you — but these are busy days."

"Of course they are." She reached out to touch his hand. "Don't worry about me — I'll have a lovely time." She looked for a clock. "My train doesn't leave till three. I'll just look around — I'd like to see the college and your fraternity house. Isn't it the same one Tommy was in?"

Gus nodded.

They started walking.

"She's beautiful, Gus," Louise murmured. "Something so special — I don't blame you for loving her."

He felt ashamed that someone like Louise should look at his relationship with Leslie and think it sweet. He wanted to explain that it wasn't so simple as that, but the words that came to his lips were, "She thinks I'm a child."

"Nonsense," Louise scolded, as a mother would her boy. "It's perfectly plain that she's madly in love with you."

He had to let it go at that.

"Gus," Louise hesitated, then laughed to show that what she wanted to say was partly a joke, "I — well, I hope I didn't embarrass you."

"No, no." He took her hand, pressed it in both of his. "No, Weezie — you can't think that."

"Well *good*," she said. "It was such fun for me."

Then it was time to say good-bye.

"State's up there," Gus pointed. "You can't miss it, I guess. The Gam house is on the street at the foot of the hill — number seventy-nine."

"I won't get lost."

"Well —" Gus smiled awkwardly. "This is it, I guess. It was swell of you to come."

Louise reached up to kiss him. "Merry Christmas, Gus."

"Merry Christmas, Yooweez."

He watched her smile, turn, and start across the street. Her heading through the strange town alone caught at his heart and he called out to her. "Louise." When she looked around, he said, "I guess you know how I feel about you."

"I think I do, Gus." And she crossed Main Street toward Harrisville's seat of learning.

That afternoon, around five, he took a few minutes off to phone Leslie. He wanted to tell her he would be working late but would drop by at nine. He could hear the landlady calling upstairs and a voice answering. When the landlady returned, she said, "Miss Crane is not at home."

"Would you please tell Miss Crane it's very urgent I speak with her?"

The landlady sighed, dropped the phone, and in a moment, the angry voice of Leslie was saying, "Hello."

"What was the point of that?" Gus asked.

"What was the point of *what?*"

"Of your lying."

There was a pause, then her tight voice, "I'm getting a little tired of being questioned about everything I do. I won't stand for it, Arthur, I won't stand for it — "

"Okay," he said calmly. "Okay. Forget it. Be seeing you." But he waited before he hung up.

"Wait a minute, Arthur — don't go. I didn't mean it. Someone's here. I didn't want to be interrupted just then. But I wanted to talk to you."

"Who is it? Who's there?"

Another pause. "It's a woman, Arthur. My high-school English teacher. Now are you satisfied? She just dropped in today."

"Okay — okay. Look, I have to work late. See you at nine."

"Oh Arthur — " her voice was distressed. "I'm afraid — look, darling, with Molly here — I can't leave her — "

"It's Christmas Eve."

"I know, I know — but we'll have tomorrow." After a moment, she said anxiously, "Arthur? You aren't angry, are you?"

"Sure I'm angry. What about tomorrow? Can I come early? Nine or so? We'll open packages."

"Nine's wonderful."

That was all — but he had to give her a lead — he had to know what she thought. "Hey, Les," he said. "Louise says you're beautiful — thinks you're swell."

"Oh? Good. I'm glad she approves."

Gus waited. "Well — I guess it's tomorrow then."

"I can hardly wait — my dear, my dear."

At eight that night, when he finished work, Gus stopped in the drugstore for a hot beef sandwich, and then, hell, it was Christmas Eve, he wandered around town, looking in store windows, buying a few trinkets in Woolworth's — some jewelry and needle work (ha ha) for Leslie, and some Santa Claus candles to give a festive air to her room. Then it occurred to him that festivity called for wine, so he dropped in the liquor store and bought a sixty-nine-cent bottle of Sauterne. On the way home, he noticed the lighted star on top of State's Doric administration building and wondered if its location had any particular significance. The Gam house was dark and empty. Only a couple of other guys were staying on during the holidays and of course, on Christmas Eve, they'd be out. But that was okay, a little sleep never hurt anybody. He listened to the radio for half an hour and turned in by ten.

Christmas day, he awoke before eight, lay in bed hating to pull out of the warm sheets to close the window, yet too excited to stay there for long. Jesus, what an ass! Wouldn't he ever grow up? You'd think that Santa had sure enough come, the way Gus's heart was pounding, the way he couldn't lie still. He jumped out of bed, pulled down the window, and stretched his way into bathrobe and slippers. Then he went to the can and brushed his teeth, sauntered downstairs to start coffee. Before Mrs. Tobin had left for vacation, she had put locks on all the kitchen cupboards so Gus and the other two guys had had to buy their own coffee and sugar. Gus got the coffee on the stove and wandered into the living room. It was a mess — hadn't been cleaned for a week and even under the best of conditions, it was a pretty dismal room. Cigarette butts and empty Coke bottles and newspapers littered the floor. A sorry-looking Christmas tree stood before the gray window. A couple of guys had put it up for the Christmas dance, decorated it with a string of lights and a package or two of icicles. Gus shook his head at the sight of it, but, shrugging his shoulders, decided he better turn it on.

Then he went to the door for the paper. As he reached for the knob, his eyes fell to an envelope which had been slipped under the door and before he picked it up, he knew it would be for him. "Mr. Arthur Gannon," it said on the outside, and inside it said, "My darling, I can't make it today — I'm leaving town. But it won't be for long — tomorrow night I must, I *must* see you — it has been too long and there's so much we must say to each other. I feel that in some way I'm failing you — not the nonsense of Christmas — but somehow, I haven't been, oh, I'm afraid, all to you that I could be. How do I love thee? Let me count the ways — Deeply, deeply. Forgive me. L."

Gus read the note two or three times, then quite mechanically stuffed it into his pocket and went to the kitchen for his coffee. While he gave it an extra couple of minutes to perk, he rubbed his hand over his unshaven chin and cheeks, over his forehead as if he were pondering a problem, but, really, his mind was quite empty. He took the coffee back to the living room, slumped into a chair. He was breathing heavily through his mouth; he squeezed his eyes tight shut — opened them — muttered, "Well, Gannon, and a Merry Christmas to you too."

His first thought was of Clark City — he should have gone home after all. And if he had? A repetition of last year — a guest in their homes — the struggle to be discreet, withdrawn from their family problems — the necessity of alcohol to break down the barriers between them. Even at Louise's that's how it would be. Each of them had a life that excluded him; they'd all gone ahead without him. Tailing along behind, it was for Gus to feel the confusion, the resentment, and yes, by God, the self-pity of desertion.

He swallowed his coffee, put the cup on the floor, and took the stairs two at a time. In a way, he was trapped. He couldn't go home, he couldn't go to Leslie. Suspended, he could wriggle and writhe. He couldn't even go to his medicine — on Christmas day, the library would be locked, the deserted fraternity house would drive him away. In his room, the little pile of presents was on his dresser — the packages from Clark City, his gifts for Leslie. He stared at them, turned slowly away. He stripped off his clothes, and, naked, walked down the hall to the showers.

The hot water beating on his head, sliding over his body, soothed, relaxed, comforted. He massaged his forehead and his eyes and his head. And what next? he asked himself. What next? He was in love — he had given her that, finally, after a year of her begging for it. And if love was the final awareness of wanting someone — no matter what — then he was in love. He had been a long time admitting it because he had assumed always that being in love meant being happy, and in all the time he had known her, he couldn't remember that she had ever made him happy. But he was a child, she told him. He had been poisoned by the middle-class ideas of his family. He was puritan and a moralist and he knew nothing of modern poetry or the civil war in Spain.

But nonetheless, she had wanted his love, his loving. During the summer when he had stayed on in Harrisville to work, she had come in from her father's ranch once or twice a week to see him. And she would kiss him frantically, then go limp in his arms, shivering at the touch of his fingers and lips, yielding, demanding up to the point of consummation, then fighting him off in a kind of terror. And pleading always to be loved.

A hundred times, more than that, he had called it off, said good-bye and walked out. Always she came for him, crawling, pleading, weeping; always, he went back. Because he was in love? He didn't think so. It seemed to be because she involved him so completely in her life — she made demands on him that struck so deep within him, touched emotions that till then hadn't existed. The easy kisses and sorority chatter of a Carol Simpson never penetrated — there were dozens of her at State who wanted first a sorority pin, then a fraternity pin, then a husband, a house, car, baby, and membership in the Harrisville Country Club. Take your pick — they're all alike, and if you lived with one for twenty years, you'd never know her from any of the others. Half the guys in the fraternity were pinned to them and would marry them in the June following commencement. The other half bought their tail at the Comet. And which half knew more about love? Either way, you were putting down your two bucks and buying a mechanical job.

Well, there was nothing mechanical about Leslie Crane, and it wasn't any two bucks she was after. Leslie wanted a pound of flesh and he had paid it until he was about bled dry. Only trouble, he never seemed to have bought anything.

Gus turned the tap to warm the water just a little, and he

soaped himself and held his head back to let the water beat down in his face. Ah, it was good. Maybe the best thing would be to spend the day under the shower, sing a carol or two, feel sorry for himself. It was funny Leslie hadn't mentioned why she was leaving, where she was going.

Bill Adamson came into the shower room, a towel slung over his bare shoulder. "Hi Art. Merry Christmas."

"Merry Christmas, Bill." Gus grinned. "How ya feeling?"

Bill regulated the shower next to Gus's, testing the water with hesitant hazarding of hand or foot; then hunching his shoulders, he stepped breathlessly beneath. Finding that the warmth had been no delusion, he relaxed. "Not so good. I was up pretty late." Bill was a stocky boy with dark curly hair and a look of the wide open country. "Women never want to go to bed."

There was one for a crack, but Gus let it go. "Why you up so early? It's practically middle of the night."

Bill rubbed his chin, smiled foolishly. "My girl's mother — well, she sorta wanted me there when they opened their presents. You know, that kind of stuff."

Gus whistled. "Boy. Are you hooked."

Bill blushed, rubbed a great lather under his arm. "Oh, hell, nothing like that. Well — you know how women are."

"Sure," Gus said. "Sure. What have you got for Betty?"

Bill's rosy face became even rosier, and he exposed it to the spray of water. "Well," he sputtered, "I got her a pin — jeweled one — pearls."

"Hey — that's great. That's news. Congratulations."

They shared a wet grip of brotherhood.

"That explains things," Bill said, able once more to face Gus. "Her mother's got her a hope chest — cedar chest, that is — and wants me there when Betty sees it." He gave Gus a smile of satisfaction and contentment.

"Gee that's swell. You really making plans."

Bill studied his toes unhappily. "Jeez, I don't know. I got another year before I graduate and the draft — "

"Yeah, the draft."

They stood pensively under the hot water and then turned off the hot, turned on the cold, danced, gasped, rubbed themselves.

Drying, Gus said, "Sounds to me like you got a pretty good set-up."

"I sure think so," Bill agreed. "You know, this may sound kind of screwy, but my mother says you can tell the kind of wife a girl will be by her mother. You just oughta see how Betty's mother runs that house — and what a cook!"

"How's her shape?" Gus asked. "Man cannot live on food alone."

"She's had five kids," Bill expostulated. Then he leered, "Wait'll I start in on Betty."

In his own room, Gus slipped into shorts and undershirt, socks and shoes. Adamson was somewhat of a jerk, but who the hell was Gus to talk? The one thing he'd wanted to buy for Leslie was a jeweled Gam pin — with pearls. The fifteen-dollar bottle of Shalimar and the Complete Greek Drama were the second choice he'd decided on when he suddenly envisioned Leslie opening the small box with the Balfour label. As Gus picked up his shaving things, his eye was caught by the bottle of Sauterne. He took that along too, and stopped in Bill's room.

"Hey, Bill," he said, offering the bottle. "Here's something — it isn't much — I just wanted to get you a little remembrance. I thought you might want it for Betty's mother."

Bill, in shorts, had been stooping to fasten a garter. He stood up, let the garter drag on the floor. "My God, Art, you shouldn't have done that." He looked from the bottle to Gus, too touched, almost, to speak. "That was a hell of a nice thing for you to think of." With his left hand, he took the bottle; with his right, he slipped Gus the grip of brotherhood.

"Oh, it's nothing, really," Gus said.

Gus passed on down the hall to the can, stood before the mirror, aud rubbed lather onto his face. The only question now was how to get through the day. He could dress up in his best suit, find a church, have dinner afterwards at the Golden Pheasant. But the thought of doing any of that alone was just too much — left him feeling as if his innards had dropped out. The movie wouldn't open till two or so and that was still five hours away; otherwise, he could spend the whole day there. The best thing was probably to walk, one end of the town to the other, or better yet, dress in old clothes, take a couple of sandwiches along, and climb the hills behind the University. Away from town, the sunless sky wouldn't seem so gray — there'd be nothing to remind him of Christmas at all and the snow would be white. He and Buddy Sawyer, when they were kids, used to take hiking trips — good days together in the hills and hot cocoa when they came back down. It'd be like that. And tonight, maybe a movie. He finished shaving with the gold razor Jack had once given him. Old Jack. And he returned to his room.

On his dresser was the pile of presents and now was as good a time as any, probably, to get that over. Sweater from Flo, shirt and tie from Eddie, wool sport shirt from Jack and Fran, tie from Sam. Louise's box should contain either a tie or gloves, but it contained instead a check for a hundred dollars and a note. He picked up the note, then decided he better not try to tackle it just now.

He rummaged around in his closet for old pants and boots. And when he was dressed, he straightened the bed. That was it. He turned the light off, looked around the room to see if he had everything. His mother's picture was on the dresser. He went to it, looked at the face, held the picture in his hands. As he replaced it on the dresser, he said quietly, "Merry Christmas, Ma." And then he left.

The night of the twenty-sixth, he met Leslie at the White Spot and arrived late because too many times now had she kept him waiting. She was on her second cup of coffee, and the ash tray was filling up with half-smoked cigarettes.

Gus nodded to Henry, who flipped the hamburgers, slid into the booth, across from Leslie. She looked at him with no expression, dropped her eyes to her cigarette. Gus noticed that her fingers were trembling.

"How was *your* Christmas," he said to her.

Leslie shrugged, didn't look at him.

"You should try Christmas in Harrisville sometime. Lovely spot — gay, friendly —" He still could get no rise out of her. He added, "Or have you tried it?"

Her eyes snapped up, her fingers drew back. "What was the meaning of that?"

"Nothing, nothing," he said wearily. "No one has spied on you.

I'm not even asking. It just suddenly occurred to me yesterday that you were probably right here — in your room. I'm not asking why."

"Go on, Arthur — if it gives you pleasure. Say anything, think anything — "

"I'm through. I've said it all — thought everything. Maybe it's your turn now."

Leslie raised her hand to her forehead. "Must we fight, Arthur?" she whispered. "Nothing you can think is bad enough, I know. But one thing you forget — "

Gus waited. "Well?"

She shrugged. "I love you."

"Okay," Gus said. "Okay. I'll try to remember."

They sat until she finished her coffee. He kept his eyes on her; she looked any place but at him. When the coffee was gone, she kneaded her palm, and then, almost as if she were frightened, looked around her. "Can't we go someplace else? I can't talk here."

"Sure — anything you say." He helped her into her coat. "Your place?"

Leslie searched through her purse for a dime, handed it to Henry. Outside, Gus stopped before the steamy White Spot window. "Well?"

"We can't go to my place," she mumbled. "Molly's still there."

"*Staying* there? But you've just got a single bed."

"Well, it doesn't matter, does it? Let's walk — any place. We don't have to stand here."

They walked — apart, cautious over the hard-packed snow.

At Main Street, Gus stopped and looked to her for directions.

With a shivering hand, she held her collar tight, and she searched the street for a way to go. "Couldn't you take me to the Gam house? I'm cold, Arthur."

"I could. It's against the rules."

"But no one need know. We'll turn all the lights on so people can see it's all right. Or we'll turn them off so they won't see anything at all." She took his arm, happy now she had solved everything. "It'll be cozy. We can really talk."

Away from Main Street, the night seemed colder, sharper, and the moon cut through the black night with the coldness of snow. The Gam house was, fortunately, dark. Gus preferred breaking rules in private to public display of virtue.

Leslie stood in the doorway while Gus turned on the tree lights. "We can sit in the dining room. Not much chance that anyone'll drop around."

He pushed two of the overstuffed chairs into the dining room, close to the radiator. The moon shone through the window, and over the backs of the chairs, the dull blur of lights was a red glow.

Leslie snuggled into her chair with the pleasure of a child playing hide'n'seek. "Now isn't this much nicer?" she whispered. "I'm really quite tired of my dreary little place — I've been thinking of looking for something else."

What she wanted him to say was that the Gam dining room was not for rent, but he would not be won so easily. "Cold?" he asked.

"Ah no, it's lovely."

And so they sat. Leslie reached for his hand; he removed it from her grasp. She twisted around so that she could smile at him; he stared stonily at the moon. When she told him she didn't think he was being very friendly, he didn't answer.

"What's the matter, Arthur?" she pouted.

"Nothing. It was my impression you wanted to talk."

"All right. We'll talk." She drew her legs up under her and folded her hands in her lap. "Now I'm ready. We'll talk."

Gus, slouched in his chair, held his hand over his eyes and made no answer.

"Number one," she said. "Arthur, what do you want of me?"

"It's no joke, Les. Maybe you'd better go. I'm not in your mood."

"No, I know." Anxiety came into her voice. "I mean it. What do you want?"

"I want you."

"Does that mean — you want me to go to bed with you?"

"Among other things."

"But why? Why can't we go on as we have?" She clutched at the arm of his chair. "It's been beautiful, Arthur. Why must you ask for so much?"

"Do I? You want it to be platonic, as they say?"

Leslie shook her head, gave a bitter little laugh. "You're right. But I can't help it — I want you so much." She pressed her chin into her hand. "Do you want to marry me?"

"Yes."

The word dropped into the dark stillness of the house and neither of them moved. The talk, it seemed, had ended. For minutes they sat, their breathing and the sizzling of the radiator the only sound.

Leslie moved to Gus's chair, forcing him to adjust his knees to hold her. She kissed his dry lips and rested her head and hand on his chest. One finger slipped inside his shirt to touch his skin. Then she kissed him passionately, groaning softly. And she opened her sweater and blouse for him, and groped for his hand. In the light of the moon, he could see the pointed little breast, white touched with pink, and he felt the weight of her thigh pressing on him. The unfulfilled need swelled through his body, and, helpless, his hand touched her.

Suddenly he turned his face from her. "No, for Christ's sake." He tried to stand, forcing her to her feet. Trembling, almost in tears, he said, "Whatever it is you want, by God I'm not giving it. I don't like your terms."

Leslie's white, fragile face was stunned, uncomprehending. She took a step toward him.

"Can't you hear me?" he yelled. "I'm through — finished — I've had enough."

She looked at him, her tongue touching her upper lip. Then she looked at her open blouse. Head low, she slowly buttoned the blouse, the sweater.

Gus reached for her coat and held it for her. She made no move. "So this is the way the world ends — " she whispered.

"This is it," he said gruffly.

"Could we go someplace — away? So it wouldn't have to be here? Some other town?"

"There are other towns."

She pushed her hand through her hair. "Molly leaves the day before New Year's. That afternoon, if you're free — "

"I'll be free."

She slipped her arms into her coat. Gus reached for his own.

"I'll go home alone," she said. "I'd rather." She started toward the door.

"Les —" he stopped her. "You forgot something. Do I buy a license?"

For a moment, she said nothing. Then she was sobbing into her hands. "Don't hound me — just leave me alone. I'm going with you — isn't that enough?" He reached out to her. "Don't touch me!" she cried, and ran out the door.

A bus station was like a railway station, Gus decided, except that the accumulated odors of urine, disinfectant, stale tobacco, and coffee were fresher, more pungent — Time's mellowing hand had not yet made them part of the shiny oak benches and phone booths and lunch counters, but had left them suspended in air. Bundled up peasants with bulging shopping bags had taken root on the benches, waiting for the local runs that would deliver them to the frozen farms — the ice-bound steppes. At five minutes to four, day, through the frosty window, was already giving way to night, so that soon this thirty-first of December could be called New Year's Eve. Sparkling letters above the lunch counter said "Merry Christmas" and "Happy New Year"; but the N had tipped so far backwards that it seemed to say "Happy ew Year," and between the friendly greetings was a red sign urging all Coca-Cola drinkers to please pay when served.

Gus held between his gloved fingers two tickets for the four o'clock bus to Pocatello, Idaho. He wore a hat and gloves and muffler and he had put off shaving until three o'clock so that he looked, he knew, like a pink-cheeked high-school boy, off to ring in the new at a church supper. The battered overnight bag at his feet contained shirt, pajamas, toothbrush, razor, fifteen-dollar bottle of Shalimar, and the Complete Greek Drama. He couldn't stand still very long and he had to watch himself that he didn't start grinning.

The trick was, he had decided, not to think. He hadn't thought for days. Leslie had refused to see him and so there had been no one to talk to. The thing that was about to happen was too big, really, too important for the human mind to grasp. It could be investigated, named, perhaps, but not conceived. And so the only solution was, don't even try. With Leslie's appearance the fact would be established and Gus had a virgin's faith that with loss of virginity all problems of the human race could be solved.

At two minutes to four, the bus was called, and the peasants rose heavily from their seats. Gus picked up his bag and rushed to the window, then out the door to look for her. He would not have expected her to be early, but a four o'clock bus leaves at four! He returned to the waiting room with some vague idea that she might have slipped in while his back was turned or emerged, smiling, from the ladies' room. Then he ran out to the bus — she might have wanted to surprise him by being there, waiting for him. He watched the peasants pass by the driver, show their tickets for the driver's punch, vanish into the dark mouth of the bus. And he stood, frozen with horror, while the bus driver himself climbed in and sealed the doors after him. He ran back to the waiting room with the desperate conviction that she must be there — she was always late! Then he sat on a bench and stared at his bag.

Gus had trained himself for so many days *not* to think that now it took time for his mind to focus. He held two tickets in his hand for Pocatello — useless now, but perhaps he could get a refund or an exchange. Exchange! Suddenly everything was clear! They didn't *have* to go to Pocatello — it could be any place on the train or bus line. He stood and ran toward the telephone booth, fumbling with a shaking hand for money, tangled in coat and gloves. But face to face with the telephone, Gus went limp. No, the landlady would say, Miss Crane is not at home. At the Gam house, waiting for him now, was a letter.

Hadn't he known all along? Wasn't it because of that he had forbidden himself to think? He picked up his bag and started from the station. The sparkling letters said "Happy ew Year," and the outside air, when he opened the door, was bitter cold.

He didn't look for the letter but went straight to his room and lay on his bed in the dark. His momentary flash of brilliance was gone and his mind had blurred, leaving him only the awareness of such sickness of defeat that he shriveled in revulsion against himself. She had denied him in every way that it was possible to be denied — as a person, as a friend, as a lover, most painful of all as an adult male. He was a child, shivering and helpless in the dark.

He lay there, God knows how long, in a half-sleep, a numbness that was indistinguishable from sleep. He was roused by a flash of light when his door was thrown open, and a voice, "Hey, Art — you in here?"

He squinted, rubbed his eyes, pushed himself up on his elbows.

"Letter for you — special delivery." It was Spide Hamilton. He tossed the letter — it hit Gus in the face — and turned on the light.

"What day is it?" Gus mumbled.

"It ain't day, son, it's night."

Gus yawned, stretched, twisted around to drop his feet to the floor. He stared at the letter. "What the hell you doing around here?"

"Me?" Spide's face grew red, his neck muscles swelled. Through clenched teeth he spat out his indignation. "Jesus Christ! I been drafted."

"*You?*" Laughter spilled through him, tied him up so that he lay back on the bed roaring with it. "As a private?"

"What's so God-damn funny?" Spide scowled. "Sure as a private. You think they'd make me a general?"

"Oh Jesus, that's wonderful," Gus said. "Hey, it'll make a man of you, Spide. Like the advertisements say. Maybe there won't be a war anyway."

"Don't give me that," Spide whimpered. "There'll be a war all right and I'll get my ass shot off."

"Maybe when the Germans hear about you, they'll surrender. That's not impossible."

"Cut it out, will you? It won't be so God-damn funny when you get it. Hey!" Spide got a puzzled smile on his face, scratched into the scrubby growth on his head. "That examination — they sure do some funny things to you."

"Well, this just shows the value of a college education. If you hadn't flunked out, you'd have till — "

"Can it, will you? Please? I can think of those things myself."

"Old Private Hamilton. What are you doing tonight?"

"What do you think I'm doing? What would you do? I'm gettin' loaded." He looked uncomfortably at Gus's letter. "I'll go take a leak or something."

Gus looked at the letter for a long time, turning it over and over, before he opened it. "Dearest Arthur —" it began and his chest tightened, the weakness returned. "I couldn't go through with it — not because of my wishes but because I know you really don't want it. I've always told you that you are better than I — and it's true, it's true. If I can't give you my best, you would not want second best. It must be the whole heart or nothing. I'm leaving —" the letter said, "Harrisville, State, you — it has all been a waste and I've made too many people unhappy — whatever I touch seems to die — I can't keep on. There's no goodness left — I'm glad about the war now — there's nothing worth saving, not until every last thing is destroyed can we start fresh, with hope. One more thing — and this you must believe — I've lied before but this is true: in you I do believe — in your success and your happiness and your integrity. You have been the one true thing in my life. I leave you — with thoughts that lie too deep for tears. L."

It was over now. He folded the note and replaced it in its envelope and dropped the envelope in a drawer. He must look at it later when he could think it through. For now, the trick was not to think.

He went to the bathroom and doused his face with cold water and squinted at himself in the mirror. He looked no different — fairly rosy, freshly shaved. Clean young man. Nice boy. He dried his face vigorously, rubbed his head with the towel, and the back of his neck. He straightened his tie and stopped in his room for his jacket.

Downstairs, Spide was stretched on the couch, reading the paper and picking his nose in sober concentration. "Hey," he looked up, "it says here the Germans have sent fifteen thousand men to Albania to help the Italians. Is that good or bad?"

"Not so good, I guess. But you'll change all that." Gus slumped into a chair, yawned, asked casually, "You eaten?"

"Yeah. Long time ago."

"Oh." Gus paused, scared to ask the question, afraid his voice would betray how much he cared. "Who — uh, who's your date, Spide?"

"Huh?"

"Who's your date tonight?"

"Hell, I got no date."

"You haven't? Well, look," Gus tried to sound indifferent. "How about if I come along. I wouldn't mind getting loaded myself."

Spide twisted around to scowl at Gus. "What's happened to that communist friend of yours? I figured you was getting it pretty regular from her."

"You need a change — variety — you know — "

"Well, sure kid, come along." Then Spide grew cagey, frowned as he sat up. "Sure you want to?"

"Look, Spide, I don't know how you feel but the kind of women I like, have to have character — they gotta be realists — "

Spide rubbed his hands along his thighs. "Hey Art — " he was becoming restless with excitement, "I got a pint out in the car. We might have a couple of short ones — "

"How about food for me?"

"Okay. Food for you."

"I'll get my coat." He ran to the stairs. "Hey Spide." He turned. "Does it really cost two bucks?"

"Three and a half. War prices."

Up in his room, putting on his coat, checking his money, Gus wanted to laugh. Everything else that had ever happened to him was crazy or else this was. Take your choice. He was growing up, tonight was the highlight of his college career — the only thing he had seen through to its logical conclusion. The highlight maybe of his life. And all for three bucks fifty. He'd have preferred not seeing his mother's picture: she wouldn't understand a thing like this. But the evening he was headed for did not call for under standing. Or remembering. The letter could wait. The trick was *not* to think. Tomorrow he might be sorry but at least he'd know.

Coming down the stairs, he called out, "Hey Spide, what was the name of that friend of yours? The one you wanted me to meet?"

"Bertha," Spide said. "Some people call her Big Bertha."

"Is she safe?" Gus asked, as if he were joking.

"Hell, kid, don't worry." Spide threw a protective arm on Gus's shoulder. "Leave that to me."

"Out with the old, then," Gus cheered. "In with the new. Big Bertha!" He threw a kiss to poor old Prometheus over the fireplace. "Big Bertha — the first lips I'll kiss in 1941."

CHAPTER 8

THERE HAD BEEN a good deal of wrangling over who should pack the lunch. Flo felt that she should do it since she was the oldest girl and hence should take over the obligations of a parent. But Louise complained that since Gus was staying at Flo's, Flo was usurping too many of those obligations and should share them with someone else. Frances spent half a day phoning Flo, Louise, Eddie, presenting her claim, mentioning Jack's position as legal head of the family, her own attachment — really stronger than any sister could feel — to Gus, her inability, because of her pregnancy, to offer any token of her regard other than a box lunch. Eddie said wearily that she would gladly give Gus five dollars to *buy* his meals — what was more deadly, more unfashionable, really, than a box lunch on the train?

It was up to Gus, ultimately, to decide, and he designated Frances, because he could more easily contrive favors to ask of Flo and Louise than of Fran. He could borrow Flo's car, he could make himself at home with Louise's icebox and living room couch. He could extract promises from both of them of fudge and cookies, detailed acounts of all Clark City happenings, clippings from the *Sentinel*.

His train was to leave at three-fifteen and he told Fran he'd drop by at noon to pick up the lunch — to say good-bye to the kids, see Jack and save her a trip to the station. That morning, he took his bag to the station to check it through. What with the family all coming down to see him off, he wanted nothing on his mind.

It was April. Gus drove Flo's car back from the station, along familiar streets. Spring hadn't quite arrived but everything was stripped clean, waiting for it. Clark City looked pretty shrunken with nothing to hide the poor bones beneath, a shiny skeleton of a city with blue sky in all the open spaces. It might have been better if he'd left directly from Harrisville, without the furlough. Something about all this, the bareness, the cry for human hands, made him sad that his own hands would be so far away. He had undergone the obscenity of the physical examination, the lines of naked men — no young gods these, but scrawny steers being measured and marked for the kill. Maybe there wouldn't be a war, people said — the German economy may crack — Churchill, England — But did anyone really believe that? The job was there for someone to do — better to get it over, with no time off for April.

A cab was parked in front of Flo's square brick house, and as Gus turned into the driveway, he noticed that the driver was slouched in his seat reading a comic book. A rough way to earn a living, Gus figured.

Inside the house, he could hear Flo's voice, saying something about Connie, and when he closed the door, she called him. "Come here, Gus. Is that you?" He smoothed his hair down with his hand, felt his tie, prepared himself to be polite. And stepped into the living room.

His first impression was of clothes — the mink coat, the beautifully tailored suit with diamond clip on the lapel, the alligator pumps. Then he said, "Babe," and it wasn't until he had named her that he really recognized her. She was seated on the couch, smoking, one shapely leg across the other. She was a beautifully shapely woman, large but perfectly trim. There was nothing in her appearance or manner to identify her as the old Babe — and yet it was so unmistakably she.

"Babe," he repeated, not knowing what to do. Should he kiss her? Shake her hand?

"You knew me," she said, with something of the old warm smile

— but it was guarded, indirect. "I wonder if I'd have known you, this way."

"He turned out fine, didn't he," Flo said with a mother's pride. Beside Babe, poor Flo looked dowdy, matronly, a little wobbly on the heels. "How tall are you, Gus? Are you over six feet?"

"It was Caesar he was supposed to look like, wasn't it?" Babe asked. "Only he's changed — he must have. Caesar wasn't very good looking, was he?"

"Augustus Caesar," Gus said. "He was handsomer than Julius."

At that, they smiled, but now there was nothing more to say. Gus waited, then slouched into the room and dropped into a chair. "Well — got my bag checked."

"Oh?" Flo said. "Well, that's fine." She folded her plump hands in her lap. "Babe is on her way to Chicago — just passing through. She wanted to see you."

Babe looked up quickly to explain. "I heard you were drafted. I thought that as a student you could be deferred."

"Till July." Gus stretched. "No point in putting it off. It's gotta be done."

"I can't believe that we'll have to go to war," Flo said. "I won't let myself believe it. Someone will take a gun to Hitler — some mother. I'd do it myself if I could get near the man."

"Have you called Louise?" Gus asked. "Is she on her way over?"

"I don't have much time." Babe searched for an ash tray. She seemed to have a trick of not looking at you when she spoke. Flo removed some chocolates from a silver dish and handed it to Babe.

"I'll call her." Gus stood. "She can be here in a minute. She'd want to see you."

Babe reached for her alligator bag and fumbled through it. "Don't bother — I haven't time. I think I better leave now."

Gus shot a questioning glance at Flo but Flo's mind was elsewhere. "I think it would be grand if you could see Sam while you're in Chicago, Babe. His training program is right near there — the navy, that is. I'm sure he could get time off to come in and see you. And wouldn't she get a shock, Gus? Of course Sam has changed just as much as Gus here."

Gus seated himself on the couch beside Babe. "Sam's not such a shock, Flo," he said. "Pretty agreeable sight, in fact."

"Is his hair still red?" Babe murmured.

"More sandy than red, wouldn't you say, Gus?"

Gus nodded agreement with Flo and the conversation dropped. He tried to think of something to say, something that wasn't taboo. It was difficult to be polite, to pretend that they were playing a straight game. In Babe's mind, in his, somewhere in Flo's, were the memories, the questions, the wounds and recriminations, but they must all carry on as if Babe's "just passing through" took care of everything.

"How's Eddie?" Babe asked suddenly. "Is she — "

"Oh Eddie's fine," Flo said. "And just the same. She's working very hard — chairman of Bundles for Britain in this region and doing a wonderful job. No one can beat her when she sets her mind to anything. And she's selling bonds. Howard — " Flo's face clouded (she had confided to Gus that Howard was rumored by her club to be wandering a little: like father, like son, they said) "he's fine too."

"Is she still beautiful?" A smile came to her face, a smile for a private joke. "Bill will want to know."

"Not so beautiful as you are," Gus said, and Babe stretched the fingers of her gloves as if she weren't listening.

"She's quite gray," Flo said. "It happens to people with that dark hair, you know. But it's very becoming, isn't it, Gus?"

"Is Jack gray, too?" Babe asked.

Flo and Gus looked at each other and laughed. "Would that he were, poor guy," Gus said. "There's nothing left to turn gray."

Babe clasped her gloves across her knee and bit into her lower lip. "He was the most wonderful — the most beautiful — I'd just die if he had changed." For the first time, she looked straight at them. "It would break my heart."

Flo made an involuntary tug at her corset. "It's not so much that he's changed: he's just *older*."

"Jack wouldn't be Jack if he weren't young," Babe said. "It's something that — that can't be imagined."

"Well," Flo said uneasily, "it happens to us all, I guess." She picked up a chocolate and handed it to Babe. "Would you care for a chocolate?" And when Babe shook her head, Flo ate it herself. "I do wish you'd let me fix a bite of lunch."

"I have to go," Babe said. She stood, reached for her coat and gloves, hurriedly, as if she feared another offer of hospitality. "You know how trains are," she said, fussing with her clothes. From the alligator bag, she took a small package and handed it to Gus. "Here."

He wasn't sure what he was to do with it. "What's this — what —"

"It's for you." She turned her back to them and spoke quickly, tensely, on the verge of tears. "I didn't know what to get — I hadn't seen you — I didn't know. And the army — what can you take to the army — "

He lifted from the box a gold watch with a gold bracelet. It almost took his breath away. "It's beautiful, Babe — "

"There!" She turned in a kind of triumph. "Bill told me I should give you money, but people don't give money — it had to be a present — but I didn't know — "

Gus went to her, took her hand, kissed her lips. "It's beautiful — just right." He looked at the watch. "But too much, Babe — "

"I must leave — my train." She touched her lips to Flo's cheek. "Good-bye, Flo." Then she turned to Gus, looked at him, raised her hand to her forehead. "Gus — "

"Look, Babe," he said, "could you drop me at Jack's? I see you have a cab. It'd be swell if you would."

"What about your lunch?" Flo asked. "Don't you want a bite here first?"

"Maybe Fran'll feed me." He took Babe's arm. "I'll be back in an hour or so."

Flo came out to the porch to stand with folded arms until they left. Gus helped Babe into the car and the cab driver tossed aside his comic book.

Gus gave the address and settled back with a great sigh. "How does the town look to you, Babe? My own, my native land — "

"I shouldn't have come! My God, I shouldn't have come." Tears started down her face and her voice was choked as she tried to talk. "But I had to — I — When Louise wrote that you'd been drafted, I thought I'd lose my mind — " She tried to find a handkerchief in her purse. "You never liked me, Gus — it was always Louise. But my God, when this happened, it seemed to me you were all I had in the world — "

"Don't, Babe — " he put his arm around her. "The only thing that matters is that you did come back."

Babe wiped her eyes and her nose. "I'm not like this — you'll all

think I'm crazy the way I've acted and it isn't true — people think
I behave well — they tell Bill. Bill thought I should come — and
look at me!"

"Don't — don't think about anything." He patted her shoulder,
tried to soothe her, to turn them both away from the unpleasant
truths. All the whys were to be avoided and only the immediate
fact considered. "Look Babe, come in and see Jack for a minute.
It'll make everything seem right — like old times."

"No." She drew away from him, blew her nose, returned the
handkerchief to her bag. "That's all over. He wouldn't want to
see me. I'll miss my train."

"Jack? Of course he'd want to see you. And he hasn't changed
so much, really. It's mainly just baldness."

She shook her head, stared out the window.

The cab pulled up in front of Jack's house and stopped. The
driver turned off the ignition, reached for his comic book.

"We're here, Babe. This is where I get off."

Babe didn't move, didn't look at him.

"It's hard to say thank you," he murmured. "That's not enough."
He waited. "And now I want to ask for something else. Will you
write to me, Babe?"

Babe was crying again, shaking her head back and forth, sobbing. "Dead! That's what I am — I wrote that to Mother and that's
how I meant it to be. But I'll write." She put her arms around him
in a powerful embrace. "I'll write."

"Okay. Then everything is all right."

"Do you need anything, Gus?" She sniffed, wiped her cheek with
the back of her hand. "A car? I could buy you a car. Or medical
school! When the war's over, I'll pay for medical school."

Gus smiled. "Not a thing. Just the watch."

He opened the door, but Babe hugged him once more. "You
write me first, Gus, and send me your address." She searched
frantically in her bag for her card and pen. "Here, you take mine."
While Gus wrote her address, Babe drew back into the cab.
"Would you tell the driver," she said, "how to get to the cemetery."

Gus kept his eyes on his writing. "City cemetery — he'll know.
Grandfather Gannon — if you can't remember, the attendant can
tell you." He returned the pen. "Thanks, Babe."

"I'll just have time," she said, looking at her watch. "My train doesn't leave for a few minutes."

Gus stood on the curb, watching Babe's taxi vanish down the street. Three blocks straight ahead, and then it turned to the right. "The city cemetery — he'll know."

Jack's house behind him was like a person's stare that you feel and finally must face. But Gus didn't want to turn — he was being drawn in too many directions — for a moment he felt a kind of panic, he wanted to run. Then he heard behind him a child's shrill "Eeee — " A screen door slammed shut; Jack IV, naked and yelling like an Indian, streaked across the porch, down the steps, and flew at Gus's leg. Gus reached down and ruffled the kid's hair. "Okay, Jackie. Let's face it."

The father Jack came out on the porch, and he, fortunately, was not naked. You never knew, though: this was the damnedest family. "Riding in cabs these days," Jack said. "The army's spoiling you."

"Yeah." Gus hoisted Jackie into his arm and carried him into the dark bungalow, tossed him onto the couch. The house was pretty messy. A bowl of half-eaten cereal was on the coffee table, amid the filled ash trays and empty highball glasses. The kids' toys were everywhere and in the only comfortable chair in the room, was a pile of unironed laundry. Fran and Roger were not in the room, but you certainly could feel their presence.

Jack felt through his pockets, looked around the room for cigarettes. "You don't have a cigarette on you, do you?"

Jack ought to know by now that Gus didn't smoke, but those kinds of facts about other people didn't seem to register with Jack. Gus shook his head. And then Jackie found a rumpled pack squeezed between the couch cushions and threw it at his father.

"Jack," Gus said, "Babe was in that cab."

"Babe?" Jack frowned. "Our sister? Babe Gannon?"

"Babe Miller."

Jack lit his cigarette, slowly, tossed the match in the general direction of the fireplace. "What did she want?"

"She came to see me. To see me off."

Jack drew on the cigarette, let the smoke curl from his nostrils. "Wasn't that a bit cheap?"

"Cheap?"

"You know what I mean. Maudlin. Showing up now. That was finished long ago."

"Funny. Her very words. She spoke of you too. Your handsomeness. She said you were wonderful."

Jack was pleased. He smoothed the rumpled vest that didn't quite reach his belt. "I have nothing against Babe as she *was*. She was a hell of a cute kid. But she isn't a kid any more — and you don't necessarily approve the adult because you liked the child."

"Maybe," Gus said. He wanted to add that probably Babe hadn't changed very much from the child she was. But Fran came from the kitchen with Roger tucked under her arm.

"Hi ya, honey." She deposited Roger in the center of the floor and came over to kiss Gus. She wore a loose cotton house coat, quite obviously nothing else, not even shoes, and when she stooped to kiss him, the great breasts opened a view all the way to her waist. She smelled of fresh soap and water; her lips on his cheek were sweet. "I don't look my best," she said, trying to collect the scattered wisps of stiff bleached hair, "but as you know, gestation does take something out of a woman."

How would he know? "Oh sure," he said.

"Look Gus," Jack said, "I don't mean to sound intolerant. I think I've been around enough to know what goes on. It's just that I can never forgive her for what she did to Mother."

"Oh sure," Gus said, sinking deeper, deeper.

"Who's intolerant?" Fran demanded. "What's going on here?" But before anyone could answer, she was saying, "Sugar, how about a little drink? Gus will think the liquor sure does pour like glue around here."

"No thanks," Gus said quickly. "I — well, I'm blurred enough already."

Fran settled herself onto the couch and patted Jackie's bare little bottom. "Well honey, I think I'll have one. Just a double Martini for me. I think we owe it to Gus."

Jack went into the kitchen and Fran, not looking at Gus, shook her head. "Honest to God, Gus, I get a terrible pain right here," she covered her left breast with her hand, "when I think of you leaving. Jack says if I break down, he'll divorce me — pregnant and all — but he doesn't know what I feel — "

Gus murmured, "Thanks, Fran."

"Oh, I know it's crazy — you're probably raring to go — get free of the family and raise Cain. But I still get that feeling."

Gus stretched. "I don't know. This war hasn't been so much fun as other wars."

"Say, you'll have the time of your life. I knew some soldiers out of the last war and I swear, there was no stopping them. And I don't think you'll have to fight. When Germany sees that we're really preparing, she'll surrender soon enough. She hasn't forgotten our boys in nineteen eighteen."

Jack appeared with a coffeepot of Martinis and two tumblers. "Do you want some food, Gus? Fran, can't you find something for Gus to eat?"

Fran went to the kitchen, the lovely flesh rippling beneath the cotton house coat, making it difficult for Gus to remember that she was his brother's wife. Jackie ran to Gus, crawled into his lap, tried to climb on top of his head. Roger kicked and gurgled.

"Quite a family you got, Jack."

Jack stood against the mantel, sipping his drink. The traces of the golden boy of Babe's dream were hard to detect; the beauty and distinction she admired had been traitors to him, deserting at the first sign of fleshiness, of baldness. Now he was the base product, the ordinary citizen of forty. There were millions of him in offices and city streets and bars.

"Where's Tommy Reed?" Gus asked. "What's happened to him?"

"He tried to enlist — you knew that, I guess." Jack stroked his head. "It's what we'd all like to do — if we didn't have responsibilities. Old Tommy. He didn't quite make it — hasn't taken care of himself too well. 4-F."

Fran called from the kitchen, "Tell him about Muriel."

"You knew Muriel Hooper?" Jack asked. "Great friend of Eddie's."

"I guess so — can't quite remember. What about her?"

"Oh, she died."

"Oh?"

"Cirrhosis of the liver. It was too bad."

Fran brought in a tray of food — half a beef roast on a platter, French bread, a big hunk of Swiss cheese, and a quart of milk. "Here's something to pick at." She bent over to clear some space on the coffee table, and the wonderful breasts swirled and dropped, readjusted themselves when she straightened up. "Where's my drink, Daddy?"

Jackie, eying the food, slid out of Gus's lap and made directly for the cheese. He bit off a corner which he dropped just out of reach of Roger's hand, then settled on the couch to munch at the rest.

"Gus — " Jack took a large swallow of his drink, leaned his elbow against the mantel. "You know that I envy you, of course — that one doesn't like to have been left out of both the grand shows of our time — "

"Oh sure."

"You're too old to fight, Daddy," Fran said. "This is for the younger boys."

Jack filled his glass and Fran's from the coffeepot. "I remember when I was a kid in high school — the bitterness of watching the others go — the parades, fellows dropping out of school. Even that man Babe ran off with — he enlisted, lied about his age."

"It's different now."

"I know it is. You're bitter for a quite different reason and I don't blame you. I want you to understand that."

"Me bitter? What am I bitter about?"

"We got you into this — my generation and Fran's."

"Well, I ain't bitter. Honest. I hold no grudges."

Jack looked into his glass as if all the answers were written there in gin and vermouth. "Not you, maybe, but your generation. Yours is the disillusioned generation — not ours; not the twenties but the thirties."

"Jesus Christ, Jack. I ain't disillusioned. I never was illusioned. How can I be *dis*?"

"That's just it," Jack said, flushed, intent. "You've lost faith. Or what's worse, you never had it."

"You want some food, Daddy?" Fran asked. She took the cheese from Jackie, cut off a slice for a sandwich, returned it to Jackie.

"Swell food," Gus said to Fran, chewing on meat and bread. "Who would have thought you could cook?"

Fran handed Jack a thick sandwich, but he frowned and shook his head. He tossed off his drink and reached for the coffeepot. "The thing I don't understand," he said, "is *why* you're going — if you have no illusions — why you're fighting the war. You can't, of course, be patriotic."

"I was drafted." Gus poured himself a glass of milk. "It's happening to a lot of guys."

"But that says nothing about *you*. That's government machinery, bureaucracy. That isn't enough."

Gus didn't understand too well what was eating Jack, but since this was his last day and since Jack was getting a little tight, he would try to be patient. "You complicate things, Jack. Hitler's evil so you get rid of him — like a doctor — you cut out the infected appendix. As Fran says, you're too old to do it so I do it."

"But do you want to do it? Do you as a person, an individual, *want* to risk your life to do it?"

Gus snorted, glanced at Fran to see if she were finding this a little ridiculous too. "Gosh, Jack. I've had to do a lot of things in my day that I didn't want to do."

Jack moved away from the fireplace, sat in a chair, very morose indeed, but that could be the gin. "Do you think we'll win the war?" he muttered.

"If we have the most resources and the best scientists we will," Gus said. "Here — don't you want a sandwich?"

Jack ate his sandwich, saying nothing, keeping his eyes on Roger. Fran was cutting off little pieces of meat and bread for Jackie, washing down her own food with sips of Martini.

"If it's another boy," Gus said, "you'll have a third of a baseball team — almost a half, including Pa. Isn't that the ambition of every American family?"

"I want a girl this time," Fran said. "I've had enough boys for a while. I want a girl that I can name Harriet."

Gus cringed a little. But Fran meant it, meant it with all her heart — and so it was right. "I hope it's a girl too, then," he said. He reached over and took her hand. "And the fourth, if it's a boy, name him Gus."

He stood up, took a handkerchief from his pocket to wipe his hands. "I'll be shoving off, I guess. Couple of things to do — and we'll probably get to the station early. The gals'll be coming down."

"Gus, I can't stand this," Fran said. She looked at Jack, stood up. "I'll get the lunch."

Alone with Jack and the two boys, Gus thought that now was the time for Jack to give him some fatherly advice. It would be interesting to hear Jack's opinions on sex and the necessity of proper precautions, or money and the necessity of a proper budget. Or the evils of alcohol, the dangers of the toilet seat.

But Jack said nothing.

Fran returned with the lunch — no shoe box this, but a sturdy carton almost the size of a hatbox. She handed it to Gus, her eyes filled with tears. She looked at Jack. "God damn you, Jack, I'll cry if I want to."

Gus lifted the top of the box. Besides the wax-paper packages of food, there were a carton of cigarettes, a pint of whiskey, a couple of Pocket Book mysteries. Gus had no doubt that somewhere within the box, Fran, predicting all the needs of man, would have packed condoms and sanitubes.

He smiled. "This is swell, Fran."

"The sandwiches are beef and ham." She steadied her chin with her fingers. "Fried chicken is sort of messy for the train."

Gus and Jack left together. At the sidewalk, Jack had to turn down the street, Gus, up. They shook hands.

"So long, Gus." Jack squinted in the sharp light of the April day.

"So long. Take care of those kids. And their mother."

"Gus," Jack gave him a crooked smile, "don't think too badly of me."

Gus grinned, slapped Jack's shoulder. "Take it easy, Jack. And good luck."

Carrying Fran's lunch under his arm, Gus headed toward Flo's. He decided to make a small detour to pass the old house and he probably shouldn't have. The place was run down and the large Mason Mortuary sign across the front of the house blocked the view from Mother's window. Eddie had been right: it would have taken an awful lot to get it in shape. All the big old houses were selling for mortuaries, it seemed — the old Governor Reed house and the big Parry house. Leslie Crane would have seen a fitting symbolism in that, but Gus could only wish that theirs had fallen into the hands of someone who cared about it. Maybe with May and June, when the vines were green and the trees came out, it would look not quite such a derelict. He walked on.

Well, this was it. A couple of hours now and he'd be on his way. For God knows what. The house had depressed him and his mouth was dry and he couldn't get a lift even remembering Jack. Was it Jack who had died the day of the crash, or was it he himself? Jack believed. In what? He kept hoping. For what? But had Gus been permitted either hope or belief? Right now, he was empty, barren, alone. Even the sidewalks were deserted. Where was everybody? Jesus Christ, it was April!

But he had to shift Fran's box from one arm to the other and he handled it carefully because the contents were precious. And he remembered that he must write to Babe. And Flo and Eddie and Louise would be at the station. Maybe the streets weren't so deserted as they looked. Maybe there was something.